The Way You Look At Me

An Rx Chronicles Book

EeJay Enekwa

The characters and events portrayed in this book are fictitious. Any similarity to real persons, living or dead, is coincidental and not intended by the author.

Cover design by: The Start Up Pro
Visit the author's website at www.eejayenekwa.com

This book is dedicated to all the hospital pharmacists out there. Keep doing your part to save lives!

PROLOGUE

Kelenna Agu hadn't been on a date in six months. Not. A. Single. One.

Ordinarily, that wouldn't be an issue. It wasn't like six months was that long for a dating drought. So many things happened within six months. A trip to the dentist. An oil change. Daylight savings time.

Your ex-boyfriend getting engaged after a mutual breakup.

It was considered mutual if he was the one who suggested it and you went along with it, right? That way, no one had the upper hand. That way, you could save face. Because if it was left up to you, maybe you wouldn't have broken up.

Should it hurt more that the person he got engaged to was Amara St. John, an ex of his that he'd claimed to have broken up with because they were better off as friends? If he was going back to exes, why didn't he come back to you? Why was Amara the one he deemed worthy to spend the rest of his life with?

Perhaps the one thing that was amplified in Kelenna's mind, as she pretended to work in her office in the pharmacy at Preston Regional Hospital, was that she lost out on a great match for her. She fell for Will within a month of meeting him, and ten months later it was over. There were no arguments, no fights, no theatrics. That was the tricky part. There'd been nothing overtly wrong with them. According to him, they'd just grown distant. "But maybe we could stay friends?" he'd offered.

But that wasn't a real option. Because how well could you remain friends with an ex, even after an amicable split? What kind of friend blindsided you with their engagement announcement? And via email?! The picture in the save-the-date message was burned in her memory. Amara's long, manicured nails were resting gently on his chest, her left leg raised and bent at the knee in a way that meant she was either abandonedly in love, or was trying to show off the red-bottomed soles of her designer shoes. His hand was possessively around her waist. They looked like the very picture of bliss.

No, they weren't friends. You couldn't be friends with someone who'd slipped through your fingers. Not when in the deep recesses of your heart—so deep that you only permitted yourself to visit occasionally—you'd assumed the two of you would have one last shot. Maybe you hadn't even entertained the thought of dating other people for that exact reason. All that meant nothing though, because while he was embarking on this life-altering journey with another woman, you were left alone to languish in singledom.

William Perry III, was not her friend. He was *The One Who Got Away.*

There was only one thing she could do now.

She had to move on.

1

The ambiance in the little Italian restaurant nestled in the quiet Atlanta neighborhood of Virginia Highland was very romantic. There were chandeliers designed to look like candlesticks hanging from the ceiling, their flame-like bulbs keeping the room so dim that you could really only see the person in front of you. All the tables were daintily covered with white silk tablecloths that had jars of flowers and candles for centerpieces. Music from what sounded like a string quartet floated across the restaurant, just loud enough for you to hear, but soft enough to not be distracting. All that was needed to fully transport you to Venice was a canal outside full of gondolas drifting slowly over the waters.

Kelenna Agu wished she was in Venice. It didn't even have to be Italy; it could be Venice in Illinois, Florida, or California for all she cared. Anywhere but here, sitting in front of her third bad date in as many weeks. Less than half an hour in, Kelenna was already eyeing the exit door, wondering how rude it would be to ask the waiter if she could get her food to go. How was it possible that this man was in the lead for her worst date of the month, slightly edging out the guy who'd been rude to their waitress and the one who'd had a distracting case of halitosis?

"Kelly Anna?"

She blinked to hide an eye roll. There was no need to correct his mispronunciation of her name since she'd already done so twice that evening.

Besides, she was fine with him calling her whatever he wanted as she had no plans to see him again.

"I said I didn't mean to interrupt you. You were saying? . . ."

"Oh, don't worry about me," Kelenna said, mostly because she had no clue what she had been saying. He'd cut her off so many times that she was almost afraid to share any more opinions.

"Oh, good. Because the stock market can be very volatile—"

Right, they'd been talking about investing. How incredibly dull for a first date. She breathed a small sigh of relief when she saw their waiter approach their table, expertly balancing a large tray in one hand with a stand tucked underneath his other arm. He placed the stand on the floor and set the tray on top of it. A big smile was on his face as he put their meals in front of them.

"*Buon appetito*!"

* * *

"The only thing good about that date was the food! Can you believe he wanted me to go home with him? Why, so he could talk my head off?!"

She heard Chika Okafor's exasperated sigh through her car's speakers. The BMW sedan was the first real thing she'd splurged on a year after landing her big girl job. Two years later, she still enjoyed its luxurious feel. "Kelenna, I'm sure he was inviting you over for other things," she said dryly.

"I know what he was inviting me over for!" Kelenna snapped. "I just can't believe he even had the nerve to try. He didn't care about anything I had to say all evening. He kept talking over me. He kept cutting me off. He kept—"

"Did you let him know any of this?" Chika interrupted.

"Let him know what?" Kelenna asked with a frown even though her friend couldn't see it.

"Let him know how you felt when he talked over you?"

"And when would I have done that? When I couldn't get a word in?"

"I'm just saying, Kelenna. This is your third date, in what, a month?"

"Three weeks," she corrected.

"Three weeks. And each time you've come up with some problem you can't get past. You pretend like you're being open and giving these people chances, but you're cutting them off over the littlest of issues."

Kelenna snorted. She should have known better than to rant to Chika. They'd grown up together in the Atlanta Nigerian community and had been friends for over twenty years. Chika was tough love all the way. She should have told her pharmacy school classmates, Zoe Callas or Sharon Ackerman. They both had supportive partners who would rather die than make them feel inconsequential. Zoe or Sharon would have been way more sympathetic.

"So what if your first date yelled at the waitress?" Chika was saying. "Maybe he was having a bad day."

"People who yell at waitresses have serial killer tendencies, that's been proven."

"Okay, what about the date with bad breath? That's nothing a good dentist can't fix."

"Hey, it's not my place to tell an adult man that he has halitosis! It's too awkward. If his family and friends won't tell him, he'll just have to live with it for the rest of his life. Chika, he tried to kiss me!" Kelenna shuddered as she remembered him leaning in, his overpowering breath almost choking her. She was glad that she'd quickly turned her face so that his lips landed on her cheek instead.

"Your negativity will get you absolutely nowhere, girl."

"I'm not being negative, I'm being real. SwipeNow hasn't worked for me in three tries. What does that tell you?"

"That you should keep trying?"

"Wrong answer," Kelenna said with an eye roll.

"Remember that time I met that guy online? And he stalked me for a month and a half? You didn't see me swear off dating apps, did you?"

Kelenna's eyes widened. "Now you're just making my case."

Chika laughed out loud and the sound grated on Kelenna's ears. "Well, what else are you going to do? You're not always going to bump into eligible guys at the grocery store, or in some woman's office at your job."

Kelenna scowled at Chika's unnecessarily specific comment. She was clearly alluding to the way Kelenna met her ex-boyfriend. It was a Wednesday afternoon, and she had been hard at work when she was summoned by the hospital's risk manager, Prudence. A lawyer had some pharmacy-related questions for her, was all Prudence had said over the phone. By the time Kelenna arrived at Prudence's office, she was a nervous wreck. She'd been prepared to meet an older man with a southern accent that matched Prudence's, but was met with the opposite. Sitting in the cozy office, his eyes completely focused on the laptop on his thighs, was a young, bald, medium-complexioned African American in a really sharp suit. She politely waited for him to raise his eyes to meet hers before she said hello. When he finally did, she couldn't look away. It was the first time in a long time that she felt that cliché stirring of attraction in the pit of her belly. It was definitely the grin that had done it. Such a cocky grin that seemed too intimate for present company but that completely disarmed her. When he stood to his full height—no more than six feet based on her appraisal—and offered her his right hand, she was flustered.

"Hello, I'm William Perry III."

"I'm Kelenna Jordan Agu, the first." Her eyes widened in shock as she took in his arched brow and obvious amusement. She cleared her throat to mask her embarrassment. "Just Kelenna. Agu. It's nice to meet you."

That was the kind of story you could tell your grandkids. You wouldn't tell a 'your grandfather didn't care about anything I had to say all evening so I went out with him again' story. It would totally set the wrong example.

"You know what your problem is, Kels?" Chika continued, clearly on a roll. "You're an idealist. You think there should be sparks the second you meet a new person. It doesn't always work that way. You're a pharmacist, you know all about chemistry and experiments, don't you?"

Kelenna narrowed her eyes as she focused on the road ahead of her. "Okay?"

"When you put two elements together, they form a bond between them and become a compound, right?"

"What's your point?" Kelenna asked suspiciously. No one created more random analogies than Chika, but Kelenna could usually follow her logic. This time she was at a complete loss.

"I'm saying, you need time to form bonds. What if sodium and chloride never took the time to form the bond and become table salt? What would we cook with?"

Kelenna stayed mute over the line to let Chika know just how bad her analogy was. When Chika barked out a laugh seconds later, she joined in. "Maybe you should leave the chemistry metaphors to me. Acids and bases literally need a reaction to form bonds and make salt. There's your immediate spark!"

"Kels, my point is, just be open. Give it time. Don't place too much importance on the presence or absence of sparks. They're not reliable."

Kelenna sighed. She knew all about unreliable sparks. Heck, the ones she'd had when Will flashed that cocky grin at her disappeared mere minutes later. Prudence had barely caught her up on the legal issue that required her assistance before Will had pounced on her like she was a witness in a courtroom and he was cross-examining her.

"Apparently one of your pharmacists gave some information about a drug manufacturer to a patient," he practically yelled at her. "Now she's suing Preston for negligence. Do your people not know that they can't release information to just anyone? What kind of operation are you running down there?"

"Hold on," Kelenna said after she was able to find her voice. She could ignore his last question, seeing as she technically wasn't the one running the operation as he'd put it. Her job title was clinical pharmacy *manager*, not pharmacy *director*. What she couldn't abide was his gibe at her people. Her fellow pharmacists. If what Prudence said was to be believed, that the patient had experienced hearing loss after receiving the popular antibiotic, *vancomycin*, then there was no one to blame. Bad drug reactions were random and could happen to anyone. "My pharmacists would never release protected information over the phone. A drug manufacturer is not protected information."

Will just looked at her like she was too stupid to understand while Prudence rushed to play mediator. "Kelenna, if a patient wants any information, we would like for them to go through the proper channels. We would have done damage control if we had known earlier. Being named in a lawsuit alongside Tinkerson Bingham is massive."

Kelenna whistled. Tinkerson Bingham was one of the largest drug companies in the country, second only to Alistair Pharmaceuticals. "Is there anything I can do?"

"Just tell your pharmacists to be careful next time," Will said with a dismissive wave. "That'll be all."

Kelenna's irritation carried her to the door of Prudence's office before a thought popped into her head. She paused and turned around. "Are we really taking this hearing loss claim seriously?"

"I'm here because we are taking it seriously," he said with a smirk. Kelenna's hand itched to smack it off his face. She managed to keep her hands to herself though. Only just.

"May I look at some of her information?"

Within a few minutes, she was sitting at Prudence's desk, going through Grace Lowry's medical records on the computer. "Looks like she was in really bad shape when she got here. Cocaine and marijuana in her urine. Unresponsive. We saved her life."

"Yes," Prudence said with a snort that contrasted her usual sweet demeanor. "We saved it long enough for her to sue us."

Kelenna nodded and stood up from Prudence's seat. When she got to the door once more, she turned back around to look at the lawyer. "For what it's worth, it's unlikely that *vancomycin* caused hearing loss in that patient. For one, she got such a low dose. Two, we didn't give her any other drugs known for causing hearing loss. And three, *vancomycin* hasn't been toxic to the ears in almost fifty years. I know this because I gave a lecture on it about it a year ago. It's more likely that the drugs she overdosed on caused her hearing loss, not *vancomycin*."

"You got all this from looking at her charts for five seconds?" he asked in such an incredulous tone that Kelenna didn't know whether to feel flattered or insulted.

"I'm a pharmacist," she said flatly. Then she let the door shut behind her as she walked out. Maybe a little harder than necessary—for effect.

She hadn't taken two steps in the hallway before she heard him behind her.

"Do you have a business card on you?" he asked when she turned around. He must have taken note of the bewildered look on her face because he added, "Just in case I have any additional questions."

She nodded once and dug into the large pocket of her white coat where she kept some business cards for situations just like this.

"Kelenna Jordan Agu, PharmD B-C-P-S," he read out loud. And even though he mispronounced her name, stressing the first syllable instead of the second, she felt those sparks return. Something told her that whatever additional questions he had would center mostly around whether she ate dinner with people she didn't know that well, and if perhaps she would like to do it with him. Two days later, he'd done exactly that.

"You still there, Kels?" Chika asked, dragging her back to the present.

Kelenna pulled into the parking spot in front of her Marietta apartment and put her car in park. "Yeah, I'm here."

"It's a step in the right direction, you know?" Chika said in a softer voice. "Going on all these dates? After Will broke up with you, it seemed like you were waiting for—"

"Will didn't break up with me," Kelenna cut in, sighing into the phone. "It was mutual."

Chika paused for a second before she continued. It reminded Kelenna that Chika had never bought into the mutuality of her break up with Will. *At the end of the day, there's always a 'breakup-er' and a 'breakup-ee,'* she'd said six months ago. "Okay fine, after your mutual break up with Will, you just sort of carried on with your life."

"What else was I supposed to do?" Kelenna asked. She was out of her car now and was gingerly walking up the stairs to her apartment on the second floor. The four-inch heels she'd paired with a black slip dress nicely accentuated her slim, five-nine frame, but had really bad wear time. Less than four hours into wearing them, she was already looking forward to the relief of taking them off.

"Exactly what you've been doing these last three weeks. Being proactive. Not watching your own love life from the sidelines and waiting for something to happen."

It all sounded positive, but being proactive didn't make her any happier. She didn't relish getting all dolled up after a long day at the hospital just to sit in front of a stranger for mediocre conversation, no matter how good the food was. "It's exhausting," she admitted. "I feel like we spend so much of our lives either being in relationships, or trying to be in one. Where does it end?"

"It ends when you get what you want."

Kelenna frowned as she slid her key in her lock. "And what's that?"

"Come on, Kels, you know you want it all. The husband. The big house in Marietta like your parents. Two kids like you and John. And maybe if you're lucky, one of them will have a friend like me who has the good sense to push them. You want that cookie-cutter, perfectly symmetrical Nigerian-American family just like the one your parents have."

2

Kelenna was still thinking about Chika's words the next evening while she was having dinner with her family. Her cookie-cutter, perfectly symmetrical family. The truth was that they *were* symmetrical. They were a perfect square. A pair of children to match a pair of parents. One boy and one girl. They were all *doctors.* John, her brother, was a cardiology fellow at Emory, a medical doctor just like their nephrologist father. Her mother, Mrs. Uche Agu—or Dr. Obidi as she was known professionally—was a pharmacist just like Kelenna. They even had the exact same job description: clinical pharmacy manager. The only difference was her mother practiced at a larger hospital. Baptist in downtown Atlanta was easily three times the size of Preston Regional.

"So Kelenna, have you joined the Nigerian Pharmacists Association like I asked you to?"

Oh, another difference between Kelenna and her mother? She had a passion for the profession of pharmacy that Kelenna couldn't match. Kelenna was darn good at her job, loved it even—which was more than she could say for many of the pharmacists she knew. She loved being a clinical pharmacist and she loved being in charge of her own program. The job wasn't perfect, but even when nurses complained about a drug delay, or doctors called down to yell at her or her staff, or there was a drug shortage and she had a devil of a time figuring out an appropriate alternative, she felt like she was doing what she was meant to do.

Her mother did all that and then some. It wasn't enough that she had her finger on the pulse of one of the busiest hospitals in metropolitan Atlanta; she was also super involved in pharmacy at the state level, national level, *and* international level. She treated pharmacy like it was a civic duty she had to perform. It was almost like it kept her going, like somehow if she took a break from serving the profession, she would drop dead from the inaction.

Kelenna exchanged looks with her brother who was sitting on the right-hand side of their father across the cherry oak dining table. When he gave her a small nod, she knew, without having to glance beside her, that her mother had pinned her with an 'over the glasses' look. It was the classic Dr. Obidi 'you better say what I want to hear' look. Kelenna had learned early in life not to mess with that look.

"No, I haven't joined NPA yet," Kelenna responded in a muffled voice.

"What's the hold up?"

Kelenna groaned inwardly, but it may as well have been an outward groan based on the sharp look her mother threw her way. "Mom, it's not that I don't want to be part of NPA." She didn't. "It's just that I don't have enough time for these extra-curricular—"

"You should have plenty of time to be part of NPA," her mother cut in firmly. "I don't see you participating in PHA, OPA, ASHP or IDPP. You've been out of school for three years—four if you count the year you spent doing your residency. When do you think you will be ready?"

Dear Lord, she barely knew what half of those acronyms meant. Did her mother belong to all of them? How much was she paying in membership dues?

"I really want your help on the education committee," her mother was saying. "That project would suit you nicely."

"I can help you with whatever projects you need, Mom. I don't need to join to do that." It wasn't like she'd been part of any organizations while essentially being her mother's personal assistant growing up. Her mother was an expert at accepting tasks from all the organizations she participated in, and then reassigning those tasks to Kelenna to complete. Kelenna remembered times when she was watching TV with her brother and her mother would show up out of nowhere with a pen and a notepad. "Stop watching your life go by," she'd say, throwing the items on the couch. "Here. Write this down." She was ten years old!

"Leave her be, Uche," her father, Dr. Emeka Agu said. "Let her do what she wants."

"Thank you," Kelenna mouthed to her father, smiling when he sent her a conspiratorial wink.

Her mother backed off with a low grunt that made Kelenna almost burst out in laughter.

She loved when her parents did that neutralizing thing they did with each other, as if they'd made a pact to never be riled up at the same time. Whenever one of them tried to fly off the handle, the other did something to calm them down. It could be as simple as a hand on the shoulder, or a subtle look. Something to let the other person know they weren't alone, but that effectively doused whatever might have been brewing. It was her favorite thing about them. Chika was right, she did aspire to a relationship like theirs. How could she not? It was damn near perfect.

"Hey, did you hear?" She felt John's foot tap her shin underneath the dining table.

"Hear what?" she asked in between bites of her food.

"Chris finally accepted the position."

Kelenna arched a brow. "Really?"

"Yeah, it happened today. Can't believe I know more about what's going on in your hospital than you do."

Kelenna snorted. "That's just because you guys tell each other everything like an old married couple."

It still surprised her how close John and Chris had become over the years. Apart from attending Emory medical school together, she didn't think they had that much in common. Her brother was serious, intelligent, and respectful. He didn't charm his way into women's pants and treat them like they were interchangeable. How did someone like him develop a bromance with someone like Chris?

"What position did Chris accept?" their father asked.

"Emergency department medical director," she answered.

"Wow, ED medical director! How impressive!" their mother exclaimed. "I have to call his mom to congratulate her. That boy has done so well for himself." It was such a Nigerian parent thing to do: congratulate a parent on the accomplishments of the child.

"He's been interim director for almost two months!" Kelenna said with a dismissive wave. She was probably being unfair, but was it *that* impressive if it was a job nobody wanted? Not even him? "They've been dangling this job in front of Chris the whole time. Glad to see he's come to his senses and taken it."

"Well maybe he's been hesitating to commit to *Preston*," John said, scooping up the last of the grains of rice on his plate with his fork. "Maybe he's trying to decide if the OTP life is really for him."

"Why would he?" Kelenna snorted, ignoring his 'outside-the-perimeter' gibe. The fact that John had adopted that snobbish Atlanta term was rich since he had in fact grown up outside the perimeter of the city. "Preston is no Emory—"

"It's not," John interjected.

Kelenna pointed her fork warningly at him until he gestured for her to continue. "As I was saying, Preston is no Emory, but we're a good hospital! Chris loves being the big fish in a small pond. He thrives on the attention and everyone in the ER obliges him. Why would he want to leave?"

John grinned. "Classic Chris. That's exactly how it was when he was a resident at Emory. All the nurses loved him. Still ask about him."

"If by classic, you mean he's an unrepentant flirt and womanizer, then sure, it's classic Chris."

John's grin turned into a grimace, an expression she was very familiar with. He always grew defensive when she made comments about his best friend. "Come on, now. He's harmless and you know it."

"Chris is only harmless to people who are lucky not to get caught in his web," she said matter-of-factly.

She knew because it was a bullet she'd dodged herself. Okay, maybe 'dodged a bullet' wasn't exactly what happened. It was more like he hadn't even pointed the gun in her direction.

Long ago, when she was a freshman in high school, and he was a junior, she had the biggest crush on him. It was hard not to. He was tall and good-looking, and even though he'd been born in Marietta like she and John, he'd spent the last six years with his family in Port Harcourt, a city in southeastern Nigeria. Those six years had done him a lot of good. He was more mature and self-assured than anyone she knew at their school, and she became so obsessed with him that she was blind to how much of a player he was. She lived for the moments when he would wink at her as he walked past her, or high-five her when they were near each other. It meant that he noticed her. But how he noticed her didn't dawn on her until one afternoon, in between periods, when she was with John standing by their lockers. Chris was walking with Brianna, a popular senior on the cheerleading squad who was clinging to his arm like she was physically attached to him. He smiled broadly at her and John when he saw them. Whenever he smiled like that, she couldn't help but return it. When he caught up to them, he put his arms around Kelenna and John, and to her horror, in that odd accent of his that made her swoon—an accent that was mostly American but had Nigerian inflections—he introduced her and John as his little cousins. "They're family," he told Brianna. Later she analyzed the comment with Chika, and in her fourteen-year-old mind, she tried to rationalize that he hadn't just 'cousin-zoned' her. After all, people who got married ended up being family, so maybe there was hope for them, right? But Chika was even less of a romantic back then. She simply said, "You said your mom and his mom are best friends, right? Best friends can be like sisters. I would hope our children think they're family."

From that day on, Kelenna dropped the rose-tinted glasses, and she could see Chris for what he truly was.

John rolled his eyes now. "His web? Jeez, Kelenna, will you relax? You make him sound like some kind of predator."

Kelenna shrugged. "No, not a predator. Just your run-of-the-mill heartbreaker. I need all my fingers to count the number of women he's had relationships with since y'all were in med school together. I can just imagine the string of women he's left in his wake, waiting for him to decide if he wants to be with them."

John was quiet for a moment before he cocked his head to the side and looked at her. "Do you think you're projecting?" he asked in a low voice. "Will's getting married, now Chris is the bad guy?"

Kelenna hissed as she glanced at her parents. They were talking to each other, but she knew they were listening. "This has nothing to do with Will," she muttered.

"Doesn't it? He's the only one who's decided who he wants to be with lately." *And it wasn't you*, he didn't add.

Not that he would have. He loved her too much to hurt her feelings just because he was trying to prove a point. Besides, she didn't think John was Will Perry's biggest fan. He'd never said anything negative about him, but one time, after they'd all hung out together, he told her that she'd been unnatural all evening. "You're not *you* around him. You were like a heightened version of yourself the entire time you were next to him. It was weird," he'd said. She never asked him what he meant by 'heightened.' On some level, she probably knew she wouldn't like the answer.

"The politician is getting married?" her mother asked, confirming that she'd heard every word they'd said.

"He's not a politician, Mom," Kelenna said with a sigh.

That politician quip took her back to the first time she introduced Will to her parents. She'd brought him over on a family dinner night, and her parents were convinced that Will had been testing them for a political campaign. "All that talk about free healthcare. He's a bit radical, but I would vote for him," her mother had said right before she angled her head. "But Kelenna, do you want to marry a politician?"

"Why didn't you tell us?" her father asked now in his slow, deliberate tone.

Kelenna snorted. Of course she didn't tell her parents about her ex's upcoming nuptials. Not when she was very single herself. Kelenna knew her parents would have taken her being married to anyone, even a 'non-Nigerian, radical politician', over being a prospect-less, almost twenty-nine-year-old.

"I didn't tell you because it's not a big deal," Kelenna said instead, as determinedly as she could manage. "I'm fine with it. Will and I broke up ages ago. Obviously, he's free to marry whomever he wants and I'm happy for him."

The hush that followed her last sentence told her that she oversold how fine she was. She could practically feel all the looks that were being exchanged on her behalf. Then without warning, she felt her mother's hand close over hers and squeeze her fingers firmly. Once. Twice. Her throat clogged up with emotion. She was surprised at that because she'd never been much of a crier. She certainly hadn't shed any tears over Will's engagement, so why was she triggered by the simple comfort her mother was offering? When she raised questioning eyes at her mother, the woman patted her hand and released it.

"For what it's worth, my dear, I really think you would have made a lousy politician's wife."

3

The pharmacy department at Preston Regional Hospital was located in the basement, secluded from the rest of the hospital and spread over 2000 square feet of space. It was built in the shape of a watch with a clock face and two straps. To the left of the main entrance were the managers' offices, including hers, and a storage room that housed boxes of old pharmacy records and cartons of fluids that were used throughout the hospital. To the right was a break room and the sterile compounding rooms where intravenous (IV) medications were prepared. Finally, right in the center, surrounded by computer stations and shelves of medications, was the pharmacy pit. It was where the pharmacists and pharmacy technicians worked—where all the action happened.

Kelenna's office was the first one in the hallway, closest to the pit. The first thing she usually did when she got to work was read her emails and review patients' charts in preparation for rounds in the intensive care unit (ICU). She liked to keep her door ajar in order to hear the chatter of the pharmacists and techs. Sometimes they talked about mundane stuff: a must-watch television show, or something funny one of their children had done. Other times, there would be a problem that Kelenna would overhear, and she would either hop out of her chair to help, or eavesdrop as they handled it. Right now, there was silence—almost as if nothing was happening out there. She liked the silence, even though it would inevitably be interrupted by a ringing phone, or someone barging into her office with an issue she had to address.

"Kelenna! Have you checked your emails?"

Case in point, now. Kelenna knew without turning around that Lisa, the pharmacy buyer, was behind her, most likely with papers in her hand and a pen behind her ear. Lisa had the distinct ability to determine whether Kelenna would have an easy day or a hard one. The urgency in her tone told Kelenna it was going to be the latter.

"I already did. Why?"

"Check again," Lisa instructed. "HQ just sent out a message telling all the buyers to stock up on IV *morphine*, *fentanyl*, and Dilaudid. There's some kind of strange shortage going on with the opioids. Our suppliers are completely out!"

HQ was the corporate office of Dynasty Corp, the twenty-hospital system Preston belonged to. For every department in the hospital, there was a corresponding team at the HQ level that served as a resource. Kelenna reopened her email, and sure enough, there was a barrage of new messages from the pharmacy leaders at HQ. As she read, she began to see the picture that was being painted. The Drug Enforcement Agency, or DEA, an agency in charge of regulating the amount of opioids in circulation every year, was mandating that the aggregate production quota for opioids be lowered.

"They're saying that the DEA wants to fight the deadly opioid epidemic by making cuts to what the manufacturers can produce," Kelenna summarized with a frown.

"By creating a drug shortage?" Lisa asked incredulously.

"Essentially. Lisa, we need to know the counts of our IV opioids. If our suppliers are out, we could be in big trouble. We use several doses of these drugs every day."

"I'll get those numbers."

"Awesome," a voice behind them said.

Kelenna and Lisa turned towards her door to see their boss, Pat, the no-nonsense, almost-militant director of pharmacy standing there.

"Awesome?" Kelenna asked, raising her brows. "This sounds a little insane, Pat."

"No, I meant, awesome, you've gotten the news about the opioid production cuts." Pat came further into the office as Lisa slipped out. "The CMO got word of it and has set up an emergency meeting for noon."

Kelenna was surprised. If the chief medical officer was already involved, it meant that Dynasty was really taking it seriously. "Who else will be at this meeting?" she asked.

"Nurse leadership, the quality and risk departments, and I think the new ED medical director. And you. It involves everyone. We'll need to deal with this before it becomes an issue. Do me a favor and look at all the suggestions in the emails HQ sent to us. That will give us a good starting point."

"On it," Kelenna replied. But first she had to get ready for rounds. The opioid crisis-shortage was going to have to wait.

* * *

She arrived at the seventeen-bed ICU located on the second floor before the majority of the rounding team. Not before Dr. Boucher though. He was one of Preston's three ICU doctors, and even though he was even-tempered, he looked impatient as he waited for the other stragglers to show up. When they did, he gestured at Paul, the nurse, to begin.

The patient in bed one was a forty-nine-year-old white woman who had overdosed on a cocktail of prescription medications, and per the doctor's notes Kelenna had read before rounds, possibly bath salts.

"This is her second admission with this kind of presentation within the last five months," Paul was saying. "The last time this happened, she was brought to the ER with hallucinations and seizures, and was so agitated that we had to intubate her for airway protection. This time around, she presented with agitation and altered mental status, but no seizures. She was intubated in the ER. Her heart rate and blood pressure have remained elevated since yesterday. Her husband actually brought the substance she took." Paul went into the patient's room and came back out with a small container. "Lah-NEP-teen," he enunciated. "*Laneptine.*"

Everyone's eyes turned to Kelenna, as they usually did when a drug was involved.

"*Laneptine* doesn't sound like any bath salt I've ever heard of," Kelenna remarked with a frown. She motioned for them to continue while she looked up the drug on her tablet.

"Her husband said that she only takes *laneptine* when she runs out of her pain meds. After the episode she had a few months ago though, he hid the drugs from her. He found this stashed away in her purse."

"Okay, *laneptine* is primarily an antidepressant." Kelenna's eyes roved over the screen of her tablet as quickly as they could. "With activity at the mu-opioid receptor!"

"In English?" Bree, the case manager asked, causing everyone to laugh.

Kelenna smiled as she rolled her eyes. "It's an antidepressant that also has opioid effects. It's not approved in the United States, but it looks like you can purchase it online from Europe or South America."

"So she's essentially self-medicating with this drug?" Paul asked, his eyes wide.

Kelenna couldn't believe it herself. "It would seem so," she said softly.

After rounds, when Kelenna got back to her office, she read some more about *laneptine*. She stumbled onto online forums where people talked about how the drug worked for them. None of them treated it like the antidepressant it was. They all took as much as ten times the recommended amount to get that euphoric feeling that only opioids could provide. Some users even injected the drug, blowing out their veins in the process. How ironic that she would stumble across this drug on the same day they received the notification about the opioid cuts. It seemed that the DEA could make all the cuts they wanted to, but a person who was addicted would find a way.

And if they found their way using a drug like this—a drug that was capable of causing an overdose similar to opioid overdoses—it was something to be very afraid of.

* * *

By lunchtime, she'd spent a good amount of time preparing for the emergency meeting, and she was confident she had a good solution to the problem. If the DEA wanted to cut the amount of opioids they could buy, then they were going to adapt by cutting back on what they used. It was going to be the easiest meeting she'd ever attended. She walked to Meeting Room B, which was set up conference room style with a long rectangular table surrounded by several collapsible chairs. She was the first to get there, but one after the other, Dr. Schwartz, the chief medical officer (CMO), and the nurse leaders trickled in.

"Hi everyone," Dr. Schwartz started in his out-of-place New York accent, adjusting the wire-rimmed glasses on the bridge of his nose. "Thank you for coming here on such short notice. I forwarded out the email I received from my boss at HQ, Dr. D. Hopefully, you've all had a chance to read it."

Amid the murmurs of assent, the door to the meeting room opened, and Dr. Tari-Douglas popped a head in. After squinting and looking around, he seemed satisfied and walked in. His scrubs—black ones like all the ER doctors wore—fit his tall, trim frame like they were tailor-made for him. He pulled out the empty chair beside Dr. Schwartz, right across from Kelenna.

"Sorry I'm late, Josh," he said to Dr. Schwartz as he sat. Then he leaned back on the chair and let his eyes travel slowly around the table. Kelenna wanted to roll her eyes when she noticed how he gave each nurse director a corner-of-the-mouth smile. She recognized that smile. It was one that said he was sure of himself, and that he knew he was the focal point of any gathering. When his eyes landed on hers, he greeted her with a slight brow raise. She responded with an even slighter nod.

"No problem. Glad you could step away from the ER," Dr. Schwartz said graciously. "As I was saying, Dr. D sent a message out to all the CMOs, and I thought it was imperative we address the issue immediately. Kelenna, would you like to tell us more about this opioid shortage from a pharmacy perspective?"

"Yes, sir," Kelenna said, sitting up straighter. The quicker they could get through this meeting, the sooner she could get back to work. "If you've been following the news, you're not surprised to hear that we're in the middle of an opioid crisis. The death toll from opioid overdoses has been steadily climbing since the early 2000s. The DEA has decided to step in and cut production quotas by about twenty percent. They believe that hospitals, physicians, pharmacists, and pharmaceutical companies are culpable for the epidemic. They blame the pharmaceutical companies for pumping the drugs into the country, the physicians for overprescribing, and the pharmacists for dispensing."

"Let me get this right," Tari-Douglas cut in. When she turned to him, he was looking directly at her. "They want to force a reduction in the demand by reducing the supply?"

"Essentially," Kelenna replied, mildly surprised that he'd been listening since he'd looked bored during her entire preamble. "If there is not enough drug, then maybe we will be forced to use less in hospitals."

She thought she heard him mumble the words *ridiculous* and *controlling* under his breath, but she wasn't sure.

"Well, what do we do now? Exactly how do you want us to handle this?" Ashleigh, the red-haired, fiery-tempered ER nurse manager asked. Kelenna couldn't tell if she was irritated or frustrated or both. She was something though.

"I've run the numbers, and they don't look good," Kelenna started out slowly. "If we continue at this pace, we'll run out of drugs—specifically the IV opioids. We'll have to cut back our own usage to match the production cuts." She paused to look at Ashleigh, and then her eyes veered over to Dr. Tari-Douglas. "And it needs to start in the ER."

Tari-Douglas frowned, his bewilderment obvious. "Why us?" he asked.

"Because the ER has the highest use in the entire hospital. Followed by the post-surgery unit—"

"Hey!" Maryann, the nurse director for post-surgery cut in. "The patients in my unit have just finished having painful surgical procedures. We can't cut off their pain meds!"

"Cut *back*, not cut *off*," Kelenna said gently. "It would make such a difference if the ER could cut back. Maybe we won't run out in two weeks."

"I think we have room to cut back in the ER," Sarah, ER nurse director and Ashleigh's boss started softly. "We deal with a lot of drug seekers in the ER. They claim to have a pain of eleven out of ten just so they can get Dilaudid. They know what to say, and the doctors give in to them to shut them up."

Tari-Douglas scowled at his right-hand woman's comments, as if she'd just betrayed him when she was simply speaking the truth. "If a patient comes in with a broken bone or with chest pain, they're going to get an IV narcotic."

"What about the ones who get a Percocet for a simple headache?" Sarah countered. "Face it, we're probably part of the problem just like the DEA says. And nurses aren't helping. We're the ones running to the doctors to get the orders for those drugs!"

"I mean, when we have patients screaming in pain, what else are we supposed to do?" Maryann cried out in a way that made Kelenna want to put a hand against her temple. She didn't think her cut-back strategy would be this controversial. What had they expected her to say? That she would manufacture opioids down in the pharmacy?

"What happens to all the training we got at the pain summit three months ago?" one of the other nurse directors chimed in. "We were taught to believe the patient when they say they're in pain. To not label them as drug seekers because of whatever bias we may have. All that goes out of the window if we're to start policing these patients because the DEA won't let us have enough drugs."

"I'm not telling you to label them as drug seekers!" Kelenna snapped. When every eye in the room turned to her, she took in a deep breath to calm herself down. She didn't want to alienate anyone before she could get her message across. "Look, if we're going to get through this shortage, we have to be serious about it. We have to let the nurses know that they can't enable patients and allow them to—"

"Kelenna, I'm sure none of our nurses' intentions is to enable drug abuse," Ken, the chief nursing officer, cut in gently. There was a hint of admonishment in his grandfatherly tone as he defended his staff. "Nurses have been trained to get on top of the patient's pain so they can minimize complaints later on. There's nothing wrong with that."

"That's exactly the culture we're going to have to change," Kelenna dug in unapologetically, ignoring the annoyed glares the nurse leaders were sending her way. "This shortage is a big deal. It means we can no longer hand out opioids to our patients at the slightest complaint. We can no longer shoot them up to shut them up."

A dramatic hush filled the room. It lasted for only about ten seconds, but it felt more like ten minutes. She'd gone too far. She could see it in the way they all turned to look at her. She could feel their eyes like daggers piercing through her.

Maryann was the first to speak, and when she did her voice shook with emotion. "I'd like you to come up to the floor and watch how we *hand* drugs to the patients. Have you ever heard a patient yell out for their pain meds? Have you ever had them curse at you when you tell them they have thirty minutes before they can get their next dose of Dilaudid? When you do, let me know how you think we're enabling these patients."

"Those kinds of patients are not unique to this hospital," Kelenna said quickly. She kept her tone kind in a last-ditch attempt to douse the tempers flaring around her. "And I don't mean to imply that any of you are purposefully enabling patients. You're not. This is Preston! Majority of our patients are used to taking opioids and other drugs, and that means they're tolerant, dependent, and maybe even addicted. Not giving them what they want will be hard, but we have to do it, otherwise there won't be opioids left for *any* patient. We'll have to manage our patients' expectations, and tell them *why* we're cutting back. We'll have to say, hey Mr. Smith, your pain may not be a zero, but we'll do our best to keep you comfortable without overmedicating you."

This time, the angry and defensive looks on the nurses faces changed to something softer. They looked like they were starting to listen. Kelenna let out a low breath of relief and turned back to the CMO.

"What exactly do you need us to do, Kelenna?" he asked her.

"The most obvious thing would be to get all the doctors on board with cutting back. We'll continue to monitor the stock in the pharmacy, but in the meantime, Dr. Tari-Douglas can ask his ER doctors to use oral opioids or non-opioids like *ibuprofen* and Tylenol. HQ also recommends that we come up with an IV to PO conversion chart for opioids."

"An IV what?" Tari-Douglas asked, looking up at the mention of his name. He didn't even manage to look sheepish about being distracted by his phone during the part of the meeting that most concerned him.

"IV to PO conversion chart," she repeated.

He gave her a blank look that said he still had no clue what she was talking about. Surely, he knew that IV meant intravenous, and PO meant oral.

"It's a chart with a list of IV drugs matched to their equivalent doses in oral form," she told him patiently. "Whenever a patient is on an IV opioid, like *morphine*, a pharmacist would be able to change it to PO *morphine* automatically." She shot a look at Dr. Schwartz. "Now, it's not going to be a hit with the physicians, so I'll need your help selling it to them."

"I'll get them on board," Dr. Schwartz promised.

She nodded her thanks and allowed Dr. Schwartz to wrap up the meeting. She knew she still had some work to do to pacify the nurses after some of the things she'd said, but right now, she was just content she'd gotten her message across.

As everyone was dispersing, Kelenna made a beeline for Maryann, the nurse director who had seemed the most offended by her words. She was glad when Maryann apologized for her outburst, and agreed to get behind the simple strategy Kelenna had outlined. While they were standing near the door talking, she felt a tap on her shoulder, and turned to see Tari-Douglas behind her, his face so close to her ear.

"Can I borrow you for a second?" he asked, his hand grasping her elbow in a totally inappropriate way that she hoped Maryann couldn't see.

"Uh, sure, Dr. Tari-Douglas," Kelenna replied quickly. "Thanks, Maryann."

She followed him—no, she was *pulled*—out of the meeting room and down the hall. "Dr. Tari-Douglas, can you slow down?"

He released her arm and stopped completely. "Still feels like you're mocking me when you call me that."

Kelenna frowned. "I'm not mocking you, I'm being professional. You're a doctor in my hospital and—"

"You would call John Dr. Agu if he worked here?" he cut in.

"Yes," she said insistently. "Because that would be the professional thing to do."

"Kelenna," he said disbelievingly.

"Chris," she countered.

"Better." He grinned, clearly proud of himself for trapping her.

Kelenna rolled her eyes but couldn't stop herself from smiling. His grin was just as infectious as his smile. Always had been. "Did you even have a reason for *borrowing* me?" she asked.

"Not really. I mostly wanted to get you away from that nurse. She was really angry with you." He seemed to look at something behind her before his gaze returned to hers. "Do you always piss people off at these meetings?"

Kelenna raised a brow at his protectiveness. It was nice of him but completely unnecessary. "Maryann is harmless. She wasn't angry *with* me, she was angry at what I said."

"That sounds like the same thing."

"You didn't like what I was saying either, but you're not angry with me," she pointed out.

Chris grunted. "It's ridiculous that the FDA plans to cut back—"

"DEA," she corrected.

"Same difference," he said.

"It's not. FDA approves drugs and makes sure they're safe. DEA stops drug trafficking. Two different agencies."

Chris waved a dismissive hand. "Fine, DEA. The DEA are being ridiculous if they think they can blame the opioid epidemic on doctors. It oversimplifies addiction and points the fingers at overworked doctors who are just doing their jobs. We have HQ and the government breathing down our necks about patient satisfaction scores, and keeping our patients happy, and the DEA goes and does this thing that will definitely make our patients hate our guts." He took a deep breath and shook his head. "That's why I didn't like what you were saying."

Kelenna's eyes widened at how serious and how . . . aware he sounded. Over the years they'd spent growing up together, even up to the last couple of years after he joined the ER team at Preston, he'd always been a devil-may-care, take-things-in-their-stride sort of guy. She didn't know this version of Chris, the person who was now responsible for outcomes in the ER, and was feeling the weight of that responsibility. All of a sudden, he seemed more relatable. "Congrats on the new role, by the way," she said softly.

"Don't remind me," he groaned.

"Why not? I know you didn't really want it, but this is a big deal. You're only thirty-two and you've only been here two years. Your team must have a lot of faith in you to let you lead them."

"Or they think I'm a sucker for taking on the job," he said with a snort. Then, as if he couldn't help himself, he launched into a speech that was decidedly whiny and made Kelenna unsure if she should laugh at him or hug him. "There's so much . . . extra work involved," he said. "I never even used to look at my emails before, and now I get a hundred a day. And I'm supposed to read them all! And don't get me started on the complaints and the problems. I never knew there were so many issues in the ER! Just the other day, Dr. Woodrow came to me to report that there were dark particles floating in the water. And I stood there wondering if I was the maintenance guy or something. He expected me to handle it!"

The laughter won out for Kelenna, most likely because she couldn't pull off a hug in the middle of the hallway of the hospital where they both worked. "Welcome to the admin life! I spend half my day dealing with audits and paperwork and coming up with solutions to problems I didn't even know existed. Trust me, you'll get used to it."

Chris let out a grunt that said he didn't believe her for a second. "You had lunch yet?"

Kelenna blinked at the abrupt change in subject. "No?"

"Good. I have half an hour to kill before my next meeting. Join me? You can tell me more about your drug shortage."

"It's not *my* drug shortage!"

But he'd already begun to walk down the hall.

4

Kelenna watched as Chris piled two different kinds of complex carbohydrates, two chicken breasts, and what she could only describe as a forkful of green beans onto a flat plate. In line behind him, she went with one chicken breast, a generous helping of green beans, and only one complex carbohydrate.

"You know you're not always going to be this lean, right?" she commented as she followed him to a small table in the corner of the physicians' lounge. They placed their plates on the table and sat opposite each other.

"Lean?"

"In shape," Kelenna said with an eye roll at his knowing smirk. "Whatever."

"I'm training for a marathon so I can afford the carbs."

"Hmm." She should have known. Chris was one of those runner nuts who could get up and run ten miles in one morning. She took a sip of water from the Styrofoam cup in front of her as she looked around the lounge. It was definitely more modern than the hospital's regular cafeteria. It had muted grey walls, fancy light fixtures, and futuristic-looking tables and chairs. Also, the food was free—for doctors. "Are you sure it's okay that I'm in here?" she asked uncertainly.

He shrugged. "Technically, you're a doctor."

"*Technically*, I have a *doctorate*," she corrected with a hiss.

He laughed. "I'm sure it's fine." If he wasn't sure, he didn't sound like he cared. "Besides, this is a working lunch," he added with a wink.

Kelenna smiled at his implication that their lunching while at work could be categorized as a working lunch. "We've never had lunch together. We don't do this."

"I've never been the ER medical director," he replied with a shrug. "Now, what was it you were saying I needed to tell my docs? Order more Tylenol and less *morphine*?"

"In a nutshell," Kelenna said in between bites. "But tell them why. Let them understand that this is not my shortage. The DEA are the bad guys here."

"Got it. We hate the DEA."

Kelenna hid a chuckle as she returned to eating her food. They spent the next minutes in companionable silence, only interrupting it to crack jokes about each other's departments. And even though his gibes were funnier—albeit super stereotypical and borderline rude (like when he said that Amazon Prime delivered packages faster than pharmacy delivered drips to the ER), she thought that she wouldn't mind having a working lunch with him again.

Suddenly the door of the lounge swung open loudly and a Black woman in a white coat walked in. Kelenna recognized her as one of the nurse practitioners with the cardiology group. She'd seen her around but she'd never spoken to her before, so she was surprised when the woman approached their table. Before long, she was standing behind Chris, dragging a not-so-subtle hand around his shoulders, and causing him to turn around.

"Oh, hey Stacy, how are you?" he drawled in a low, almost sexy voice that Kelenna certainly hadn't heard all day.

"I'm good. Hey, I left you a message yesterday. Did you get it?"

Chris frowned. "I don't think so. You have the right number?"

Stacy called out a number and he nodded, satisfied that she had the right one. Then he did a double take at Kelenna, almost as if he only just remembered she was there. "Do you know Kelenna? She's the pharmacy director here."

Kelenna's eyes widened at his claim. "No I'm not!"

"No?" He looked truly confused so she knew he wasn't teasing her. "You're not the director? What are you then? Why are you always bossing us around?"

"I do not!" she huffed, kicking him under the table. "And I'm the clinical pharmacy manager. How do you not know my position here?"

"No, we haven't officially met," Stacy interrupted, turning to Kelenna for the first time. Her saccharine smile failed to reach her eyes as she stretched out her hand. "It's good to meet you."

"You too." Kelenna accepted the offered hand. "If you need help with anything drug related, I'm your gal!"

"I'll keep that in mind." Stacy said, her tone dry and just a tad unfriendly. Then she turned back to Chris, effectively dismissing Kelenna. "So do you think you're free on Thursday? There's a show at the Fox Theater that everyone's going to. I've got tickets."

Kelenna couldn't stop her eyes from widening once more in fascination as she took in the scene. Did Chris walk around being overtly hit on like this? Even while he was sitting with a pretty girl? She looked down at herself. Okay, so she didn't look as flawlessly put together as Stacy did. Half of her long braids was piled in a haphazard bun on the top of her head, while the other half fell down her white coat and hit her waist. Her face was devoid of makeup, and her nails were short and could do with a manicure. In her defense, she had to keep them short and free of nail polish on the rare occasion that she was needed to prepare a drug in the sterile compounding room. The amount of bacteria fingernails could harbor was astounding. Stacy, on the other hand, looked like she'd just stepped out of a hair salon. Her long tresses—half of which Kelenna suspected were hair extensions—fell in bouncy curls well past her shoulders. Her bright red nail polish could be seen a mile away. And she wore heels. Heels! Who wore heels to walk around a hospital?

Chris didn't miss a beat when he apologized and told her he wasn't free. "We have that thing on Thursday, don't we, Kels?"

"Hmm?" she said, startled at being included in the conversation. And also, that he'd just called her Kels. He never called her that. She remembered because she wasn't the biggest fan of her own name growing up, and he'd unwittingly played a major role in changing that. It didn't matter how often her parents told her it was a beautiful name, or that it meant 'Thank God,' which was a prayer of gratitude, as her mother liked to say. She only cared that it sounded like a bootleg version of Helena or Elaina, and so she went by the much cooler Kels or Kelly. It wasn't until she re-met Chris after he returned from Nigeria, and he asked her, "Do you remember me, Kelenna?" that she heard for the first time how nice her name sounded. From that day forward, she embraced her full name, and only Chika and John had a free pass to call her Kels.

She tried to read him now, to see if he was giving her some kind of non-verbal cue, but his eyes were blank and unhelpful. Why didn't he want to go out with Stacy? She was totally his type. Average height, light-skinned, cute. He could easily start and end a relationship with her in the span of a month. Matter-of-fact, she'd seen him start and end relationships with women just like her in the span of a month. A light bulb went off in her head. Maybe calling her Kels was the cue. He most likely knew it would trigger thoughts about John. She blinked as she tried to think about what her brother John would do if he were there with Chris. He would cover.

"Yes?" she said, her response sounding more like a question than a definitive statement. She saw Stacy's entire demeanor drop with that simple three-letter word and regretted covering for Chris that very second. She knew what it felt like to want to be noticed by Chris, even if it was when she was a teenager fifteen long years ago. When she glanced at Chris once more, he looked so relieved that she had corroborated his fib that she decided to give

Stacy a glimmer of hope—the opposite of what Chika had given her back in high school. "Maybe next time? I'm sure Chris would love to take you to a show. Maybe we'll even double date." She smiled sweetly at Chris but he didn't return it. He just stared at her with a look she couldn't interpret.

"Next time, then," Stacy said, and this time her smile reached her eyes. Kelenna smiled back at her as she turned to walk away, happy that she had removed herself as a threat to whatever Stacy wanted from Chris. Let him deal with it.

"See you, Stacy," Chris said. Instead of turning around to leer at her backside like Kelenna expected him to, he leaned forward and let his eyes bore into hers. "Double date?" he asked incredulously. "What was that?"

"You were blowing her off! I had to say something!"

"All you had to do was stop at yes!" Chris said with an exasperated laugh.

"I was trying to soften the blow," she said with a shrug. "I'm not good at lying on the spot."

"You're not good at lying, but we're going to double date? With your *boyfriend?*" His index and middle fingers made the most annoying inverted commas as he said 'boyfriend'. "The last fella I saw around you was that uppity lawyer, and that was a year ago."

"It was six months ago, and he's not uppity," she said with a scowl. But the longer she thought about it, the more she could see how someone like Chris would think Will was. They were opposites. Chris took himself far less seriously than Will did. "Anyway, this isn't about me. You can't charm a woman and then act all surprised that she wants to go out with you."

"I *charmed* her? All I said was hi!"

Kelenna lowered her voice and gave him as seductive of a look as she could manage. "Hey Stacy, do you have the right number?"

Chris choked on a laugh. "I definitely don't sound or look like that."

She grinned at him. "What's the big deal anyhow? Why didn't you just take her up on the offer for Thursday? Is it too short notice? You have to do your hair? What?"

Chris completely ignored her jokes and gave her a confused look instead. "We *do* have a thing. Thursday Night Football? Your brother's football watch parties are practically tradition. You *are* coming out, aren't you?"

"Oh," she said sheepishly. "Completely forgot about that."

"Yeah, you thought I was just lying."

"How was I supposed to know you would blow off a night with a beautiful woman for a football game?"

Chris raised a finger. "Not just any football game. The first game of the season. Falcons versus Saints. I'm not missing it for some concert."

Kelenna could only stare at him. "This is no way to treat your future ex-girlfriend."

Chris shook his head and smiled. "Something tells me you couldn't care less what I do with her."

She raised her cup in mock salute. "Excellent deduction, doc."

* * *

After work on Thursday, Kelenna made the twenty-minute drive from her apartment in Marietta down to John's condo in Buckhead. Technically, the condo belonged to their parents. They'd snapped it up in the late 2000s when the housing market crashed and properties were foreclosing left and right. As the economy improved, they rented it out to a series of students and young professionals, stopping only when John graduated from med school. It had been their gift to him—the keys to the condo and the responsibility for its upkeep. The first thing he'd done was pull in Chris to be his roommate, and they'd gone on to live together for the following three years while they were both residents at Emory, paying a fraction of what it cost the rest of the masses to live in that upscale, overpriced part of town.

She parked her BMW in the empty spot next to John's ancient Jeep Liberty, the car he'd driven since they were in high school (he was so very frugal), and headed for his door. Now that he was a fellow and made a little bit more money, he was able to live alone comfortably. She rang the doorbell twice, and when there was no response, she withdrew a spare key from her purse and opened the front door.

"John?" she called out as she walked into the condo. It had an open floor plan with bright white walls, hardwood floors, and high ceilings. There were en suite rooms on the top and bottom floors, and a half bathroom a few feet away from the entrance. There weren't that many places he could be if he didn't hear her.

"Really?" a shirtless John asked, coming down the stairs. "I want my key back."

"What?" she said, her eyes going wide in protest as she choked down on a chuckle. "No, I thought you weren't here!"

He gave her a disbelieving look. "You thought I wasn't here, but you saw my car outside?"

"I don't know." She shrugged defensively. "You could have gone for a walk, or could have been dead asleep." She looked at his sleep-tinged eyes and snorted. "Clearly the latter."

He scowled, stretching and yawning at the same time. "I was so tired, I slept all day. I was up for forty hours straight at the hospital. I almost canceled this watch thing."

"Yeah right." John was a natural host, just like their mother. He would host even if he had to sleep on the couch while everyone else watched the game. She was pretty sure he'd done that before.

"What'd you bring?" He gestured at her hands.

"Wine coolers." She placed the six pack on the kitchen counter and followed him out to the living room. It was minimally furnished with a three-seater couch flanked by a loveseat and the most comfortable, out of place, leather recliner chair. That was her seat. She plonked down on it and let out a deep sigh.

Today had been a particularly difficult day. Apart from the fact that they'd lost a twenty-nine-year-old patient to a heart attack at the hospital, it was the one-year anniversary of the day she and Will Perry had gone official.

Facebook took it upon itself to remind her about a status she'd posted exactly a year ago, around 10:53 pm.

Today was a good day. #LetsDoThisThing

To most of the people on her friends list, the vague status could have meant anything. A new job. A promotion. A carefully laid trap to get people to join a pyramid scheme, as Chika had posited. How could anyone have known that the four-word hashtag was exactly how Will had asked her to 'go steady'? It happened about three months after they first met in Prudence's office. He'd invited her to a cocktail event his law firm was hosting, and she'd worn this royal blue, fitted dress that really popped against her brown skin. It had a little ruching around the middle and gave her an illusion of a waist that seemed to hold Will's attention, the way he kept his palm permanently attached to it throughout the evening. Normally, corporate events were not her scene, but she'd enjoyed this one. She got caught up in the way Will worked the room, steering her through the crowd as he did so. They ate the expensive-looking hors d'oeuvres and drank champagne while he introduced her to his fellow senior associates, and they schmoozed with the partners of the firm and other important clients. She was a little tipsy when he drove her home, but she felt so warm and content. As she kissed him good night and let him know what a good time she'd had, he caressed her cheek and looked deeply into her eyes. "You were a natural tonight, Kelenna," he told her. And then almost like an afterthought, he ran a hand down her arm and caught her hand in his. "Hey," he said. "Let's do this thing." In her mildly intoxicated state, she beamed and nodded yes. The next morning she woke up with a small headache, but a big smile on her face. She'd gotten what she wanted after all—an official label for her and Will's relationship. It was crazy how much of a contrast she was feeling now, a mere year later. Now, the status floated around in her head and the words she thought were impossibly cute once upon a time seemed to be mocking her.

"You good?" John asked, pulling her back to the present.

She closed her eyes and did not answer his question immediately. After a few seconds, she opened them to see him looking at her expectantly, his expression telling her that he knew she wasn't 'good', and that she had better give him a satisfactory response. She sighed once more and decided to go with Henry Kingston—the less pathetic answer. "We had this patient today. He stuck with me. Probably because he's about our age."

"Yeah?"

"Yeah. He had a heart attack during sex."

John's brows went up. "Like in the act?"

"Yes. Collapsed on top of his fiancée. She called 911 and started doing compressions. By the time the ambulance arrived, he'd gone into cardiac arrest. They shocked him, and that's when he got to our ER."

John gave a knowing nod. "What kind of heart attack was it? A STEMI?"

"Yeah. Hundred percent blockage of the LAD artery."

John whistled. "The widowmaker."

"The widow what?"

"It's called the widowmaker heart attack because it's so swift. It makes widows out of people. Get it?"

"Got it. I guess his fiancée is not technically a widow, is she? Since they weren't married yet?"

"He didn't make it then?"

Kelenna shook her head. "He was down too long. The CT scan showed brain injury. His mother and fiancée decided to pull the plug."

"Damn, that's a sad story."

"Yeah. How was he supposed to know he was having a heart attack? He was twenty-nine, for crying out loud!"

"Chest pain?"

"He had some chest pain throughout the week, according to his fiancée, but he thought it was indigestion. And why wouldn't he? I would take a Tums too if I had chest pain!"

John nodded knowingly. "What about his family history?"

"Unremarkable. No history of heart attacks in any of his parents or grandparents."

"High cholesterol?"

"Lowest I've ever seen."

John looked at her. "That low?"

"His LDL was twelve." LDL was the bad cholesterol that was usually the culprit in most heart attacks. Kelenna didn't understand how he was able to create blockages in a major artery with essentially no cholesterol.

"That is low. Drug use?"

"Not recently. His fiancée said he gave them up years ago."

"Did y'all check his urine?" he pressed.

"They did. It was clean."

"Damage could have already been done. If he's from Preston, cocaine is not a reach. We're talking vasospasm and constriction of the vessels."

"Yeah." She wasn't a fan of his Preston stereotype, but it wasn't unreasonable. Preston was a blue-collar town thirty minutes north of Marietta known for being the drug capital of Georgia . . . or at least that was how it was portrayed on the local news. During rounds, his fiancée was in tears as she described how he'd turned his life around two years ago. He'd gone back to school, gotten a good job, and had become a mentor to young boys and girls. How could he have known that the damage was already done?

"I feel bad for the woman," John added. "One minute you're having sex with your fiancé, the next minute he's dead. That's pretty traumatic."

Kelenna put a hand to her head. "The mental picture is bad enough without you spelling it out."

"Sorry, sis. Do you need a hug? You seem really down about this."

"No, no," she said, waving him away. "Go put a shirt on, your guests will be here soon." He'd helped more than he knew. Apart from the fact that it distracted her from anniversaries she didn't want to think about, their talk reminded her about the fragility of life. This twenty-nine-year-old man's life was cut short right in his prime, but he'd lived and loved. Maybe she could take a leaf out of that book.

She was contemplating that when she felt her brother's arm wrap around her shoulders from behind her. She smiled and patted his hand.

"You'll be all right, Kels."

Somehow, she knew he wasn't just talking about Henry Kingston.

5

By 8:45 p.m., John's condo was filled with guests that were a combination of some of their high school friends and friends from John and Chris' days at Emory. Kelenna knew everyone except for one medical resident and a woman who spent most of the first quarter of the game talking to Chris by the door.

"Who is that girl?" her best friend Chika asked from the arm of the recliner.

Kelenna glanced back at Chris and the woman. Her big curly hair hid most of her face, but her hands were gesturing wildly. Chris was looking down at her with an amused smile. "I don't know, maybe a new girlfriend? You know how Chris is."

"I mean John. Why is she all over him?"

"Oh." Kelenna looked over at her brother who was sitting on the middle cushion of the three-seater couch. There really was a woman practically hanging onto his arm as they cheered the play on the television. "Relax, she's harmless." It was Keisha, a girl from his med school class that Chris had gone out with while they were first or second years at Emory. There was no way John was getting involved even if he was interested. "That's bro code violation territory."

"Bro code violation?"

"You know how Chris is," Kelenna repeated.

Chika raised her brows and smiled satisfactorily. "God knows I can't stand the guy, but if he's keeping John single by dating every woman around him, then he's good for something."

Kelenna laughed at Chika's joke. It never got old when she put on her crush-on-John act. It may have been true once upon a time, when they were much younger, but now, it was just a part she played when she was in between boyfriends or dates. If Chika were even remotely serious about it, Kelenna could reel off a dozen reasons why she and John would be poor fits for each other. Heck, Chika would add a dozen more to the list. The most obvious ones were that she didn't have the patience it took to deal with someone as distracted and as driven as John, and John thought she was flighty and a little ridiculous.

When her phone vibrated in her back pocket, Kelenna pulled it out and looked at it. It was work. She let out a groan and hopped up. "Watch my seat, will you?" She hit the answer button as she walked into the kitchen, crossing her fingers that it was nothing critical. You never knew with Kurt, the evening shift pharmacist at Preston. She sat at the breakfast table, and for the next twenty minutes, she went over details of the issues he had encountered that evening. For some of them, she was just a sounding board, affirmation that he'd done the right thing. He hadn't on one instance, but it was a minor issue she could handle in the morning. By the time she got off her phone and returned to the living room, Chris had commandeered her recliner, and Chika was nowhere in sight.

She stood in front of Chris, blocking his view of the television. When he looked at her, she motioned for him to stand up. He didn't. Instead, he shifted to the left and patted the space beside him. She narrowed her eyes at him. In all the years they'd hung out at John's to watch football, he'd never contested the seat with her. Not even while he lived there. Still, there was enough room for her, so she could be magnanimous. She sat beside him and rested against the recliner.

"Where've you been?" He sounded aloof, as though he wasn't really interested in her answer. She wondered why he even asked.

"Work." She held up her phone. "Where's your friend?"

"Who?" He'd been leaning forward, so he turned back to look at her.

"The pretty one with all the hair."

"Nara? She had to go to work. She's on call. OBGYN."

"Ooh, a doctor." She wiggled her eyebrows. "Oh, is she the reason you blew Stacy off?"

He pursed his lips and shook his head. "Is this going to be your new thing? Running a commentary on my love life?"

Kelenna raised her brows in pretend shock and nudged him with her elbow. "So you're in love, huh?" she said with a teasing chuckle. "That has to be a first for you."

He snorted and turned his attention back to the game, ignoring her laughter beside him. She thought she saw his lips turn up though, like he was trying hard not to laugh as well.

Her phone rang again and she had to lift her hips awkwardly to pull it out of her back pocket. Chris gave her an odd look as she moved around beside him.

"Do you need help?" he asked dryly.

"I got it," she replied with a glower. "Hey, Zo," she said into the phone when she was finally able to answer. As she listened to Zoe Callas, her friend and former pharmacy school classmate, her eyes got progressively wider. "I'm closer than you are," she said in a hushed tone. "I can be there in five minutes."

"Something wrong?" Chris asked after she ended the call.

"You know my classmate, Nichole?" When he mimed an hour-glass figure with his hands in response, she rolled her eyes. Nichole Masterson did have the small waist-to-hip ratio thing going for her, and what looked like a triple D chest to match, but Kelenna could do without the objectification. "Yeah, that one."

"Okay?"

"She was robbed," Kelenna told him as she picked up her purse. Just then the Falcons scored a touchdown and John was hi-fiving everyone around him. "Tell John I left. And Chika, wherever she is."

Chris grabbed her arm. "Hey, is she all right?"

"I don't know. That's why I'm going."

But Chris held onto her arm. "I mean, is it safe? Is the robber gone? Have the police been by?"

"Oh," she said softly, touched by his concern. "Well, she was robbed at the pharmacy where she works, and now she's at home, so I would say the coast is clear." When he still didn't let go of her arm, she gave him a puzzled look. "If that's all right with you?"

"Go on." He released her arm and sat back. "I'll let John know."

"Thank you," she murmured, grabbing her purse and slipping past their friends and out of the condo.

* * *

`Hey guys, I was robbed at work. Just got done with the police. Headed home now.`

That was the simple message Nichole had sent to The Classmates group chat an hour ago. Kelenna saw the message over and over again in her mind as she covered the short distance from John's condo to the high-rise where Nichole lived. She parked in the garage and made her way to the corridor that led to Nichole's apartment.

"Kelenna, wait up!" she heard from behind her. She turned to see Dev Patel, another former classmate, jogging lightly towards her.

"I didn't know you were coming," she told him after he gave her a quick one-armed hug.

"Me either, I was on a date when Zoe called."

Kelenna looked up at him. "You blew off your date for this? I'm sure Nichole would have understood."

Dev shrugged. "It's fine. To be honest, the call rescued me. Kristy was just too . . ." He made a face that Kelenna couldn't interpret.

"Kristy? I thought you were seeing Becca?" She distinctly remembered the name of the last girl he'd brought around the last time The Classmates had all hung out. When he gave her a look that said Becca was long gone, Kelenna let out a low laugh. "Why am I not surprised?" she asked as she knocked on Nichole's door. Dev was the biggest player she knew. He loved women and they loved him and his Bollywood good looks right back.

"Hey, this is what single people do." He glanced at her. "You know what I'm talking about."

Before she could ask him what he meant, they heard Zoe call out to them and turned to see her running down the hall.

"Hey guys," she said breathlessly. "Did you knock already?"

"Yep."

"Everything all right?" Zoe asked, looking between them.

"We were just talking about how your call interrupted Dev's date," Kelenna said quickly, ignoring Dev's warning look.

Zoe gasped. "Oh no! Tell Becca I'm sorry."

"No, not with Becca," Kelenna corrected with a cheeky grin. "This one is Kristy."

"Dev," Zoe said with a disappointed head tilt. "Already?"

"What? Becca and I aren't exclusive!"

"You're still an 'are'?" Zoe's eyes bulged out.

"Is Nichole in here or not?" Dev knocked on the door three more times, loud enough to simultaneously drown out Kelenna and Zoe's laughter, and bring Nichole to the door.

"Guys, you didn't have to come," Nichole said after she let them in.

"Nonsense, Nic, of course we were always going to come." Zoe leaned down to hug her. She was the nurturer of their little crew, always ready with a hug or a quick word of encouragement. "Are you okay?"

"I'm fine."

Kelenna stepped forward and hugged her next. When she released her, she held her at arm's length. Nichole didn't look fine. She looked drained and, for lack of a better word, forlorn. She was wearing a fluffy robe over a t-shirt and a pair of sweatpants when she shouldn't even be cold. She looked like she needed something more than warmth from it. Something more akin to comfort. Even her hair looked dull. Nichole had thick, long natural hair that she always wore in different creative styles. Right now, it was twisted up into a knot at the top of her head and its usual luster and vibrancy was gone. She was not fine. Not even a little. "Are you sure you're okay? Do you need to talk to your mom? Someone?"

"My mom will just worry. I'm fine, seriously. Just shaken up."

Dev put an arm around her shoulders and led her to her living room. His six-two frame towered over her five-three one as he guided her down to sit on the couch. "I'm so sorry you had to go through that. I mean, you read about these things, but you never think it could happen to someone you know."

"What did happen?" Kelenna asked, sitting carefully on an armchair that was way too close to the glass side table for her comfort. Everything in Nichole's apartment was so fragile.

"Hold on, let me call Pete and Sharon." Zoe pulled out her phone and video-called the Ackermans, the last two people that completed their six-man crew. They'd all been a part of the same study group in pharmacy school and had managed to remain close in the four years following their graduation. Within seconds, the five of them were listening intently to Nichole's tale about the robbery.

"Y'all," she said after she explained how a man dressed in all black had gone from politely asking to purchase insulin needles to pointing a gun in her face. "I thought I was going to die. That's what I can't get out of my head. He was willing to shoot me over some needles and some Oxy!"

"Addicts." Pete's curse came through the phone. "They'll do anything for their next fix. They case pharmacies and try to hit up the ones that seem empty."

"Well they came to the right one," Nichole said with a snort. "I'd just sent my tech home, and y'all know how Dexter's is. We're all the way in the back, secluded from the rest of the store. I was alone back there."

Every pharmacist worth their salt had been inside a Dexter's pharmacy at least once in their lives. It was the largest chain of retail pharmacies in the country. The convenience store that fronted the pharmacy rivaled any superstore, but the pharmacy in the back left corner was the real money maker. The stock behind the counter of the pharmacy was easily worth millions. If he wanted Oxy, there would have been a lot of Oxy to give him.

"I gave him everything he wanted. I figured I just had to keep him happy so he wouldn't hurt me. But by the time I got to the safe, I remembered there was a panic button right on the side of it. So I pushed it." Nichole went on to explain that the panic button triggered an alert for the local authorities and the store manager. The store manager could look at the cameras while the police made their way down. "He got greedy and wanted everything we had. That's the only reason he was still around when we heard sirens outside. And that was when he used me as a human shield."

"I'm sorry, what?" Zoe was aghast.

"Yep." Nichole nodded gravely. "The sirens freaked him out. He tried to jump out of the drive-thru window, but there were bars on them. So he came up with the next best plan. Me. I felt like I was a hostage in some kind of horror movie. He made me walk him out to the front, and no one looked at us twice. I wanted to scream out loud for help, but I couldn't." She rubbed her lower back. "I can still feel his gun digging into me."

Kelenna was having a headache just trying to picture the events. "Please tell me the police were at the entrance."

Nichole dragged her breath. "They were. We got up front, and there were like three of them, guns drawn. At us. And I freaked out because I was scared they would fire and hit me." When she shuddered, Zoe grabbed her hand and squeezed. Kelenna sat ramrod still as Nichole finished her story. She'd dropped to the floor when the police had asked them to, and the robber had clumsily lost his gun. "He was an amateur," Nichole said with a snort. "One of the cops cuffed him while another pulled me to the side. I've never been so relieved in my whole life."

"We're not safe out there, man," Pete said.

"No, we're not," Zoe agreed. "And on top of that, we're treated like machines. Sometimes I wonder if it's worth it."

"Do you have to work in the morning, Nic?" Sharon asked.

Nichole gave a tired smile. "No. I already had the weekend off, so it worked out. I just need the time to get my mind right, you know?"

* * *

About half an hour after Pete and Sharon disconnected to put Carter Rose, their adorable twenty-two-month-old daughter, to bed, Nichole threatened Kelenna, Zoe, and Dev with eviction unless they a) changed the subject from the robbery, and b) agreed to share a bottle of Merlot with her. It took some cajoling for Kelenna, who never drank on a work night, but soon the trio was doing their best to distract Nichole from the awful events of the night. Dev shared more about his date from hell with Kristy while Zoe talked about a fellow professor at the pharmacy school where she taught. "He has a PhD in pharmaceutical sciences and he patented this compound he sold for millions. He's slumming it with us at the university. Marcy, who teaches medicinal chemistry, snuck a look at his jacket and the label said Armani. Who wears an Armani suit to teach?"

While the others laughed at Zoe's story, Kelenna spared a minute to look at her messages.

Chika: Where did you go? I was talking to Trent. He and some buddies of his have a startup and I was talking about doing some PR work for them. Isn't that exciting? Plus he's super cute.

Kelenna didn't even know who Trent was, but she wasn't surprised. Chika was a public relations specialist slash brand consultant slash one of those Gen Z jobs that was so nondescript that Kelenna didn't quite know what she did. She hopped on whatever opportunity she saw to grow her clientele.

John: Sorry to hear about Nichole, say hi to her for me. P.S. Your friend is talking my guy's ear off. Something about PR work? Does she have to solicit clients while we're watching a football game?

Okay, so it seemed that Trent was one of John's doctor friends.

Chris: Are you alive?

She smiled at his attempt to mask concern with aloofness and replied immediately.

Kelenna: I'll be sure to let Nichole know you're glad she's fine.

His response came back in seconds.

Chris: That she is

Kelenna: You're hopeless :)

"What's so funny?"

Kelenna looked up to see Nichole looking at her inquisitively. "Nothing," she said quickly. "Well not nothing. John said to tell you hi. He's sorry this happened."

"Oh, that's sweet of him," Nichole said softly. "Tell him I said thanks."

"I will."

"And since you won't tell us what was really funny, how about you tell us what's new with you? And nothing about your perfect job, please. I don't think I can take it."

Kelenna pursed her lips to hide a sigh. She was used to Nichole's digs about her 'cushy' pharmacy job that she loved so much, which was a sharp contrast to how Nichole felt about hers. Nichole had worked at Dexter's Pharmacy for many years, even before pharmacy school, and she was very vocal about how much she detested it. Right now, with the DEA-engineered opioid crisis-shortage bearing down on Preston, Kelenna's job was anything but perfect, but she knew Nichole wouldn't want to hear about that. She decided to go with the most imperfect thing about herself she could think of. It was a no-brainer. "Um, I joined SwipeNow?"

Kelenna watched as the bomb she dropped permeated through her friends' minds. Being on a dating app was like breathing to some people, but her friends would understand that it was completely out of character for her.

"You what?" Nichole asked incredulously at the same time Dev said, "That's not news."

"Wait, what?" Kelenna frowned at him. "What do you mean it's not news? You know?"

"Was it supposed to be a secret?" he asked, puzzled. "I'm on SwipeNow too, you know. I saw you."

Kelenna gasped. "How in the world did you see me?"

"I have SwipeNow set to a fifty-mile radius," he replied with a shrug.

"This is mortifying!" Kelenna cried out, pulling out her phone to open the SwipeNow app. "I can't believe you've known this whole time!" Sure enough, there he was. He was shirtless in his display picture, and looked like he was at the top of Stone Mountain. His 'about me' section was short. It was a lecture they'd all heard before on how to pronounce his name. "It's pronounced 'Dave,'" he'd written. No doubt he got more action with that three-word bio than she did with the paragraph she had on hers.

"Come on, it's not mortifying. We're a social media generation. This is how we meet people. It would be weird if you weren't on it," Dev said. "I'm on at least four apps."

"How does someone like you need four apps?" Zoe asked, sounding a cross between amazed and perplexed. "You meet women on the street!"

"I may not need them, but having them exponentially increases my chances of meeting these people in real life."

Kelenna frowned. "I don't follow."

"Okay, listen. My phone is always on me, whether I'm jogging at Piedmont Park or working out at LA Fitness. That means my location is on. That means people who are swiping may or may not spot me. I don't know what it is, but girls have infinitely more courage stepping up to a stranger they've just seen on an app than actually messaging them through the app. I was at Whole Foods the other day and a woman came to me and said, 'I thought that was you.'"

"Helps when you look like a Bollywood actor," Kelenna muttered.

"Ooh, did she think you were the actual Dev Patel?" Zoe asked.

"No, she saw me on the app! And what does that mean, the actual Dev Patel?" Dev rolled his eyes. "I look nothing like that man."

Kelenna didn't think it was a bad thing if he was mistaken for Dev Patel, the actor, but she didn't say that.

"Kelenna, dating apps don't have to be an extreme sport like the way Dev has approached it," Nichole said. "I'm on a couple, and it's no big deal. Think about it like Facebook or Twitter. You only go on when you're bored, and maybe you'll get a free dinner or make a new friend."

That was easy for easy for Nichole to say. She traded out boyfriends like she was on an app called *SwapNow*, not SwipeNow, and she didn't think twice about it.

"That's the problem, you see," Kelenna said with a frown. "I have enough friends already, I'm not interested in making any more. I'm trying to make a real connection, as crazy as that sounds, and so far, it's been slim pickings."

She went on to tell them about Bad Breath, Yells At Waitresses and Talks Over People. "I've been chatting with this professor for the last couple of days. He seems promising but with my luck, he'll probably turn out to be a serial killer!"

"Kelenna, you can't expect too much from these quickie dating apps," Dev started, his tone patient like he was talking to a six-year-old. "It's not like TruMatch where you actually pay for people to figure out how well you and another person fit together. This is all superficial. You're never going to find your future mate on SwipeNow."

"Don't say that, Dev! I've heard stories!" Zoe cried. "Marcy met her fiancé on Tinder!"

Dev looked exasperatedly at Zoe, probably wondering how she'd managed to live as long as she had with her idealism intact. "Marcy doesn't sound real."

"She's a professor I see every single day at work!"

Kelenna tuned them both out. If Dev was right and there was no hope of meeting anyone special, then what was the point of even being on the app? She could be intentional all she wanted. She could make a list of the kind of people she would only swipe right for. She could even decide to chat with them for some time before she agreed to meet, and still it could amount to nothing. It seemed like a colossal waste of time.

As if he could read her mind, Dev patted her shoulder. "Kelenna, my point is, you don't need that kind of pressure. Don't overthink it. You like their profile? Swipe right. You don't like what they're saying? Ignore them and move on. Just have fun."

"I agree with Dev," Nichole said. "The most unlikely things happen when you're not trying. I mean, look at Zoe. She met the love of her life at nineteen. In the library. And oh, he just happened to be the star wide-receiver for her school."

"And I fought it for half a semester," Zoe said with a wistful grin. Then she turned to look at Kelenna, her face growing serious. "I'm all for you stepping out of your comfort zone, girl. It's a good thing. I just hope you aren't doing it for the wrong reasons."

"I'm not!" Kelenna protested. When Zoe did nothing but stare at her, she let out a sigh. "I just want to make a real connection," she said, repeating her own words from earlier. "This isn't about Will." *And the fact that he was getting married in six and a half months*, she didn't add. She may or may not have pulled up his save-the-date email last night. Or the last several nights. She also may or may not have gone to his wedding site to stalk the wedding plans. The wedding countdown may or may not have been so visible on the page that it felt like a clock ticking in her ear, reminding her what a loser she was.

"I didn't say anything about Will," Zoe replied knowingly. "You did."

6

Vinings was a charming, posh community in Cobb County with the perfect mix of modern buildings and older, more quaint structures that Kelenna had romanticized growing up. Even now, as her Uber driver pulled up at her destination, she was enthralled by the picturesque block of stores accented by a street made entirely of cobblestones. She'd never been to this particular spot before, but she was glad she'd chosen it for her SwipeNow date. If things didn't go well with the professor, at least she would have spent her Saturday at such a pretty place.

"Here you go, young lady," the older, African American driver said to her. He had to be somewhere between fifty and sixty, but he looked considerably younger. He'd made the short trip from her apartment more interesting with his incessant chatter. First he mistook her for an undergraduate at Kennesaw State, and when she corrected him, he went on a three-minute rant about how young she looked and how he couldn't believe she'd been a pharmacist for four years. "Bet the boys are intimidated by you!" he'd said. He was even able to finagle that she was going on a first date. By the end of the drive, she felt like she'd been adopted by the man.

"Thank you," Kelenna told him when she got down from the car.

"No problem, sweetheart! Make sure he got a real job, now! A pretty woman like you gotta be careful! You don't want no moochers!"

Kelenna let out a good-natured laugh and assured him that she would. After she spent a second watching him drive away, she turned towards Lila's coffee shop and took a deep breath to gather her nerves. "Let's do this," she said to herself.

She spotted the professor immediately through the glass doors of the small shop. How could she not? He was sitting in full view of the door and anyone who would walk in. Kelenna paused outside the coffee shop as she stared at him. His SwipeNow display picture didn't do him justice. He was much hotter in real life. And bigger. The chair he was sitting on was far too small for him. He seemed confident that it would bear his weight though, the way he spread his legs and leaned back against it. One hand was on his thigh while the other rested on the table, moving up and down on his phone. The sleeves of his button-up were rolled up, emphasizing how big his arms were. Was he a professor or a body-builder? Her eyes continued to look him over until they reached his face. He looked younger than the thirty-seven-year-old he claimed to be. He was bald and light-skinned, but she already knew that. Those glasses. He didn't have them on in any of the pictures. Why not? Didn't men realize that they would get more right swipes if they could pull off looking hot in glasses? His were modern, black-rimmed, square-framed and sat on really high, really sharp cheekbones. Involuntarily, her hand went up to her own cheeks. She spent a lot of her teenage years despising them. She inherited the fullness of them from her mother who'd promised her that she would appreciate them later in life. "When you're fifty-five, you'll look forty," her mother had said numerous times. But Kelenna knew she would be okay with looking fifty-five at fifty-five if she had cheekbones like the professor's that could cut glass.

"Coming in?"

Kelenna snapped out of her thoughts to see a white man in a t-shirt and cargo shorts holding the door open for her.

"Yes," she said quickly, mildly embarrassed by the length of time she'd spent gawking at her coffee date. "Thank you."

The doors to the coffee shop had one of those bells that announced the presence of every customer that walked in. She caught the professor's quick glance at her, and quick dismissal, before he returned his gaze to hers and held it a bit longer. She didn't look that different from her own SwipeNow picture, did she? She mentally assessed her appearance. An oversized, mustard yellow sweater that fell off one shoulder over denim pants and leopard-patterned ballet flats. Not a stitch of foundation on, just lip gloss and a little eye-liner. She'd put her natural hair, now out of braids, into a high bun that she'd had to tame by tying it down with a scarf for several hours just so it could lay as flat as she wanted. She looked good for a late morning date. Simple, but good. She hid her disappointment at the fact that the professor had had to do a double take at her and walked up to him. To his credit, he scrambled to his feet and beamed at her. Nice, straight teeth that blinded her and rendered her almost speechless met her. Forget body-builder, was he a model?

"Kelenna?"

"Professor," she replied in a low voice, then shook her head quickly, mortified. "I mean, Darrell." She shook her head again, completely flustered. "Sorry. Dillon. Jeez." How had she managed to call him professor all this while and not have committed the name Dillon Warner to memory?

He took it in stride. His chuckle was disarming and cut through the awkwardness of her gaffe. "I think I like professor the best," he said with a confident grin. "A definite no to Darrell." His hand swallowed hers as he shook it. He looked even bigger up close, much taller than she was, anyway. Kelenna wanted to snatch his phone and rewrite his dating profile. *I'm a six-six professor in a body-builder's body with a voice like a radio presenter. Yes, I'm not real.* That would have encapsulated him properly. The fact that she would have swiped left on him if she'd read that wasn't the point. The point was that he'd sold himself short. It was like getting catfished, but in reverse. There was no way she'd been prepared for him.

"Please, sit." He gestured at the chair across the small table from where he stood.

"I'm so sorry, Dillon," she said with a self-deprecating laugh. "I think I may be nervous."

"I get it," he replied kindly. "It's not the same as chatting back and forth, is it? It's nice to finally meet."

She let out a small sigh of relief. "Same here."

There was another awkward moment of silence before he suggested that they go to the counter to get something to eat and drink. They did, and she chose a blueberry scone and a strawberry lemonade tea. He chose a coffee of some sort and a sandwich. She let him pay for her items and thanked him as they sat back down.

"No coffee for you?"

"I don't drink coffee," Kelenna said with a slight wrinkle of her nose. She only did it in jest because she knew it amazed coffee drinkers when an adult could function without it. "Never have, never will," she added cheekily.

"No? Why are we in a coffee shop then?"

"Oh, the blueberry scones here are to die for," she said without missing a beat.

That was a bald-faced lie, seeing as she'd never been in this shop before. Maybe she would tell him the truth when they got to know each other a little better. After her series of bad evening dates, she decided to try out this two-part first date strategy. The first part, or pre-first date as she was calling it, would be a quick date at an obscure location where she could properly assess the man. If he passed, he would graduate to a proper first date at a bona fide restaurant. Chika thought it was crazy, but hey, she could bear bad hour-long coffee dates if they spared her from horrible two-hour dinner dates in the future.

"Really?" He gave her an almost disbelieving look that made her wonder if she needed to defend her lie about the scone a bit more. "You mind if I . . ." He stuck a plastic fork and broke off a piece of her scone. Then he slid the piece into his mouth and chewed it slowly. All without breaking eye contact. "You're right. It's pretty good."

Her mouth went dry as she stared at him. "Told you," she managed to squeak out.

"So, Kelenna, tell me more about yourself. You're a pharmacist, right? One of the doctor ones?"

"One of the doctor ones?" she repeated.

"You know, like how some people have PhDs in pharmacy, and others don't."

"Oh, no. The degree is a doctor of pharmacy—PharmD, not a PhD." She went on to explain the difference between a PhD in pharmaceutical sciences or pharmacology, and a PharmD. Then she talked about the years and money it cost to get a PharmD. She stopped abruptly when she caught herself rambling about how the PharmD program started in California in the '50s, and had been optional until the early 2000s. "Sorry," she said looking down at her hands sheepishly. She didn't want to look back on the date and realize that she'd spent half of it giving a pharmacy history lesson. She shook her head to clear it. "I tend to get carried away."

"No, it's impressive," he said softly. She liked how he looked unblinkingly at her, like if he spared the second it took for his eyes to flutter, he would miss something. It was unnerving and thrilling at the same time. "I like that you're so passionate. I had no clue how pharmacists got to where they're at. I just knew they worked at Dexter's and made a lot of money."

She smiled at his admitted ignorance but didn't say anything else. She was mostly blown away by the fact that he was even listening to her. It was a refreshing contrast to the last man she'd sat across a table from.

"I told myself I wouldn't ask, but I have to." He leaned back against his chair as he regarded her. "What's a woman like you doing on SwipeNow? Don't get me wrong, I'm happy you were on it, because it's brought us here today. But I just can't believe there are that many blind men around you in real life."

"Have you looked at yourself?" she blurted out. When she slapped a hand over her mouth, he let out a hearty laugh. He didn't stop until she joined in.

"And a sense of humor too," he said with a smile that produced crinkles around his eyes. They were the cutest smile lines she'd ever seen. "Where have you been all my life?"

She rolled her eyes but smiled into her tea. When she was done with that sip, she looked up and met his eyes. If he liked her humor, would he also like her vulnerability? "I wanted to try this because I wanted to open myself to possibilities. I wanted to put myself out there and make things happen, you know?"

"I know exactly what you mean. SwipeNow gets a bad rap for being a hookup site. How does it matter how you make the connection, as long as you make the connection?"

Kelenna smiled broadly at him. "I totally agree," she said, wishing Dev and Nichole could hear him and see how wrong they were about her expectations of SwipeNow. Sometimes all it took was patience, and someone with similar ideals.

Within the next few minutes, they were actively trading information about themselves with each other. She loved that he was a big talker. It was a far cry from anyone she'd ever known, including Will. Will made you earn getting to know things about him. While she'd been intrigued by his mystique once upon a time, she didn't realize until now just how limiting it had been.

Dillon talked about growing up in New York, moving to DC for college and grad school, and eventually relocating to Atlanta for work. When he said he taught at the all-girl Spelman College, Kelenna joked that she was sure that his class was a popular one on campus. He'd choked so hard on a laugh when she added that she could picture girls lining up outside his office to ask for 'extra credit' that Kelenna knew it wasn't far from the truth. Using humor to try to tame the ridiculous attraction she was having to him was working thus far.

They kept things relatively light until she casually mentioned her Nigerian heritage. That was when he went from flirty to full-blown professor of African American studies. Before she knew it, she was pulled into an African black versus American black discussion—what he called the Black Divide. If it was possible, he got even more attractive. Was there anything better than a man who had a passion and was willing to share it? She felt like she was getting a glimpse into how he operated in a classroom, and it was fascinating to her, even if at certain points she felt defensive of Africans. "What do you think?" he asked, after his last comment where he said African blacks ride the waves of the opportunities created by American blacks while looking down them.

"Trust me Dillon, I understand you. And I know I'm not an expert like you are, but the way I see it, Africans who come to America have a different struggle. They know that failure is not an option, and because of that they'll seize every opportunity they find. I just think that like with any other thing, if we broaden our scopes, stop the generalizations, and learn to think of people as individuals, we'll gain a little more insight into each other."

"Insight into each other," Dillon echoed, looking at her with another intense gaze. He seemed to be weighing her words in his mind, like she was one of his students and he had to grade her. She was almost afraid that he would tear them to shreds. "Fair point, Kelenna. We both have different issues. I just think there needs to be a little more understanding."

"I agree. And it starts with open dialogue."

"I want a second date with you."

Kelenna's mouth fell open with his abrupt change in subject. How did they go from talking about the relationship between black Americans and black Africans to second dates? Had he been testing her in some way?

"Brunch," he continued when she said nothing. "I know how you women love that. I'll even cook." Then he leaned forward and placed a hand over hers, turning her palm around in his and drawing slow circles on it. "You have the kind of mind I want to explore."

He was seducing her openly, in the middle of the afternoon, in this small coffee shop that she'd found by googling 'small coffee shops near me.' Normally, it would have raised her heckles, because who said things like, *I want to explore your mind?* Normally, she would have run far away from a guy who was coming on too strong too quickly. But she was doing this thing where she was putting herself out there, and he was unbelievably hot, and anyway, the only thing she could fix her mouth to say was, "You cook?"

"I'm an amazing cook." If it was possible, his already deep voice dropped by at least another octave.

"Okay," she whispered.

"Good." He released her hand and probably released her from the spell he'd put her under. "It's a date."

7

"Ooh, someone looks good today! Hot date after work?"

Kelenna snorted at Ji and walked further into the pharmacy, placing her handbag on the worktable in the middle of the pit and looking down at her outfit. She had traded in her usual uniform of maroon scrubs for a pair of wide-leg pants and a dress shirt. She'd even spared a few minutes to put on eyeliner and some eyeshadow. "If I had a date, I wouldn't be wearing the clothes now."

"No, it's her birthday today!" Siya Desai chimed in. "Happy birthday!"

"Oh, that's right. Happy birthday! How old are you now?" Tricia asked.

"Thanks, guys." Kelenna smiled as she pulled out a chair and sat on it. Ever since she turned twenty-six—that annoying age where you were considered late twenties, but still felt like you were in your mid-twenties—birthdays had become just another day for her. A reminder that she was getting older. But she liked to at least look good while she was doing it, hence the extra effort in her appearance. "I'm old. Twenty-nine."

"Twenty-nine isn't old!" Tricia protested. "When I was your age, I was living in Atlanta and working at Dexter's. I went out every other night. Being single was fun." Now, Tricia lived on a farm with actual animals out in Cartersville, Georgia, about thirty minutes away from Preston. "I have a different kind of fun now, but I wouldn't trade those days for anything. Even though I was considered old when I got married."

Oh boy. Kelenna knew what was coming next. Once a derivative of the word 'marry' was uttered in the vicinity of the trio of pharmacists, it was a clarion call for them to begin their good cop, bad cop, and indifferent cop routine. Siya was mostly always the bad cop, telling her to stop being picky and settle down. Tricia was the good cop, imploring her to take her time and choose right. And Ji was the indifferent cop, almost like the record keeper, listening to the conversation, repeating what was said for verification so that no one missed a detail, but not giving any real opinions. It amused her to no end that they were worse than her Nigerian parents when it came to her being single. It didn't help that she was the last unmarried person in the entire department. There was literally nobody else for them to pick on.

"Anyone new?" Siya eased into the subject with as much subtlety as a bull in a china shop.

"What about Dr. Tari-Douglas in the ER?" Tricia asked. "Speaking of ER, have you done a walk-through over there lately? There are some cute nurse practitioners and physician's assistants over there. You have to go with one of the techs when they're restocking the ADM. Maybe one of them will see you and just fall in love."

"Wow." Kelenna smiled dryly. The ADM or automated dispensing machine was a glorified vending machine for drugs. There was one on every patient floor, and the pharmacy technicians were responsible for filling it with the most frequently used medications in that area. "It's that simple, huh?"

Tricia shrugged looking like she was on the verge of laughter. "Sure."

"I thought Tari-Douglas was your cousin?" fact-checker Ji interjected.

All right, she may have told them that Chris was her cousin when he first started working at the hospital a couple of years ago. He was always calling the pharmacy and asking to speak to her. It was never really for anything personal, but it had been enough to make them suspicious. After one of the techs sighted him, they declared he was tall and good-looking enough for Kelenna to consider as a potential mate. It was easier to go with the cousin lie. She knew that Chris would have corroborated that without needing to be coached.

"Did I?" she asked now. "I must have said he was like a cousin to me."

"I specifically remember—"

"But I met someone new," Kelenna said, interrupting Ji before she could access her memory vault and repeat whole conversations from years ago verbatim.

She gave them a rundown about Dillon. She tried to keep it light, because it had been only a week since she met him and there was still so much to discover. But as she talked, her tone, as she feared it would, belied her excitement. It was hard to not be hopeful about him. Apart from the fact that he was so hot, he had the maturity of an almost-forty-year-old that didn't believe in playing games. He was the kind of guy who was secure enough to say that he liked what he saw when he saw it. She loved how detail-oriented he was. When he sent her text messages, they were always in longhand, written out with every single letter, as though he wanted to make sure he got his words right when he communicated with her. Even though they hadn't met up yet for brunch like he'd promised, they'd talked about plans for fall break, when he would be done grading midterms.

"Seems like you hit the jackpot with this one, Kelenna!" Siya remarked. "You seem smitten!"

"It's still so early," Kelenna said modestly.

"Trust me, if it's meant to be, it'll happen quickly," Tricia said in the voice of someone who was speaking from experience. Everyone in the pharmacy knew that she married her husband three months after they first met. "Y'all just have to be honest with each other."

Before Kelenna could respond, the phone rang, the doorbell buzzed, another phone line went off, and the little downtime they'd had disappeared. She slinked away from the busyness and went to her office down the hall to prepare for rounds.

* * *

Later that evening, Kelenna slipped her key into the lock of her parent's front door and let herself in.

"Birthday girl is here!" she called out as she shut the door behind her and twisted the lock. When no one responded, she walked through the foyer into the kitchen and to the adjoining dining area. She beamed when she saw the spread on the dining table.

"There you are," her mother said from behind her, giving her a hug and a kiss on her cheek. "Happy birthday, my dear girl."

"Thank you, Mom. This is too much, you didn't have to go to all this trouble."

"Nonsense. It's not every day my only daughter turns twenty-nine." She squeezed Kelenna tight before she released her. "Get your dad and we'll start dinner. Your brother will be here soon."

John joined them about twenty minutes later, announcing his presence from the door right before they heard him shut it. He materialized in front of them moments later and soon she felt his arms go around her shoulders in a hug. "Happy birthday, sis."

"Thanks, twinnie!" she said with a mischievous smile. It was a dance they did every year. He stopped being her big brother on her birthday in October, and became her twin until his birthday in mid-January when he became older again. That he was in denial about their Irish twins situation was none of her concern. Even now his hug had tightened considerably. He was definitely punishing her for challenging his seniority.

"Ow!" she cried out, unable to keep the laughter from her voice. "You're smothering me!"

"Was I?" he said disingenuously, his arms still tight around her. "So sorry, little sis. With strong emphasis on little sis." He gave her a quick kiss on her cheek and squeezed her shoulders before he released her. "Oh, and I found this one outside." He gestured behind him, and Chika appeared out of nowhere, arms stretched wide in the universal 'ta-da' gesture.

"Hi Aunty and Uncle!" Like a well-trained Nigerian, she went round to hug the older adults first before giving a loud shriek and pouncing on Kelenna. "Happy birthday, darling! Welcome to twenty-nine!"

"Join us, my dear." Mrs. Agu motioned for Chika to help herself to the food at the center of the table. "How are your parents? Do you see them?"

"They're fine. I saw them last weekend," Chika replied stiffly. She was always stiff when she had to talk about her parents. Kelenna knew it had to do with her overbearing mother. Six years ago, Chika was a second-year at Emory Law when she abruptly dropped out of school. Her mother still hounded her to complete the degree all these years later. Never mind that she was thriving in a career that suited her personality better than law would have, and also that she'd thoroughly hated every second of law school.

"Good, make sure you say hello to them for me."

"Yes, Aunty." When she turned to Kelenna, the stiffness was gone from her expression and her eyes danced with anticipation. "So, we're all dying to know. How was the date with the doctor?"

If looks could kill, Chika would have become a pile of ashes from the fiery look Kelenna sent her way. To her credit, Chika recognized that she had spoken out of turn.

"Oops. Is this the first time y'all are hearing about him?"

"Chika! What part of this," she shot her the exact murderous look, "did you not understand?!"

John laughed at her discomfort. "Come on, tell us about your date. Who is this person?"

"And a doctor?" her mother added, sounding way too excited. "What a lovely birthday surprise! Do we know him?" Only her mother would view Kelenna going on a date as a birthday surprise when it wasn't even her birthday.

"Where does he practice?" her father asked.

"He's not that kind of doctor." She resigned herself to the fact that there was no way she was leaving the table without spilling everything. "He has a PhD in African American studies."

She saw her father's face wrinkle, probably in displeasure, but definitely in judgement. "So he's a teacher?"

"Yes, Dad, he's a professor. An accomplished one." She had no idea if he was accomplished at anything, but her father didn't need to know that.

"I think I meant to say professor," Chika added distractedly. By that time, Kelenna had had enough of her. She proceeded to talk about her date in full detail, all the while making sure to let them know that there were no expectations.

"He sounds interesting, dear," her mom said, her earlier excitement cooling off. "Just make sure you're careful with these people on the internet."

They spent the rest of the dinner talking about other things, and Kelenna was grateful for the break in the talk about her love life. When her parents retired to the living room, Chika resurrected the topic once more.

"Okay, now that Aunty and Uncle are gone, tell me the good stuff. Did you kiss him?"

"Chika! It was our first date!"

Chika shrugged and muttered under her breath. Kelenna thought she heard the words *prude* and *innocent*. If she was a prude for not kissing Dillon on their first date, then so be it.

"Can you at least tell me if he was hot?"

"Painfully so," Kelenna sighed. "Think Common, the rapper, but taller, bigger, talks a little bit quicker, and oh—glasses."

"Common in glasses! That's my dream guy!" Chika grabbed Kelenna's hands and began a happy little dance.

"Dear God."

They both turned to John at the sound of his voice. He was still sitting across the dining table from them, looking highly unimpressed.

Chika blew him a kiss and grinned widely at him. "Only second to you, Johnny!"

"Yeah, right." He rolled his eyes. Was he blushing?

Chika turned back to her. "Okay. So let me see if I have it right. Hot, older, professor, never married—"

"Hold on. Never married? I don't know about that. I didn't ask." Not that it mattered whether or not he was a divorcee, but she was surprised that she hadn't even thought to ask.

"You didn't ask?" Chika's eyes widened as she pulled out her phone and started punching at it. "Does he have kids?"

"I don't know!" Kelenna said worriedly. What kind of person had kids and didn't bring them up during a first date? "He would have said, right?" she added weakly.

"Probably not! Let me guess, you didn't check to see if he's currently married, did you?"

"Check? Why would a married guy be on SwipeNow?"

Chika paused midway through the assault on her phone and glared at her. "It's like you don't read any of the links I send you. John, tell your sister that men don't see marital status as a hindrance to being on a dating site."

"Huh?" John asked.

Chika ignored him. "What's his middle name?"

"How am I supposed to know?"

"I thought you said you went out with him?"

"I did. It was a date, not an interview!"

"Don't you see? That's exactly what these things are! Interviews! You do your research before and after you catch feelings!"

"I haven't caught feelings for him!"

"Right," she scoffed. "Even I have caught feelings for him."

"Wow." John stood up and stretched. "Men are not worth all the detective work." With that, he walked out of the dining room, Kelenna guessed to join their parents.

"Ignore him, he's one of them. Here it is . . . Oh."

"What?" Kelenna leaned over her friend's shoulder.

"Is this him?" She showed Kelenna a picture of a white woman holding a child, standing next to a man holding a second child. They were standing in a garden looking like a magazine ad for the perfect interracial family. This was the kind of picture that could tug at the side of her that wanted a family, but today, it made her blood boil.

"How dare he?" she gasped, snatching the phone away from Chika and scrolling through Dillon's wife's profile. Her name was Melissa, and even though Dillon had no page of his own on Facebook, he was featured heavily in hers. Why didn't people make their profiles private more? Did they want other people to admire them and be jealous of how blessed they were? And how blessed were you anyway if your husband was lurking around on an app trying to date other people?

"What are you going to do?"

"I'm going to give him a piece of my mind."

"Ooh, I like feisty Kelenna." Chika clapped happily.

Kelenna ignored her excitement. "I mean, what was the plan? Did he want to make me his second wife?"

"Definitely wanted to get into your pants."

"You know what he said to me? He said that I had the kind of mind he wanted to explore."

"Sounds like a euphemism for pants," Chika said with a frown. "From the 1990s apparently."

Kelenna ignored her once more. "And oh, get this. He told me he wanted to cook brunch for me at my place. I was going to let him into my apartment! I guess we know why he couldn't do it at his!"

"Hmm," Chika said thoughtfully. "He was going to cook for you? Maybe he really likes you."

Before Kelenna could say what she thought about Dillon liking her, her phone vibrated, indicating that she had received a new text message. "Aha, speak of the devil! He can't actually call me, because he's at home with his family and they would hear him talking to me!"

"Now you're learning!" Chika laughed.

"*Happy birthday again, beautiful*," she read out loud, "*I hope dinner with your family is going fine.*" She sighed in regret. "Damn. He has perfect text diction."

"Text diction is not a thing." Chika rolled her eyes. "Now, tell him off!"

Kelenna started to craft out her response. She deleted some words here and added some words there, until she was satisfied. She handed the phone to Chika to read.

"*Thank you, dinner was great. So, how's your family?*" Chika read out loud. "I was expecting some fire, but the coolness works. Send it!"

Kelenna laughed, happy that she could see the funny side of Chika's obvious pleasure at the entire situation. She hit send.

"Now we wait." Chika rubbed her hands together gleefully. "This will be quick."

She was right. Dillon's response came almost immediately.

"*I was going to tell you, I was just waiting for the right moment. We are separated and have been for some time.*" Kelenna snorted and shot a knowing look at Chika. "Do you think his wife knows that their marriage is on the rocks?"

"Doesn't seem like she does," Chika said, playing along. "I mean, she just posted about their cute little family last week."

"If you are indeed separated," Kelenna dictated as she typed, "it doesn't look as though your wife got the memo. I really hope you both are able to make it work, and leave unsuspecting women out of it."

"Always so classy," Chika mused.

"Well, listen to this!" She read his next message: "*You know nothing about my marriage, so I would appreciate it if you didn't judge me.*"

"Whoa," Chika said, eyes wide.

"You know what? Enough is enough." Kelenna typed out one more text, hit send, and then slammed her phone down on the dining table.

"What'd you say?"

"Told him I was sorry if I sounded judgmental. Then I blocked him and deleted his number. I'm done having that conversation."

Chika placed a hand on her shoulder. "Are you all right? This is a really crappy thing to happen on your birthday. I feel partly responsible."

Kelenna thought it was a crappy thing to happen on any day. "It's better that I found out now rather than later," she said tersely.

"That's a good way to look at it. And the next time you meet up with someone from the app, you can be even more prepared—"

"The next time?" Kelenna asked, aghast. "Chika, I did nothing wrong and I still almost became a homewrecker." She stood and picked up her phone. In three quick steps, she uninstalled the SwipeNow app. "There. A permanent SwipeNow break. I feel better already. Come on. There's cake in the living room."

"There you are," John said, barely looking away from his phone when they walked in. "So what's the verdict? Married or not?"

"Married with two kids," Chika said as she sat beside him on the two-seater leather couch.

"Damn you, professor, I had faith in you! I owe you a ten, Mom."

"You bet on whether or not he was married?" Kelenna asked disbelievingly, sitting beside her mother and tucking her feet underneath her.

"Just a friendly one, my dear." Her mother patted her knee reassuringly. "I'll put it on your tab, sonny."

Kelenna shook her head. "I just don't get it. If a man needs a way out of his marriage, why does he have to get involved with someone else in the process? Mom, did you ever have to go through this before you met Dad? Were the men of your day this disrespectful?"

Chika snorted. "Men of any era are the same."

"We need to work on your cynicism." John frowned at her and received a shrug for his observation.

"I wouldn't know," her mother said. "I never dated anyone before your father."

"You what?" If Chika's eyes could pop out of their sockets, they would have just then. Kelenna was surprised for a different reason. She'd heard before about how her parents met. About how her father was the first man her mother had given a real chance to and how she'd been older than all her friends when she'd done so. This was just the first time she believed it.

"I seriously thought you told me that so that I wouldn't want to go out on dates in high school!" Kelenna said.

"Were you and Uncle an arranged marriage?" Chika asked, clearly still surprised.

"No, nothing of the sort. Back then, I was completely focused on my career. Also, most of those young men held no appeal for me. I was like you, Kelenna. I didn't consider marriage at all. Thought it wasn't for me."

"That's not what I'm doing!" Kelenna protested.

"No?" her mother asked, her piercing gaze betraying the innocence in her tone. "I wasn't sure. Anyway, I was at the APiH Convention. African People in Healthcare, that is. The organization no longer exists, but there used to be an annual conference. That was when I first spotted your father. I knew on sight that I would marry him."

Chika swooned. "How sweet!"

"Mom, come on," John said with a disbelieving scoff. "How did you look at a stranger and know on sight?"

"It's difficult to describe, but it was a feeling that the man could mean something to me one day."

"Hmm," Kelenna said noncommittally. She'd had immediate attractions before, obviously, but never any strong feelings like what her mother was describing. "What happened at the convention then?"

"To start with, I had known of your father, but I'd never met him. The Nigerian community was small then, so everyone had at least heard of everyone else. On the last day of the convention, he came to me and asked for my address."

Her father, who had been quiet the entire time, laughed. "So you won't tell them the whole story? When I first saw your mother, she was standing with two of her friends, telling one of her stories. She was so animated that I found myself wanting to be a part of the conversation. When I walked up to them and introduced myself, she barely looked at me. Her friends actually had to tell me her name."

"I don't remember that part," her mother said, feigning ignorance. Even Kelenna had heard the story of her giving her dad the silent treatment all those years ago.

"Oh, the whole weekend was like that. I wondered if you were the same person. You got quiet when I came near, and then when I left, you would start talking again."

"Don't mind your father. I threw him off because I wasn't all over him that weekend. He didn't understand it. You should have seen those women. He couldn't take one step without one of them ambushing him."

"So you caught his attention by playing coy?" Chika clapped. "Oldest trick in the book!"

Her mother winked. "It's good for men to sometimes not be too sure of themselves. They only appreciate what they work hard to get."

"It took some work definitely but eventually I got her address." Her father smiled in memory.

Her mother let out a good-natured snort. "And showed up at my apartment. You couldn't ask for my phone number like a normal person?"

"A man has to go after what he wants."

"Your father says this now, but I did have to wait for him to get done with his girlfriend. I wasn't going to be the so-called side chick."

"Daddy!" Kelenna gasped. "You had a girlfriend while you were chasing Mom?"

"Told you! Men of any era. All the same," Chika said with a vindicated smile.

Her father smiled as he shook his head. "I did have a woman in my life. She was a family medicine resident while I was doing internal medicine. When I met your mother in the final year of my fellowship, I had been in a long-distance relationship for the better part of four years. It was all but over, and I ended it."

"So to answer your initial question, my dear," her mother said, turning to her. "People will treat you the way you allow them to treat you. If you want a man to respect you, don't tolerate disrespect from him."

It was a classic Dr. Obidi response. She always thought that things were as simple as one made it. If only the affairs of the heart were so.

8

"Do you all need anything?"

Dev was hovering, and it was a little annoying. It was the weekend after her birthday, and she and The Classmates were at Dev's family's Diwali celebration—an event they marked with elaborate lights to usher in the Hindu New Year. Kelenna wanted to tell him to relax, but this was typical of him. Whenever they were at his family's home, he changed from his usual carefree self to an eager-to-please, stressed-out host.

"Oh, don't worry about us," Zoe said waving him off. She was right. They didn't need him to entertain them because they were doing a good enough job keeping themselves company in the corner of one of the many living rooms in the house. Actually, house was too tame a word for the behemoth of a place. It was more of a mansion. A mansion that comfortably housed four generations of Patels: Raj, Dev's cardiologist older brother and Mya, his dermatologist wife, their two children, Dev's parents, and Dev's grandparents. Dev was the prodigal second son who'd broken tradition to live out in Midtown, far away from his family in Kennesaw.

"Worry about her," Nichole muttered under her breath. Kelenna, who was closest to her, and the only one who'd heard her, had to stop herself from laughing out loud.

Her was a pretty blonde named Hayley, a girl Dev had invited to the party as his date. The date he met just last week at a doctor's office while he was supposed to have been working. The date he made sit with them while he ran around greeting other guests. The date his very Indian parents had patently ignored when they came over to say hello to The Classmates. The same date who Dev was now whispering to, and who he was now walking out of the front door because she'd probably had enough of feeling out of place.

"Oh, Dev," Sharon said when the odd couple, Dev in a traditional Indian outfit, and Hayley in a tight, short halter dress, were well out of earshot. "He'll never learn."

"Don't guys ever get tired of dating every woman out there?" Kelenna mused.

"Don't look at me, I married the only woman I want to date." Pete leaned down to give Sharon a kiss in a rare show of PDA. Zoe and Nichole clapped in solidarity while Kelenna grinned as she looked on. You couldn't tell from looking at him now, clean-shaven and all, but back when they were in pharmacy school, Pete was the quintessential California dude with shoulder-length hair that he wore up in a man bun, and jeans that were probably too skinny. He looked more like a rock star than an aspiring healthcare professional. Somehow, he clicked with Sharon Brown, the most southern, sorority girl in their year, and didn't look back. They were married a month after graduation day.

"Such a good answer, babe," Sharon said now, reaching up to caress his cheek.

When Dev returned sometime later, he looked even more frazzled than before as he planted himself on the leather sofa next to Zoe.

"Tea?" Zoe offered him her cup.

"I need a shot," Dev murmured. Of course, there was no alcohol in sight. The Patels did not imbibe. "Oh, that reminds me. I'm having an informational dinner for our new drug, Scalitz, at The Westin in a couple of weeks. You all are welcome to attend. I'll send an invitation so you can RSVP if you're free."

"Uh, do you have to ask? It's The Westin and free food. Count us in," Pete said.

"What's Scalitz, and am I going to be harassed about it by your drug reps?" Kelenna asked uncertainly.

Dev barked out a laugh. He worked as a medical science liaison (MSL) for *the* Alistair's Pharmaceuticals. Majority of his job entailed going into doctors' offices and hospitals and speaking about his company's drug products. "Come on, Kelenna, we do not harass you!"

Kelenna gave him a knowing look. He knew as well as she did that Dynasty Corp did not like drug reps peddling their new drugs at any of their facilities. They didn't want their doctors being swayed by new and potentially very expensive drugs. Suffice it to say that the physicians were not fans of Dynasty Corp's bigwigs. "Dev, I get tons of calls from drug reps every month. That's the definition of harassment."

"I'm not a drug rep, remember? I only come in when *you* want to know clinical details about the drugs. Why can't you be more like your mother? Dr. Obidi *calls* me to come to Baptist and talk to her staff and doctors."

"That's because my mother just wants free lunch!"

Dev laughed once more. "Whatever her motives are, she helps us meet our quota," Dev said with a grin. "But really, our target for Scalitz is hospice patients, so Preston isn't going to be on our radar. It's essentially *fentanyl* but with a different delivery mechanism. You'll learn more about it at the dinner. It's pretty exciting stuff."

"Dev, I think those girls are trying to get your attention," Nichole said, discreetly pointing to a couple of young women some distance away from them. The girls immediately turned away when they discovered that they were being observed.

"Doesn't look like they want him to know that they're looking at him," Sharon mused.

"Well they've been staring at us all night. Who are they? Cousins?"

Dev left Nichole's question hanging for a beat as he stared unabashedly at the girls. "I've never seen either of them before."

Kelenna couldn't help but notice his confusion and she pounced on it. "Do you think your parents have finally taken my advice and have found a woman for you? The one in the purple sari is especially pretty."

Dev gave her a look that either meant that the thought was way out of the realm of possibility, or that it was too horrible to contemplate. Once again she had to stop her laughter in its tracks.

"Excuse me for a minute." He left the group, but did not head in the direction of the girls. Instead he walked to where his mother was. When he returned, they were all at the edges of their seats.

"So who are they?" Zoe pressed. "Cousins you don't know?"

"One of them is a niece of a friend of my aunt from England," he said stiffly. "My parents wanted us to casually meet each other this weekend."

Kelenna gasped, putting her hand over her mouth in shock. "I was right? We're in the middle of a marriage set up?"

* * *

"What is he waiting for, true love? Tell your friend to go out on a date with the girl and see what happens. Or does he have something against Indians?"

It was the following Monday and Kelenna had just returned from ICU rounds and was now making small talk with the pharmacists before their daily huddle began. She felt bad about using Dev's situation as a diversionary tactic, but she just didn't want her coworkers to delve deeper into her close call with becoming a homewrecker. It was bad enough that she couldn't stop thinking about how she'd missed the signs with Dillon without having yet another set of analyses from them.

"Of course not, Siya! Knowing Dev, he just doesn't want to disappoint anyone. His parents. His aunt. His aunt's friend. The girl. Too many people could be offended if this doesn't work out."

"Well, I think he's overthinking it," Siya said defiantly. "He has to approach it with an open mind, otherwise it's doomed from the start." She muttered something under her breath, and Kelenna only caught the word *Americanized* before they all heard Pat's platforms bringing her to the pharmacy pit.

"Good, we're all here. Let's get started please, today is a busy day." Pat took her place at the center of the huddle. "Any shortage updates, Lisa?"

"There are a few," Lisa began, "but our major one is the IV opioids. We've been keeping an eye on it for the past few weeks, ever since we first heard about the DEA cutting back on supply. It looks really bad now though. We haven't been getting anything in."

"How are our numbers?" Kelenna asked quickly.

"I ran them this morning. About two hundred small doses of *morphine* and Dilaudid hospital-wide."

"And in our vault?" Kelenna pressed.

"We're pretty much empty."

"Two hundred doses in the entire hospital?" Anna, one of the techs asked incredulously. "That'll be gone in a day and a half! We have OR, ER, ICU, post-surgery. Forget the opioid crisis, *we're* in a crisis!"

"She's right," Tricia added. "If we run out of opioids, our patients will leave AMA! Although I'm not sure if that's a bad thing."

Pat let out a rare chuckle. It was a running joke that the quickest way to get a patient out of Preston was to cut their pain med supply off and watch them leave 'against medical advice.'

"No one's going to leave AMA," Pat said. "We're just going to have to get creative with what we *can* get. Kelenna, what do you think?"

Kelenna cleared her throat, knowing she was about to incur the wrath of the pharmacy techs. "I've kept this card in my back pocket since the DEA made their announcement," she started slowly.

"What card?" Anna asked suspiciously.

Kelenna grimaced. "I really hoped we could avoid this, but the fact is, if we're this low on IV opioids, and we have nothing coming in, we have no choice but to unit dose."

There was a collective groan from the pharmacy technicians and Kelenna wanted to groan along with them. Unit dosing was fancy pharmacy talk for drawing up smaller doses of drugs from bulk products into syringes. The techs would have to prepare hundreds of doses of the opioids, label them, and store them. Basically, the pharmacy would become something akin to a factory, without machinery to carry out the repetitive tasks. It was going to be exhausting, but Kelenna couldn't see a way out. The DEA's opioid shortage was truly an inconvenience in every possible way.

"There's no way we have the staff to unit dose opioids! We have other crap to make! You'll need a second tech in the IV room just to pull this off!"

"You'll let me worry about the staff, Anna. That's what they pay me for," Pat said dryly. "Any other concerns?" When Molly, another tech, raised her hand like she was in a classroom, Pat pointed at her. "Molly?"

"Y'all said weeks ago that the ER was going to cut back on using all that Dilaudid and *morphine*. I can tell you right now, that ain't happening. They're not even trying. We have to restock their ADMs every single day. There's your real problem."

Kelenna knew Molly was right. She'd been tracking IV opioid usage for the last couple of weeks, and the trends were clear. The ER was behaving like there was no crisis-shortage. They'd never bought into the conservation strategy, and because of that, they—the pharmacy department—were going to suffer for it.

"You've made a good point, Molly," Pat said. "I'm sure Kelenna won't mind talking to our ER physicians one more time, to remind them that there is a real shortage, and that our drugs have to be reserved for critical cases."

"Yes, I can," Kelenna replied. *For all the good it would do*, she didn't say out loud.

Pat nodded and turned back to the group. "We are going to work on a process for unit dosing the two major opioids we use, *morphine* and Dilaudid. We'll share that process with you soon. Huddle out." As she began to walk away from the pit, she turned back. "Kelenna, a second, please."

Kelenna followed her boss down the hall to her office. When they were in, Pat gestured at one of the office chairs for Kelenna to have a seat before she shut the door and took hers.

"Okay, Kelenna," she started with a sigh. "How are you doing?"

"I'm fine," Kelenna replied quickly, wondering where the concern for her welfare had come from. Not that Pat didn't care about her staff, she did, but not in this *'there's clearly something wrong with you'* kind of way.

"I ask because you've seemed distracted here lately. In the past, I've been able to rely on you to handle shortages like this. You've been very good at finding solutions and executing them. But ever since we heard about the opioid shortage, you've taken a very passive approach. Have you even been monitoring our stock?"

"Of course," Kelenna said defensively. "I've been tracking our usage ever since we learned about the crisis. That's why I know where our problem areas are."

"You know where our problem areas are and yet you need Molly, one of our techs, to remind you to speak to the physicians again?"

"Pat, the doctors don't listen—"

"Physicians need constant reminding, you know that." Pat took a deep breath. "Do you have a unit dosing plan?"

"Not yet," she replied, catching Pat in the middle of another sigh. "But that's because I wanted to put it off till it was absolutely necessary," she added quickly. "I knew it was going to be a big undertaking. I've been working on the IV to PO conversion chart for opioids. Once I get that approved by the doctors, that should help a good deal."

"An IV to PO conversion chart is obviously not an immediate solution," Pat said through gritted teeth. "There's no excuse for not having a unit dosing plan that's ready to go right now. These are opioids we're talking about, not Tylenol. There could be legal ramifications if we don't do this right. And now that it seems like we have to do it soon, we're nowhere near ready. Have you even asked Lisa if we can purchase bulk vials of *morphine* and Dilaudid? Have you looked into how long they're stable after we unit dose them? Have you looked into storage? Do they have to be refrigerated or kept at room temperature?"

Kelenna had done none of those things. She stayed mute while Pat continued, disappointment evident in her voice.

"If I'm going to rely on you, I have to be kept in the loop when you're in over your head, but you're going to have to be able to recognize when you are."

Kelenna nodded apologetically. What else could you do when your boss essentially called you out for dropping the ball? And Pat was right, she *had* been dragging her feet, waiting and hoping for the problem to take care of itself. As if the DEA was going to magically change their minds and lift the opioid cuts. Her voice shook a little when she spoke next. "I'll get right to working on a process."

"Thank you." Before Kelenna could leave Pat's office, Pat signaled to her. "Oh, Kelenna? Make sure it's a seamless one. We have to make sure everyone in this department can speak to whatever process we develop. Keep me updated."

The first thing Kelenna did when she returned to her office was draft a memo to the physicians. She kept the message short, not wanting them to tune her out without reading it. She reminded them about the opioid shortage, emphasizing that it was unprecedented and not expected to improve any time soon. She injected some fear, telling them that the drugs would run out in twenty-four hours if usage remained the same. And then she tried to temper that fear by saying that the pharmacy department would continue to work on ways to provide the drugs to the best of their ability. After sending the message out, she switched to developing and outlining a process for unit dosing the opioids.

Twenty-four hours later, they ran out of IV opioids.

Chaos erupted in the pharmacy as angry nurses from units all over the hospital called down to report that their ADMs were out of *morphine* and Dilaudid. Pharmacy technicians scrambled to move drugs around, borrowing from units that had some and giving it those that didn't have any. Word traveled fast, and even more calls came down to the pharmacy. Kelenna felt like a telephone operator, getting on call after call to explain the situation to doctors and surgeons and the administration team. Yes, they had run out of opioids. Yes, they were working on a solution as quickly as they could. No, surgical cases did not need to be canceled. And no, the hospital did not need to be put on diversion!

* * *

"I wanted to die when Ron asked if he needed to tell ambulances to divert patients to other hospitals. He's the CEO! Usually when we have system failures, we mop it up before it ever gets out of the department! It was humiliating and exhausting at the same time! And don't get me started on the unit dosing process. On paper, it seemed like a good idea, but when it came down to it, it was a nightmare! We had to call in techs on their day off to help draw up *morphine* and Dilaudid into smaller syringes. Then we had to count them, label them, and store them. We did this for five hundred syringes! Five hundred!" Kelenna paused in the middle of her rant to take a deep breath. She was sitting on her chair in her brother's condo, and only one person in the small crowd gathered for another Falcons' game—this time against the Panthers—was paying any attention to her. "And we had to do it in batches of twenty-five, because otherwise it's not sterile, and if we don't keep it sterile, patients will get infections and die! Do you know how many twenty-fives there are in five hundred?"

"Twenty," Chris replied coolly from beside her. They were sitting shoulder to shoulder on the massive recliner, sharing it for only the second time. She suspected it would be his new thing.

"Yes! Twenty batches of syringes of Dilaudid and *morphine.* I'm tired all over again just thinking about it. I'm surprised Pat didn't fire me on the spot for letting it get to that point."

"How long do you think that many doses will last?" Chris asked softly.

"It doesn't matter, they all expire in seven days. If they don't get used, we're throwing them away." She knew she was whining, but she couldn't help it. Pharmacy did such thankless work sometimes. All hell broke loose for the hour when there were no opioids in the hospital, but no one recognized the massive effort it took to rectify it. She turned to him. "I'm curious. Did you read my email from a few days ago?"

"The one where you said there was a shortage and that you would take care of it? Yeah, I read it."

"That's what you took away from it?"

Chris shrugged. "It was literally what you said. You said you had a backup plan, which I assume is this tedious unit dosing thing you're doing."

Kelenna frowned and leaned away from him. Something about his tone grated on her nerves. "What's wrong with having a backup plan? Did you expect me to say we're running out of *morphine* and Dilaudid, and we'll just let it happen?"

"No," Chris said calmly. "I just think that if you're trying to put fear in us, then maybe don't tell us that you have any backup plans in the works."

Kelenna was dumbfounded for a moment. Did he hear himself? How did he expect a hospital pharmacy to function without any backup plans?

Without a word, she stood from the recliner and walked out of the living room and into John's kitchen. She didn't want to say anything she couldn't take back. She'd just spent the last twenty-four hours trying to salvage the fact that she'd slacked on the job, and there he was indirectly minimizing her efforts.

She wasn't surprised to find that Chris had followed her, even though he should have known better than to leave their recliner empty for any of the other guests to pounce on it. Before she could point that out, he came and stood right in front of her.

"Do you have a problem with something I said?" he asked.

Kelenna was quiet for a second before she chuckled mirthlessly. "This is weird. This isn't us. We don't do this."

"What's weird?"

"This." She gestured first at herself and then at him. "We don't fight about work. We don't fight about anything."

Chris narrowed his eyes and looked at her like she'd lost her mind. "Fight? We're not fighting, we're just talking. And we talk all the time."

"Okay, here's the thing." She closed her eyes and took a deep breath. When she opened them back up, she saw him looking intently at her, waiting for her to speak, his dark eyes telling her to say what was on her mind. She let out a sigh. "You're the only doctor I know personally at Preston, Chris. I thought you of all people would listen when I told you about the shortage. I'm a little pissed that you and your team didn't take me seriously about this opioid issue." There, she said it.

Chris' eyes widened. "Whoa, whoa, whoa. *We* didn't take you seriously?"

Kelenna shrugged. "I told you four weeks ago that the ER would be crucial to our conservation efforts. We had a working lunch where we talked about the message that should go out to your doctors. Did you even send it?"

He gave her an affronted look. "Of course I did."

"You did?" she asked with a head tilt that she hoped told him she didn't believe him at all.

"Yes!"

"Please, Chris, I looked at the numbers. Not once did you or your doctors even try to cut back. It was business as usual in the ER. You used up all the *morphine* in the hospital without caring about how we were going to take care of the rest of the hospital. It was irresponsible. It was selfish. It was—"

"Oh, come on, Kelenna, it was a bad plan," he cut in.

Kelenna shook her head. "No, it wasn't! You guys just have zero perception of your ordering habits. Cutting back a little would have kept us afloat a little longer."

"And then what, Kelenna?" Chris snapped. It was so uncharacteristic of him that she had to lean back. She could tell he noticed because he let out a low hiss and continued in a gentler voice. "After that, what would have happened? You would have found yourself back at this same spot. Kelenna, relying on doctors for conservation was always going to fail in the ER."

"Why? Why are you so opposed to the strategy when every hospital in the nation right now has to do it?"

Chris threw up his hands. "Because we're ER doctors! We treat patients in the moment! That's literally our job. We're not going to *conserve* medications for Mr. Jones who's going to show up in week with a broken arm! I don't *know* if Mr. Jones is going to show up in a week with a broken arm!"

Kelenna closed her eyes and let out a frustrated breath. He had a point, but his point was not helpful in the least. "Fine, we'll just keep doing what we're doing. I just hope our techs don't quit because we're running them into the ground. I hope I don't get fired because I come up with bad plans." She tried to walk around him, back to the living room, but he caught her arm to stop her.

"Hey, they're not going to quit." He ran his hand briskly up and down her arm like she was shivering and he was trying to provide some warmth. "And you're not going to get fired. Your team is great. *You're* great. Everyone knows it."

"Do they?" she mumbled disbelievingly.

He tapped her chin lightly, either in encouragement or as a reprimand for being what he probably considered dramatic, she couldn't tell which. "Of course. Just work out the kinks in this unit dosing thingy and make it work."

Kelenna lifted shrewd eyes at him. "You didn't understand any of what I described, did you?"

"Not even a little," he said with a light chuckle. "But hey, even if it doesn't look like it, we do listen to you. Sarah and Ashleigh got marketing to make posters for the ER the other day. It'll be like an advertisement to our patients, a way of telling them that basically, we're not going to feed any opioid addictions."

"Oh," she said softly. "That's great." It was even more passive than the conservation strategy he detested so much, but at least it was something. "Whose idea was it?"

"Ashleigh's."

Kelenna smiled in surprise. Ashleigh, the ER nurse manager, was so obsessed with doing everything by the book that Kelenna couldn't believe she'd come up with an original thought. "Thanks for telling me this."

"You're welcome."

At that moment, they heard a collective groan from the living room. "You better go. It sounds like the Panthers may have just scored a touchdown."

Usually, that would have been enough to pull Chris' attention away, but this time he ignored her. "Are we good?" he asked, looking down at her. Then he grinned mischievously. "Did we survive this fight?"

Kelenna snort-laughed and slapped his upper arm. "Just go watch your game."

9

The following weekend, The Classmates were at The Westin seated at a round table that had been specially reserved for them, and eating hotel-catered food as they listened to Dev talk about Alistair Pharmaceuticals' new drug, Scalitz. Dev was in his element, talking a little about the research behind the drug, before focusing mainly on its novel delivery system. Kelenna listened as he described what seemed like a cross between an insulin pump and a patient-controlled analgesia pump. He played a video that showed how it worked. It was applied with an adhesive to the surface of the arm just like a *fentanyl* patch, but there was a little needle that punctured the subcutaneous layer of the skin. On the device was a blue button that the patient could push for a tiny dose of *fentanyl* to be delivered through their skin. The device would monitor how many doses the patient self-administered throughout the day. It was supposed to be difficult to overdose on it.

Kelenna was proud of Dev's performance, but that was where it ended for her. How much was she expected to care about a drug that was essentially repackaged *fentanyl?* It was remarkable to her that drug companies could simply change the delivery mechanism of an existing drug, and charge an arm and a leg for it. Besides, they were smack in the middle of an opioid epidemic. Was it wise to put yet another one on the market? She kept these thoughts to herself as she watched him work the room and answer the questions his doctor audience threw at him. At the end of the presentation, The Classmates waited in the wings while Dev spent some one-on-one time with his guests. When he was done completely, they rushed up to him and shared hugs and congratulatory words.

"Thanks for coming, guys." Then he asked if they had time for a quick drink. "I want to run something by you."

"Is it about the girl your parents want you to marry?" Nichole asked, sounding hopeful as they followed him from the meeting room down to the hotel bar.

Dev shot her a bewildered look. "No, it's about work. And her name is Priya. Before you ask, she wants nothing to do with me, and the feeling is mutual. So we'll go on a few dates and let our parents know it didn't work out. Problem solved."

Kelenna blinked. "That was fast! You didn't even give it a chance!"

"Chances are for people who are interested," Dev said with a shrug. "This way."

Down at the bar, Dev ordered a whiskey, neat, and downed the contents of the glass in one gulp. He slammed the glass down and asked for another.

"You okay there, buddy?" Pete asked, concern etched on his face.

Dev dragged a breath after he threw down the second drink. "I think I may have inadvertently stumbled upon something big."

"Okay, Dev, come on." Zoe pulled him gently away from the bar in the direction of a chair. "Kelenna, get this guy a glass of water, will you?"

Kelenna got a glass of water from the amused bartender and took it to the table where the rest of The Classmates were already seated. She placed it directly in front of Dev and heard him let out a light snort before he took a sip.

"All right, Dev, spill it," Kelenna said sitting on the empty chair beside him. "What happened?"

Dev looked around like he was trying to make sure the coast was clear before he leaned closer to the center of the table. "One of the doctors today was just asking me about an executive speaker engagement package for Scalitz."

Kelenna looked at her friends' expressions and was sure hers mirrored theirs. Dev was going to have to tell them more if he wanted them to understand why he was so agitated. He must have realized that because his next words were a bit more ominous.

"It's a deal that doesn't exist. We do pay a speaker's fee for physicians to talk about our products at various specialist meetings all over the country, but what this doctor was asking for is some kind of payment deal to the tune of anywhere between fifty and a hundred thousand dollars a year. And it's under the guise of speaking, but it's really more of a compensation for prescribing the medication."

Kelenna's eyes widened in shock. "That sounds illegal!"

"It is. And it's bad enough that subsidiaries of Alistair are all over the news for essentially price gouging—"

"Please don't get me started on price gouging," Kelenna interrupted, shaking her head. "Last year, Alistair's raised the price for that blood pressure medicine from about fifty bucks a vial to seven hundred dollars! I had to tell my doctors to stop using it!"

"Oh, and remember the time they rebranded that medication for gout?" Sharon asked. "They took a really old drug that was dirt cheap and added a new patent to it, now it's super expensive. You know they're going to do the same thing with *aspirin* next. Just watch!"

"Rebranding drugs that were grandfathered by the FDA ages ago is a scam," Pete added with a derisive snort. "There should be a way to stop them from doing that."

"How long have you guys hated the company I work for?" Dev asked somberly.

"Not yours in particular, darling," Zoe corrected gently. "Big pharma."

"There's nothing wrong with big pharma," Dev snapped. "And rebranding drugs is not a scam. Why should old drugs get a pass because they were made before the FDA passed all their safety and efficacy laws? It takes us ten years and a ton of money and research to bring one drug to market. I hate to be the one to break it to you guys, but we live in a capitalist country. How else can we recoup our investments if we don't place a high value on our products?"

"Your profit margins are astronomical," Zoe countered. "You value the product at a hundred times the cost of production. That's highway robbery!"

"For good reason! After ten years or so, we lose the patent, and the price comes down when generics enter the market."

"And that's when you create the extended release version to try to extend your patent," Zoe retorted. "Sneaky."

Dev closed his eyes as if doing so would force them all to keep quiet. Kelenna reached over to pat his shoulder and shook her head at the others, silently telling them to change the subject. Nichole sounded pensive when she spoke up next.

"I have no personal issue with big pharma. Except for when they try to buy doctors. Or when they try to flood the market with opioids to turn a profit. Dev, that *is* what you're describing, right?"

"I think so," Dev replied in a low voice.

"Dude," Pete said with a head shake. "Could this doctor be lying?"

"I don't know. I guess I could find out. I could look into sales, and then look at the regions where he said this deal exists. Run numbers to see if there is high usage of Scalitz over there. Maybe I could ask some insiders for—"

Kelenna waved her hands to cut him off. "What are you now, a detective? If they're bribing doctors to overprescribe the medication, at the risk of patient safety, then that's a problem. If you start asking too many questions, and there *is* something going on, it could go bad really quickly. For you."

Dev shot her a thoughtful look before he let out a resigned breath. "I don't know. I just want to get to the bottom of it. I wish there was someone I could talk to. Like a lawyer. Just to get an idea of how much I should even be digging into this."

"My ex is a lawyer. He may be able to give us some insight." Kelenna regretted her words as soon as she uttered them. She hadn't corresponded with Will since the one-word congratulatory text she'd sent to him after she learned about his engagement. The one he'd responded to with a polite, 'Thank you, Kelenna.' But Dev looked so distraught, and she'd said the first thing that popped into her head. "Or Zoe, your dad's a lawyer, he can give Dev some advice."

Zoe shook her head. "Bad idea. My dad's a judge *and* a former DA. If there's a sniff of impropriety, he will escalate it. Besides, he's in Greece seeing my grandparents."

Dev turned back to her. "Kelenna, do you mind? I know I couldn't ask any of my exes even if they were lawyers. For whatever reason, they can't stand me."

"Gee, I wonder why," Nichole said.

Kelenna tried to hide her sigh as she dialed Will's number. If she was lucky, he wouldn't be available.

She wasn't lucky.

"Perry."

She hadn't been prepared to hear his voice. Especially not if he was going to answer her call with his last name, the way he'd done the entire time they were together. Like he had some kind of deadline to meet and didn't have time for formalities. Later in their relationship, when she would respond to his curt answer with a, "Hi, Will," he would come back with a soft, "Hey, baby." A wave of nostalgia washed over her so strong that she almost expected to hear him say just that.

He did not.

"Kelenna?"

"Hey, Will. So sorry to bother you. I had a quick favor to ask you. How are you?" She wanted to hit herself for sounding nervous and letting her words run together.

Will's reply was smooth. "Hey Kelenna, I'm good. How can I help?"

Once upon a time they wouldn't have been so formal. She sighed inwardly once more and proceeded to give him a quick summary of what Dev had told them.

"If he's there, you can put me on speaker."

Kelenna obeyed and placed the phone on the center of the table. The Classmates drew closer to the phone like it was a crystal ball that would tell them the future.

"Hi Dev," Will began.

"Hi Will," Zoe practically yelled. She'd always liked him.

"Oh, everyone's there? Hi guys." He didn't wait for a response before he continued. "First of all, this isn't legal advice. You probably can't afford me." That bit of cockiness got a few laughs. Kelenna didn't join in though. It reminded her of too much.

"It depends on what your end goal is," Will continued. "If you go around and start asking questions and there *is* something going on, they could try to silence you somehow. They could fire you, have you blackballed in the industry, enforce that non-compete agreement you signed—"

"I didn't sign a non-compete agreement," Dev interjected.

"Did you read every document you signed when you got hired?"

"Not every single word."

"You signed a non-compete," Will said dryly. "But I think if you're careful, and can find out valuable information, you could—"

"Become a whistleblower!" Nichole interrupted, sounding excited as she slapped the table. "This is like any good TV show!"

"No!" Kelenna blurted out. Everyone at the table paused and looked at her. She could even feel Will's eyes through the phone. "We're not whistleblowers," she said in a more measured tone. "We do our job, make our money and mind our business. If we disagree with the mission or vision or the processes of the companies we work for, we leave."

After an even longer pause, she heard Will's deep voice through the phone. "Who is *we*?"

"People like us? Young professionals? Children of immigrants? I don't know, take your pick. Anyway, this is all moot unless Dev has solid evidence that this is even happening. There has to be a chain-of-command somewhere that he can follow. His supervisor or something."

"For the record, I was going to say, dig deeper for information before you overreact, Dev. But it would serve the dual purpose of keeping you a step ahead, and protecting yourself in case anything happens. If this is what it sounds like, then you almost can't trust anyone. Not even your supervisor. You would have to be careful about throwing accusations around."

"Hmm, that's good," Dev said.

"Another option would be to change jobs. Sounds extreme, but it would be the easier thing to do. That's something to consider."

"Wow. I don't envy you, bro." Pete shook his head. "You give this great presentation and twenty minutes later, you're faced with a moral dilemma."

Kelenna frowned, thinking about the opioid crisis. Alistair's would go down in a heap of flames if they were truly involved in bribing physicians to use their drugs. She really hoped for Dev's sake that it wasn't the case.

"Thanks, Will. I appreciate the talk," Dev said.

"You're welcome. Feel free to keep me posted if you like."

Kelenna picked up the phone and took him off speaker. As she walked away from her friends towards the corner of the bar, she thanked him for even answering the phone.

"Of course you can call me when you need something. You know that, Kelenna."

Kelenna hesitated before she spoke again. "I wasn't sure. I only called because Dev needed help and . . ." she trailed off.

"Well, now you know." There was a pause as he cleared his throat. "Look, I wanted to talk to you for a little bit while I had you on here. I wanted to . . . Listen." Another pause. "There just hasn't been an easy way to have this conversation, has there?"

He wanted to do this now? While she was at The Westin with her friends who were now unabashedly staring at her? And why was he stumbling over his words? He was the most composed person she knew. She'd pictured them talking about his upcoming marriage several times, and not once did she imagine it would play out like this.

"Kelenna?"

She couldn't do it. Not today.

"I'm sorry, Will, but I have to go. Can I call you later?"

She heard Will's sigh. It was almost as if he knew she was using later as a synonym for never. "Sure. Bye, Kelenna."

"Goodbye, Will."

10

With the first Wednesday in December came the sixth and final pharmacy and therapeutics (P&T) committee meeting for the calendar year. This was the one meeting where Kelenna took the reins. Sure, they had a P&T chairman, but he was Queen Elizabeth. His real name was Dr. Yang, and he was an even-tempered spinal surgeon who presided over the meeting in an almost aloof way. His presence there was ceremonial, a requirement of the bylaws of Preston Regional. She, on the other hand, was the prime minister. Churchill or Thatcher or Tony Blair. She did the leg work.

Her job was to collect all the items for discussion and do her best to sway everyone's vote towards whatever option was most economical for the hospital, but at the same time, was non-compromising where patient care was concerned. She'd had to learn the art of diplomacy with the physicians; how best to keep them happy while not giving into their every request. The amount of give and take she'd had to do over the years rivaled any under-the-table deals politicians made in Washington. She would promise to add drug A to the hospital formulary if a physician would support letting go of drug B. Or let a physician have his or her way once so she could have her way down the line. It was an exhausting game, but she played it as well as the best of them.

She especially loved when she didn't have to play any games. When good old-fashioned literature was the difference between a drug getting approved or rejected by the committee. Today, she knew before she even started that she would win her first battle. Dr. Reddy, one of the cardiologists, wanted an intravenous drug that cost over ten times its oral sister drug. Her passion as she defended the need for the pricey medication was admirable, but it was really no match for the numbers Kelenna was able to lay out. They debated back and forth for some time until Dr. Reddy finally conceded.

"For now," Dr. Reddy added, looking at her through narrowed eyes. It was as though she'd seen the mental fist bump Kelenna had celebrated her minor victory with. "We need to be able to revisit this at a later time."

She hid a smile as she nodded, accepting that she had won the battle for now. After Dr. Yang made the motion to reject the request, it was seconded by Dr. Reddy and they moved on.

"The next item on our agenda is an addendum to our existing IV to PO conversion policy. Pharmacy would like to add opioids to the list. This is a recommendation from HQ to help combat the opioid shortage. To be honest, we've been late in implementing this, but only because I've wanted to come up with the most accurate conversion chart for the opioids we use."

"So HQ wants *y'all* to switch drugs on *our* patients without asking us first? Based on a *chart*?" Dr. Atkins asked incredulously. Dr. Atkins was one of the general surgeons, known as much for being generally insufferable as he was for his surgical skills.

"Yes," Kelenna said as jovially as she could manage, despite his acerbic tone. He would be all right once he laid eyes on the chart, she was sure of it. "Based on a validated chart. And based on other existing criteria for IV to PO conversion."

"What criteria? Every time I turn around, one of your pharmacists has changed my IV drugs to a pill. I wish y'all would let us be doctors and let us decide when we need to do things for once!"

Kelenna's brows furrowed. This wasn't how this portion of the meeting was supposed to go. She could lose the room if Dr. Atkins started a *'pharmacy wants to practice medicine'* debate. She had to nip his rant in the bud. Before she could get the words out, Pat cut her off.

"The IV to PO program has been in place for over a decade now, Alex. Surely, you're not just now developing a problem with it?"

Alex? Kelenna's eyes widened at Pat's use of Dr. Atkins' first name. They didn't call doctors by their first names at Preston. It was either doctor, then their last name, or their last name alone, but never their first. Why was Pat being so familiar?

Atkins didn't seem to notice though. "Just because you've always done it doesn't mean it's safe!" he retorted.

"It's perfectly safe," Pat countered coolly. "We agreed then—and we still do—that it's better to give patients drugs orally. It reduces the risk of infections that could prolong their stay in the hospital."

Dr. Atkins snorted. "And don't forget, it helps to save a penny here and there, as you all like to do."

Pat's voice became tight. "That usually is a factor, yes—however, seeing as we're dealing with an actual drug shortage, saving money is irrelevant."

"Well, I don't believe there's a shortage at all," Atkins continued belligerently. "I go to other hospitals and they never seem to have these problems."

Pat threw up her hands in disbelief. "Are you implying that we are making up a shortage of this magnitude so we can take on extra work because we want to save a few pennies?"

"It wouldn't be the first time."

"Oh, please," Pat huffed. She shifted around on her seat and literally turned her back on him.

"I think it would help if we saw what you were proposing," Dr. Yang said gently, gesturing to Kelenna to advance the PowerPoint slides.

"Right." Kelenna closed her mouth, which had apparently been hanging open for several seconds as she watched Pat and Atkins go at it, and quickly clicked over to the next slide that displayed her chart. "Here are some of the most commonly used IV opioids and their doses. The chart gives first and second line options for oral opioids if the patient can tolerate them."

"That's the problem," Dr. Atkins interrupted once more. "Explain to me how you can know for sure that a patient can swallow a pill all the way from the basement? You do *not* see the entire clinical picture! You do *not* know what we know in the moment! Your pharmacists change patients from IV to PO and place them at risk of choking!"

"If you have a complaint about the pharmacists, you should bring them to me," Pat bit out stiffly. "With specifics. I can't handle wild and random accusations because I wouldn't know what to fix. That's if there's anything to fix."

"It's not my job to babysit your staff!" he snapped. "I make my complaints as they happen. Hell, Kelenna hears about them. They fall on deaf ears for all that's being done. My vote is an absolute no for this. We will be putting patient care at risk."

Kelenna froze when he mentioned her name. The *one* time he'd ever brought an IV to PO related issue to her was two years ago, and they'd resolved that misunderstanding. The fact that he would make it seem otherwise in front of all these people touched a nerve, and even though she knew from experience that she should never take Atkins' comments personally, she felt the annoying prickling of tears. She tried to stave them off with a smirk that said, *good old Dr. Atkins.* Everyone in the room had at some point or the other been at the receiving end of one of his attacks, even some of the physicians. She succeeded but barely. She would not be known as the girl who Dr. Atkins made cry at her own meeting.

"If we're going to throw respect out of the window, then I'm done here." Pat's chair scraped the floor as she pushed it back and stood up. Her voice was low and soft as she leveled her gaze directly at Atkins. "Before I go, let me be clear. We have an opioid shortage. My staff is working their behinds off to repackage bulk doses of opioids so that no one feels like we've run out. So that patient care is not compromised. If you think that it is out of our scope to do the most simple form of clinical work a pharmacist can do, then so be it. But I'm not going to sit here and listen to my entire department be insulted by you." Without a glance at anyone else, she walked out of Meeting Room D.

Kelenna stared at the door in shock, but only for a second, before she let her eyes sweep over the room. The other P&T members around the table had similar expressions of shock, but it was the look on Dr. Atkins' face that irked her. He looked surprised, almost as if he couldn't imagine what he had said to rile Pat up. That was what did it. She felt some steel return to her spine. A minute ago, her voice would have cracked with emotion if she'd dared said a word. Now she felt empowered to take back control of her meeting.

"I apologize on Pat's behalf," Kelenna started disingenuously. She wasn't the least bit sorry. If she could have applauded Pat's exit without putting her job at risk, she would have. She turned to Tessa, the recorder for the meeting. "Tessa, can you please note Dr. Atkins' comments for the minutes?"

Tessa gave her a sympathetic nod. "Yes, I can."

"I think Pat—" Dr. Atkins started.

"I want to try to allay everyone's concerns about this," Kelenna interrupted forcefully, cutting Atkins off. "We're dealing with an opioid shortage because the DEA thinks we're contributing to overdose deaths by overmedicating patients. And in a roundabout way, we are. Part of it is us giving these patients IV opioids that we know they can't go home with. They get a quick high, and it wears off a short while later. But for the most part, these patients do not need IV *morphine* or Dilaudid when they can swallow a tablet. Pharmacists do not need a special kind of skillset to know when to give a patient a tablet. And it's one less thing off the doctor's already full plate."

"Okay, I think we've all heard enough," Dr. Yang said. "Let's go ahead and vote. Those in favor of this addition to the policy, please say aye."

They voted four to one in favor of the addition. Only physician members of P&T were allowed to vote, and fortunately, the ones who were quiet during Dr. Atkins' outbursts weren't swayed by it. All Atkins could do was huff and mutter that no one listened to him. Kelenna couldn't care less about how he felt, but she knew she had to smoothen things over with him before long. After all, there could come a time when she would need him to scratch her back. It was all the part of the game.

* * *

"Pat!" Kelenna burst into her boss' office after the meeting. "Oh my goodness, what was that?"

"Congrats," Pat said calmly, like she hadn't just caused a ruckus that would travel through the hospital before the day was done. "I heard you got what you wanted."

"Yes, I did, but at what cost?" Kelenna sat in one of the chairs across from Pat's. "Atkins is going to get you written up for insubordination!"

"Oh, please. He's going to try, but I'm two steps ahead of him. I stopped at Ron's office and let him know what happened. I've been given a *'strong warning.'*" Pat wiggled her eyebrows.

Kelenna nodded at Pat's mention of Preston's CEO. Ron would be fair and wouldn't be swayed by whatever Dr. Atkins had to say.

"Okay, I've got to ask, Pat." Kelenna regarded her boss through narrowed eyes. "Who in the world is *Alex*? That entire exchange sounded so personal."

Pat grimaced. "Picture Dr. Atkins thirty years younger with less of a receding hairline, and less of a pouch, and you have Alexander Atkins, class president at Preston High," she said. "We were classmates. He was as full of himself back then as he is now."

"Oh, wow," Kelenna laughed. "So did you two . . ." she trailed off, gesturing back and forth at Pat and the direction of Meeting Room D.

"Date? God, no. Listen. Alex is a damn fine doctor. If I need to have my appendix taken out, he would be the first person I'd call. But he's a bully, and you have to stand your ground with him or he'll be happy to walk all over you."

Kelenna sobered up. "I could never say any of what you said to him," she said softly. "I may be thinking it, but I wouldn't ever say it."

"And you shouldn't. You were doing a fine job being professional and saying all the right things. I'm sorry for cutting you off and putting you in an awkward position, even if it did feel good to stand up for the department. Maybe you'll be able to do the same thing one day. When you have some tenure."

"Hopefully by then all the physicians will be a little bit more pharmacy-friendly. Any chance Atkins is close to retirement?"

"People like him never retire, Kelenna. And if they do, another one will pop up. Pharmacists have been told to stay in their lane for years. You're going to have to keep fighting *that* battle."

* * *

"Mom, do you find that you have to continue to fight to expand the clinical roles of your pharmacists?"

Kelenna was at dinner with her parents, and had just recounted Dr. Atkins v. Preston Regional Department of Pharmacy. Before her mother could respond to her question, the alarm on the front door went off, and they could hear footfalls most likely bringing in John, the habitual late-comer, to dinner.

Kelenna wouldn't have turned around, but hearing her mother squeal and seeing her jump out of her chair made her do so.

"Hey, my own mother is more excited to see you than me," John said.

Chris was beside him, basking in the attention. Kelenna looked on at the spectacle, watching her mother put an arm around Chris' back as she led him towards her dining chair. Before she knew it, her mother, father, and Chris were conversing in Igbo, catching up like three buddies who hadn't seen each other in a while. Kelenna exchanged an amused look with John who had taken his usual seat adjacent to their father. They were probably thinking the exact same thing. Chris was definitely a show off. Neither of them were very good at understanding Igbo, and they could speak it even less. When Chris was done flexing his language skills, he walked over to her, greeting her with a shoulder tap as he took the long way around the table to sit next to John.

"You're bringing strays home now, John?" Kelenna asked as he sat down. When their eyes met, she sent him a cheeky grin. He shook his head and smiled.

"You're not funny," he told her.

Ever since their 'fight' in John's kitchen last month, things had returned to normal between them. She'd even stopped by the ER to look at the posters he and his team had displayed on their walls. They warned of the dangers of the opioid epidemic and highlighted Preston ER's commitment to safe use. When she popped her head in his office to tell him how impressive they were, he simply grunted. "They're running our patients off."

John cut into her thoughts. "We were playing basketball at the rec center. Chris was hungry, so I invited him over."

"The answer to your question, Kelenna, is yes," her mother said. "It's a never-ending battle because we pharmacists are very hungry. We're always looking to plug ourselves into one hole or the other. Always looking for a bit of autonomy. And we inevitably push some physicians' buttons with our continued ambition."

Kelenna nodded, returning her focus to the discussion she was having before the boys joined them. "You ever yell at a doctor?"

"Oh no, I'm much too calm for that. But then again, I worked with the majority of my attendings when they were green residents. It's almost like dealing with your children. They're very respectful towards me."

Kelenna knew how respectful everyone at Baptist was towards her mother. She'd been there for over thirty years and had helped train several medical and pharmacy residents. Heck, she was the only non-physician doctor Kelenna knew who actually went by the title *Doctor* in a hospital setting. Everyone, from the CEO to the janitor, called her Dr. Obidi.

"It's the tenure thing," Kelenna said thoughtfully. "I just don't have it yet."

"There's nothing wrong with being able to keep your head while others are losing theirs. As for tenure, only time can bring that. Until then, before you present anything, make sure you have your ducks in a row so that the detractors have no leg to stand on. You understand?"

"Something happen at work?" John asked as he dished out his food. When he was done, he started to put food on Chris' plate. They really were like a married couple, those two.

"Nothing really."

"Hold up, I heard about this." Chris raised a finger as if he was trying to jog his memory. "It was about Atkins and the pharmacy director coming to blows." He turned to look at her. "I thought you said you weren't the director."

She hissed at him. "I'm not, and they did not come to blows!" It was crazy how much of a telephone game this had turned out to be. "How did you hear about this?"

"I think it was Ashleigh who mentioned it." Chris shrugged. "So there wasn't an actual fight?"

"No, there wasn't! I wish people would get the story right if they're going to spread rumors. We're one step away from saying my boss punched Dr. Atkins!"

"Well, whatever happened, people think your director is a legend. Atkins has gotten away with this sort of thing for too long."

She knew that, but still the entire ordeal bothered her. With his outbursts, Dr. Atkins had managed to reduce the entire pharmacy department to mere drug suppliers who operated from the basement, despite all the work she'd done for them to be seen as more than that. When she was first hired at Preston three years ago, Pat gave her the responsibility of the clinical pharmacy program and asked her to advance it. She'd just completed a pharmacy residency out in Augusta, and the job was probably too much for her, but she'd worked hard to do just what Pat had asked. Today, pharmacists were on the floors interacting with doctors and nurses and reviewing medications to make sure everything was correct. Her team was responsible for managing dangerous medications like *warfarin* and *heparin* that could make a person bleed if they weren't careful. They monitored patients with infections to make sure they were on the right antibiotics for the right length of time. Basically, they were doing their own bit to keep patients safe and save lives, but apparently there were still people out there who thought they were pests, or that they weren't good enough.

Just then, the doorbell rang and startled everyone at the table.

"Are you guys expecting someone?" John pointed at each person, making sure they were complete and accounted for.

Her mom shook her head before her eyes widened. "Yes! The Igbokwes!" She stood up quickly, making her way to the kitchen as she directed John to open the door.

John did as he was told while Kelenna sat still, her mind running at a mile per minute. She didn't care about the Igbokwes, whoever they were. If news about the P&T blowout traveled around the hospital, did everyone think like Chris? Or were there some people who sided with Dr. Atkins' side and thought that pharmacists should stick to counting pills and mixing drugs? A hand on her shoulder jolted her out of her thoughts, and she turned to see Chris sitting on the dining chair beside her. She raised quizzical brows at him.

"You good?"

"Yeah." She cleared her throat to say it more assuredly. "Yes."

"Hmm." He continued to look at her, a frown on his face, the hand still on her shoulder as if it belonged there. In a weird way it felt good. Grounding. They were the only ones left at the table, and it was quiet, but faint sounds from her family and their guests floated over from the living room. "Whatever happened at your meeting really got to you, didn't it?"

"Maybe," she said evasively.

"Well, stop thinking about it. It says nothing about you in particular."

She looked at him sharply. She had just been wondering if she was less competent at her job than she gave herself credit for. The events of the last few weeks certainly supported that notion. "You don't even know what happened."

"I don't need to know," he said dismissively. "Look at you. You look like you're contemplating changing jobs."

Before she could respond, she was summoned to the living room by her mother yelling her name. Chris let his hand fall from her shoulder and motioned for her to go. She smiled and mouthed her thanks to him.

When she got to the living room, she saw the guests seated across from her parents on the leather loveseat. She couldn't remember exactly who they were until—

"Kelenna, you remember Aunty Carol and Uncle Sam?" her mother asked.

That was who they were! "Yes, of course!" She went over to greet the older couple with hugs. "It's good to see you, it's been so long." They were friends of her parents who used to live in Atlanta before they moved to Rhode Island over a decade ago. Or was it Connecticut? She couldn't remember, but she did recall that they had at least five children, all of who were older than her.

"Yes, it's been so long. Sit down, my dear."

Kelenna did as she was told, squeezing awkwardly between the woman and her husband on that loveseat.

"Wow, you've grown to be so beautiful!" Aunty Carol declared exuberantly. She seemed so surprised that Kelenna made a mental note to take a closer look at her childhood pictures. "Are you single?"

Kelenna's eyes widened at the unexpected question. She spared a quick glance at her parents. Their smiles gave nothing away. John, on the other hand, looked like he was a step away from bursting out in laughter.

"Um, yes, I am," she said truthfully, dreading but knowing that the woman was about to play matchmaker. The glint in her eye could not be mistaken for anything else.

"Perfect! I want you for Landon, my oldest. You remember him?"

She did remember him. He had to be at least seven years older than she was. Fifteen years ago, that age difference would have been insurmountable, so she knew that there had never been much interaction between them. She didn't even know what he looked like now.

As if the woman heard her thoughts, she whipped out her phone and showed her a picture. Kelenna blinked at it. He looked like Blair Underwood, was what he looked like. She looked closer. Okay, he was a poor man's Blair Underwood—his gaze was less penetrating—but any version of the actor was still handsome.

"I think I remember him," Kelenna said softly. "Vaguely. He's a doctor, right?"

"Oh, they're all doctors," Aunty Carol dismissed proudly. "He's the one who went to Harvard. Our neurosurgeon."

A Harvard-trained neurosurgeon who had to be in his late thirties, and looked that good. Why was his mother going on the prowl for him?

"Carol," Uncle Sam chided gently. "Leave the young lady alone. I'm sure she doesn't want to hear all about Landon."

But Aunty Carol ignored him. "Ah, I wasn't sure you would be here tonight otherwise I would have brought wine with me! We would have been doing this properly!"

The wine joke was a bit too much for Kelenna, as it was one of the highest statements of intent to marry amongst her people. She fidgeted uncomfortably on the chair as she shot her mother a glance that begged her to intervene. *Make it stop*, she silently told her.

If they had better telepathy, maybe it would have worked. No, her mother apparently interpreted her horrified look to mean, *egg her on*, because she smiled and started cracking jokes. "How *is* Landon, anyway?" the traitor asked. "He was so well-mannered back then! Emeka, remember when they would all come to visit, and he would straighten up before they left? He was so little, but he insisted!"

Kelenna felt further betrayed when her father joined in. They were two seconds away from betrothing her to this woman's son! As fine and as well-to-do as he was, it was too weird for her. For the first time, she identified with how Dev felt that night of the Diwali. Already, her mind skipped past all the positive possibilities and over to what could go wrong. After all, lately, that was the only way things had gone.

"He now works at Johns Hopkins. He's done very well for himself." Aunty Carol's eyes shone with pride. "I have to make sure he finds the right kind of girl. My dear, you will give me your number, and he will call you."

Kelenna looked to her parents to deliver her from the aggressive clutches of this woman, but once again they sent her encouraging smiles. She had no choice but to recite her phone number. She could only hope that Landon was not a mother's pet like John and wouldn't do everything she asked him to do.

By the time Chris walked into the living room to announce his departure, she was ready to leave with him.

"Another son?" Aunty Carol asked in bewilderment, probably sizing him up for one of her daughters.

"Oh no," her mother corrected. "That's Chris Tari-Douglas."

Kelenna watched in amusement as the woman made a spectacle of herself trying to greet Chris. It was easy to forget just how much fanfare Chris' family name garnered. His grandfather, Dr. TMT Douglas, was an economist and physician turned politician who played a really significant role in Nigeria becoming independent from Great Britain. A lot of historians claimed that were it not for the politics of the time, he would have been selected as the first president of an independent Nigeria ahead of Nnamdi Azikiwe. Kelenna was pretty sure Chris and his family were Kalabari-Nigerian royalty.

While Aunty Carol was distracted asking Chris questions about his family, questions that he was patiently answering with a smile plastered on his face, Kelenna and John stood up to say their goodbyes to their parents.

"I know this was a set-up," Kelenna whispered in her mother's ear as she hugged her.

"What?" Her mother's blank look was a dead giveaway, but she didn't have time to analyze it if she wanted to make a clean escape.

"We'll talk about this later."

Five minutes later, the trio was outside the house, leaning against John's Liberty and breathing exaggerated sighs of relief.

"We don't know how much longer they'll be in there," Kelenna remarked. But no one made any move to get up from the car. It was a warmer than usual December night, but it was still cold. She lifted her face to feel the cool breeze and looked up at the sky. There were so many stars. "John, remember when you went through that stargazing phase?"

"Yep," John chuckled from beside her.

"There are stars?" Chris asked from his other side.

"Yeah," Kelenna said slowly.

"You can't see them?" John asked. "Dude, I told you, you need glasses."

Chris sighed like glasses were the most inconvenient thing in the world. "I know."

"She was the most aggressive woman I've ever met," Kelenna mumbled. Not even her mother, who was as take-charge as they came, could match her.

"She asked me for my dad's direct number in Nigeria," Chris said with a snort. "As if I would just hand that out."

"Careful how you talk about Kelenna's future mother-in-law," John said, barking out a laugh.

Kelenna scowled. "What do you remember about this man Aunty Carol is going to have call me anyway?"

"He's at least forty," Chris muttered under his breath.

Kelenna's head whipped to the right as she leaned over John to look at Chris. Had he meant for her to hear him? She didn't know he'd even been paying attention at her parent's house. "I was talking to John. He remembers everything. I didn't even know you knew him."

Chris scoffed. "Who doesn't know Dr. Landon Igbokwe? Dude just got published in the New England Journal of Medicine."

"Really?" she asked, her eyes wide. Okay, that was ridiculously impressive. The New England Journal of Medicine was only the most important medical journal in the world.

"Yes," John said, agreeing with Chris. "His mother's right, he's very accomplished."

"Probably read *Gifted Hands* by Dr. Carson and modeled his entire career after him." Chris let out a derisive snort. "So cliché."

"I thought all of you became doctors because of that book. You sound like you have a problem with him."

"Sure, I read the book, but I'm not the neurosurgeon who works at Johns Hopkins. And I don't have a problem with him. He's perfect."

John laughed. "You could definitely do worse than him."

"Hmm," Kelenna said, less comforted by that comment than he probably wanted her to be. "Guess it's kind of his mother to consider me for him, then. There's no way he's looking at me twice."

She felt John's frown before she heard his next words. "What do you mean by that?"

"I'm just saying. If he's that great of a person, he's probably dating other neurosurgeons or, I don't know, politicians? Socialites? Whoever people date in the DMV area. Or he's on the other extreme and wants the perfect little homemaker to help raise their future genius children."

"I thought we raised you to have more confidence than that." John's disappointment was clear in his voice.

"Raised me? Please. Last time I checked, we are still in our twin phase! And I'm confident enough to know when people are out of my league."

"Can you stop saying that?" He elbowed her ribs. "No one is better than you. Chris, tell her."

"No one is better than you," Chris parroted.

"I didn't say he was better than me. I said he was out of my league."

"What's the difference there?" Chris asked, suddenly more interested in her love life than she would have preferred.

Kelenna sighed. "It's not easy to explain without you boys thinking my confidence is in the gutter. I just think there are levels, and he's on a different one. Not higher or lower. Just different."

"The word *level* implies height and depth," Chris argued.

"And writing him off without giving him a chance because *you* don't think he would give you a chance is illogical," John added. Then he began to mutter about how women overthink every little thing they do.

"It's not illogical," she snapped. "It's just easier!"

"Easier in what way?" John asked softly.

It was much easier to avoid heartbreak by not opening the door in the first place, she thought. She didn't say the words out loud though, but knowing John, he probably heard them. They had better telepathy. "Never mind, ignore me. I'm just going to go home." She raised up off the hood of his car and headed for her car which was parked behind his.

"Kelenna, wait up." John caught her arm. "Did something happen after the married man?"

"What married man?" Chris asked, sounding like he was ready to defend her honor. She appreciated his brotherly concern for her, but she didn't need him thinking she was incompetent professionally *and* personally on the same day.

"Ignore him," she said, sending John a quelling look.

John ignored *her*. "You know where I am if you ever need to talk, right?" he asked.

"Yes, of course." Then, because she wanted to smooth over his concerns, she reached up to hug him. "Thanks, big bro."

John had always felt responsible for her. Just the other day, he told her a story from when they were five years old. They had been riding their bikes in circles in the yard. Kelenna, in her attempt to keep up with him, fell off hers, scraped her arm, and had begun to cry. John ignored her and kept riding. When their mother came out, she made sure Kelenna was all right before pulling him aside to chastise him. She told him that as the big brother, it was his duty to make sure nothing happened to his little sister. "And I took her words way too seriously," he said. "It was a long time before I realized that she really just wished that I had come to get her when you fell."

"You're good, right?" John released her now and kept her at arm's length to search her eyes.

"I promise."

Behind him, Chris was looking at her with an inscrutable expression. It didn't change, even when she smiled weakly at him.

11

Have you heard from him?"

Kelenna didn't bother pretending not to know who *him* was. She put her purse down on the living room floor and exhaled. "As a matter of fact, yes I have."

She'd been summoned back to her parents' house on a non-Wednesday to help her mother with a project for the Nigerian Pharmacists Association, and she'd wanted to get right into the work, but her mother was full of questions of a different variety—the neurosurgeon kind of variety.

"And what did you think?"

"We didn't talk for too long. There wasn't much for me to go on."

It was the truth. Three days after talking to Landon Igbokwe, she was still analyzing the call. His voice had been very calm—almost hypnotic—and their conversation had been quite nice, but was it the start of something new? She had no clue.

"My mother mentioned that she saw you last week," he said after he introduced himself and they'd gotten the pleasantries out of the way.

"It was good to see her," Kelenna replied. "It's been what, over ten years?"

"More than that. I remember coming over to your parents' house and seeing you and your twin brother. You couldn't have been more than ten or eleven then."

She didn't corrected his twin comment and she made a mental note to laugh about it with John later.

"My mother tells me you're a big-time pharmacist somewhere outside Atlanta. Nice."

"Me? What about you? Double Ivy? Neurosurgeon? Johns Hopkins? You just got published in the most renowned journal in the world—"

"Jesus." He cut her off with a wince that made him sound like he was in pain. "I've asked my mother not to go around reciting my resume."

"Oh, no, she didn't tell me all that. I—" That time she cut herself off. She was about to expose herself as a creative stalker.

She was too late.

"You researched me," he completed for her, letting out a low chuckle that sounded either cocky or flirty, she couldn't decide which.

"You've caught me. In my defense, your mother gave me too little to work with. Just a picture of you from ages ago. I had to see what you looked like now, and boom! Turns out you're all over the internet!" She was much better at teasing than flirting, and she hoped that it would work out in her favor.

It did, and she knew it because he laughed out loud. A more genuine-sounding laugh. "Okay little girl, you're the one I remember as an actual child. And I haven't been lucky enough to see a picture of you as a—how old are you now?"

"Twenty-nine. Not so little anymore. Hang on for a second." She turned her camera on, smiled as wide and goofy as she could, and snapped a quick selfie. Before she could analyze it too much, she sent it to him via text. "You should be getting a picture in five, four, three—"

"Oh." He laughed once more, clearly noting that she hadn't been attempting to send him her best picture. "Very cute." If blushing was audible, he would have been able to hear hers, but as it was, she could hide behind his next words. "And you just sent me a picture without putting on your face, as you young folks say nowadays."

"I think you'll find I'm not your typical young folk." She hit herself then for sounding like she was a contestant auditioning for *The Bachelor*. Why did she feel the need to separate herself from other *young girls*? There wasn't anything wrong with wearing makeup if that was the person's preference.

They reminisced some more about their childhoods before he abruptly cut her off. "Hey, I have to go, but it's been nice catching up."

"It has been indeed."

That was when he hit her with, "Don't be a stranger."

Don't be a stranger. What did that even mean? Was he going to call her again? Did he want her to call him next?

"Let's talk more about this later," her mother said now, interrupting her thoughts. "I need this presentation finished by tonight. It's a proposal for an educational trip to Nigeria." She handed her laptop with PowerPoint open on it over to Kelenna. "My student has already worked on some of it. We just need to finish the rest."

Kelenna nodded as she skimmed through the presentation. It seemed like it focused primarily on the importance of improving physician and pharmacy relationships, and expanding the role of pharmacists in hospitals. Last year, her mother visited three or four teaching hospitals in Nigeria and she was in essence summarizing her findings in this presentation.

"This is no different than what we continue to strive to do down here," Kelenna noted.

"That's right. The only difference is that they are in the beginning stages. Include this phrase on the second slide." Her mother paused to collect her thoughts before she continued on with her dictation. "The healthcare system in Nigeria is imperfect, but we must work within its confines. It is important to have open discussion with their physician leaders to see how we can match their goals."

Kelenna finished typing and let her fingers hover over the keyboard. "Will they be receptive to change?"

"Not if you come in trying to change everything all at once," her mother said. "That's the easiest way to get the door slammed in your face."

Kelenna blinked at that. "Wow. So where do you start?"

"We keep it simple and start from where we can have a measurable and sustainable impact. New slide, please."

Her mother went on to dictate the ideas she had to increase pharmacy's visibility in hospitals. She talked about how they would need support from the doctors with the big titles. They were the ones who the people on the ground would listen to. Then she finished up with ways for the pharmacists to monitor the effects of the changes they implemented.

Kelenna wrapped up her typing and saved the document. As she handed the laptop back to her mother, she shook her head in wonder. "This is all so impressive, Mom. I don't know how you manage to be so passionate about this."

"The passion is the simple part, my dear. It's easy to be passionate about the things you love, especially when they are important. And this is very important. We know from numerous studies that clinical pharmacists can save lives when they're used to their maximum potential. We catch medication errors and we make sure the right drug is being used in the right situation. Without the pharmacy department, the hospital cannot function. There are hospitals that either don't understand that or don't want to understand that. There are even pharmacists who don't want to live up to that. And that's what continues to drive me."

Kelenna understood all that, but still. "Don't you ever get discouraged? Don't you get *tired*?"

"Depends on the day and the situation. But when there's a will, there's a way. Remember that."

Kelenna nodded. "Well, I hope you get the funds you need. This project seems really promising."

"Thank you, my dear." Her mother turned hopeful eyes to her. "*Now* will you join NPA?"

Kelenna rolled her eyes and laughed. She should have known her mother wouldn't abandon this request from months ago. "Fine, I'll join NPA," she acquiesced.

"Aha! You can join me on my next trip!" Then her mother launched into her plans to visit even more teaching hospitals in Nigeria. "We can start small and spread out quickly. If we're lucky, we can influence several areas in the country." Kelenna found herself getting excited as she listened. She wondered if passion could be obtained by osmosis. Not long after, her mother closed the laptop. "Okay, now, back to Landon Igbokwe."

Kelenna groaned. "Mom, there's nothing—"

Her mother held up a hand to silence her. "You have no idea what I am going to say. I spoke to John a couple of days ago. He told me what you said about Landon, and he wanted me to talk to you."

Kelenna groaned again, this time it was louder and prolonged. "John misunderstood every single word I said!"

"I'm sure he did. But I understand what you meant quite well."

"You do?" She was prepared to defend her comment to John the Tattler, not to have an unlikely ally in her mother. Weren't parents supposed to be all about believing their kids were the best?

"Sure. You and your brother are alike in some ways, and very different in others. John is Mr. Popular, Mr. Overachiever, Mr. Go-Getter, you name it."

"And I'm not any of those things?"

Her mother shook her head in a way that made Kelenna want to clutch at her chest. How brutally honest! "Not to the same extent, no. When you were younger, yes, you showed signs that you could go toe-to-toe with him. You caught up to his height by the time you were two, and you started reading when he did. There was even a time when I bought him a bicycle for your birthday. You would have been four then."

"Hold up." Kelenna laughed, suppressing her wonder about yet another bicycle story. "You bought *him* a bike for *my* birthday?"

Her mother shrugged. "I always bought you both gifts on one person's birthday so the other wouldn't feel left out. You were the one to throw a tantrum on John's third birthday, so I did it up until you were old enough to not be too jealous. Anyway, I bought him a bicycle with those training wheels attached, and got you a tricycle. You took one look at his, hopped on it, and refused to come down. We had no choice but to take yours back and get you the same one."

Kelenna laughed once more. She truly did love hearing her mother's little stories about things she couldn't remember. The toddlerhood aggression she described seemed so far away from her current personality she couldn't help but wonder if her mother was exaggerating.

"Where was I going with this again?" her mother asked.

"You were telling me how different I am from John," she replied, still smiling.

"Oh, yes. At the time, we thought it was wise to keep you both in the same grade, since it was an option then. We thought you were like a little genius. In hindsight, I'm not so sure we didn't hurt you a bit by doing that. Where John blossomed, you retreated. It was almost as if his presence meant you didn't have to work as hard."

Kelenna frowned. "What does that mean? I may not have been valedictorian of our class like he was, but I was a good student!" It wasn't her fault that John felt the need to reassert his seniority over her by graduating from high school with enough credits to be a junior in college. If anything, it said more about him than it did about her.

"Yes, you were. Yes, you could make good grades without studying, but I mean more than that. You were content to stay in his shadows while he was around. It wasn't until you went to pharmacy school that I saw you come into your own."

"You make it sound like I used John as a crutch. I may have been an introvert, but I had my own life!"

Her mother sighed and abandoned the point she was doing a terrible job of making. "I say all this to say that John doesn't know a situation that he can't own. He could be the doorman and still carry himself like the owner of the building. It's why he didn't understand you when you told him that you didn't think you were good enough for Landon."

"But you do?"

"Of course. I understand that you're very pragmatic. That you realize that he has accomplished more than the average person. More than you have."

"Yes! And those are facts. I don't see what's so wrong about acknowledging facts!"

"The only problem with it is when you diminish yourself in the process."

This time when Kelenna rolled her eyes, she made no attempt to hide it. She leaned back into the couch almost petulantly. "I should have known you would find a way to turn this back on me."

"Ah, my dear, I'm doing no such thing. Think about it. Everything you know about Landon is on the surface. His job description is just one aspect of his life. We really do not know much about his character. But you? We know your character and your qualities. We are the ones who should be concerned whether or not *he* is worth *your* time."

Kelenna digested her mother's words. These were things she knew in theory, but they were things she applied to other people, not to herself. It dawned on her then that she was pedestalizing the doctor. She placed him so high in her mind and convinced herself that he was too *big* for her. But maybe, just maybe, if they both stayed in their lanes—he in neurosurgery, and she in pharmacy—they could meet on a different plane.

"I would love it if you and Landon got to know each other and decided to start a relationship," her mother was saying. "Believe me, you're not getting any younger, and I've always thought you would do well with a doctor."

"Really?" Kelenna's nose scrunched up as she ignored the subtle reference to her age. The woman didn't have a leg to stand on when it came to getting married later than her peers. She didn't marry Kelenna's father till she was thirty! The way Kelenna saw it, she had a solid year before her mother could pester her. "I've never thought I would do well with a doctor. They work far too much."

"Nonsense," her mother dismissed. "It's good for a man to work. An idle mind is the devil's workshop."

"Said the workaholic."

Her mother laughed. "Kelenna, it doesn't have to be Landon. I didn't orchestrate a meet up with Carol to unite the Igbokwe and Agu families. I'm not that underhanded."

Kelenna didn't buy her mother's act for a second. "No, you're not underhanded. You're just a puppet master that likes to make people dance to your bidding." She mimicked a puppeteer's action of pulling the strings on a marionette.

"What a rude child!" Her words were in direct conflict with the smile on her face. "One would think that at your age you would have better manners."

"This is the second reference you've made to my age today. What's up?"

"I do worry a bit about you not being married yet." She held up her hand as though she knew Kelenna was about to protest. "I know, I know. You're waiting for the right person."

"I'm waiting for the feeling you had when you saw my father," Kelenna said cheekily.

"Ah, it'll be different for you," her mother replied, clearly not catching Kelenna's jocular tone. "You don't have a spontaneous bone in your body. You will overthink the entire thing. I wouldn't be surprised if you've already dated your future husband. Or at least met him."

Kelenna frowned. "Will?"

"No, not that politician," her mother scoffed. "Who it is, isn't the point. I just don't want you to bank on having a feeling that may never come."

"I know it may not," she said somberly. It broke her heart a little to admit it because who didn't want that storybook feeling? The one that came with seeing someone and knowing that they would '*mean something to you someday*'? But she was nothing if not a realist, and she knew her mother was right.

"And I'm not getting younger, myself," her mother was saying. "I would like some grandchildren that I can see every once in a while."

"Once in a while? You'll be babysitting them every weekend!" Kelenna said, laughing when she saw her mother's horrified face. "Mom, do you make these requests of John?"

"Of course," her mother said, her face serious once more. "Boys are different. All they need to do is find a girl and settle down. Now, John is more like me. If he sees the right girl, he will be married in under six months. You, on the other hand, may not know the right person if he stood in front of you."

There she went again. Beneath the jokester exterior lied a very perceptive woman. Suddenly Kelenna wondered if her mother knew something she didn't know. "Mother, do you want to tell me who I'll end up with? Save me all the time?"

"Tell you so that you can run in the opposite direction? No, better to let you figure it out on your own."

"Mom!" she said exasperatedly. The woman was now bent over, laughing at her.

"Ah, my dear girl. How can I know for sure when I'm not God? Just be happy that I'm not like the Okafors otherwise you would be getting married in Nigeria this month. Have you eaten?"

"The Okafors?" she mumbled, following her mother who had begun to make her way into the kitchen. "No, I didn't get a chance to have dinner."

"By the way, how is Chika getting ready for her wedding? You know, her mother never got over her quitting law school. I tell her all the time, let the girl find her own way, she will end up where she's supposed to be. Perhaps this will satisfy her, for now."

Kelenna was too stupefied to call her mother out on her hypocrisy. If she or her brother had even thought of dropping out of pharmacy or medical school, their mother would have lost her mind. "Mom, stop. What are you talking about? What wedding?"

"You didn't know? Chika's mother said the *iku aka* will likely happen this Christmas."

12

Iku aka literally meant 'to knock.' In the Igbo culture, it represented a visit paid to the family of a woman by the family of her significant other. It was the first step in a series of rites that led straight to marriage. If Kelenna's mother was right, it meant that in two weeks, Chika was going to be practically engaged. To someone Kelenna had never heard of. How was that even possible?

"Hold this one." Chika handed her a red cocktail dress still attached to its hanger. Kelenna spared it a cursory look before she took it from her and dropped it in the cart she was absentmindedly pushing in front of her. They were walking through the aisles of Nordstrom Rack in Buckhead, making a great pretense of clothes shopping. At least that was what Kelenna was doing. It had been Kelenna's idea to go shopping in the first place. She thought that maybe if they were in Chika's natural habitat, that is, surrounded by stylish clothes and off-price designer items, Chika would feel comfortable enough to share her upcoming engagement. So far it wasn't working. Chika seemed more interested in talking about Dr. Landon Igbokwe for some reason.

"You know Dr. Landon and Ada Ozim are cousins, right?" she was saying. "I was talking to her the other day, and she said she had just seen him in D.C. last week. You absolutely need to call him. That guy is dreamy. He looks like he's pure, but also like he could do wicked things. Why are you looking at me like that? It's true!"

"Are you going to tell me that you're getting married or not?" Kelenna blurted out, surprising herself a little, and Chika a lot.

"I-I I'm not getting married," Chika stammered.

"Don't lie, your mother told mine about your *iku aka* this Christmas!" Kelenna whispered harshly. "I didn't even know you were going to Nigeria this year!"

"Oh, come on, I go to Nigeria every year."

"Not to go get engaged, you don't!"

"I'm not getting engaged," Chika said weakly. "We're just going to do an introduction and we'll see how it goes."

Kelenna's eyes bugged out. "You think you can just do an *iku aka* and walk away? I can't believe you didn't tell me any of this."

"And when would I have told you?" Chika snapped back. "We're always talking about your issues. When have you ever asked about me?"

Kelenna recoiled like she'd been slapped. "Don't try to turn this back on me, I'm not the one keeping things from her friend! You're getting engaged to someone I don't know! Do you hear yourself?"

"There you go again, somehow making this about you. You want to know why I didn't tell you?"

"Isn't that what I've been asking?"

"Because you would never have understood!"

A few heads turned their way, and Kelenna all but scowled at them.

"Let's go somewhere private," she said in a low voice. She made her way out of the store fully expecting Chika to follow her.

"Don't you want to buy any of those clothes?"

"No." She was resolute as she kept walking to Chika's car. When Chika opened the car remotely, Kelenna got in the passenger seat and waited for Chika to get in the driver's seat.

"Now explain why I, *of all people*, would never have understood this?"

Chika let out a sigh and started her engine. "His name is Daniel Okocha, and he lives in Lagos. His family is friends with my mother's cousin. They're a good family. My mother just wants me to meet him and make a formal decision while we're there."

"So you'll meet him for the first time and decide if you want to marry him that day?"

Chika's second sigh gave Kelenna the feeling that she was saying the wrong thing. But what else could she say? "See? I knew you would never get it."

"Then explain it to me," she implored. "What am I missing? It seems like your mother is setting you up in a weird *Married At First Sight* situation and you're just going along with it!"

Chika tapped her steering wheel absentmindedly. "My last real boyfriend was three years ago," she said. "Every other guy has been a waste of space since then. I'll be thirty soon, I can't wait forever."

"We'll all be thirty next year!" Kelenna snapped. Why was everyone acting like thirty was synonymous with senior citizenship?

"Well, maybe thirty looks different for different people. You may not have the clock ticking in your ear, but that doesn't mean I don't. There's all this pressure around me, and it's about time for me to start a family."

Kelenna wanted to shake her friend. "Chika, you don't believe in pressure!" How did a girl who always marched to beat of her own drum suddenly succumb to pressure in the most important decision of her life?

"I'm just tired of the endless arguments and the constant put-downs. You're the golden child in your family, Kelenna, you don't get it. The thing about pressure is eventually, it gets to you."

"John's the golden child in my family," Kelenna mumbled.

Chika gave her a look that said she wasn't even going to debate that with her. "My older brother and younger sister are both married."

"Your little sister is an anomaly who got married at twenty-two! She doesn't count!"

"And according to my mother, she had a child and still managed to finish dental school. My parents think I'm a failure, Kels. And before you say anything, I know I'm not. They think all that matters is having a graduate degree and a six-figure salary, and anything short of that means I've brought shame to the family. So would it hurt if I just consider this one thing for them? It's no different than what I've preached to you for months now. I've told you to join apps, go on dates, and keep your mind open. How is that different from what my mother wants me to do?"

* * *

Later that night, Kelenna sat in her bed with a glass of wine on her nightstand and the TV turned on for some background noise. Whenever she was upset, or at a loss for how to truly respond to a situation, she turned to what calmed her down the most—journaling. It was a habit she'd picked up in undergrad and she only did it sporadically. She found that putting pen to paper helped to arrange her thoughts and remember things with more clarity. And right now, clarity was what she needed.

She hadn't succeeded in getting Chika to shun her own mother, cancel her flight to Nigeria, and completely forget about the *iku aka*. They'd talked for over an hour in that Nordstrom Rack parking lot, and everything she'd done to pull Chika from the brink of making the worst decision of her life seemed to push her further over the edge. It was like she had found a noble cause and was determined to martyr herself for it. She'd seemed eerily at peace with it, even cracking jokes about her potential last name. "How does Chika Okocha sound?" she'd asked.

Kelenna looked up from her notebook at the TV screen. Maxine Shaw had just made a snarky comment about Regine's hair on an episode of *Living Single*, and the TV audience had responded with raucous laughter. She snorted a low laugh. A little part of her wished her final comments to Chika in the parking lot were about something as irrelevant as her hairstyle. In her defense, Chika had provoked her with a quip about how passive Kelenna was, and how she was always waiting for things to happen, rather than making them happen. That was when she'd called Chika desperate and told her that she would regret letting her mother dictate her future. Chika had shut down after that. Kelenna could see that she was fighting tears.

It was just as well. Chika was an expert at dishing it out, but wasn't as good at taking it. She could use a little tough love. Besides, what kind of friend would she be if she couldn't say how she felt for fear of hurting her feelings?

But something about Chika's comments about her own passivity stayed with her. Chika had accused her of *'waiting for something to happen to her'* before, but Kelenna hadn't thought twice about it. Maybe because it felt like she *was* doing something by joining SwipeNow and going on all those dates. Either way, it reminded her of the relationship between drugs and the human body: pharmacodynamics and pharmacokinetics. In its simplest meaning, the former was all about what drugs did to the body, while the latter was what the body did to the drug. Was it really her nature to let things happen to her rather than to take charge? Were all the dates she'd gone on truly indicative of how in control she was? Or were they more examples of just how passive she was? Suddenly, Landon's words, *Don't be a stranger,* echoed in her mind and took on a new meaning. Perhaps he was gauging her interest in him, putting the ball in *her* court, ceding power to *her.* In this day and age where gender roles were being questioned in the relationship arena, where the guy didn't have to always make the first move, why couldn't she be *kinetic* and *do* something? If she liked Landon, what was stopping *her* from giving him a call?

She wrote down the words: 'Be Kinetic' and circled it. Then before she could overthink it, as she was wont to do, she put down her pen and picked up her phone. She scrolled to the number that had called her exactly a week ago. When the phone rang for the third time without anyone picking up, she almost hung up.

"Hello?" It was a woman's voice. "This is Landon's phone."

Kelenna's eyes widened at the sound of the voice. It was well past 9 p.m., but one never knew with surgeons. He could be in the middle of some kind of emergency neurosurgical procedure. "Hi! I'm sorry, I was trying to reach Dr. Igbokwe. I'm a friend of his—"

"Oh right," the woman cut in. "He's been playing phone tag with a friend. You're the one from Yale, right?"

"No, I'm from—"

"Harvard?"

"No, from Atlanta," she said quickly, before the woman could run through the other Ivy League universities.

"Atlanta?" The woman's voice sounded incredulous, as though Atlanta was in a foreign country and Landon would never have heard of the place. "Babe!" she yelled.

Babe? Was she his girlfriend? She was contemplating hanging up when the woman returned to the phone.

"What's your name?"

"It's Kelenna. Look, if he's busy I can just—"

"It's Kelly Anna from Atlanta!"

Before she could correct her, she heard shuffling of feet, and then Landon's voice in the background.

"Kelenna?"

"Hi Landon." She was flustered from all the ceremony that had happened just to bring him to the phone. "I didn't mean to call on a bad night. It sounds like you're busy with your girl . . ." she trailed off, hoping he would take it from there, but he was silent, and it became increasingly awkward the longer he kept quiet. "Anyway, I just called to say hi." She laughed nervously. "Trying not to be a stranger and all that."

"Hi Kelenna." His voice was warm and patient. "Thank you for calling me." He made it sound like she had done him a favor just by calling. "I have a fundraiser to attend right now, so it really isn't a good time. Hold on." There was a brief pause. "I'll be right there, Ming!"

"I'll let you go," she offered quickly.

"Sorry Kelenna. But hey, we'll be in touch."

They hung up.

We'll be in touch? Could he be any more vague? Plus, who was this Ming woman who called him babe, and was so obsessed with Ivy League schools?

She flopped back onto her pillow in frustration.

* * *

By the time Wednesday rolled around, Kelenna was ready for the upcoming weekend. First of all, she had to get through this family dinner where her mother was in a special mood. It was all Kelenna's fault though. She should have known better than to bring up Chika's situation in the manner that she did. Her mother was the least traditional Nigerian woman she knew, but she was still Nigerian.

"Everyone is different," her mother said. "You can't apply your preferences to others and expect them to abide by them. There's nothing wrong with considering a young man your parents introduce you to for marriage. That's all she's doing. One day, you'll understand."

"Come on, Mom, this is way past considering! You don't invite someone to knock on your door if you don't plan on opening it! If Chika goes through with this *iku aka*, Aunty Mercy will make sure she stays married! I'm never going to understand why Chika thinks she should bend to her mother's wishes. Marriage is not necessary for her happiness!"

Her mother sighed, and Kelenna heard her unspoken admonition loud and clear: marriage better be necessary for *your* happiness.

"Kelenna, let it go," John said gently. "We all know Chika. She's not going to go through with this. She never follows through with anything."

Kelenna scowled at him. She knew he was alluding to Chika's short law school career. He'd been disapproving when she quit, and had always seen it as a character flaw. "Did you ever ask Chika why she dropped out of Emory law?"

"I know why," he answered with a smirk. "She changed her mind. She changes her mind at the slightest difficulty, and she'll change her mind when she gets to Nigeria. She—"

"Wrong," she cut in firmly. "Law school was easy for Chika. She was top of her class when she quit. You know how hard it is to be top of anything at Emory, don't you?"

"Yeah?" John murmured.

"Chika quit because she realized she didn't want to be a lawyer," Kelenna said softly. "She's not flighty like you think she is. She's strong-willed. And it's because of people like you that she feels like she has to do this thing and ruin her life!"

John's eyes widened. "People like me? What the hell did I do?"

"It's people like you who make her think she's a non-conformist."

John shrugged. "She is, in fact."

"And there's nothing wrong with that!" Kelenna retorted. "Now she's settling just to fit into some role her mother wants for her. It's crazy!"

"We agree on that."

"Will you two stop it?" her mother snapped from beside her. "Who says Chika is settling? What do I always tell you? Look for the character. You know nothing about the character of this man her mother has chosen for her."

"Neither does she," Kelenna said under her breath, but her mother heard her and turned to give her a stern look. Kelenna shrugged defensively. "Mom, the truth is, you can't trust desperate mothers. They make the worst choosers. They're so eager to marry their daughters off that they'll say yes to any guy who breathes. I told her she's going to regret it."

"Chika doesn't need you telling her what you think is right according to the school of Kelenna Jordan Agu," her mother said firmly. "You need to be supportive. Call that girl and apologize at once."

"Apologize? She said some crazy things to me too! Why do *I* have to be the bigger person?"

"If you have to ask, then I've done a horrible job raising you."

"Fine," Kelenna mumbled. She was annoyed by how easy it was for her mother to reduce her to a ten-year-old with just one comment. A ten-year-old eager to not disappoint.

In that precise moment, it dawned on her that maybe Chika's feelings were valid. Kelenna just wished Chika didn't have to prove that she was the dutiful daughter by committing her future to a total stranger.

They finished the rest of the meal in silence and retired to the living room shortly after. Her father got a call from the hospital and went to his office to deal with it, while John promptly passed out on the couch.

"So, how is work going?" her mother asked.

Work was usually neutral ground for them, but it wasn't to be tonight.

"Busy. Stressful. Take your pick. The opioid crisis-shortage is affecting us big time. I feel like I'm some kind of pain medicine police."

"Really? How so?"

"Nothing we do is enough. We draw up Dilaudid in syringes, and they get used up before we're even out of the IV compounding room. We work hard to switch patients to PO opioids, and before we blink, the doctor comes and switches them back to IV. It's been non-stop the last few weeks trying to stay afloat with not having enough opioids, and trying to save what we do have."

Her mother nodded sagely at her rant. "It comes with the territory, my dear." She then proceeded to veer off on a tangent about how solving problems was tantamount to being a manager, and that she should embrace it.

"I like problem solving well enough, Mom," Kelenna protested. "Just not when there is no answer! I was in a meeting today with some of the nurse managers, and this one named Ashleigh talked about a patient who had to be Narcaned by paramedics. She should have been thankful for her life, but what does she do when her boyfriend comes to see her? Slips a *fentanyl* patch into her mouth. In her mouth! She had to be put on a Narcan drip after that. We have to face it. Fighting a chronic problem in an acute hospital is impossible. It's a losing battle. And frankly, we worry so much about these patients who have no regard for their own lives. Maybe we should let them take themselves out."

"What do you mean take themselves out?"

Kelenna let out a breath. "I mean, we're willing to do so much to save these people when they're not willing to save themselves. We give them Narcan for free, but we charge an arm and a leg for other life-saving drugs like *insulin.* Instead of forcing these people to stay alive, maybe we need to shift our attention. To help other people who actually want our help."

"You can't possibly believe that." Her mother was aghast. "You ought to have a little more empathy for addicts than you do. It's a disease, just like diabetes. You can't just hope the problem will go away, Kelenna. Part of solving a problem is having the patience to see it through!"

Kelenna looked up to the ceiling as if she needed help from above. "I don't think I can say anything right today." When her mother said nothing, she turned to find her looking at her shrewdly. "What now?" she snapped.

"You are letting disillusion set in. How can you be this jaded when you've barely begun your career? At this rate, you'll burn out before you're forty. Listen, you have to know the why behind what you're doing."

"The *why*? I know the why. The DEA thinks opioids are being overprescribed and has decided that cutting off manufacturers is the best way to stop it. Never mind that they've probably never worked in a hospital in their lives. They have no idea how—"

"I don't mean the textbook why," her mother interrupted harshly. "Anyone can memorize that. The *why* is the patient. Whether or not you think the patient is worthy is not up to you. Their life is important. We are not God to decide who needs saving!"

Kelenna sighed. Her mother was right. And the more she thought about it, the more she recognized that all the measures she'd taken to minimize the impact of the opioid crisis-shortage were impersonal. Asking the doctors to cut back on prescribing. Unit dosing *morphine* and Dilaudid. The IV to PO conversion program. None of them had had anything to do with the patient. Every step of the way, the patient had been an afterthought. It was easy to look at the computer, and see that a patient was getting too many opioids, and react to the amount, without knowing what their pain truly was, and if they were addicts, without caring about their psychological health. It was easy to be judgmental when you couldn't put yourself in another person's situation. "You're right, Mom," she said feebly. "I'm sorry. I think I'm just . . . stressed."

"It's okay. Just remember what I've said. Your problems will be half-solved when you can connect to the why. The next time you look at a patient, really look at them."

Kelenna nodded. She didn't yet know what changes she was going to make, but she knew it would have to start with a change in her mindset.

"I think your conversation put me to sleep," John mumbled, rising out of his slumber.

"Really?" Kelenna said with a laugh. "It wasn't the fact that you were on call last night?"

John snorted as he stood up from the couch and stretched his long limbs. "No, I'm pretty sure it was Mom using her Dr. Obidi voice that lulled me to sleep." He leaned down to give their mother a kiss on her cheek, and then turned and did the same to Kelenna. "Listen to Dr. Obidi, Kels. She knows best."

13

The next day after work, Kelenna found herself knocking on Chika's apartment door. A scowl greeted her when the door opened, confirming that Chika was still angry with her.

"Hey, girl," Kelenna said softly, trying to look as contrite as she could. "May I come in?"

Without a word, Chika opened the door wide. It looked like a tornado had swept through her usually tidy apartment.

"Winter cleaning?" Kelenna asked, side-stepping a pile of shoes by the corner of the door.

"I'm packing for my trip," Chika replied sullenly.

"Already?"

"Yes." Chika walked past her and into her living room. "I always pack early. What do you want?"

Kelenna's eyes widened at her friend's hostility. Maybe she deserved it, but couldn't Chika cut her some slack? "I wanted to apologize. I crossed the line with you, and I'm sorry. I just want you to know that I support whatever decision you make. Specifically regarding marrying David."

"His name is Daniel," Chika said with a snort. "And I told you, I'm not marrying him."

Kelenna shifted some clothes on the sofa to make room for herself and sat down. "I didn't come here to fight, I came here to make peace. Do you need help?"

Chika rolled her eyes and nodded. "Grab that pile of clothes and follow me."

When they got to Chika's bedroom, she dumped the clothes on the bed, and together, they began to fold them and tuck them in suitcases. As they worked, Chika told her about Daniel.

"My mother says he's a businessman. He's into trade and all that. He goes to Dubai a lot."

"Oh, so he's well-traveled?"

"I'm not sure."

"How old is he?"

"No idea."

"What's his middle name?"

Chika groaned. "Stop trying to quiz me about him. Whatever I don't know now, I'll find out over the next two weeks."

Kelenna stopped folding and sat heavily on the bed. "Doesn't this feel weird to you?"

Chika sat beside her. "A little."

Kelenna snorted. "You know, over the years, we must have talked about who we'd want to end up with a thousand times. Remember?"

"Yes." Chika stared wistfully at her suitcase. "I thought I would end up with John and you thought you would end up with Chris."

"Right." Kelenna chuckled as her mind went briefly to her teenage crush on Chris. It amazed her just how much time had changed everything she and Chika were back then. How could they both have had romantic interests then that they wouldn't even consider now? "We thought we had it all figured out, didn't we? We wanted it all. We called it The Whole Nine. Tall, dark, handsome, intelligent, good morals . . . What else was there?"

"Hold on, let me think." Chika looked up at the ceiling, as if she expected to see the answers written up there. "Great job, nice body, non-smoker. God, I can't remember the last one."

"I think it was nice teeth?"

"Nice teeth!" Chika laughed. "I can't believe we put that in our criteria!"

Kelenna joined her. "Man, we were hopeless romantics."

Chika started to laugh once more, but then she stopped abruptly, almost as if she decided that she didn't deserve to laugh. "Well, lucky for us, as we've gotten older, we've learned that men like that only exist in romance novels. Or if they do exist in real life, they aren't interested in us. Now, the whole nine means more practical things. Like, is he alive? Is he not ugly? Now, we have to take matters into our own hands."

Kelenna could hear the resignation in Chika's words. And the cynicism. She stared at the suitcases on the floor, the stark reminder of her friend's decision to take matters into her own hands.

"Remember your date with the rude guy who wouldn't stop cutting you off?"

Kelenna raised a brow. "Yeah?"

"You said something interesting. You said that we spend so much of our lives either being in relationships, or trying to be in one. I've thought about that a lot since that day, but I keep falling back on the same answer. What else can we do if the alternative is that we end up alone?"

"We're not going to end up alone." Kelenna waved a dismissive hand, even though she wasn't sure. She could just imagine a statistician punching in numbers and calculating the odds based on their collective dating history. The odds would be very poor indeed.

"No, we won't. Not if we take matters into our own hands. Not if we ditch the fairytale we filled our heads up with when we were younger, and go into things with a clear mind. Do you understand me now?"

"Yes." She understood that the fear of winding up alone was a big motivator. Had she not felt that same fear herself after Will got engaged? She handled it by joining SwipeNow and going on dates. Who was she to judge how Chika handled her own fear?

Chika squeezed her knee. "Now, about you. I know you've given up on the dating apps, and you'll never be open to Aunty Uche matchmaking—"

"My mother knows better than to—"

Chika raised a hand. "I get it. But did you never call Dr. Landon back? I think he could be the Will replacement you've been looking for."

Kelenna's eyes widened in horror. "I have absolutely not been looking for a Will replacement!"

"You have," Chika said smoothly. "That's why every person you've met after him has fallen short."

"Not because they weren't Will!"

Chika gave her a knowing look. "All I know is that Dr. Landon won't fall short. He's just your type. Good looking, a little arrogant, bookish. Probably has good text diction too."

"You don't know any of that for sure." Also, Chika made her type sound horribly shallow. Were those really the leading traits of the men she gravitated towards?

"But you can find out," Chika was saying. "If you get off your butt and give the man a call!"

"As a matter of fact, I did call him." Kelenna pursed her lips as she remembered the call she had with Landon. She recounted the experience to Chika, especially highlighting the fact that he had a very real girlfriend.

Chika couldn't hide her grin. "Come on, you're not a hundred percent sure she's his girlfriend. She could be his roommate for all you know."

"As if he would need a roommate. He's a neurosurgeon. Did you not hear when I said she called him babe?"

"So? Maybe she's from California." Chika shrugged. "They call everyone babe over there."

Kelenna let her eye roll tell Chika just what she thought about Ming being from California.

When the phone in her hand rang out of the blue, she looked down at the lit screen. Her eyes widened when she saw who it was, and she threw the phone away like it was evil. It had to be, because it had conjured the very person they'd just been gossiping about.

"What's the matter?" Chika reached over to pick up the phone. It took her only a second to register who it was, and she tossed it back on Kelenna's lap. "Oh my goodness, talk about the devil! Answer it!"

"What if he heard us?"

Chika ignored her and hit the accept button. "Hello?" she said in such a low voice that Kelenna wondered who in the world she was mimicking. She let out an inaudible gasp and grabbed the phone from Chika just as she heard Landon respond to Chika's greeting.

"Kelenna, it's me, Landon. How are you?"

"Hey, I'm fine." She tried to sound aloof. Nonchalant. Cool. It wasn't easy to do because her mind was racing at the same time, trying to predict what he was calling her for. After last Saturday when she called him in that impulsive, put-herself-out-there way, she silently bid Dr. Landon goodbye and vowed that she would never be that forward again. Now, he was calling her out of the blue. What could he possibly want?

"You sound preoccupied. Is this a good time?"

"Yes, it is." She had to elbow Chika who was now leaning heavily against her shoulder, trying to get an earful of the conversation. Against her better judgment, she hit the speaker button. "What's up?"

"I guess I'll just get right to it then. I'll be in Atlanta before the holidays for an interview at Emory."

"An interview?"

"Yes. Emory has been trying to bring me into their neurosurgery program for about a year now, and I think it's time that I see what they're about."

"Wow, that's nice." She had no doubt that he was the kind of person that was highly sought after by several prestigious neurosurgery programs. Why was he calling her to tell her about it?

"I wanted to let you know because I would like to meet you. Or, I guess I should say, it would be nice to see you again."

"Oh." She had to swallow hard to stop herself from squealing and launching into a small victory dance. Chika, on the other hand did not hold back. She'd had the good sense not to squeal, but she actually got up and started dancing. Kelenna cleared her throat and tried a nonchalant tone once more. When she spoke though, it came off as coy. "I'm sure I can fit you in my calendar."

His smooth baritone came back almost immediately. "I want you to do better than that. There's a winter benefit gala at The Ritz that weekend. I want you to say you'll be my date."

She dropped her coy-cool act that second. "I would love to. It would be great to see you."

"Great. Listen, I have to run, but I'll send you a message with the details and we'll talk later."

She ended the call and stared at Chika who was already staring back at her, frozen like a statue.

"Unbelievable," she said slowly, the wonder evident in her voice as she thawed out. "Do you understand that *the* Dr. Landon just asked you out? To a gala at The Ritz? Oh my God, what are you going to wear? I wish I was going to be here! Will you call me and tell me everything after?"

Kelenna laughed, secretly wishing that her excitement didn't wear off the minute Chika started spouting off her questions. "Could you be any more excited?"

"Why aren't *you*? Just as we're talking about him, Landon rings you up! If that isn't a sign from the Universe, I don't know what is!"

Kelenna didn't believe in signs from the Universe. She was more concerned about practical things. Like, did Landon break up with his girlfriend in the five days since she last spoke to him? Was she just a girl he wanted to keep on the back burner, in a different area code?

"Oh no you don't." Chika wagged a finger in front of her face. "I can see the wheels turning in your head. Don't sabotage this before it happens!"

"What do you mean, sabotage?"

"I know you. You're thinking about his roommate again."

"She's not his roommate, she's—"

Chika placed her hands on Kelenna's shoulders and cut her off. "Girl. Don't overthink it. It doesn't have to be more than you meeting up with an old friend." She paused and let go of Kelenna's shoulders to begin clapping excitedly, maniacally. "With the potential to become more! I swear, Kelenna, you're a lucky girl!"

14

Monday, Tuesday, Wednesday, Thursday, FRIDAY! The week had flown by without a hitch and Kelenna was grateful for it for two reasons. One, Pat was on a cruise vacation to the Bahamas and Kelenna was subbing in for her as the highest-in-command. Kelenna had only been required to be responsible for the department a few times, but whenever she was called upon to do it, she preferred that no issues arose. Two, she was excited about Saturday, when she would be at The Ritz on Landon Igbokwe's arm. He'd texted her on Wednesday to give her more details about the gala, and like the conscientious girl she was, she'd Googled it. Landon had been so very modest. Not only was he slated to receive some kind of award at the gala, it turned out that the mayor of Atlanta was expected to be in attendance. Apparently, a mayor wasn't worth mentioning in Landon's eyes. What was the big deal about a mayor when you'd been handed an award by the president of the United States? That same evening, she called Chika in a panic, begging for her help in finding the perfect dress. Chika relished the chance to style her, and picked out a black, floor-length ball gown that cost entirely too much. "Feel the fabric," Chika told her, pushing the dress into her fingers. It was made from the softest velvet material. "Dr. Landon won't be able to keep his eyes off you! And hopefully his hands too!" The dress was now hanging in front of her closet, and every time she walked past it, she let her fingers travel along its skirt. She couldn't wait for her date with Landon, but first, she had to get through Friday.

She'd gone to work at her usual time of eight o'clock, and had immediately begun preparing for ICU rounds. The ICU was full, each room occupied with a patient that seemed sicker than the next. It took the team over an hour to make it around the entire unit, and right when they got done, the work mobile phone in Kelenna's pocket rang out loud.

"Pharmacy, this is Kelenna?"

"Kelenna!" Prudence, the risk manager's voice came through the phone. "We need you! How quickly can you come down to my office?"

The older woman's tone sounded so weary that Kelenna didn't ask any questions before heading directly to her office.

She felt self-conscious the moment she opened the door and saw the crowded room. Bertha from the quality department, and a couple of nurse directors occupied the small space, and barely made eye contact with her. Her mind raced, wondering why she'd been summoned. Had she unknowingly violated a hospital policy?

"Kelenna, dear, come on in. I called the pharmacy and they reminded me that Pat is out on vacation."

Kelenna shut the door behind her and leaned against it. There was no literally nowhere else for her to go in the office. "Yes, she's been gone the whole week."

"Something terrible has happened. This morning, Dr. Tari-Douglas found Ashleigh unresponsive at her desk. We found empty vials of Dilaudid and a needle around her."

Kelenna raised a brow. Drugs and a needle? She looked around at the faces of the people in the office. Were they all just going to sit there while Prudence implied that Ashleigh was shooting up on the job? Ashleigh, the straight-shooter? The hardest-working person in the ER? The no-nonsense champion of the hospital's opioid reduction cause in the ER? Just the other day, Ashleigh had told her how they'd found narcs in a patient's pocket and had had to confiscate it. *That* Ashleigh was shooting up?

"Forgive me," she started after she realized that she hadn't said a word out loud for some time. "I'm just a little surprised. First of all, is she okay?"

Prudence's hesitation in answering made Kelenna take a closer look at everyone else. Their eyes were all red-rimmed and even Ken, the chief nursing officer, who was usually so stoic, was shaking his head.

"She did not make it."

Kelenna gasped as she clutched her chest. "I'm sorry? Are you serious? Ashleigh *died*?"

"Yes, dear," Prudence said somberly. "I'm so sorry to have to tell you this. We're all so crushed. Ashleigh grew up in this hospital, you know. She volunteered here as a teen, and went from patient care tech to staff nurse, then charge nurse, and now nurse manager."

Kelenna was frozen throughout Prudence's mini speech. She couldn't believe that the woman she spoke to so often about general issues in the ER was gone. Just like that. When she was able to collect her thoughts, she nodded. Ashleigh was a known staple at Preston. She'd even been born at the hospital, so there were jokes about her having been there for over thirty years.

"We're planning to meet with a broader group of people at two o'clock today. If Ashleigh has been stealing our medications, it's anyone's guess how long it's been going on. That's where you come in."

"There's doubt that it could be ours?" Kelenna asked in a hushed tone. "If you give me the lot number and expiration dates of the drugs, I can tell you if it's from our stock."

"Great. I'll send you an email with pictures of the items that were found in her possession. I can't physically hand them over because the police are involved."

"That should work," Kelenna replied quickly. She was still stunned but she managed to keep her composure. "Where will the meeting be?"

"Meeting Room B. We need to know how she got her hands on those medications. If there's a loophole, we need to find it, and close it."

Kelenna wasn't sure how she made it back to the pharmacy. She was in such a daze that she couldn't have said if she took the stairs or the elevator down to the basement. She paused at the door for a moment to collect herself before she hit her badge against the sensor and walked in. It was immediately clear that everyone had heard the news. They were all huddled in the pit, their work abandoned, their tongues wagging. There was such despondency on their faces that Kelenna wished she could tell everyone to go home.

"Kelenna, is it true? Is Ashleigh really dead? Is that why Prudence called three times trying to hunt you down?" one of the techs asked her.

Kelenna shook her head sadly. "Yes, it's true." And before they could ask her more questions, she held up a hand. "I don't know all the details yet, but I've been asked to see if there have been any discrepancies."

"Discrepancies?" another tech asked uncertainly. "Pat isn't here, and the last time we pulled you into a discrepancy issue, you didn't know your right from your left."

Kelenna winced. That was two years ago, when she was still green from residency. She'd learned considerably more since then, and even though she had nowhere near the level of expertise Pat had, she knew the basics. The counts of all the narcotics had to match up, otherwise there would be a discrepancy and someone would need to resolve it. Resolving it was the harder part, because the explanation could be that a person—a nurse, a pharmacist or a doctor—was diverting the hospital's medications. With all the laws surrounding narcotics, no one wanted to be the one who was accused of diverting or stealing one of them.

"I'll just need some help, that's all. Where's Cassie?" Kelenna looked around. She wanted—no, wanted was an understatement. She *needed* Cassie's help. Cassie was the ADM expert at Preston, and if there was a report that could be run, she knew how to run it.

"Check the break room," Siya said. "Ashleigh was her classmate in high school. She's taking this hard."

Kelenna found Cassie drying her eyes when she got to her. She also appeared to be wrapping up a telephone conversation. When she got off the phone, she looked inquisitively at Kelenna. "What's up?" she asked.

"I need your help." Kelenna went straight to the point. She told her about Prudence's request to find out how Ashleigh got the drugs she overdosed on.

"Oh my God, so it really was an overdose? We thought they were kidding about that! I thought it was a heart attack."

Kelenna frowned. How much did everyone really know? She had no doubt that a statement would be released by the hospital administration soon, and she didn't want to say too much before then.

"I'm sorry, I heard you guys were close. It's crazy, right?"

"Yes! It's unbelievable. Drugs? Ashleigh wouldn't even touch a cigarette in high school. Are you sure it wasn't her heart?"

Kelenna arched a brow. "She had heart problems?"

"No, but you never know, right? Don't they say heart disease is a silent killer?"

Kelenna shook her head sympathetically. "It is, but not in an otherwise healthy young woman who died from a drug overdose." She shook her head again when Cassie tried to protest. "I know you don't want to believe it, but there was no heart disease. We don't know what caused her to do it, but what we *can* do is find out how she got the drugs so that we can stop someone else from doing it." She let out an exhale when she saw Cassie nod in agreement. "I think I need the discrepancy report?"

"There's been no discrepancy today. If there was one in the ER, I would have heard about it by now."

"What about discrepancies in other departments? Could Ashleigh have gone to the ADMs on other floors? Gotten meds from there?"

"No, she only has access to the ADM in the ER. That was how I set her up. She doesn't work anywhere else."

"Hang on." Kelenna snapped her fingers at her sudden realization. "Ashleigh is a manager, so technically she doesn't take care of patients. Why would she need to go into the ADM anyway?"

"She could be filling in whenever they're short-staffed," Cassie pointed out, sounding almost defensive. "She could be helping other nurses with their patients while they're on lunch."

"True," Kelenna conceded. "If that's the case, though, she wouldn't need to go into the ADM too often, would she? Can you print a report of all her ADM activity in the last month? I want to see the patients she's been dealing with, and the drugs she's been removing."

"Sure. This is so crazy. If Ashleigh has been taking our drugs without creating a discrepancy, this could have been going on for a long time. I wish Pat were here, she would know where to begin. No offense, but Pat just knows all the ways people can steal our drugs."

Kelenna wanted to roll her eyes and point out that Pat did not know about this particular method of stealing if there was no existing safeguard against it. But seeing as she also wished Pat were around, she couldn't do anything but smile. "We're going to *be* Pat. We're going to think through this and you are going to tell me if I'm missing anything."

Over the next two hours, Kelenna and Cassie worked side by side. Lunch was forgotten as they pored over reports and looked at medication administration records in the computer. Prudence had sent Kelenna the email with pictures of the drugs Ashleigh had in her pockets and on her desk. There were vials of Dilaudid, *morphine*, and *ketorolac*, and they matched the lot numbers of the products in the pharmacy. That helped to put the doubts about where she'd gotten the medications to rest.

In the end, they found Ashleigh's most likely method of stealing. They couldn't confirm it without a confession, but the patterns were so consistent that Kelenna was pretty sure they had it right. The challenge now was how best to—as Prudence put it—close the loophole.

When it was close enough to two o'clock, Kelenna stuffed her notes in the pocket of her white coat and made her way up to Meeting Room B. She took an empty seat close to the door and let her eyes scan the room. She hadn't realized that when Prudence said 'broader group of people', she'd meant every single leader in the hospital, from the CEO to the director of security. It would have been intimidating if it were any other situation, and not a death of an employee on hospital grounds.

She hadn't been sitting for too long before the door opened once more. In walked Sarah, the ED nurse director, and Chris close behind her. Kelenna was saddened by Sarah's swollen eyes, but it was the haunted look in Chris' that undid her. He'd taken the seat directly across from hers, and that usually meant winks and subtle eyebrow raises to elicit some kind of reaction from her. This time, his eyes were completely blank. It was almost if he didn't see her. *Couldn't* see her. That was when she remembered that he was the one who found Ashleigh. She hid a sigh as she tried to imagine what he'd been through over the last few hours. She felt a strong urge to hold his hand . . . to offer him some little comfort. She clenched and unclenched her fists discretely, and only stopped when Prudence started to speak.

"Thank you, everyone, for coming to this impromptu diversion team meeting. We're going to try to keep it short so we can all get back to work. We're all devastated by the death of Ashleigh, our colleague and our friend. I know many of us have known her for years, and have worked closely with her, and are hurting right now, but we feel like this is a good time to discuss this occurrence, so we can make sure it never happens again."

Kelenna's eyes flitted over the people in the room once more. The mood was so low that she could almost palpate the sadness. She wanted to run away—do anything but say what she knew she was soon going to have to say.

"I want us all to understand," Prudence continued solemnly, her voice quaking, "this is a judgement-free zone. We are not here to point fingers or to discuss her condition or her state of mind. It also goes without saying that this is confidential. What we discuss here needn't leave the four walls of this room. We will let you know what we want you to relay to your staff. We believe it was an accidental overdose, however, the police are involved, and an autopsy will be performed by the coroner's office. Now I know we don't all participate in the monthly diversion team meetings, so I think it's reasonable for us to go over how controlled substances are handled at Preston. Kelenna, please."

Kelenna sat up straighter and cleared her throat. There was nowhere to hide now.

"First of all, I have to say, I'm so sorry about this. Ashleigh was an amazing person, and this entire situation is unbelievable." She waited for the murmurs to subside before she continued. "We keep very close watch on our narcotics. From when we buy them, to when they are stored in the pharmacy, taken to the floors, placed in the ADMs, given to the patient, or thrown away. There are checks at every point, signatures on paper, documentation showing that we know where everything is. If we are over or under a pill or a vial, we give ourselves forty-eight hours to figure it out. We have a very robust diversion control program."

"Let me get this right," Chris said, his eyes training on her for the first time since he walked in. "You say you all have this foolproof method for controlling the narcotics, correct?" Before she could correct his use of the word foolproof, he continued. "How was Ashleigh able to get these drugs out, under the radar?"

Kelenna sighed inwardly. She knew the question would come up sooner or later, but she wasn't prepared to hear it from Chris, and laced with insinuations that pharmacy had dropped the ball in some way. "It's not foolproof," she admitted. "If a person is familiar enough with our system, there are ways to evade the checks we have in place."

"Kelenna, were you able to figure out what happened?" Prudence asked.

"We think we know how she did it, yes, but without video evidence or a confession, it's all speculation." She pulled out papers from her pocket and spread them on the table in front of her. "We ran a report of all the meds

Ashleigh took out of the ADM. Then we went to the computer to match them with her scan records. She was perfect. Every time she told the ADM she was taking out a medication for . . . John Doe, she went to John Doe and scanned that medication. Scanning is important. It's the only way for us to know the drug was given. It puts a time stamp in the computer, and it lets us know who did it."

"But just because she scanned the medication against the patient doesn't mean she gave it," Ken said slowly.

"Exactly," Kelenna said. As chief nursing officer, Kelenna knew Ken would grasp the implication of her words quicker than the others. "But since we assume that there's no foul play when drugs are scanned, that's one way to work under our radar."

"Hold on, something doesn't add up," Sarah said, in between sniffles. "Are you saying Ash would take a drug out of the ADM and scan it, but not give it to the patient? Have you *met* our patients? If they have Dilaudid ordered and they don't get it, they'll raise hell!"

"Absolutely," Kelenna said. "Unless it was never ordered to begin with. Or they were given something else instead of the opioid to help with pain."

"*Ketorolac*," Prudence said softly.

Kelenna responded with a slow nod. "Of course it can't be proven, but it's something that has happened in other hospitals. Nurses divert opioids by giving *ketorolac* and keeping the opioid for themselves. They can get away with it because *ketorolac is* a shot and would provide *some* pain relief."

"And I do want to point out, for those of you who don't know, that Ashleigh did have at least ten vials of *ketorolac* in her pocket," Prudence added.

Kelenna nodded in agreement. That detail was what completed the puzzle for Kelenna and Cassie. "Right. Even if she had a patient with an order for only one dose of *ketorolac*, she would have been able to remove as many as she liked from the ADM."

"Wouldn't the ADM have been able to catch that the count was off for the *ketorolac*?" Ken asked.

"The ADM would only know what it's been told. If there were twenty vials of *ketorolac* and Ashleigh told it she was removing only one, then it would think there are nineteen left. No matter how many she took out."

"And there's no way to definitively say that Ashleigh removed more *ketorolac* than was ordered?" Dr. Schwartz threw in.

"No. What we *do* know is that someone *has* been removing more than what they're telling our ADMs. We've had to replace *ketorolac* more often. Nurses call us to restock *ketorolac* when our records show there should be several vials left in their machine."

"Foolproof was the wrong word," Chris sighed. "It's not foolproof at all. How long have you known this?"

Kelenna let out a low wince. She could practically feel disappointment at her department oozing from his words. Or was it disappointment at *her*? She gave her head a mental shake and kept her tone even. "Maybe about a month. According to my techs, Pat had plans to add a blind count to certain drugs that could be used as decoys to steal narcotics. *Ketorolac* was one of them."

Chris frowned. "Blind count?"

Before she could respond, Sarah spoke up. Her eyes were dry now and her voice was clear. "Blind count is when we have to tell the machine how many doses of the drug there are. And hope it matches with what it thinks is in it."

"Right. It's what we currently do with our narcs. That way, the ADM knows what the count is supposed to be, and if a nurse tries to take out more than what the doctor ordered, it would alert us to a discrepancy in the count."

"Let me get this right," Prudence intercepted. "You believe Ashleigh was removing medication from the ADM, scanning it against the patient to document that it was given, but giving them *ketorolac* instead, and taking the opioids for herself?"

Kelenna nodded. She was certain. It was the only thing that made sense.

"You said something else," Chris said, his tone sharp and almost accusatory. "Something about there being no orders for the opioids. Explain that."

"That's correct. We believe she may have been falsifying orders." Kelenna sifted through her pile of papers once more and settled on the ones that showed Ashleigh's orders. "We went back thirty days to look at the patients she took out opioids for. She put in each of the orders herself. Under a doctor's name."

"My goodness," Prudence gasped. "How can you be sure?"

"Yes, how do you know the doctor didn't give her a verbal order?" Chris added defensively. "We do that all the time. I tell the nurse what I want, and they put it in for me."

"That wasn't what happened in this case," Kelenna told him.

"How are you so sure though? If we—"

"Because our computer system tracks everything, Dr. Tari-Douglas," she cut in softly, managing not to snap as she did so. Inside she was seething at Chris' behavior. Didn't he realize she was only doing her job? She hated that he kept interrupting her and questioning every little thing she said. "When a nurse puts in a medication order for a patient, they're required to put in the source of that order, and they have two choices: telephone or verbal. That way, you, the doctor who gave that order, can get a notification that there's a nurse out there putting orders in your name, and you can confirm that you authorized it."

"Okay?" Chris said, sounding like he still didn't know what her point was.

"Ashleigh did neither," she said finally. "She put those orders in as protocols. A protocol would bypass the notification system, and the doctor would never know. She's been ordering opioids under different ER doctors for months now."

"Is there a protocol that allows nurses to order opioids in the ER?" Prudence asked hopefully. "We don't have a lot of protocols, but maybe it's an old one . . ." she trailed off.

"No, it's against the law," Kelenna said with a solemn head shake. "But it is the perfect way to stay under the radar."

There was a collective gasp that echoed throughout as the implication of her statement hit everyone. She knew how they felt because she felt the same way. It was scary that despite all their hard work, diversion could be happening on such a wide scale. It was scary to see someone actually die from it.

"I understand why *we* would never know, but why wouldn't pharmacy? Does no one verify these orders?" Chris asked, clearly still on a mission to single out the pharmacy department. "Why isn't this something that could have been caught on your end?"

Kelenna looked directly at him. It took all she had to keep her voice level. "We've never had a reason to audit Ashleigh before today. And no, we don't verify ED orders. They're considered urgent, so we don't interfere unless it's something we have to mix in the pharmacy."

"This is a lot of information, Kelenna," Prudence said. "Thank you for researching on such short notice. And with Pat gone too."

Kelenna nodded. She felt a knot in her chest loosen as she let out a slow exhale, underscoring just how tightly wound she'd been since she walked into the room. She'd never spoken so firmly in front of this group of people, and definitely not about an issue this serious.

"I assume we have plans to close this loophole?" Ron, the CEO said, speaking up for the first time. His deep country accent made him sound cavalier sometimes, but there was no mistaking his expectations. Ron definitely wanted immediate action. "What can be done?"

"I asked Connor, our IT pharmacist, and he's going to turn off our nurses' ability to use the protocol order source," Kelenna said. "And Cassie, our automation technician will turn on blind counting for *ketorolac*, *promethazine*, and Benadryl. If anyone tries to take more than they should, we'll know when it happened."

"Those are great action plans," Prudence said, her hand moving furiously over a piece of paper as she took down notes. "Does anyone have anything else to add?"

"I do," Kelenna said quickly. "Months ago, Pat put in a request for cameras to be placed in the medication rooms where we keep our ADMs. I'm not sure what's going to happen, but I think it's vital that we move forward with that as quickly as we can. If we had video surveillance in the ER, we would have known more than we do about this case."

Ron nodded and turned to April, the COO. "April, can you prioritize this?"

"Certainly," April replied.

"Please take care of yourselves. Love on your staff extra hard today." Prudence clasped her hands imploringly. "And keep Ashleigh's husband and three little angels in your thoughts."

The sound of feet shuffling and chairs moving filled Meeting Room B as everyone stood up to leave. Kelenna kept a smile plastered on her face as she walked out, not even stopping when she heard Chris call out her name.

15

Kelenna didn't know how long she had been staring at her ceiling for, but she knew it was probably close to an hour. The minute she walked into her apartment after work, she changed into a tank top and a pair of yoga tights, ate some leftovers from the night before, and went to lay down on her sectional. She should have known better than to think the week would go by without a hitch. The excitement she'd felt going into the weekend had been drained away by a single day's event, and she felt powerless and unable to rediscover it. After the impromptu diversion team meeting, she'd gone back to her office to take second looks at her notes. She'd even gone as far as printing off scores of ED orders for opioids and benzodiazepines, trying to see if there were other nurses with the same habits Ashleigh had. She fell down a rabbit hole so deep that she didn't climb out of until around six o'clock. At least she'd had the good sense to pack up and leave then. It had been the most unproductive use of her time, and she didn't discover anything new. Instead, she arrived at home feeling low and on edge. It didn't help that she couldn't put her finger on what was bothering her. Sure, Ashleigh's death, and the manner in which it happened, was a factor, but something else was clawing at her.

She gave a start when she heard a knock at her door. She wasn't expecting anyone, so she didn't rush to answer it. Instead, she picked up her phone and opened her doorbell app. A little over a week ago, John had installed a camera over the peephole on her door. She could see through it now, and standing there, in a hoodie and sweatpants, looking like he was lost, was Chris. She hopped up and ran to her door. Her hand was on the knob, ready to flip the lock open before she paused. There was an antique mirror hanging on the wall right beside it, a random purchase from a garage sale in her parents' neighborhood, and she looked at her reflection. She looked tired, like she hadn't slept in days, and she was certainly in no mood for company. Why was he standing at her door after all the grief he'd given her earlier at work? Since when did Chris come to her apartment unannounced? Since when did he come to her apartment at all? She unlocked the door and opened it, managing to startle him. They stared at each other for a moment—he, looking like he was surprised to see her, as though she had come to his house and not the other way around.

"I haven't been here in years," he remarked needlessly. She knew that. "Can I come in?"

She took a step back to let him in, and locked the door when he had fully entered. She leaned against the door and watched as he went further into the living room. He looked around as though he needed to get his bearings. There wasn't much to her apartment. The front door opened straight into the living room, which was furnished with the most comfortable sectional ever, and a coffee table. She had a four-seater dining table to the left, right beside the kitchen fitted with stainless steel appliances and fluorescent lights.

"I haven't been here in years," he repeated, sounding as uncertain and unsure as she'd ever heard him. "I had to see someone. I got home and didn't move from my couch for about an hour. I just got in my car and drove. I wasn't even sure you still lived here."

Kelenna took in a deep breath and let it out slowly. He may as well have been describing what she did when she got home from work. "Do you want something to drink?" Those were the first words she'd said all evening. She didn't realize how dry her mouth was, or how hoarse her voice was.

"Water's fine."

She nodded and lifted herself off the door. She walked into the kitchen and opened her tumbler cupboard. After filling a tall glass with cold water from the filter attached to her fridge, she handed it to him. He leaned against the counter and drank the water in a few gulps.

"More?" she asked. When he said no, she nodded once more and picked up the cup from where he'd placed it on the counter. She was about to turn and place it in the sink when he caught her wrist and forced her to look at him. She put the cup back on the counter.

"Kelenna." He held on to her wrist, and she looked down at the contact. "I'm sorry I lashed out at you today. At the meeting? I'm sorry."

She nodded her acceptance of his apology, and this time it was his turn to sigh. "It's fine," she added, not meeting his eyes.

"Kelenna, look at me," he said softly. She obeyed his order and raised her eyes to his. "I know you heard me call your name after the meeting. I know you were upset at me."

She held his eyes then. "Why *did* you lash out at me? I was already so nervous, and the situation was bad enough without you attacking everything I said! Or blaming pharmacy for everything!"

"I don't know." He turned her wrist in his palm and held onto her hand instead. "I don't know. I wanted answers, and you were the only one giving them. But you weren't saying what I wanted or needed to hear."

But you weren't saying what I wanted or needed to hear.

That was what pushed her over the edge. They triggered the tears that frankly had been beneath the surface since she left Prudence's office that afternoon. By the time he was aware of them, she had been silently crying for a few seconds.

"Jesus, Kelenna," he groaned, pulling her into his arms. "What did I say?"

She shook her head against his shoulder where it was now resting. Saying actual words would have made her sob even harder, so she stayed mute and allowed him to comfort her. Even though her tears must have been soaking through his shirt, he didn't seem to mind. He just kept running his hand up and down her back, and shushing her gently.

She finally knew what had made her so upset about Ashleigh's death. And it was interesting that it took Chris coming over for her to figure out what it was. Someone whose only other reason for ever being in her apartment had been to assist John in helping her move into it over two years ago.

He released her just as her sobs died down and used his thumbs to wipe away the last of her tears. "I don't think I've ever seen you cry." He tipped her chin up to look at him as if he was inspecting her for signs of further water works.

"I try not to make it a habit," she mumbled, trying to tuck her chin down, away from his eyes. But she was not strong enough, and he lifted her chin once more.

"Are you good?" he asked. When she nodded, he let go and placed his hands on her shoulders to turn her around and propel her back to her living room. "Go on, sit down. Tell me what I said."

"It wasn't just what you said." She sat down on the sectional, raising her knees to her chest and wrapping her arms around them. "It was a combination of everything. Ashleigh's death. Opioids. My mom."

He sat close beside her. "Your mom? What does she have to do with this?"

"I may have been dismissive of addicts in her presence, and she didn't like that. About a week ago, she told me I was becoming disillusioned. That I was too young in my career to lose my empathy for sick people. And I thought she was just being dramatic because Dr. Obidi has her moments—"

"John does that too," he cut in with a smile.

"Does what?"

"Calls your mother Dr. Obidi sometimes."

Kelenna laughed for the first time that day, and it felt good. "It's what we call her when she goes into disciplinarian mode. She was right though. I wasn't interested in doing anything to affect the opioid epidemic at our hospital. And it's because I hadn't seen its impact up close. Not like this. I didn't care enough about the illness of chronic pain or addiction to inconvenience myself."

"That's not true. You've done a number of things to try to make us cut back on prescribing narcs."

She dismissed his attempts at making her feel better. He seemed to have conveniently forgotten that he'd called her initial plan to reduce opioid use a bad one. "I was just doing what I had to do so we could continue to operate as a hospital." She burrowed further into the chair as though she needed comfort from it. "And then you said what you just said in the kitchen, and I couldn't help feeling like I've not done enough."

"What did I say?"

"You said that I had the answers, but they were not what you wanted to hear."

"If you thought I was still blaming you for Ashleigh's death—"

"No, Chris, I don't think that. It just helped me realize that I need to approach this in a different way. It's not about making sure we don't run out of opioids. It's about making sure we don't let people use us as an access point or gateway for them. We have no idea how many Ashleighs there are at Preston. We have to make sure no one ever finds any of them with a needle up their arm."

She heard Chris' wince before she remembered again that he was the one who discovered Ashleigh. For the first time, she thought about the words he uttered when he first walked through her door. He said that he had to see someone. For whatever reason, that someone was her. Had she even taken a second to ask him how he was feeling?

"My goodness, Chris." She placed a hand on his knee. "I'm sorry, I wasn't thinking. How did you . . ." She let her unspoken question linger in the air. She knew he would get it, and his slow intake of breath told her that he did.

"I went looking for her. We had a meeting, she, Sarah and I, and I went looking for her. She wasn't at the nurses' station where you could usually find her, so I went to her office around the corner. It was locked."

Kelenna frowned. "It was locked?" There weren't that many doors that locked with a key at Preston. "Why did she need a door that locks?"

"I don't know, but that question came up and the lock has been removed."

"How'd you know she was in there?"

"There's a narrow glass panel on the door. It's not too easy, but you can see through it. I could see her head on the desk. I thought she was sleeping, so I knocked on the door to wake her up."

"But she didn't wake up, and you were losing time."

"In hindsight, I see that we were, but in that moment, I thought she was just really deep in sleep. By the time Sarah came with her set of keys, and we got the door open, she was unarousable. We saw the drugs on the table, but I didn't really look closely to see what they were. I told Sarah to call a code blue when I didn't feel a pulse, and I got to work. I had her on the floor by the time they came with a gurney—it had to have been under two minutes. I didn't notice the syringe and needle till after she was lifted off the floor."

Kelenna stifled her gasp by covering her mouth with her hand. The locked door aside, they'd lost even more valuable time by not recognizing that it was an opioid overdose.

"The needle was on the floor, on the other side of her chair. That was when I picked up the vials and noticed what they were. Empty vials of Dilaudid and a syringe. That was when it clicked. And you have to understand, it was so chaotic. Sarah had climbed on the gurney, and was doing compressions as they wheeled Ashleigh out of her office and to an empty room. I had to chase them down to tell them to Narcan her." He was staring into space as though he had physically transported himself back to Preston, and was watching the scene play out before him. "It was too late."

"Chris, I'm so sorry." She shifted as close to him as she could get, and leaned against his shoulder. Now that she had a better idea of what happened, she had no doubt that he was blaming himself for not being able to save Ashleigh. She could hear his heart pounding, and she wanted to do something to slow it down. "I know she was important to you, but you have to know that it wasn't your fault."

"I know it wasn't in theory, but we lost a lot of time because—"

"Because nothing," Kelenna cut in firmly, turning to face him. She grabbed his face, feeling the whiskers on his unshaven cheeks scratch her palms. She wanted him to hear her. Really hear her. "How could you have known?" she asked. "How could you have known she was an addict?"

Chris shut his eyes and put a hand on her wrist. "That's the thing, I didn't even consider that. Until the meeting with all your evidence, I thought it was a suicidal overdose."

"Really?" Kelenna cocked her head and released his face gently. It hadn't even occurred to her that it could be an intentional overdose. If she had approached her research into the stealing with those blinders on, she would never have uncovered the truth.

"Yes. Because how could we not know that we've been working with a functioning addict for however long?"

"You know as well as I do that addicts are experts at hiding these things," she chided softly.

Chris snorted. "I guess so."

"We don't know what she was going through, Chris. It could have been anything."

"Sarah mentioned that Ash had been on pain meds for chronic back pain. There was an accident a few years ago. I didn't even know that."

Kelenna exhaled as she sat back down beside him. Poor Ashleigh. Some surgeon or ER doctor had probably given her a prescription for some pain medicine after her accident, and then she'd gotten sucked into the dreaded triad of tolerance, dependence, and addiction. "We have to get real about the opioid crisis now, Chris," she said, resting her head against his shoulder once more. "This tragedy can be the catalyst for us to do something meaningful."

He put an arm around her shoulder and squeezed once. "Whatever you need, Kels," he promised gruffly.

16

Kelenna painstakingly applied her makeup in preparation for her date with Landon. She'd chosen subdued hues for her eyes so that she would look understated but classic, and a deep red lipstick to show that she could be unpredictable. She'd flattened her hair down to a low ponytail to give her an adult, sophisticated look. When she was done she stared at her own reflection. She looked great, she knew that, but that wasn't the only thing she saw. Somehow, her bathroom mirror had turned into a screen, and on it, images of the events from the night before floated through.

Chris didn't leave her apartment till well after midnight. It seemed that once they decided to do something about opioid overuse at Preston, both were eager to start brainstorming immediately. So they ordered pizza, drank wine, and traded several ideas between them until it became a contest where they tried to one up the other with the most outlandish suggestion. It was only when Chris suggested that they remove all opioids from the hospital formulary that Kelenna gave up and declared him the winner.

Kelenna couldn't think of another time when she simply enjoyed hanging out with a guy. It certainly helped that there wasn't the added pressure of trying to impress or entertain him, but it was more than that. Just being in his company changed her mood from dismal to rather pleasant. By the time Chris was ready to go, she had dozed off on the arm of the sectional, and he'd had to wake her up. When she walked him to her door, he enveloped her in his arms, and thanked her for cheering him up. That hug threw her for a loop. In all the years they'd known each other, the hugs they'd shared were mostly quick, one-armed, side hugs. She didn't know this Chris who provided comforting hugs, like he'd done earlier in her kitchen, or wrapped her up in his arms and buried his face in her neck, like he'd done right before he left her apartment. She definitely didn't know the Chris who'd kissed her twice as he rose from the longer than typical hug. The first time right below her left ear, and the second time on her forehead. She didn't recall her reaction, but that was probably because she'd just stood there, dumbstruck. Luckily, she could blame that on her grogginess, and perhaps the single glass of wine she'd drunk. "Get some sleep, beautiful," he whispered before he walked out.

Beautiful.

Fourteen-year-old Kelenna would have been over the moon to hear Chris call her that. Heck, twenty-nine-year-old Kelenna was still thinking about it a day later. And she didn't know why she was so fixated on that single word. Just the other day, some stranger called her beautiful after she thanked him for holding the door open for her at the convenience store. She didn't spend the next eighteen hours analyzing what he could have meant while she got ready for a date with another man. Granted, he had to have been seventy-five years old, but a word was still a word.

She was not the least bit surprised when she heard the rap on her door right at 7 p.m. She'd made a wager with herself that Landon would be very prompt, and she was right. It was a good thing that she was already in her shoes, sitting down, and watching the clock so that all she had to do was grab her clutch and house keys. She stamped down her nerves as she spared one last look in that antique mirror. Exactly as she'd done the night before when a different man stood on the other side of her door. Would tonight end on the same beautiful note that last night had? She shook her head to clear it. She needed to get a grip and focus on what was in front of her—Landon. With that, she took in a breath, unlocked her front door and pulled it open. A man was standing there, on the phone, his back facing her. He turned around mere seconds after the door had opened, and told the person on the line to text him with updates.

"The hospital." He sounded apologetic as he slid his phone into his trouser pocket. Then he proceeded to look her over, his eyes traveling slowly from her head to her toes, appraising her, like he wanted to make sure she was worthy of being on his arm. She was almost ready to take a step back before he spoke up. "My mother was right, you *have* grown up. And you're so tall."

"It's the shoes," she dismissed with a smile. He was shorter than she remembered, not even six feet, but without her heels, he wouldn't think she was so tall. She did some appraising of her own and she liked what she saw. He looked a little different than the picture his mother had shown her, but he still looked good. The fitted tux, the flecks of gray on either temple, it all came together to produce a distinguished look that she could definitely get behind.

"Where are my manners?" He held her elbows and leaned closer to give her a kiss on either cheek. "It's good to see you again." She hadn't anticipated that European move, but she was glad that she handled it well, and didn't come off like a bumbling idiot.

"It's good to see you too."

"Shall we?"

Soon they were seated in the back of a black town car and being driven by a young white man down I-75. She sent surreptitious glances down Landon's way. He seemed content to watch the highway rather than talk to her. She hoped that he wasn't one of those dull types with no conversational skills.

"Was Emory able to sway you into moving back to Atlanta?" she asked, trying to break the silence.

His chuckle sounded more like a snort. "They tried, but it's left to be seen."

She hid a frown at his short answer, and his tone. Was he being superior? She didn't work at Emory, but as a Georgian, she felt protective of it. Surely, a person could do worse than one of the Ivy Leagues of the South! She said as much to him and this time, there was no mistaking his condescending smirk.

"There are a lot of stipulations that would have to be met for me to come down here. My decision will be based on whether it's worth the effort or not."

Never mind. Sometimes, superior could be sexy. She smiled at him ruefully. "I guess that means you're at Johns Hopkins for the foreseeable future."

"We'll see about that. But enough about me." He shifted to face her. "What about you? Preston Georgia, huh?"

"What do *you* know about Preston?" she teased.

He let out a patronizing laugh. Or was that all in her head? "Don't forget, Kelenna, I used to live here. Everyone knew about Preston. I never went out that way because we were warned that nothing good happened there. If there was a drug to be used, they used it."

"I'm sure that was an exaggeration," she said stiffly, thinking about Ashleigh as she covered for the entire city of Preston. "There are drug addicts everywhere, and we have our own share, but Preston Regional is so much more than that. It's important to the entire county. The hospital employs a lot of locals, and keeps people out of trouble. It's a great environment, and has been a good place to work."

"Okay, but do you ever see yourself wanting a bigger challenge at a different hospital?"

"I wouldn't mind leaving when the time is right."

"Oh really? And what does the right time mean for you?" he pressed.

She tried to stop herself from shrugging, but she couldn't. If she came off as not being interested in changing anything about her career, it was because she wasn't. She was comfortable at Preston, and the hospital was growing fast enough to challenge her. "I guess I don't know. When I stop liking my job, I'll leave."

"Hmm." He shifted in the seat, turning towards her. "I'll admit, my line of work is so specific that I don't really interact much with pharmacy, but I have to imagine that you would get a bigger challenge at an urban hospital. You see the worst of the worst there."

"I mean, you're not wrong, but I don't think the work done in community hospitals should be minimized. These hospitals in rural areas are sometimes the only hospitals that people have access to. Some of them treat us like we're their primary care. Is it right? No, but if we aren't there, then what would they do?"

He smiled slowly at her and nodded. "You sound like you have a purpose out there in tiny Preston."

He reminded her of John, with his almost condescending views of the small town. "I tell my brother this all the time. Preston is no longer tiny. It's a town that's growing and spreading out. It's not Baltimore or D.C, but I bet it's thriving more than what you remember from twenty years ago."

"Fifteen, my dear," he chuckled, and she laughed at his correction.

The mood in the town car lightened considerably after he backed off, but for a moment, she wondered if there was something about her that screamed mediocrity. She hadn't even been in his car for ten minutes before he started trying to tell her what trajectory her career should take. It was almost as if he had asked her out just to see how malleable she was to changing things in her life. Her thoughts halted when she saw him looking at her expectantly, and she realized that he had asked her a question.

"I'm sorry, what?"

"I asked about your twin. How's he doing?"

"Oh, John. He's great. He's not my twin though," she replied sheepishly. She knew she'd had an opportunity to correct him long ago.

"No way, this whole time?" he laughed. "I just remember him being boisterous, and you being reserved. I used to think that you had to be the most different pair of twins I had ever met."

She liked that he remembered her. She liked that they had a shared history even if it was incorrect. "And I just remember you being an adult and too old to hang out with us kids," she teased.

"Too old, huh?" He smiled once more at her. "You still think I'm too old?"

She looked at him, thinking she had heard an insecurity in his tone. But if there was, he was very good at schooling his features, because it was not apparent on his face. She shook her head.

"Very good." He looked out of the window as the driver pulled up in front of The Ritz. "We're here."

He got out of the car while the driver helped her out of her side. When she reached him, he offered her his arm. "May I?"

She accepted it, placing her hand in the crook of his arm as she walked gingerly through the glass doors. "Be patient with me," she told him, "this dress doesn't have too much give."

"You do look amazing, though." He didn't see her blush, but he patted her hand after she muttered her thanks. Compared to everyone else she saw as they made their way in, her choice of a one-shoulder black dress was pretty sedate. Still, she was excited about the evening. She had never been inside The Ritz before, and the opulence of the hotel stood out to her immediately. Before they entered the ballroom where the event was happening, they had to show identification and their belongings had to go through a scanner.

"Because of the government officials here," Landon explained.

As far as first dates went, it was pretty atypical. What else could be said about sharing your date with three hundred other people? Or not being able to talk too much so you didn't come off as uncultured at the table filled with older, wealthy couples? Or the biggest one, finally realizing the gravity of your date's importance at the event? It was wild enough that he was being honored, but the reason why was even more impressive. Their tablemates had all read the brochure, and had figured out who he was. Now they were making small talk with him. She was listening in, as they talked about the surgeries he had performed for people in low income countries.

"I didn't know you did these things. That is so cool," she whispered to him when he had a moment's respite from all the questions that were being thrown at him.

"I'm not doing it alone," he whispered back modestly. "My team and I have been going on biannual trips to different locations for about three years now. Without our work, some of these people would not . . . let's just say we're their only hope."

"You and your team sound amazing." She grinned at him, and he smiled in response.

Turning back to listen to the lady at the podium, Kelenna wished she knew what he wanted from her. Was this a trial date to see if she was someone he wanted to get to know? Was that what the questions in the car were about? Did he want to gauge how willing she was to leave her Georgia safety nest? For a life in a bigger city as he alluded to? Baltimore perhaps? The loud applause that filled the room interrupted her overthinking session. She sighed inwardly as she joined in the clapping. She really needed to get a grip and stop projecting a future from something as simple as a reunion with an old family friend.

The hour after the lovely three-course dinner dragged. She knew that because she kept sneaking glances at her phone, hoping for things to move faster. She was probably going to hell for thinking it, but fundraising galas were unbelievably dull. It turned out that listening to people and companies talk about themselves was not one of her favorite pastimes. Landon, on the other hand, didn't seem to think it was boring at all. He was paying close enough attention to laugh and clap at appropriate times. It didn't seem like he would be interested in playing a game of people watching with her. That was a pity, because there were so many interestingly-attired people sitting at the tables around them.

Finally, they announced the three recipients of the highest award for the day. When Dr. Landon Igbokwe's name was called, the applause was the loudest. It felt like the Oscars, because everyone at their table stood to cheer him on. They even reached over to congratulate *her*. She felt like a fraud for not correcting all their assumptions, but what could she say? That they were old family friends who hadn't seen each other in over fifteen years? No, all she could do was thank them, and say, yes, she was very proud.

Landon was the last one to give his thank you speech. His voice held everyone captive as he thanked the foundation, his team, and his family. "I've been blessed to be able to use my hands to be a blessing to others, and the work that's done here to raise funds is paramount to our project. And it changes lives. So thank you very much."

Her phone buzzed on her lap, startling her. As everyone clapped once more, she looked at it. She'd left it on vibrate in case something happened at the hospital and someone wanted to reach her. It was a text message.

`So you and Gifted Hands, huh?`

Her head jerked up immediately. Chris had to be right there, in the ballroom, with that book reference. She looked behind her and around her, but didn't see him. She was about to text him and ask where he was when her phone buzzed again.

`One o'clock.`

She looked up in front of her to get her twelve o'clock bearing first, then let her eyes veer slightly towards the right. She found him a few tables away. He caught her eyes and raised his wine glass to her in a greeting. She smiled and nodded like she was the queen and he was her subject. How had they spent a whole evening together and not realized that they would be at the same event the following day? How had he managed an invite to such an exclusive gala? Just then, he leaned down towards the person sitting next to him to listen to what she had to say. The woman's big hair was so distracting, practically all over his face. Kelenna only knew one person with obnoxiously big hair and bright skin. It was Tara, Chris' OBGYN friend. Before Kelenna could stop it, a frown crossed her face. He was never with the same woman for any real length of time, but somehow this one had managed to establish a presence. Was he serious about her? Another buzz of her phone stole her attention.

`See you after?`

She responded in the affirmative just as Landon was returning to his seat. She put her phone away to gush over him.

"Excellent speech, Landon!"

"I wrote it on the ride to pick you up," he confided, causing her to laugh. "Once you've given one speech like this, you've given them all."

It took another half hour for the gala to officially end, and Kelenna was glad for it. She stood some ways behind Landon as he was greeted and spoken to. It was like he was a famous author at his book signing, the way he stayed in one spot waiting for his *fans* to come to him. She felt a light tickle on her waist that made her jump. She turned to see Chris and Tara. Her eyes dropped down to their entwined hands, and she didn't understand why she had a visceral reaction to it. When she looked back up at Chris, he was studying her carefully.

"Kelenna, this is Nara," he said. "Nara, Kelenna. She's John's sister."

So it was Nara, not Tara. She looked very svelte in her inappropriate slinky red dress, and her hair looked even bigger up close. It was so typical of Chris to date such an obvious beauty. He couldn't simply—

"It's so nice to meet you!" Nara's bubbly voice cut into her thoughts. "I love John!"

"Nice to meet you as well," Kelenna said as sweetly as she could muster. It was definitely *too* sweet, and probably sounded like it was anything but nice to meet her. She chastised herself. What was her problem?

"Nara is a fan of the great Dr. Landon," Chris added, as if being a fan of anyone was something to aspire to.

Landon turned around—probably because he heard his name—and squinted in their direction. "Chris?"

"Doc," Chris drawled, walking forward in his lazy swagger to shake Landon's hand, and exchange one of those one-armed bro hugs. She looked back and forth between them in surprise while Nara smiled eerily. She didn't know Chris and Landon had any real familiarity. "It's been a while. Congratulations on everything."

"Thanks, man. How's your family?"

"Everyone's fine. It's good to see you, man."

"You too."

"Hi, my name is Nara!" a shrieky voice cut in. "I am just so excited to meet you!"

Chris slipped away, pulling Kelenna along with him and leaving Nara to no doubt talk Landon's ear off. They went to a nearby table and leaned against it side by side, watching their dates interact.

She nudged him lightly. "I didn't know you and Landon were best friends."

He nudged her back. "I didn't know you and Landon were dating."

"Oh, it's all very new. We're just seeing where it goes." She scoffed internally at her embellishment of the truth. For all she knew, she would never see Landon again after tonight. But Chris had his Nara, and being the loser at the gala was not something that appealed to her.

When Chris didn't say anything, she followed his gaze to where his girlfriend and Landon were talking a few short feet away from them. Nara was one of those annoying people who always had to touch the person they were talking to. She couldn't tell if Landon was placating her or enthralled by her. Was Chris jealous? "No, we're not best friends, but he did use to live in Atlanta. And I'm not that forgettable."

Kelenna laughed at how matter-of-fact he was. He was right though, people did not easily forget him. "Your girlfriend is really enthusiastic, isn't she? I should rescue Landon." She rose from the table, but Chris caught her waist with both hands and pulled her back beside him.

"Stay," he said, letting his hands linger at her waist. "Let her have this moment."

So she stayed. And she felt his fingers move against her side. It created a sensation she didn't understand, and she glanced up at him.

"It's very soft," he murmured.

Oh, the material. "It's velvet," she replied, not missing the irony that it was Chris and not Landon who fell into Chika's carefully laid trap of the touch-worthiness of her dress.

"It's nice," he said, finally lifting his hands. But one hand didn't go very far. Instead, it curled around her shoulder, and she didn't think twice about letting herself relax into him.

"How are you doing after yesterday?" she asked softly.

He squeezed her shoulder. "I'm fine. What about you?"

"I'm okay too. Did you go into the hospital today?"

He dragged his breath. "Yeah, not for long though. Everyone was torn up. Also, apparently, we've been getting some stick online."

She turned to him. "We? As in the hospital? About Ashleigh?"

"Yes. It was all over social media that we had a nurse die from an overdose. The comments were pretty hateful. Things like, what do you expect from a hospital in Preston, Georgia? There were other people saying that she was a known druggie in high school."

"Really?" She snapped her head in anger. "Ashleigh never even touched a cigarette in high school!" she said, borrowing Cassie's words from the day before, even though she had no idea if they were true or not. "What is wrong with people? Why would anyone say these things at a time like this? Her family is grieving, for goodness' sake! I'm going to go online and report as many comments as I can find. I'm not—"

"Is everything okay?"

She turned to see Landon and Nara standing in front of them, concern on their faces.

"Everything is fine. Kelenna just heard some upsetting news," Chris said, hugging her closer to him. She caught Landon's quick look at the two of them. Chris must have seen it too, because he released her shoulder and let his hand rest at the small of her back.

"Really? What's wrong?!" Nara practically yelled.

"Work," Chris and Kelenna said in unison. When she turned to him there was the whisper of a smile on his face.

"It's good to see you again, Chris," Landon cut in. "Nice to meet you, Nara. I'm afraid I have an early flight tomorrow. Kelenna, are you ready?"

Kelenna looked at his face for signs of irritation or annoyance, and found none. Good. He was not the unreasonable, jealous type. She accepted his arm as they said their goodbyes, and allowed him to steer her out of the ballroom. They were stopped along the way by a few more people before they finally got to the town car that was waiting for them outside the hotel.

"You have fun tonight?" Landon asked once they were settled and the car was on the road.

She yawned and stretched at the same time. "I had a great time." That was a stretch of the truth, but what did it hurt? She relaxed into the leather seat as much as she could, which wasn't much at all.

"It was good to see Chris again," Landon said. "It's been so long."

"I was surprised you remembered him at all."

"Really? I've always wondered why it is that people think you lose the memories from your youth when you become older."

"It's less about age and more about fame."

"Come on, I'm hardly famous."

"Were we at the same gala? You had everyone eating out of your palm. People like you tend to forget the little people like those of us in *Preston, Georgia*." She stuck out her tongue at him.

He laughed. "I'm sorry I looked down on your town."

"Apology accepted."

"You're more feisty than I expected, you know."

Kelenna narrowed her eyes at that. In her experience, being different from men's expectations was code for: *you're not my type.* "Is that good or bad?" she asked.

"Oh, it's good. You never know what to expect when you're set up by your mother. Especially with someone you haven't seen in fifteen years. I guess, what I'm trying to say is that you're refreshingly real."

Kelenna smiled warmly at him. "You remind me of my ex. That's totally something he would say. Matter of fact, I believe he actually did say it after we first met." When Landon was quiet, she turned to see him appear to be mulling over her words. That was when she realized she'd stepped in it. What guy wanted to be compared to a girl's ex? "I mean it in a good way," she said quickly, mentally chastising herself. "Will always said the nicest things."

"If you say so. I can tell you now, you don't remind me of any of my exes."

"Not even Ming?"

This time his head turned to her sharply, and she slapped a hand over her mouth. What was up with her? She couldn't remember the last time she put her foot in her mouth, and now she'd done it twice in under a minute.

"Ignore me, please. I didn't mean to say her name. I don't even know who she is to you. And I don't need to know. I'm going to stop talking now."

He chuckled, and even though he probably meant for it to be light, to wave away her comment, it seemed a bit forced. "I guess I shouldn't be too surprised, since you did talk to her. Ming is an old friend. We dated on and off for the last few years, but we're off now. For good."

Where had she heard that story before? Oh yeah, Will Perry. And he was getting married to the woman soon. But she knew to keep quiet this time. "It's none of my business, honestly. She's not here now."

"No, she isn't." After a brief pause, he turned to her. "And what about you and Chris?"

"Chris?" She frowned. "What about him?"

"What's the deal with you two? I could sense there was something. The way he was looking at you."

"The way he was looking at me?" She was truly bewildered. How in the world had Chris looked at her?

"It's hard to explain, but I felt like I was stepping into his territory, by having you with me."

"With me? And not his actual girlfriend?" she tried to clarify. Maybe he was confused about who Chris was truly territorial about.

"Who?"

"The girl he introduced to you as his girlfriend?"

"Nara?" Landon actually laughed out loud like she was the one who was clueless, and not him who didn't even remember the girl he had been talking to. "No, she's not his girlfriend. Besides when she talked to me, she offered to . . ." He cleared his throat. "Let's just say she didn't act like anyone's girlfriend."

Her eyes widened at his implication. What was Nara to Chris then? Friends with benefits? Either way, for whatever reason, this little bit of info made her feel better about Nara. She no longer wanted all her hair to fall out. No, not even after finding out that she'd probably hit on Landon. It didn't matter in the end, because Kelenna was the one in the car now.

"So you and Chris are not a thing?"

"No!" she insisted. "He's like a cousin to me." The below-the-ear kiss Chris had given her the night before chose that exact moment to float through her mind, but she quickly pushed it aside. No matter how weird the feelings she had about that were, it did not negate the fact that they had never been in a relationship with each other. She smiled at Landon and he smiled back. He picked up her hand and placed a kiss on the back of it.

Just then, the driver pulled up in front of her apartment building, and they both got out. He took her hand as they walked up the flight of stairs to her front door.

"I was serious when I said I had an early morning." He stood back as she unlocked her door. When she opened it, she turned around.

"I didn't invite you in," she said cheekily, putting her hand on the door frame and taking off her shoes. She flung them to the corner by her door. "Sorry, I had to get those off." She caught his appreciative glance now that she was reduced in height by over four inches. What was it about tall-*ish* men being insecure about tall girls?

He chuckled and took a step closer to her. "Would you have invited me if I could stay?"

"Maybe," she said coyly.

"I like this better." He put both hands on her shoulders, and pulled her even closer. "I'm going to have to see what to do to convince you not to wear heels."

"You won't be able to," she said softly, distracted by his hands on her.

"I won't?" He cocked his head, so sure of himself, pulling her even closer until there was nothing more than a hair's breadth between them. "Will you come visit me?"

"You want me to come visit you in Baltimore?" she asked stupidly. Did he know that his proximity was making her nervous, so that she could hardly speak?

"Yes, I do. May I?" he asked, tilting her chin up and swiping her lower lip lightly with his thumb. If his hand wasn't on her face, she would have thought he was asking her to dance. She gave an infinitesimal nod before he closed the gap between their mouths, covering hers with his. He was a good kisser, and there were enough sparks for her to want to prolong it, which she did. When his lips left hers, she slowly opened her eyes. "I don't foresee any other galas or hospital interviews in Atlanta in the nearest future, so I won't be able to finesse a meet up with you again."

Her eyes flickered to his. On the one hand, she was so flattered that he was interested in her, but on the other hand, she was perplexed. Why in the world had he felt the need to do anything big to get her attention? She was simple. She didn't need anyone to try that hard to impress her. She wanted to say something to that effect, but he must have read the consternation on her face, because he smiled and placed a chaste kiss on her mouth.

"I'm going to send you a ticket soon. Say you'll come see me."

"I can buy my own ticket, Landon," she replied primly.

"I know you can, but it will be my treat." He caressed her cheek. "I have to go now. I'll be in touch."

She nodded as she gave a little wave. She was a little more at peace than she was the last time he'd used those words on her. Because she believed now that he would actually be in touch with her.

17

The lull that usually accompanied the holidays at Preston dissipated exactly one day after New Year's. It was as if patients held on to their ailments and waited for the second the holiday was over to storm the hospital in droves. In the early days of the new year, Preston saw an uptick in business. The hospital was running at 110 percent capacity, and it seemed like every day, they admitted more patients than they discharged, and there was nothing they could do but hold patients in the ER or slip second beds into the bigger rooms. Every department, including pharmacy, was stretched to its limits trying to keep up with the workload.

In the meantime, Kelenna was doing something she'd never truly done before in her job as a hospital pharmacist. She was connecting to patients. She certainly hadn't planned it the first time it happened. All she'd wanted to do that day was pacify an outpatient whose drug order had been messed up by someone on her team—one of the techs mixed the drug in the wrong fluid and it created a reaction that produced white floaty particles in the bag. To make matters worse, it was the last dose in the hospital, and they weren't going to be able to get any more in until the next day. "Mr. Gore is not going to be happy about this," the nurse at their outpatient center huffed when she was told. But Kelenna went all the way down to the clinic anyway.

It was in a building adjoining the east wing of the hospital, a busy office with five rooms that saw a steady stream of outpatients for eight hours every weekday. The nurse was right, Mr. Gore was very angry. He complained so much that Kelenna let him wear himself out. She even had to grab a nearby stool to sit and keep listening to him. His complaints transitioned to tears, and she felt sorry for the diminutive man battling cancer, and the nausea and pain associated with it. She would never have known how difficult it was for him to get to their clinic if she hadn't sat with him, or how he was struggling to cope with his wife's recent death from a different type of cancer. All she could do was promise to call every hospital around town until they found his medication. And when their courier was occupied, she hopped into her car and made the thirty minute drive to Jefferson Medical Center to pick it up herself. It was crazy how grateful he was for her efforts, despite the fact that it had taken an additional hour. When she told her mother later that evening, the woman took full credit for it. "Aha! You see what I told you? When you can connect to the patient, half your work is done!"

She didn't know if she agreed that taking time to talk with patients cut her work in half. Not when it was actually taking up her spare time. Just the other day, she spent a literal hour listening to a patient, when all she'd needed to know was what kind of allergic reaction she'd had to a medication. The patient's nurse had refused to be the middleman and give her the information. "I would do anything for you, Kelenna, but Ms. Hunt, bless her, will never let me out if I go back in. And I have five other patients! But you can come ask her!" Emily was right, and by the time Kelenna got out of the room, she knew all about the woman, her jolly third husband, ex-con second husband, deceased first husband, and one more random detail: if she got a single dose of that medication, she would swell like a blowfish.

During that same period, Pat made operational changes to improve security over opioids at Preston. They added blind counts to several medications that could be used as decoys for diverting opioids. Drugs like Benadryl, *promethazine,* and *ketorolac* were now monitored more closely than they ever had been before. The admin team approved *and* implemented video surveillance in all the medication rooms in under a week, and everyone agreed that it was the fastest they had ever moved on anything in the hospital's history. Already, the cameras had been accessed and reviewed for several reported suspicious activities. Pat's workload increased tremendously after the addition of the cameras, and she became disillusioned pretty quickly. "If one more person calls to tell me that they saw a nurse slip something into her pocket, I'm going to pull my hair out," she said more than once.

It was all more than Kelenna could say about any clinical changes *she* had made since Ashleigh's death. In her defense, no one was holding her feet to the fire to get anything done. But every day, she would spend a little time writing down ideas about what she could do. *'A more meaningful approach to curbing opioid overuse.'* She repeated that phrase like a mantra. She texted pictures of her notes to Chris and sometimes they would have a small back and forth about them. Other times they would meet for a working lunch to discuss the ideas that were brewing in her head. So far though, none of them had truly taken root. She still didn't know exactly what they were going to do.

It was a week into the new year when Kelenna got her first pharmacy students in a long while. Their names were Parker and Tracy, and she knew from the very first time she met them—when she mistook Parker for the white guy, and Tracy for the Black girl—that they were going to be impressive. They were both in the top ten percent of their class, and were so eager to learn and to please that she oscillated between wanting to show them everything and wanting to tell them to take a chill pill. Not long after they started, they mastered the computer system and were speaking up confidently during rounds. That was why she knew instinctively that she could enlist their help in her plans. She made it part of their grades to research programs across the country, review protocols and guidelines, and come up with a solution that matched her mantra. There were no better researchers than students whose grades depended on it. Besides, the relationship between her, a preceptor, and a pharmacy student was a mutualistic one. She taught them about pharmacy in the real world, and they assisted her with whatever projects she had that needed completing. Quid pro quo.

One snowy Wednesday morning after rounds, Parker and Tracy appeared at her office door with several sheets of paper in their hands, looking really proud of themselves. Kelenna put down her pen and looked at them expectantly.

"We sent you a few emails, but we wanted to go over what we've found with you," Tracy started, coming further into her office.

She spent the next half hour reviewing the papers they presented to her. They'd found emergency departments that had developed protocols that completely avoided opioids for pain. As they looked through the drug options, Kelenna added notes to some parts and crossed out words in others.

"This is just what we need," Kelenna said. "But I want these validated. Make sure we know the evidence behind using a drug like—" She looked down at the paper in her hand. "*Ketamine.* Using *ketamine* for abdominal pain."

"*Ketamine* is a potent hallucinogenic that's used primarily for sedation. At low doses it produces analgesic effects," Tracy said. Kelenna had to stop an eye roll in its tracks. Students in the top ten percent of their classes were such know-it-alls.

"Right," she said patiently. "But I want real world evidence of use. Numbers that show that actual humans benefited from these drugs. If we're going to think this far outside the box, we have to make sure it works."

"Excuse me." Pat was standing at the entrance of her door with a grim look on her face. "Emergency huddle, Kelenna. The snow is coming down hard, and it's sticking. We'll need to make plans for inclement weather. Everyone who isn't essential may go home." She eyed the students sitting in front of Kelenna before she walked away.

"Looks like you're getting a snow day," Kelenna said, standing up and walking around her desk to leave her office. She had to hide a small chuckle when she heard Parker whisper to Tracy about how scary Pat was. "We'll pick this back up later. Good job so far. Stay safe on the roads." She slipped into the pharmacy pit just as Pat was updating the team.

"Brian from security just let us know that we're expecting a couple of inches of snow and black ice. The roads are going to be dangerous tonight and tomorrow morning. If you're supposed to be here in the morning and you don't think you'll be able to make it back, do not leave the hospital. Cots are being set up in the meeting rooms as we speak for anyone who wants to spend the night in the hospital. There'll be food in the cafeteria, and for showers, they will be closing off a few rooms on the second floor to make it available for employees. Kelenna and I will work on getting the night shift pharmacist and tech to come in a little early while the roads are still safe. Now, I need a headcount. Who's staying and who's leaving?"

* * *

"Hey John," Kelenna said after she hit the answer button on her cell phone. She was back in her office later that afternoon, finishing up some of her audits of the pharmacists' clinical activities. Part of her job was to make sure her team intervened whenever opportunities arose to do so. Clinical pharmacy was a cost-saving service rather than an income-generating one, and making interventions was one way to show the value of their program.

"You good?" John asked. "I know how you hate to drive in the snow."

Kelenna chuckled. "You know me well. I packed a bag when I saw the weather report this morning. Change of clothes, toiletries. Pat already has a cot with my name on it."

"A cot? You're sleeping at *Preston*?"

She let out a dismissive snort. "You make it sound like I said I was sleeping in prison. I'm sleeping at the hospital."

"Why do you have to sleep there anyway? It's supposed to melt by the morning."

"Good. Then the roads will be perfect for me to drive home tomorrow after work." When he didn't say anything, she continued. "What's the big deal? Aren't you sleeping at work as well?"

"Yeah, but I'm a fellow, and I'm on call. I'm used to this. You should be sleeping in your bed. It's crazy that you're trapped in the hospital because of a little snow."

"Two inches of snow in Georgia is like ten in Chicago."

"And I bet you they still go home."

"Well, we're not in Chicago."

John sighed. "What about Chris? He lives close to you. He may be able to take you home."

Kelenna wasn't exactly sure where Chris lived, but she knew it was in a development just within the borders of the exclusive East Cobb community, not too far away from her apartment complex. Two years ago, while the homes were being erected, a billboard advertised just how much owning one of them would cost. She remembered thinking it was way beyond anything she would ever spend.

"I have no idea if Chris is even here today," she told her brother. "Listen, John, I have to go. How about I call you later and let you know how fine I am?"

Kelenna worked till five-thirty that evening, past her usual hours, until she couldn't stand to look at her computer any longer. She picked up her phone and called Landon. She smiled when he answered on the third ring.

"Kelenna! You caught me at a good time. How are you?"

"Hey, Landon, I'm good. I'm still at work waiting for—"

"Work?" he cut in. "This is pretty late for you, isn't it? You're usually done by four-thirty."

She liked that he knew her schedule. It wasn't worth being part of the information he retained in his head that was already filled with incredible knowledge, but he did anyway. "I know. I'm waiting out some bad weather. Snow." Then because she didn't want to go into it, she changed the subject. "There's a lot of noise from your end, what are you up to?"

"It's the wind," he replied quickly. "I'm in Chicago. Got consulted on a case out here. I thought I mentioned it to you."

He hadn't, but that was fine. Even though they'd talked almost every day in the three weeks since the gala, they were still getting to know each other, and she didn't need to keep tabs on him. "How did the case go?"

She leaned back against the chair and listened to him describe the case he had helped operate on. He got too technical at times, but that was all right. She enjoyed hearing the passion for his work in everything he said.

Just then her office landline rang out loud. She glanced at the caller ID screen and saw it was from the ED office.

"Landon, I hate to cut this short, but I have to call you back. A doctor's trying to reach me."

"Okay. Call you tonight?"

"Yes, please. I may be in this hospital for a long time and I'm sure I'll want the company."

"Great. Later, then."

She ended the call on her cell phone with one hand and picked up her landline with the other.

"Pharmacy, this is Kelenna?"

"Hey, it's me," the familiar voice said. "John asked me to take you home. Something wrong with your car?"

Kelenna rolled her eyes. She should have known her overprotective brother would go behind her back to contact Chris. "Ignore John. My car is perfectly fine. Thank you for checking."

"So you can make it home?" he pressed.

"I think so. I'm just not going. I think it's best that I stay in the area, just so I can make sure I'm here for work tomorrow."

"Here? At a hotel?"

Kelenna snorted. "Hotel Preston, sure."

She heard an impatient sigh on the other end. "Kelenna, get ready. I'll take you home."

"Chris, you don't have to. Seriously."

"Do they need you at work now?"

"No, but—"

"Meet me at the ER main entrance in five minutes."

"Really, you don't have to, I—"

"Kelenna," he cut in firmly. "In five."

After she hung up, she slipped her work computer into her laptop sleeve, picked up her small overnight bag and headed out to say goodbye to the pharmacy staff that was left in the department. When she arrived at the main entrance of the ER, Chris was already there, wearing a winter coat over his scrubs and a pair of glasses she'd never seen before.

"Here." He reached for her bag and transferred it to his left hand.

"Nice glasses," she commented. They were just the kind she liked too. Black-rimmed and square-framed.

"You don't think they suit me?"

She laughed when he turned his head to the left and to the right, as if he was modeling his angles. The problem was that they suited him too well. "They'll do," she replied. He didn't need his head getting bigger than it already was. It was also weird how just having them on made it look like he could see her better. Had he always had such a piercing gaze?

"I can't believe I've been struggling all these years. Is this what having twenty-twenty vision feels like? Everything is so much clearer."

She followed him outside, walking gingerly on the ground that was already covered with a layer of snow. It made for a nice picture, the flakes that were falling from the heavens. It was too bad that something so pretty would end up leaving disaster in its wake. Atlantans had no idea how to handle a couple inches of snow. She already knew the streets would be littered with wrecks and abandoned cars by the morning.

He stopped at the passenger side of a black Ford F-150 truck and pressed a key fob to unlock it. He opened the door and gestured for her to get in. "Careful."

"Where's your Mercedes?" she asked when he joined her in the truck. She'd never seen this vehicle before.

"My baby is home. In the garage. Safe from all this." He gestured at the falling snow.

She burst into laughter as he started the engine. He hit buttons that turned on a blast of heat, and then started to defrost his windshield. Soon they were on the road.

As he pulled onto the interstate, she admitted her anxiety about being on the road in wintery conditions. It all stemmed from the time she was in college and witnessed an eighteen-wheeler ram into an SUV that was stuck on an unsalted, slippery highway.

She leaned back against the head of the passenger's seat and closed her eyes. "That's why I didn't want to go home. But if you drive slowly, I'll be fine. I think."

"You need me to hold your hand?"

Her eyes flew open. "No! Hands on the wheel!"

Chris lifted his hands in surrender, abandoning the steering wheel altogether.

"Chris!" she screeched.

"I'm sorry," he said contritely, settling his hands at the ten and two position on the steering wheel. "I won't move them."

It took them an extra forty-five minutes to get from Preston to Marietta, and for majority of the time, Chris kept to his word and did not take his hands off the steering wheel. She felt safe in the large truck that she was sure had more traction than her sedan could ever dream of.

When he pulled up to the small hill that led to her apartment complex, he slowed down. There were cars parked along the side of the road, and branches on the street.

"It looks like folks aren't making it up this hill with their cars," he remarked.

"I see." There were two people trudging on the sidewalk, their heads down to ward off the snow as they made their way up the incline. It would be unpleasant, but she could make it up to her apartment on foot if she had to. When she mentioned it to Chris, he completely ignored her.

"Do you see those men?" He pointed out of her window. "That looks like a transformer they're standing by. I think you may have wires down."

"Okay?"

"So your power could be out. Or there could be live wires on the ground."

"I knew I should have stayed at work," she muttered under her breath.

Somehow Chris heard her. "Change of plans." He looked left and veered back onto the street.

"Where are we going?"

"My place." Before she could protest, he raised a hand to stop her. "I'm not letting you walk on the street and risk electrocution just so you can get home and freeze to death."

Kelenna blinked at the bleak and dramatic picture he painted. "Dude, I was just going to say I could get a hotel room somewhere close. I have a change of clothes and everything. I don't want to put you out."

He let out a low chuckle. "Well, you're welcome to stay at Hotel Chris."

18

Kelenna followed Chris into his brick townhouse. The front door opened directly into a small foyer with a console table that had three decorative vases strategically placed on it. Matter of fact, there were vases everywhere. One on the floor beside the front door. Another on the bookcase beside the window in the living room they'd just walked into. On floating shelves on the side wall. On the floor right beside the TV. It was like he was putting on an exhibit called the house of a thousand vases. When she told him this, he barked out a laugh.

"I'm telling my sister you said that. Belema prides herself on her interior designing skills."

Kelenna gasped and grabbed his arm threateningly. "You better tell her I said she has excellent taste and nothing more!"

Chris laughed out loud. "She does have excellent taste. My parents stay here when they come to visit, and she wanted it to look good for them. Come on, I'll show you to your room."

Her room was on the first floor, down a short hall away from the front door. The queen-sized bed was done in all white, and there was a lone painting on the wall behind its headboard.

He placed her bag down and pointed to a closed door. "The bathroom's over there and it's completely stocked. Just let me know if you need anything else."

"Thank you," she said softly. "I'll stay so far out of your hair, you won't even know I'm here."

He gave her an odd look. "Kelenna, relax. You're not interfering. Feel free to do whatever you want. I don't mind."

"Okay."

"Good." He turned and walked away.

"Thanks again, Chris!" she called out to his retreating figure.

"Stop thanking me!" he shouted back.

She chuckled as she shut the door behind him. Then she called her brother and semi-chewed him out for going behind her back to get her out of Preston.

"You're welcome for getting you out of sleeping on a blow-up mattress," he said.

After that, she indulged in a luxurious shower (the body wash in the bathroom was actually called Luxurious Showers), and when she was done, she changed into the pair of yoga tights and large t-shirt she'd packed to be her sleepwear at the hospital. It was well past 8 p.m. when she left the guest room and retraced her steps to the living room. Chris was there already, so engrossed in whatever he was working on that he didn't notice her walk in.

"What are you doing?" she asked, tucking herself into the other end of the couch he was sitting on. She looked around now that the recessed lights in the ceiling were on and illuminating the room. Somehow there were more vases that she'd missed earlier. There was a blue-green one on a window sill, and a gold one at the center of the dining table adjacent to the living room. "I think I know what to get you for your birthday. Another vase for your collection."

"It's not a collection, and it's not my birthday," he murmured distractedly.

"I know. Your birthday's in July."

Chris snorted out a laugh and turned to her then. "You know, earlier when you said I wouldn't know you were here? Is it too late to take you up on that?"

"Shut up!" Kelenna said with a gasp, tossing a throw pillow at him that landed right on his head. She laughed and clapped at her perfect aim.

"Really?" His smile betrayed his serious tone. "Are you twelve?" He placed the pillow on the floor beside his feet, well away from her reach. When he caught her cheeky grin, he shook his head and turned back to his laptop.

"You didn't answer my question. What are you doing?"

"I'm charting."

"Oh? I thought you didn't see patients today."

"I didn't. We have 24 hours to finish our charting. This is from yesterday."

"Do you like it?"

"Do I like charting? Not really. But it comes with the territory. Everything has to be documented, I'm not going to complain about it."

"No, I mean the whole thing. Being an ER doctor. I know you hate being the ED medical director."

"I don't hate it."

"The other day you said you hated the tons of emails and—"

"I know what I said before," he cut in quickly. "Give me a second." She watched him type some more before he seemed satisfied and shut his laptop. He placed it on the side table and turned to her. "Okay, bored girl. Your first question. Do I like being a doctor?"

"I'm not bored!" she protested.

"You're asking existential questions in the middle of a snowstorm."

"It's hardly a snowstorm," she mumbled weakly.

He gave her a look that said he won that debate. "You know, I always knew I would become a doctor. You know how Nigerian parents are. There has to be one medical doctor in the family otherwise they feel like they've failed at parenthood."

Kelenna nodded with a rueful smile. "Don't I know it."

"So my grandfather was a medical doctor—"

"The original Tari Douglas," she interjected knowingly.

"Yes, the original Tari Douglas," he said with a smile. "Everyone knows him as the economist slash politician, but he really loved practicing medicine. My dad and I were both named for him, and we took after him in our own ways. My dad took after the economist part, and it seemed like fate that I would take after the medicine part."

"I didn't know you were named for your grandfather."

"He was Tari Michael Tamunotonye Douglas. My dad got Michael and I got Tamunotonye. Christian Tamunotonye Chukwudi Tari-Douglas."

"Tamunotonye," she repeated.

He gave her a look she couldn't decipher but that sent a little shiver up her spine. Had she completely butchered the name?

"Did I say it wrong?" she asked.

"No, you got it right."

"You said it very melodically," she said softly.

He chuckled. "My language is very melodic," he replied in an even softer tone.

"Yeah? What does it mean?"

"God's plan."

"I like it."

"Me too."

They shared a smile that was a little too warm for her comfort and she averted her gaze. When she turned back to him, he was fiddling with the cushion on the couch.

"There were times I didn't want to go through with it. I thought it was too much work. Plus it was really cramping my style." He looked back at her. "Do you know how hard it is to study when all you really want to do is go out with pretty girls?"

Kelenna burst out laughing, and the warm, uncomfortable moment was gone. "I know for a fact that you didn't let that stop you!"

Chris grinned. "No, I didn't. But you know why John's my guy?"

"Why?"

"He wouldn't let me blow it off. There you had this twenty-year-old kid in medical school, and he was the most driven of us all."

Kelenna smiled. She knew how driven John was. She'd lived with how driven he was.

"I'm not sure I would have made it through medical school without him."

Kelenna thought that maybe he was giving himself too little credit, but it was nice to understand how much her brother meant to him. "I know John credits you with keeping him balanced throughout school." She left out that she snorted every time John told her that.

"Yeah, well, someone had to show him the ropes."

Kelenna rolled her eyes. "And since he was your little cousin, it had to be you, huh?"

"My little cousin?"

"That's what you called us back in high school, remember?"

"Did I?" he asked, sounding puzzled. "I don't remember."

"You don't?" How could he not remember uttering the very words that had effectively ended her crush on him fifteen years ago? She wanted to press, but before she could, he had already moved on.

"I think I chose emergency medicine because I wanted the detachment. Yeah, I love saving lives, but I wanted to do it in a way where I could leave the craziness at work. Deal with my shift and go home. Come in the next day and attack a new set of problems. Not have to follow-up with patients. But then I come to a place like Preston where you can't really detach. Not when patients show up in the ER every month like we're their primary care doctors. I've even had some who ask for me specifically."

"The ladies, right?" she teased.

Chris didn't answer but she thought she caught a smile as he shook his head. "Anyway, I think I've started to see my role as ED medical director differently. And it all changed after Ashleigh died. It's not a chore or a headache. It's something I *need* to do well. Does that make sense?"

She nodded wordlessly. He'd gone far deeper than she expected him to in that moment, but she knew exactly what he meant.

"It's like what you said that night. That you'd just been going through the motions, and that you wanted to do something meaningful. Remember that?"

"Yeah?"

"I think that's the way we all feel in the department. Ashleigh's death has brought us all closer. It's an entirely different vibe. I've had fewer complaints from the staff. We're checking in more with each other. We're helping out more. It's like we've learned that we're going to be useless to the patients we serve if we're not connected with each other."

"Connected," Kelenna muttered, thinking about her own connection encounters with patients.

"What was that?"

"That word just keeps coming up." She shared some of her stories with him. She even told him about her plans to encourage the other clinical pharmacists to embrace opportunities for patient interaction. "We're a small department, and we don't have the manpower, but I think it's important for patients to see us. They may not know what we do behind the scenes to help them, but if we're able to show them once in a while that we're here and we see them, that's something, right?"

"Yeah," he said, sounding thoughtful. "It is."

* * *

"Make sure you give him a nice tip," Kelenna whispered from behind Chris. The slight turn of his head was the only indication he gave that he'd heard her.

"Thank you." Chris handed a signed receipt back to the delivery man who had just given him a bag full of the food they'd ordered.

"Drive safe!" Kelenna called out from behind him.

Chris shut the door and turned to look at her. "You're so cute."

Kelenna scowled at his patronizing tone. "I can't believe you made a delivery guy come out in this weather."

"Did I or did I not get us food?"

"Yes, but he could have been hurt!"

"Maybe you shouldn't project your fears of driving in the snow on business owners." He handed her a carton of the shrimp fried rice she ordered. "You're welcome."

She glowered at him as she accepted the food. "Thank you," she said begrudgingly.

They sat on the large area rug at the center of the living room and spread out their food on the coffee table. As they ate, Chris turned her earlier questions to him on her.

"My mother always tells this story about me from when I was a baby. She said she knew I would be a pharmacist after my first word. I'm pretty sure she groomed me to be one from that very day."

"Now I need to know what that word was."

"*Vancomycin*."

Chris laughed out loud. "There's no way that's true."

"That's what I said, but my dad says it's true too. I'm not surprised since they argue about the drug all the time."

"Why would they argue so much about *vancomycin*?"

Kelenna shrugged. "My mom is an infectious diseases pharmacist and my dad's a nephrologist. They disagree about whether or not *vancomycin* damages the kidneys. Sometimes my mother comes back home with proof that it doesn't, and she's the winner until my dad comes home with a case where he claims that *vancomycin* shot the kidneys."

"Claims," Chris said with a huff. "I can already tell what side of the fence you're on."

Kelenna's head snapped up at him. "I'm a pharmacist, Chris. I've studied the drug. It's not as black and white as you would think."

"Studied the drug? What about the doctors who've actually *seen* the effects of the drug on their patients? Should they just be ignored?"

"*Vancomycin* is removed from the body by the kidneys, Chris," Kelenna said patiently. "If the kidneys go bad, it's literally trapped and has nowhere to go."

Chris wrinkled his nose in thought. "That's like saying you're trapped in a fire that you started yourself."

Kelenna could only stare at him. She was certain that this was exactly how her mother felt whenever she was having a *vancomycin* debate with her father. Then because it freaked her out a little, she shook her head. She was not re-enacting her parents' life with Chris. It was too weird. "We can agree to disagree."

* * *

"At the very least, you have to agree that it's equal," Kelenna said, throwing the empty carton from her food in the kitchen's trash can. "It's like the chicken or the egg. Did *vancomycin* make the kidneys go bad, or is the *vancomycin* level high because the kidneys went bad? Which happened first?"

He stroked his chin as he narrowed his eyes in thought. "I'll give you sixty percent *vancomycin's* fault. You got me down from eighty-five. Accept it."

"It should be sixty in *vancomycin's* favor!" she cried out exasperatedly. She turned her back on him in disgust and began to wash her hands in the kitchen island double sink. Against her better judgement, she'd continued to argue with Chris about the antibiotic. She didn't understand why she couldn't make him see reason. He came beside her to wash his own hands, moving the faucet and interrupting the water flowing on her hands to get better access to it. She rolled her eyes. "I don't know why I'm still talking to you about this, you don't know the first thing about *vancomycin*."

"Of course I know all about *vancomycin*. I use it all the time."

She turned to him. "Yeah? Do you know what class of drug it belongs to? Exactly how it kills bacteria? Do you understand its pharmacokinetics?"

He took a step closer and looked down at her. "No, I'll leave that up to you," he said in a voice so low that she swore she felt another small shiver up her spine. Why did that keep happening? "I know the most important thing. When to use it."

She took a deep breath. "Fifty-one, forty-nine."

"Fifty-one for which one?"

"*Vancomycin*," she managed to spit out, ignoring the smug smile on his face. It went against everything she knew but irrationally, she needed to end the discussion with a win.

"Fifty-five, and we have a deal."

She mulled the deal over in her head for a few seconds before her mouth dropped open and her eyes grew wide with realization. "I can't do it," she whispered. "Is this what they mean when they say every woman eventually becomes their mother?"

From beside her, Chris burst out into laughter.

* * *

"You never answered my question," Chris said from his sitting position on the floor, half a yard away from her feet. He was mindlessly scrolling through television shows on his streaming app. She wished he would just pick one and watch it.

"Yeah, I did."

"No you didn't. I asked if you liked your job, and you went on a rant about *vancomycin*."

Kelenna put her hand on her temple to remind herself that she would surely get a headache if she dared engage with him on that topic again. When she looked down at him, away from her laptop, he was completely focused on the television. "I do like my job," she said to the back of his head. "I like being in charge of how we use drugs at Preston. I like the people I work with. It's funny how when you spend so much time in an enclosed space with the same group of people, you get to know everything about them. I haven't met some of their husbands or kids, yet I know their names, their ages and what they like to do." She chuckled. "It's been a great three-and-a-half years, but sometimes I do wonder if I'm just comfortable. If I need to be more ambitious and try to go to a bigger hospital with a different kind of challenge. But then I ask myself, why should I leave when I feel content? When I feel truly needed? When I have some autonomy, and am trusted? I like being the one who's responsible. Who *knows* things." She paused to consider her own words. "Gosh, how egotistical do I sound?"

"I don't think you have an egotistical bone in your body," Chris replied softly. "And for the record, I hope you don't leave. I like having you around."

Kelenna smiled at the back of his head.

* * *

Kelenna's eyes widened in shock as she double-clicked on the most recent email in her inbox. "I can't believe those kids," she muttered.

"What kids?"

"My overachieving students! I sent them home early today, and it looks like they decided to work from home. Look at this!"

She didn't expect him to actually get up from the floor and sit beside her on the couch, but when he did, she tilted the computer to show him her email.

"They're doing our work for us?" Chris asked, inching closer as he read the message. She smiled at his use of the word *'our.'* It truly was *their* project.

"I made it one of the projects for their rotation."

"Yeah?" he asked, leaning back to lounge comfortably on the couch. "What did they come up with?"

Kelenna opened up the attached document and scanned it quickly. "All I asked them for was evidence," she whispered. She certainly had not expected Tracy and Parker to go this far beyond her request. They'd collated the medications they'd found earlier and explained how each could be used to treat pain. Many were outlandish, but below each drug, they'd listed their references. Lots of them.

"This isn't just Tylenol and *ibuprofen*, is it?" Chris asked in wonder. "Is that *prochlorperazine*? The drug for nausea?"

"Right. It's also a really old drug for schizophrenia."

"And now your genius students want us to use it for migraines."

"*Prochlorperazine* does have an off-label use for migraines," Kelenna said with a shrug. "It's worth a shot."

Chris grunted and continued down the list. "Does that say *ketamine*?"

Kelenna nodded and turned to grin at him. "Isn't it cool?"

"Kelenna, inhaled *ketamine* for bone fractures and abdominal pain? Really?"

"Chris, I asked them to find opioid alternatives and that's what they've done."

He leveled a look at her. "I'm all for thinking outside the box, but what exactly are we trying to do here? Hallucinate the pain away?"

"Look at this reference. A cohort study in thirty patients at a hospital in Colorado. Not one patient complained about pain afterwards. Only one claimed to experience hallucinations. That's not bad."

Chris let out a dismissive snort. "Colorado? That's who we're taking advice from? They give their patients marijuana over there!"

Kelenna tried to keep a straight face at his joke, but soon she was doubled over in laughter. She was laughing so hard she couldn't get out any words. She wanted to add that marijuana would be a good opioid alternative if it were FDA approved—the CBD part, that is. Instead, she worked on regaining her composure. She felt Chris' palm rub her back gently as though he were trying to assist her.

"You good?" he asked her.

"You're horrible," she managed to gasp out, wiping away the laughter-induced tears that had formed in her eyes. Finally, she sobered. "Why are we working so late anyway? We're worse than my students." She closed her laptop and placed it on the cushion beside her. Then she scooted back and joined him in resting against the couch. "How about I review this and we can discuss it later? Maybe you'll like *ketamine* a little more by then," she said just as a yawn came over her.

Chris laughed. "You're tired," he stated rather than asked.

"Yeah." When she yawned again, she felt his arm go around her shoulder to pull her closer to him. Without a second thought, she rested against him. "So should we watch a movie?"

19

Chika returned from Nigeria the next day and was at Kelenna's door the evening after that.

"I brought us dinner," Chika said by way of greeting. In one hand was a box of pizza, and tucked under her other arm was a bottle of wine.

Kelenna collected the box of pizza from Chika and shut the door behind her. Soon, they were both sitting on Kelenna's sectional, eating and drinking.

"Tell me everything," Kelenna finally said.

"I couldn't do it, Kels," Chika started with a head shake. "We were at the family home in our village, and my mother wanted me to wait in one of the bedrooms to be presented." She snorted at the word presented like it was the most ridiculous notion. "Anyway, when it was time, she sent a relative to bring me into the living room."

"Was Daniel there?" Kelenna asked.

"I didn't know where Daniel was. There were three men laughing and chatting with my parents so I sat and said hello to them. I thought it was a traditional thing I wasn't familiar with. Like, I was in another room, so maybe he was in another room too."

Kelenna frowned. "That's strange. Why would they bring you out first? You would think they—"

"I know!" Chika cut in. "They didn't bring him out because he was already there!" She reached out to clamp a hand on Kelenna's knee. "Kelenna, he was an . . . an uncle!"

Kelenna froze and the slice of pizza she held was suspended midair. Chika called any adult Nigerian man over the age of fifty uncle. "Nooo!"

"Yes, he was!" Chika cried. "With a beer belly, and questionable dress sense, and everything! I had to stop myself from calling him sir the whole time we were there!"

"Chika, why would your mother try to marry you off to a fifty-year-old?"

"She thinks he's forty-two," Chika replied with another snort. "I'm in PR, Kels. Even I can't sell that man as a forty-two-year-old!"

Kelenna shook her head to clear it. "What happened next?"

"They asked us to step out into the compound to talk and get to know each other. The minute we got outside, he started firing these questions at me. He asked me my age, what I do for a living, and what kinds of food I like to cook. That was when it dawned on me."

Kelenna leaned forward. "What dawned on you?"

"It was all an audition, Kels. And I was failing it. I'm not twenty-seven. I don't cook any of his favorite Nigerian soups. He thinks my job is a hobby."

"What does being twenty-seven have to do with anything?"

"Apparently, he was told I was twenty-seven, not practically thirty. He seemed so disappointed. He actually asked if I was sure about my age!"

"Nooo," Kelenna said with a gasp.

"Yes! And I just kept thinking while I was out there with him, that I was only there to please my mother who already disapproves of me. Why should I sit there and be judged by a fifty-year-old pretending to be forty-two?"

Kelenna nodded sympathetically. "What did you do?"

"I got the hell out of there! I went back in the house and told my parents that I would be in my room till after the guests left." She sighed deeply. "It was a whole dramatic scene. My mother called after me, but I didn't respond. I was so hot, Kels, if I wasn't in our remote village with no airport access for three hours, I would have driven the hell out of there."

Kelenna's eyes widened. "How angry was your mother after they left?"

A small smile played around Chika's lips. "I stood up to her for the first time. Every other time, I've just avoided her disappointment. This time I called her out. I told her that she didn't care enough to vet the person she chose for me. To see if we would fit. You know what she said? She told me that was exactly what she did."

Kelenna's mouth dropped open. "She thought that he was the right kind of man for you? Why?"

"She said I needed someone to tame my big personality," she replied thoughtfully. "That I needed a strong man who could put his foot down."

"She's wrong, Chika," Kelenna said quickly. "You don't need an older, traditional man to dominate you. None of us do."

Chika was quiet for a moment. "I hated what happened. But it led to my mother and I having our first heart-to-heart in . . . ever. You see, she doesn't know a thing about independence. She married my dad when she was twenty and she thinks she has a good life now because she had the good sense to choose a man who was already made. I wanted so much to tell her that we weren't the same. But I don't think that's true. I think I would have the good sense to choose a made man if I were compatible with him. Just like she did. I guess we're just like our mothers at the end of the day, right?"

"Right," Kelenna said softly, remembering that she'd said the exact thing to Chris two nights ago. Before she could let her mind wander to that night, she spoke quickly. "Well, I'm glad you both came to an understanding."

"Yeah, I think we did," Chika said with a smile. "There were no more talks of me meeting any more uncles. You can feel free to say I told you so, by the way."

Kelenna laughed and shook her head. It wasn't an *'I told you so'* moment, not when despite everything her gut had told her, she'd wanted Chika to come out with the unlikely match. She put an arm around her friend and hugged her. "I think we'll be all right."

Just then, her phone rang out loud. Chika leaned forward to pick it up. "Ooh, it's Dr. Landon! There's no boys allowed on girls' night, but I'll let you break the rules for this one." She handed the phone to Kelenna.

"Break the rules," Kelenna muttered under her breath. Breaking the rules was what had got her in the mental rut she'd been in for the last two days. She took the phone from Chika. "You can just call him Landon, you know."

"Seems disrespectful to do that. No, I'll call him Dr. Landon."

Kelenna laughed, but she still didn't answer the phone. It'd been two days, and she still didn't know how. She'd texted him, but she hadn't spoken to him.

"Go ahead. Answer it."

"I'll just call him back later," she mumbled as she hit the silence button on the side of her phone.

Chika sat up. "Kelenna. What's wrong?"

Kelenna looked up to the ceiling for a second before she looked back down at Chika. "I kissed Chris."

* * *

Two days earlier . . .

They had a devil of a time choosing what movie to watch. She wanted to watch something light—like a romantic comedy—while he wanted something with a little more action. "Otherwise I'm going to fall asleep," Chris proclaimed.

She laughed. "Let's do this," she said, allowing herself to get more comfortable against his shoulder. "You scroll through the options, and when I say stop, we have to watch whatever you land on."

"All right." She could hear his amused tone. "You ready?"

"Start." She waited a millisecond before she grabbed his wrist. "Stop."

Chris laughed. "You didn't even let me scroll!"

"Rules are rules." Her hand was still on his wrist, so she pressed the button to hit the synopsis. "A teacher in a small town falls for the father of one her students in this thriller with a—"

"*Thriller*?" Chris interjected, sounding aghast.

She chuckled as she pressed the play button. "Do you need me to hold your hand?" she joked, borrowing his line from when they were in the car on their snowy drive down from the hospital. Before he could respond, she slid the remote out of his hand and replaced it with her hand.

Maybe she should have expected what happened next—she'd certainly been flirting with it all evening—but she didn't. She didn't expect him to turn her palm over in his and then slowly interlace her fingers with his. She didn't expect that in a matter of minutes, they would go from lounging about on the couch to essentially holding each other.

For the next five minutes, all she could do was stare at the television. It wasn't like she needed to pay any real attention to the movie. She'd seen it before. It wasn't a good movie. They really should stop watching it. But oddly enough, it felt like the natural progression of the evening. The falling snow. His concern for her comfort. The teasing, the debating, the overall banter. An awesomely bad movie experience to cap off the night while his hand gently stroked her arm. Did he even realize he was doing it? For her, it felt like her arm had nerve endings that were being ignited by his fingertips. Why couldn't he feel it?

"Kelenna, are you awake?" She felt his breath against her forehead, and his hand squeeze hers.

"Mhmm," she murmured. There was a tingle from where his lips had just been near.

"This movie sucks," he whispered.

She raised up from his chest and leaned back to look at him. "You're trying to break the rules!" she said, eyes wide in mock horror.

He rolled his eyes in response. "And we both know how much you hate to break the rules."

"What are you talking about?" she asked with a frown. Somehow it felt like he was talking about more than the movie.

Chris shrugged. "I'm just saying. You're so by the book. So straight-laced. You came up with this rule five minutes ago, and now we're bound to watching this silly movie. For all I know, you rigged it and—"

She cut him off by leaning forward and planting a closed-mouth kiss on his lips, not wanting to hear any more of her faults. When he simply stared at her, she raised a challenging brow. "I can break the rules."

He cocked his head to the right as he pinned her with a gaze. He'd removed his glasses, but they were so close to each other, it was just as piercing. "What rule did you just break, Kelenna?"

There was a calm intensity to his tone that almost paralyzed her. She held his eyes for a second before she spoke. "We don't kiss."

"Yeah?" he said, somehow drawing her closer. Or did she move towards him? "Is that similar to the *'we don't fight'* rule?"

She wanted to smile at that. Those were her exact words from the last time they watched a football game at John's condo. But she couldn't smile. Not when it seemed like all her energy was being used to keep her heart rate normal. And it was barely working. All she could muster the strength to say was, "Maybe."

"Maybe?" He tilted her chin up. Or did she lift it on her own? Either way, he was staring at her lips in a way that made her anxious. Soon, his index finger followed his eyes. "We survived that fight, didn't we? It was a proper fight too. What was it about?"

"The opioid crisis-shortage," she whispered, unsure how she was able to come up with that answer when she was so rattled.

"Are you cold?" he asked gently.

She glanced down at her arms. Goosebumps were raised on her skin. How could she be cold when she was feeling warm all over? She shook her head once.

By now his mouth was mere inches away from hers. "Want to see if we'll survive this?"

She was the one who closed the gap between them.

She was tentative at first. Shy even. Her hand cupped his cheek as she took his upper lip between hers in a slow smooch before moving on to capture his lower lip. He allowed her only that head start before he took over. Boy, did he take over. She might have guessed that he was an expert kisser, but never in her wildest imagination would she have thought it would feel like—*this*. When his hand found her waist and lifted her onto his lap, she followed willingly, not breaking contact for even a moment. She swore she could feel him everywhere. He kissed with his entire body. It was too much and not enough at the same time.

Her heart was pounding when she broke apart from him and her fingers involuntarily rose to her lips. They felt fine, even though she was sure they would feel swollen. It should have felt odd sitting on his lap with his hands loosely around her waist, but it didn't. Without saying a word about what they'd just done, she turned to settle more comfortably on his legs and rested her head against his chest.

And that was how the night continued. With the awesomely bad movie playing on the screen, the one they were pretending to watch (because rules were rules), they traded kisses. He would lean down and pull her closer for a mind-numbing kiss before he released her. And when she couldn't take the separation anymore, she would reach up to kiss him long and slow. In between the give and take, they tried their best to keep up with the movie, laughing at the absurd parts, and gasping at the shocking ones. They were both in sync, like they understood that the entire day was an anomaly. They understood that when the sun came up, they would go back to what they truly were: Family friends who just happened to work at the same hospital.

But for tonight, she could allow herself to just feel. Feel his arms around her every time they came back to each other, and the sensory overload it created. Feel the tender way he caressed her cheek, or mindlessly let his fingers glide up and down her arm.

When it was past 2 a.m. and they couldn't stay awake any longer, he walked her to her room. And no matter how much they both wanted to touch each other, they refrained. No matter how itchy her palms felt, and how much she wanted to use them to pull him closer. No matter how he kept his hands planted on the door frame and stared at her mouth. They kept their goodnight very professional.

"Car service leaves at seven-thirty," he said with a grin.

When she woke up the next morning and looked at the phone she'd largely ignored for most of the previous night, she saw two missed calls and a text from Landon.

`Just wanted to make sure you got home safe.`

* * *

Chika was staring at her with her mouth agape.

"Say something," Kelenna said with a sigh.

"I'm just surprised," Chika replied softly. "I guess I didn't realize you had a thing for Chris."

"I don't!" Kelenna protested. "People kiss other people all the time! It doesn't have to mean anything."

"People, Kelenna. Not you."

"Aren't you always telling me to do something different? Be open? Try new things?"

Chika raised a hand. "Chris is the opposite of new things."

"It doesn't mean anything," she repeated determinedly. She wasn't sure if she was trying to convince herself, or if she was trying to wipe the smirk off Chika's face. "What?"

"If it doesn't mean anything, why are you avoiding Dr. Landon?"

"Because!"

"Because what?"

Kelenna sighed again. "Remember the fundraising gala Landon and I went to?"

"The beginning of the fairytale? Yes, of course."

Kelenna gave her a weary look before she rolled her eyes and continued. "Landon thought there was something between Chris and me."

"He did?" Chika made a face. "Why?"

"I don't know. Something about the way Chris was looking at me."

"How in the world was he looking at you?"

"That's what I said!" Kelenna cried. "Anyway, I think that's why I'm avoiding Landon now. I mean, I basically told him he was seeing things, and then I go and spend the night at Chris' place and make out with him! Landon and I were supposed to catch up later that evening, and I completely blew him off." She looked at Chika. "In a weird way, it feels like I've cheated on him."

"Kissing isn't cheating," Chika said dismissively. "Besides, you and Landon aren't exclusive, are you?"

"I think I want to be exclusive with him," she said in a small voice. "He's the right kind of guy for me."

"Who is?"

"Landon! Chika!"

"Just checking," Chika said with a light chuckle. "I mean, just yesterday you were kissing Chris. Maybe he's the right kind of man for you now."

"Chika, please be serious."

"I am serious!" Chika laughed. She was thoroughly enjoying herself at Kelenna's expense. "How good of a kisser is he anyway?"

Kelenna grimaced at that. She could go with the truth. That he was so good that she was pretty sure she'd never really been kissed before. That he'd made her completely forget about Landon for the night. But while those things were true, it didn't matter in the grand scheme of things. Because no matter how the kiss made her feel, she wasn't going to read anything into it.

Chris wasn't interested in her, and she was interested in Landon. It was as simple as that. "It was fine," she said finally.

"Just fine?"

"It's Chris," she said with as indifferent a shrug as she could manage. "I don't think anyone would ever accuse him of being a horrible kisser."

Chika gave her a disbelieving look that let her know that her answer wasn't satisfactory in the least. "Kelenna, we still think Chris is a commitment-phobe, man-whore player, right?"

Kelenna winced. Had she really ever had such harsh views about Chris? She'd seen such a different side of him lately that she'd forgotten how she'd characterized him in the past. He'd stepped up at work, and he'd shown her how dependable and attentive he could be. Wasn't that what her mother always said? Look for the character? But she'd kept quiet too long and Chika was giving her a hard look.

"Kelenna. This is what you're going to do. You're going to put this . . . this kiss behind you." She said kiss like it was a dirty word. "You grew up with a crush on Chris, your teenage-self saw an opportunity to complete a fantasy and you took it. The end."

Kelenna nodded, even though she didn't believe for a second that her 'teenage-self' controlled the decisions she made.

"And call Dr. Landon," Chika was saying. "You can't get the exclusivity you claim you want by avoiding him."

20

The next morning, Kelenna mustered up the courage to call Landon. She'd been prepared to hear about how distant she'd been, and was ready to defend herself with excuses about work, but he didn't let her do that. He was so understanding that she almost asked if he was for real. He acted like she hadn't missed three of his calls, and hadn't replied his texts with short, clipped answers. According to him, it was refreshing that she had her own thing going on. "I understand too well how busy a person can get. I would be a hypocrite if I complained about it." Kelenna was glad that he was so mature, but deep down, she couldn't help but wonder whether his being fine with poor communication was a symptom of a larger issue. If the shoe were on the other foot, she would think that he wasn't interested in her. How could he be so sure that she was? She needn't have worried though, because a couple minutes later, he was talking about trips.

"Remember that ticket I promised you?" he asked. "My offer still stands."

"Landon, I told you I can buy my own ticket."

"And I told you that I wanted to do this. How's next week for you?" He paused as if he needed to collect his thoughts. "Kelenna, I really want us to see if this can be something. How do you feel about that?"

"I want to see too," she said softly, a smile growing on her face. Inwardly, she was excited that they were on the same page about moving forward.

She could hear his smile in his next words too. "Good. I have a clear surgery schedule next week. Come visit? Let me show you my city."

"Okay," she whispered.

Later that night, she joined The Classmates for a gathering at The Bistro. It was a hole-in-the-wall sports bar they'd found during their second year of pharmacy school. The first time they went there was to celebrate after they learned that they'd all passed a particularly hard pharmacy therapeutics exam. The drinks were cheap, the food was passably good, and there was this table right in the center, large and misshapen, that looked like it was carved from the trunk of an ancient tree. That was *their* table.

She'd conveniently planned the meet-up to coincide with the NFL playoffs party her brother was hosting at his condo for the game between the Falcons and the Packers. She told herself that it had nothing to do with switching from avoiding Landon to now avoiding Chris, that she just wanted to hang out with her friends.

Now at The Bistro, there was a sea of red all around them. Majority of the patrons for the evening had on Falcons paraphernalia, and as the night wore on, they became louder and more boisterous. The Falcons were winning, and everyone knew that this was their best chance to get to their first Super Bowl in twenty years. Kelenna and the other Georgia natives in the crew, Zoe and Sharon, were also feeling the buzz. Dev hadn't arrived yet, and Nichole was poring over the menu like she usually did, trying to find something to suit her fad diet of the moment.

"I have to eat soon," Nichole declared, looking at her watch. "I'm doing a combination of the keto diet and intermittent fasting. I don't want to have to stretch my fast tomorrow to compensate."

Just then, the restaurant erupted in cheers and all their attentions were dragged to whatever TV screen was closest to them.

"Touchdown!" Zoe yelled, and she, Sharon and Kelenna stood up to join in the celebration. The Falcons now had a fourteen-point lead, and there was only one more quarter left. They looked down at Nichole and Pete who were both playing on their phones, oblivious to the commotion in the restaurant.

"Can y'all show some respect?" Kelenna asked, narrowing her eyes down at them. "We rise up when the Falcons score in this city."

"Last time I checked, Nic and I are transplants," Pete said with a laugh. "My loyalty is to the 49ers."

"That's right, I'm from Tennessee," Nichole added. "I don't have to pay allegiance to this team."

Kelenna gasped in mock horror. "You're lucky this place is so loud and no one heard you just now. Don't get us kicked out of here!"

Pete laughed out loud. "I don't think there's a risk of that happening. Just like I don't think there's a risk of the Falcons winning the Super Bowl. Not against the Patriots."

"Ooh, good one!" Nichole gave him a high five.

"Oh, come on!" Zoe protested, planting herself back in her seat. "Look at how easily we're handling the Packers. We're not scared of the Patriots. This is our year!"

"And if it doesn't happen this year, next year will be your year," Pete countered dryly. "I swear, you guys are worse than Cowboys fans."

Kelenna didn't think any team had worse fans than the Cowboys, but she didn't say that. She was the only one left standing, and perhaps that was what gave her a better view of the entrance. She sat down slowly and looked at Zoe who was defending the fanaticism of Falcons fans like she was some kind of spokesperson for the team.

"Zoe?" Kelenna started, clearing her throat and pulling everyone's attention towards her. She lifted her chin, gesturing at the door. "Why is your boyfriend here with another girl?"

"No way!" Nichole said. "He is?"

While the other classmates started asking more questions, Kelenna looked more closely at Zoe. Her face had drained of color and she looked like she was barely holding it together.

"Nick and I are on a break," Zoe said solemnly.

"A seeing other people kind of break?" Sharon asked carefully.

"Apparently," Zoe mumbled.

"Zo," Nichole said, putting a hand on Zoe's arm. "What happened?"

Zoe shrugged. "Nick has some . . . issues to work through. He doesn't trust me."

"Since when does Nick not trust you?" Nichole demanded. "You guys have been together for over a decade!"

They had. Twelve years, to be exact. They were an odd couple, or at least Kelenna thought so. They had to have been odd in college. The popular student athlete hardly ever dated the smart girl on campus. But Zoe and Nick had managed to stick together all these years in a way that made you believe that opposites truly attract. Kelenna looked back over at him. Nick Costello always looked like he had a permanent tan, something Zoe attributed to his Italian heritage. He was tall and still had that slim but powerful build of a wide receiver. He'd been a shoo-in for the pros until injury struck during his senior year of college. It was a career ending one and he never made it to the NFL. Now her eyes traveled down to his hand and she saw how tightly he gripped the woman's behind him. She looked a little like Zoe. *A less attractive version*, Kelenna thought loyally. Their long, auburn hair and olive complexion was where the similarities ended. Zoe was much taller, as tall as Kelenna, and used makeup to enhance her features, not create them like this new girl apparently did. As Kelenna watched them look around, she hoped they wouldn't find seats and would have to leave.

"I can't believe he's here with . . ." Zoe took a deep breath and abruptly shifted her chair backwards. "Excuse me, guys. I need to go to the . . ." She darted off in the direction of The Bistro's bathroom.

Kelenna exchanged glances with Nichole and Sharon, and within seconds they were out of their chairs tailing Zoe.

The light in the bathroom was dim, which was probably a good thing because it was a rather ugly bathroom. The walls looked like they needed a good coat of paint, and some of the doors to the stalls were practically hanging off their hinges. Zoe was pulling out paper napkins from the dispenser on the wall and wiping her eyes with them.

"I'm okay, guys. I just needed a minute," Zoe said. But then she blew her nose in a way that made it clear she wasn't okay at all. Kelenna manned the door while Nichole and Sharon rushed up to her to put their arms around her.

"Talk to us, Zo," Sharon said. "What happened?"

Zoe turned to lean against the sink and sighed. "He's already moving on? I don't understand it. How can he erase twelve years in . . . twelve days?"

Kelenna let out a breath. She knew all about people moving on quickly, but she didn't know this. She and Will had been broken up for six months before his engagement. They hadn't been taking a break like Zoe thought she and Nick were.

"He was holding her hand," Zoe said. "He brought her to *my* spot! He wanted me to see!"

"Did he know you would be here tonight?" Nichole asked.

"I don't know," Zoe said exasperatedly. "He moved out, you guys. We've lived together for seven years, and he moved out just like that." She paused and two large tears fell on her cheeks as she wrung her hands together. "I don't know who I am without him."

Kelenna's eyes widened. She'd never seen Zoe like this. Zoe was their mother hen. Always put together. Always secure. But then again, she'd never known her without Nick. "Can you tell us why you were on a break?" she asked softly.

Zoe sighed again. "Remember that really wealthy professor from my school?"

"The one who you said wears Armani suits to work?" Nichole asked.

Zoe sniffed and nodded. "His name is Dr. Benjamin Fine. He kissed me last year."

Before Kelenna could say a word, Nichole let out a loud gasp. "Did you want him to?" she asked.

"No, of course not!" Zoe cried. "I stopped it the moment I could!" She went on to tell them about how Ben had invited a few of the faculty to a comedy show that he'd gotten tickets for. "Somehow everyone else backed out except for me, and we ended up going together. He told me he liked me after the show. That was when he kissed me."

"That is so inappropriate, Zoe. You work together!" Sharon said.

"Not to mention, you have a boyfriend!" Nichole added.

"He didn't know I had one," Zoe said softly.

"How did Nick find out?" Kelenna asked.

"We had a faculty Christmas party last month. When I introduced Nick to Ben, Ben apologized for coming on to me."

Nichole gasped again. "The sneaky bastard! You hadn't told Nick, had you?"

Zoe shook her head. "No. I didn't think it was a big deal. I'd stopped the kiss so I didn't think I had to say anything."

"But Nick did, didn't he?" Kelenna asked.

Zoe nodded. "It was bad, guys. Nick and I had a huge fight, and that's when he said he couldn't trust me if I could kiss another man." She sniffed once more just as the main bathroom door opened. Kelenna stepped aside to let a girl walk in. It was her. Nick's date. Kelenna almost looked down at her hand to see if it was mangled from how tightly Nick had gripped it.

"Excuse me," she said in a deep, sultry voice as she sashayed to the sink. Kelenna willed the other three women to keep quiet.

"Your sweater is lovely," Zoe said to the stranger, disobeying Kelenna's silent order.

"Oh, thank you," the woman said, making a show of straightening the large sweater. "First date. I'm pretty nervous."

Zoe smiled even though her eyes were shimmering with tears. Kelenna looked at Sharon and Nichole who were also eyeing the door, looking for the best way to get the hell out of there.

"We should go before Pete gets asked to give up The Table, Zo," Kelenna said softly.

"Don't be nervous," Zoe said, ignoring Kelenna completely. "All you have to do is be yourself. I'm sure he's a . . . a great guy." Her voice quivered on the last three words, and it immediately spurred them into action.

"All right, that's enough," Nichole said, grabbing Zoe's arm and pulling her towards the bathroom door. "Let's go."

"Wait, is she okay?" the woman asked with concern in her voice.

"She'll be fine," Kelenna said stiffly. And then because it wasn't her fault that Nick couldn't stay out of a relationship for two seconds before jumping into a new one, she sighed. "Enjoy your date."

Back at the table, Dev had finally arrived. Beside him was a petite Indian woman who looked vaguely familiar. Sharon took her seat beside Pete and leaned down to catch him up, while Nichole assisted Zoe with sitting in her chair.

"Pete said Nick is here with some other woman?" Dev asked Kelenna on the side. "How is she?"

"Not good," Kelenna replied under her breath, glancing at Zoe. She was staring, transfixed at something behind Dev. When Kelenna turned to look, she saw Nick staring back at Zoe, the woman from the bathroom beside him. From where she stood, Kelenna caught Nick's slight nod before he turned and walked out of the restaurant.

"Damn, did you just run Nick off?" Kelenna asked her.

"This is my turf," she replied, her voice significantly more steady than it had been just two minutes ago. Then she looked at Dev's date. "It's nice to see you again, Priya."

Everyone's eyes turned to the woman next to Dev. It *was* Priya from the Diwali. Kelenna wasn't surprised that Zoe had recognized her. Part of what made her such a nurturer was her ability to never forget a face, and to nearly always remember names. What was surprising though, was that the girl was here at all. Hadn't Dev said that they weren't interested in each other? She raised a questioning brow at Dev, but he wasn't looking her way. Instead, he'd placed an arm around the back of Priya's chair, and had leaned down to whisper something in her ear. When he lifted his head, he looked at each of them, almost like he was warning them to be cool. "Guys, this is Priya. Priya, these are the Classmates. Sharon is Pete's wife. And these lovely ladies are Zoe, Nichole, and Kelenna."

They all talked over themselves just to say hello to her. Dev shook his head.

"It's so nice to meet you all, truly. Dev's told me so much about you. I believe I could have guessed who was who without the introduction." Priya's large, doe eyes made her look earnest as she spoke to them, and her English accent came as a shock. Had Dev even mentioned that she was British?

"And Dev left us completely in the dark," Nichole said accusatorily.

"What?" Dev said, looking around. Then he stood up from his seat abruptly. "Where is the waiter?" he asked, his blatant change in subject causing laughter all around the table.

"The first time he did that around me, I was convinced he had gone quite mad," Priya said, joining in with a light laugh.

Kelenna grinned at her. She liked her already.

"So where are you from, Priya?" Sharon asked.

"Just outside London. My parents and brother still live in England. I moved to America to attend dental school."

Kelenna mouthed the word dentist to Dev and nodded approvingly. He responded with a smile that he tried to cover with an eye roll. "If you all are done with the inquisition, Priya and I would like to order something to eat now."

"Oh, we're not nearly done," Zoe said, clapping gleefully. "But we'll let you get some sustenance first." She waved down a waiter, and the man hopped over to their table.

The Falcons beat the Packers decisively and punched their ticket to the Super Bowl. Amid the fanfare, Kelenna listened as her friends peppered Dev and Priya with questions. She even asked one or two of her own. But as she watched Zoe pretend to be fine, she couldn't help but think about kisses. If a one-sided kiss could end a relationship like Zoe and Nick's that was practically common-law, then intentional kisses like the one she shared with Chris could definitely stop her and Landon's almost-relationship in its tracks.

Particularly when she couldn't stop thinking about it.

21

Kelenna poured herself into her work over the next week. She met with her clinical pharmacists to inform them of the goals for the year. At the top of the list was making sure antibiotics were being used properly, and getting better control of patients' blood sugars while they were hospitalized. She also put out a newsletter that provided the rest of the hospital with updates from the pharmacy department. At the same time, she was putting finishing touches to what she was now referring to as the R-O-I project. R-O-I—Reducing Opioids Initiative—was going to be the way Preston contributed to managing the opioid crisis-shortage.

Chris liked the name too. He said so in response to the email she sent telling him about it. They hadn't spoken to each other since the snow night, so she had no idea whether he pronounced ROI like it was an abbreviation or an acronym. Not that there was a wrong answer, but she did wonder. Their communication via email proved to be very efficient and productive. The first time, she had Tracy and Parker type up her vision and sent it to him. After he reviewed it, he asked for more edits. Back and forth, they made changes. Chris wanted the drugs arranged by the type of pain they could treat. "It would be easier for the doctors to order if they could just go to the section for abdominal pain, and select from the options there," he'd written. She agreed with that, but she also wanted the drugs listed by hierarchy. "There should be first-line, second-line, and last resort therapies for each type of pain," she'd replied via email. His only response to that was, "Please make *ketamine* a last resort option." She'd laughed out loud at that.

On Thursday, right after lunch, Tracy and Parker came to her door with more sheets of paper in their hands.

"We sent you emails as well," Parker said. "This is the final draft."

Kelenna collected the papers and let her eyes go over them. Everything looked good. The drugs, their doses, and how often they would need to be given were all neatly arranged in a clear order. If she could trust the ER physicians to buy into it, the ROI project would be super successful. "Guys, I think we've done it," Kelenna said with a proud smile. "Good job!" She acted like she didn't see the fist-bump her students shared with each other as they left her office.

Just then, the hospital intercom buzzed:

Code Runner, ER main entrance. Code Runner, ER main entrance. Code Runner, ER main entrance.

"What's a Code Runner?" Parker asked, popping her head back through the door.

Before Kelenna could answer, Tracy flipped up his Preston hospital badge and read from the list. "Code Runner means patient elopement. What is that?" he asked.

"It means there's a patient on the loose. Running away."

"Running away? Like, escaping the hospital?" Parker asked.

"Sure," Kelenna murmured distractedly.

"Why do they care if a patient leaves? Don't they have the right to come and go as they want?" she pressed.

Kelenna looked up then. "Not if they're psych patients who are at risk of harming themselves or other patients. Don't worry about it, security will handle it."

* * *

"Kelenna, did you hear?" Anna, the pharmacy tech burst into her office a few hours later, closely followed by Cassie. "Your cousin got stabbed!"

Kelenna sat up in alarm. "Who?"

"Tari-Douglas!" Cassie cried. "Our ER is becoming worse than a prison yard!"

Kelenna frowned. How many people had she told that cousin lie to? "He's not my—" She shook her head and cut herself off because that wasn't the point. "What do you mean he got stabbed?"

"I overheard nurses talking about it in the medication room," Anna replied. "They said some patient cut him!"

"That's why they called the Code Runner earlier!" Cassie added.

"The nurses said he stitched himself up," Anna continued. "How do you even reach over to do that?"

"What part of his body was cut?" Cassie asked. "If it was his leg, maybe he could reach down to stitch it himself?"

"I wouldn't be able to look!" Anna gasped. "All that blood!"

Kelenna tuned the pharmacy techs out as they took turns shuddering over how squeamish they would have been over a laceration. Her hands were unsteady as she pushed buttons on her cell phone and put it to her ear. She listened to the phone ring until it went to voicemail. "He's not picking up," she muttered. She dialed Chris' number again. No luck.

'Maybe he's gone home by now?" Anna offered.

"I'll check with the ER." They left her alone while she dialed the ER on her landline.

"ER, this is Jessica?"

"Hey, Jessica, this is Kelenna from the pharmacy. Is Dr. Tari-Douglas there?"

"I just got here for my shift. Hang on, I'll look."

Kelenna waited as she heard a recording about Preston Regional Hospital play through the phone. Soon, Jessica returned to the line and called her name. "Yes?" she answered.

"He's gone for the day, sweetheart. You need another doc?"

"Oh no, that's fine. Thank you."

She let out a breath after she hung up. She thought about calling Chris' cell phone a third time, but she stopped herself. She wasn't going to harass the man now when she'd been actively avoiding him all week. Just the other day they ran into each other in the hallway after one of her meetings, and he had invited her for a working lunch. She turned him down with such a lame excuse that she could tell for sure he didn't buy. He just looked at her through his new glasses like they gave him some sort of x-ray vision and he could see right through to her soul. No, she was going to call the next best person.

"What's up, sis?" came John's voice over the phone.

"Hey, John. How are you?"

"I'm good. I'm at the clinic today, you know how that goes."

"Oh, nice. Short day for you."

"Right. It feels long though. I put one of my patients on a fluid restriction when I discharged her from the hospital yesterday, and what does she do? She goes home, drinks a two-liter bottle of coke, and she's back today at the clinic in fluid overload. I love my job."

"Wow. Fun stuff," she said distractedly. She didn't know how to say that she didn't care about his non-compliant patient.

"You don't care about my non-compliant patient," he said, reading her mind. "What do you need?"

"I was just wondering. Have you heard from Chris today?"

"Yeah. Some psych patient cut him at work. I think he's at home now."

Kelenna let out a sigh of relief. If John wasn't concerned then she didn't have any reason to be.

"Are you two okay?"

"Who? Me and Chris?"

"Yes."

"Of course," she said quickly. "Why?"

"I don't know. He asked me how you were doing on Saturday at our watch party. Wouldn't tell me why. I told him you were with your friends. Now you're talking to me instead of him. Just seems like you're avoiding each other. Did he do something to piss you off?"

"Of course not. We're working on a project together and I couldn't reach him. Now that I know he's okay, everything is fine." She hoped the combination of half-truths would satisfy her brother. He could be really perceptive and she didn't want him to see too much. Heck, she wasn't sure what she didn't want him to see.

"Okay. Look, whatever this project is, cut him some slack today, all right? I can't imagine a psych patient lunging at me with a knife." Then he went off on a tangent about how she and Chris risked their lives working at Preston. As if the hospitals in Midtown or Downtown were completely free of mentally-ill and aggressive patients.

Shortly after she ended her call with John, Kelenna left her office and headed home. At least that was where she thought she was going until she reached that hill that led to her apartment complex. The same one Chris assessed was unsafe to drive on in the snow just a week ago. She closed her eyes as she released her foot from the brake and let her car continue down the road ahead.

She managed to retrace her steps to his neighborhood, and as she drove, without the distraction of the falling snow, she could see its beauty. There were rows of identical brick townhomes, lined with manicured shrubs that an HOA was probably charging an arm and a leg to maintain. The only problem was that she couldn't remember exactly where his house was. Was it the second house after the first right turn? Or the first house after the second right turn? She went with her gut and pulled her car into the empty driveway of the second house on the street. The only sign of life was an old Dodge sedan in front of the mailbox. Within minutes, she was ringing the doorbell, hoping she was at the right place. The door opened almost immediately and she came face-to-face with a young, very pretty, Hispanic woman.

22

I'm sorry," Kelenna said, smiling to put the young woman at the door at ease. "I think I have the wrong house. I'm looking for Chris?"

"Chris, *si*." The woman opened the door wider and stepped aside for Kelenna to walk in. She spotted the first vase and let out a sigh of relief.

"The house of a thousand vases," she muttered as she walked further in. She let the tips of her fingers touch the tallest one on the console table in the foyer. There was a little dust on its rim.

"Chris!" the woman screeched from behind Kelenna, startling her into almost knocking over the expensive-looking vase. When she turned a questioning glare on the woman, she managed to look sheepish and apologetic.

"Living room," she said, and took off for the nearby stairs. Who was she anyway?

"Isa?" she heard Chris' sleep-tinged voice from the living room behind her. When she whirled around, he was standing there, wearing a confused look on his face. "Kelenna?"

"Hey, Chris," she said tentatively, taking in his disheveled state. He was shirtless, and the sweatpants he wore hung low on his waist. His arms looked more powerful than she remembered. It was one thing feeling them around her last week, and quite another actually seeing them in broad daylight. And those abs. There was no way he got them only from all those marathons he ran.

"What are you doing here?" he asked as he tried to stretch his sleep away. Before he could catch her ogling his V-cut lower abs while his arms were raised, she averted her gaze.

"I heard you were attacked in the ER," she replied. "I tried to call, but you didn't pick up."

"Painkillers." He turned around and walked back into his living room. She followed him and watched him pick up a faded t-shirt from his arm chair and put it on. She was sorry to see that torso covered. "I know what you're thinking. This goes against our ROI project, and I should have taken a Tylenol, not a Percocet."

"The *R-O-I* project," she corrected, placing her purse on the coffee table. "I just knew you would call it ROI."

"What's wrong with ROI? It's one syllable. Rolls off the tongue."

"One syllable," she said with a snort. Men were so lazy. They had to simplify every little thing.

"Besides, doesn't R-O-I mean something else? Return on investment?"

"So what? ROI sounds like some . . . guy."

Chris gave her an incredulous look, then chuckled lightly. "Why are we arguing about this?"

Kelenna smiled. "I think it's what we know how to do best." She looked around her before she sat on the nearest chair. It was an antique-looking chair that seemed like it was removed from out of an 1800s ladies' drawing room. It looked out of place in the modern living room. "This wasn't here the last time," she remarked.

"Belema brought it over. Said it ties the place together. I'm convinced she buys things for herself, and when they don't work for her, she dumps them on me."

Kelenna laughed and sat on it. She moved around to test its sturdiness. "It's sturdy," she announced.

"That's because you're tiny."

"No, I'm not!" she protested, because one couldn't be five feet nine inches tall and tiny.

"Relatively," he said with a shrug and sat on that three-seater couch that Kelenna could barely look at without remembering. She swallowed and asked to see his arm. He lifted his right hand and showed off his bandaged forearm before letting it fall slowly. "I'm too drugged to move anymore. Come here."

She moved over to the couch and sat beside him, allowing her fingers to lightly hover over his arm. "How did you stitch the cut yourself?" When he raised inquiring eyes at her, she read his mind. "Small hospital. Word travels."

He grunted. "Word travels wrong. All I did was assist." He wiggled his fingers on his left hand. "Helps to be left-handed."

She nodded and placed her hand on her lap. She watched him rest against his couch and shut his eyes. "I was worried when I heard," she started in a low voice. "My co-workers barged into my office and told me that my cousin had been stabbed, and . . . and when you didn't pick up my call, I—"

Chris opened one eye to look at her. "Cousin?"

She ignored him. "Why didn't you tell me?"

He snorted. "What would you have done? Come to hold my hand?" When she gave him a pointed look, he sighed. "I was fine," he said in a gentler tone. "It was Benjamin Anderson," he said like she would know who the patient was. It was clear though, that he was a frequent flier at the hospital. "The worst thing Ben has done before today is smear feces on the wall of his room, and try to drink his urine." He glanced at her just as she tried to hide her cringe. "Too graphic?"

"God, yes."

He smirked. "I should have made sure he was properly searched. You should always ask if a psych patient has been stripped of their belongings before you enter their room. No matter how well you think you know them. And you definitely shouldn't think you can handle them alone after they pull out a knife. Lesson learned."

Kelenna held in a gasp. Her mind went to how much worse it could have been. She could just picture him fighting against a lunatic wielding a blade. Trying to wrestle the weapon out of his hand. What if the man had been stronger? What if Chris had actually been stabbed?

"He fainted at the sight of my blood," Chris said, letting out a low, mirthless laugh. "Blood was gushing out of my hand and this guy faints. But it gave us time to confiscate the knife and get me out of there." He paused and looked at her. "I'm sorry I didn't think to send you an email about it."

"Oh," she said, shifting uncomfortably on the couch. She knew his email comment was a subtle dig at her.

"You didn't think I'd notice you not replying to my texts and only sending me emails, huh?"

She glanced at him without saying a word.

"You actually signed the last one with 'best.' Who says best?"

"People say best," Kelenna said weakly. Then because he was still looking at her questioningly, she threw her hands in the air. "We got so . . . so carried away that night. I don't know what it was. The snow, maybe? Anyway, it shouldn't have happened. I guess I was just embarrassed a little."

"Mm," he said with a noncommittal nod. Without another word, he rose to his feet and headed in the direction of his kitchen. She followed him and watched him push buttons on a coffee machine plugged into an outlet in a corner wall of the kitchen.

"Isn't it a little late for coffee?" she asked.

"I'll need it if I'm going to stay awake and listen to you blame the snow for what happened last week."

She was taken aback by how his calm tone failed to match his harsh words. "What does that mean?"

"You weren't embarrassed, Kelenna," he said softly. "Not even for a second."

"You don't know what you're talking about," she said with a scoff.

"No?" He took a step towards her and stood so close that she almost leaned back. "You think you avoided me all week because you were embarrassed?"

She lifted a challenging palm. "You tell me, since you know me so well."

"Embarrassed is the wrong word." He stepped even closer. "I think you're a few things. Doubtful. Scared." He raised his left hand to palm her cheek, and when he did that, her mouth parted involuntarily and a small gasp escaped. She knew he heard it because his eyes flickered down to her lips. "And your brain has probably gone into overdrive thinking about it."

"Thinking about what?" she asked. She wished he would remove his hand from her face so she could process words better.

"You and me."

"I don't think about you that way," she whispered.

He gave her a conceding nod. "Maybe not before last week. But I was there, remember?" He caressed her cheek and pulled her closer with his injured arm. She didn't have anywhere to put her hands so she left them in between their bodies, just hovering over his chest. "If you weren't thinking about me before then, you're thinking about me now."

"You're so full of yourself," she said, shrugging herself out from his arms. Once she did, she could think clearly again. "You think everyone is into you. Get over yourself. So I responded to your kiss? Big deal. I'm sure I'm not the first person you've ever had chemistry with. It was probably just latent curiosity from when I was in high school." She was babbling now, but she couldn't stop. "I admit it. I've been curious about what it would be like to kiss Christian Tari-Douglas for a long time, and it was everything I thought it would be. Now my curiosity is satisfied and we can both move on."

He stared at her with a knowing look on his face. "How long did it take you to memorize that?" he asked.

She glowered at him and walked out of the kitchen. "I came here to see how you were doing, and now that I see you're fine, I'm leaving," she called out over her shoulder.

"Got it," he said, not missing a beat. "I'll be on the lookout for your next email."

She rolled her eyes and went to the handbag she'd placed on the center coffee table. She knew she wasn't leaving when her hand grasped its handle. She stared at the frayed straps for a moment before she sighed and plonked down on the couch. "I had a really big crush on you back in high school," she said. It was the first time she'd ever said those words out loud in his vicinity. "Did you know?"

"I could tell," was all he said.

She chuckled at that. "You were all I could think of that year. I don't think you knew I existed."

"I knew you existed." He went to sit beside her. "You were also fourteen."

She glanced at him thoughtfully. "And after?"

Chris let out a long breath. "You became this beautiful enigma." He picked up her hand and intertwined her fingers with his. He lifted their hands to his lips and planted a kiss on the back of it. "So beautiful." Another kiss. "So untouchable." Kiss. "You think I'm so sure about myself with women, but that's not true. I've never been sure about you. Not until last week." When she opened her mouth to speak, he put a finger on her lips. "And it's not about chemistry. Although I should kiss you again to make you respect chemistry a little bit more." That finger slid off her lips and she closed her eyes as she felt him cup her cheek again. This time in a strange caress, almost like he was feeling for something. When he exerted a little pressure with his fingers at the base of her neck, her eyes flew open to look at him. He was totally trying to find her carotid artery. In a weird, sensual way, he was checking her pulse. "It's wild," he murmured.

"My heart is beating to keep me alive," she said dismissively. "It means nothing." But then her heart betrayed her and started beating even faster.

"Kelenna," he said tenderly.

"Don't say my name like that," she whispered, melting just a little. Like earlier, she couldn't think when he was surrounding her like this.

"No? How about a nickname? Sugar?"

She laughed and shook her head mutely.

"Pumpkin?" he asked, his lips twitching just a little.

She snorted at the one.

He looked at her thoughtfully for a second. Like he was trying to read her. "Sweetheart," he said once. And her traitorous pulse went into overdrive beneath his fingers. She felt his fingers push against her artery just a little harder, continuing his experiment. "Sweet. Heart," he repeated.

She could hear her own heart pounding in her ears. How was she to know that she really liked the way he called her sweetheart? It was such an overused term of endearment in the South, heck, half the people at work called her sweetheart, and yet when he said it, it sounded unique. She whispered his name then, wondering again how he could make her feel so much. In response, he leaned over her and covered her lips with his, running the fingers of his injured hand along her thigh. How she'd missed that mouth! Her hands were already cradling his face and deepening the kiss when she heard a shrill voice call out his name. In the next second, Kelenna had disconnected from him and was sitting so primly an entire cushion away from him.

She scowled when she caught him trying to stifle a laugh. "Your friend wants you."

"Come with me." He stood up and stretched out a hand to her. "I have to pay Isa."

"Pay her?" she asked stupidly, placing her palm in his and allowing him to pull her up.

"She's my cleaner."

"Oh."

Kelenna followed him to the foyer but remained in the corner while he chatted with Isa. Now that she was away from him, and she could think clearly, her mind went into overdrive, just like he predicted it would. She wondered how long he'd felt like this about her. It couldn't have been too long since he had a girlfriend just the other day. Plus, Chika was right. He was a player and a heartbreaker. It would be irresponsible of her to join his string of women just because she enjoyed his kisses.

"I leave you for two seconds and you start thinking again."

She snapped out of her thoughts at the sound of his voice. Isa was gone, and Chris was just standing there, staring at her. "You know me. Always thinking."

He didn't respond to that, instead he smiled slowly and took a step closer to her. She took a step back, right into the wall behind her. She cursed her unfamiliarity with his house.

"Hey, Kelenna," he said softly, cupping her cheek. "Don't be nervous." His hand drifted down to her neck as he planted a lingering kiss on her forehead. "It's just me."

She closed her eyes against the onslaught of feelings. That was the problem. It wasn't *just* him. He was too important to her family for them to risk it. If they crossed that line and it didn't work, would their friendship recover? She could hardly think as his hand slid further down to her waist while the other tilted her chin. When he kissed her sweetly, gently, she wanted to cry. She sank into it for only a few moments before breaking apart from him. "Chris, we can't."

He looked down at her, and it was only when he swiped at her cheek that she realized there were tears actually coming out of her eyes. She sighed, annoyed that she couldn't stop herself. And since Chris was hell-bent on not giving her space, she had no choice but to think out loud.

"What about John?"

"John?"

"How many Johns do you know?"

Chris smiled at that. "What about him?"

"He's your best friend. I'm his sister. Isn't there some kind of bro code?"

He looked at her like that was the most ridiculous thing he'd ever heard. Either that or he'd never heard the term 'bro code' in his life. "I'm sure John will be fine."

"Really? He won't get angry at you for trying to do anything with his little sister?"

"You've been watching too many movies," he scoffed. "Come on, we're adults. Besides I've known you both the exact same length of time."

"Yes, but you're closer to him," she argued.

"I'm closer to you right now!" he protested, gesturing at their proximity.

The idea that he was closer to her than he was to John because they happened to be in the same room at the moment was so comical that she wanted to laugh out loud.

"Go on," he said knowingly. "There's more, isn't there?"

"What about Lara?" she blurted out.

"Who?"

"Lara, Zara, Tara, whatever. The light-skinned girl with the hair." She knew exactly what her name was, but she was determined not to commit it to memory.

"*Nara.*" He smiled. "She's just a friend. We tried the dating thing a long time ago, it didn't work."

Kelenna snorted and walked back to the living room. She walked up to the vase by the television. It was so tall and looked like it was made of brass. It was beautiful. "The last time someone said that to me, they got engaged to the woman six months after we broke up."

"The uppity lawyer?" he called from behind her, his tone sounding incredulous. "You think I'm like *him*?"

"I didn't say that," she replied, moving on to a smaller vase in the corner by the couch. This one was blue and so shiny that she could almost see her reflection in it. "You could do worse than being compared to Will, you know. At least he's not afraid of commitment."

He frowned. "I'm not afraid of commitment."

She waved her hand dismissively and settled back on the couch. "All the hundreds of women you've dated would disagree."

He came to sit beside her then, barely giving her an inch of space. The length of their bodies touched, and she could feel him move every time he took a breath. "Kelenna, I've never claimed to be a monk, but that doesn't mean I'm afraid of commitment. You're the one who never dates. Maybe *you're* afraid of commitment."

"I don't *never* date! And that's not the same thing at all!"

He looked like he was going to debate that point further, but then thought the better of it. "Look, I've had my share of relationships." When she raised a brow at him, he rolled his eyes. "Fine, I've had many peoples' fair share of relationships. Some were short, some were long, none of them lasted. But I don't regret any of them."

"Really? Not even Patricia from when you were a senior in high school? She was really mean."

He caught her teasing glint, and they shared a smile. "Learned not to date mean girls."

"And Latasha, from your med school class? Sydney? Brianna?"

He let out a dramatic sigh. "Of all the girls to fall for, I fall for someone who's known me so long."

"You're falling for me?" she asked slowly, her eyes wide.

"What the hell do you think we've been talking about?"

She opened her mouth and closed it as words escaped her.

"Use your words," he prompted, bumping her lightly with his hip.

"No wonder you've dated a hundred girls. If you fall for everyone you kiss, that's a lot of women."

He chuckled briefly at her joke. "I want to date you, Kelenna. You. Not a hundred other girls. And if my track record makes you think I'm not serious, I'll prove it right now."

"How?" she asked curiously.

"I'll call John and I'll ask him for his permission right now. We'll break the bro code and—"

She didn't hear the rest of his sentence because she burst into laughter. A minute ago, he didn't know what bro code was, and now he was going to try to use it to prove a point. She sighed deeply and leaned against his shoulder. Unlike that night a week ago, he didn't put his arm around her. "A bro code isn't something you break. At least not that way. I don't need you to ask John for permission to ask me out," she said in a low voice.

"No?" His voice matched hers.

"No."

"What do you need, sweetheart?" He said this against her temple. It felt like a kiss, the way his lips brushed against her skin. Maybe even a promise. Like he would do whatever she needed him to do.

"I don't know," she whispered.

She felt him sigh beside her. Saw his chest rise and fall. "There's something here, isn't there?" he asked, sounding thoughtful. Almost hopeful.

She paused for a moment before she nodded slowly. She didn't know exactly what that something was, but she couldn't deny it. There *was* something. He rewarded her honesty with a lingering kiss on her forehead. That was when she remembered. Throughout the evening, he hadn't even crossed her mind once. She was going to see Landon tomorrow. The man she was hoping to take things to the next level with. She raised up and looked at Chris. He was doing that thing where he tried to read her.

"I get it," he said finally. "You need time for your brain to catch up. You've always been so rational. Everything has to add up for you."

She shook her head slowly. "It's not that. I'm flying out to Baltimore tomorrow to see Landon." She wrung her hands together. "We've been . . . talking, and things have been moving forward."

Chris didn't say a word. If she hadn't felt him stiffen beside her, she would have thought he hadn't heard her. Was he upset? Surely, he wasn't too surprised by the news. He was there when Landon's mother played matchmaker with her and Landon, and he was there, along with the three hundred other fundraiser attendees, for their first date.

"Say something," she whispered.

He snorted. "What do you see in that guy anyway? He's an old, overeducated, Dr. Carson wannabe, do-gooder."

She smiled at his attempt to make Landon's attributes sound like faults. "Aren't we all overeducated?" She sighed. "I thought you liked him."

"So did I. Now, I don't think I can stand the guy."

She pursed her lips at that. "Well, he likes me."

"It doesn't take too much to like you, Kelenna," he said, failing to mask the derision in his voice. "He doesn't need an award for it. He gets enough of those apparently."

Kelenna sighed once more. When she walked into Chris' townhome that evening, she was content with her almost-relationship with Landon, and she had convinced herself that she felt nothing more for Chris than concern for an injured friend. Now, she wasn't sure at all. But she knew she wouldn't find the answers sitting beside Chris, clouded by all the feelings he stirred within her. Feelings were great, special even, but they weren't the be-all and end-all of a good match. If she wanted to truly know, she had to go to Baltimore.

As if he heard the resolution she made in her mind, he blew out a breath. "So Baltimore, huh?"

"Yeah," she said softly.

Somehow, their hands found each other of their own volition. It was as if they were sneaking around in the dark, not wanting anyone to see. And in the privacy of the crevice between their thighs, their fingers interlaced and held on.

23

The city of Atlanta—no, the entire state of Georgia—was awash with hysteria in the week leading up to the Super Bowl. In what would be their first appearance at the championship game in over twenty years, Atlanta was gearing up to face the Patriots, and it was being touted as the matchup of the decade.

John was probably the most hysterical fan of them all. "We're going into the game as the favorites. We're not the underdogs here," he said a number of times. "And that's hard to be against the Patriots." He even told their mother, who was inexplicably a Patriots fan, that her support for the team would be negative energy, and that he would be skipping Wednesday night dinner to avoid it.

For Kelenna, it was crunch time of a different kind. When work resumed on Monday, she went right into Pat's office, and showed her the finished product of the R-O-I project.

"Wow. This is remarkable," Pat said. "And crazy. Twenty years ago, everyone got *prochlorperazine* for nausea. No one uses it now."

"That's the point, Pat." She sat on one of the chairs across from her boss. "We're going to reduce opioid use by providing alternatives. And isn't it crazy that we don't have to go too far to find these things? We just have to start using drugs that have been right under our noses. There are entire hospital systems that have already rolled out programs using medications just like this in their ERs. We're playing catch-up here."

"I love it," Pat said, nodding her head firmly. "It's going to help with the opioid shortage and the epidemic if we can get everyone on board. You said Dr. Tari-Douglas has seen this, and is satisfied with it?"

"Yes, we worked together on this."

"Good. Pain management committee meets on Wednesday, correct?"

"Already have it on the agenda."

"Great. Way to step up for our patients, Kelenna. Good job."

Kelenna blushed under Pat's praise as she stood to leave. "Thank you."

"Is this *ketamine* for abdominal pain I see here?" Pat called out.

"We researched it thoroughly," Kelenna said, immediately defensive. "It's legitimate, I promise."

"Hmm," she muttered. "You better keep Tari-Douglas in the loop, then. You may need his help in defending this to the pain team."

If only Pat knew how much time Chris was spending in a thought loop in Kelenna's head. Since she left his house last Thursday (which coincidentally, was the start of her inability to stop thinking about him), they'd switched from her avoiding him to *him* avoiding *her*. Or at least, that was what it felt like. His silent treatment was worse. At least she sent emails during hers. All she got was radio silence. He even left her on read when she texted him to ask him if he would be available to attend the pain management meeting with her. That was Tuesday night, and that was when she broke down and called Chika.

"Chika, I think I miss him."

"Well, hello to you too!"

"Hi," she replied with a sigh. "What should I do?"

"Why do I have the feeling that this person you think you miss is someone other than the talented doctor who cuts into people's brains?"

"Because he is someone other than the talented doctor who cuts into people's brains?" Kelenna said in a small voice.

"Damn it, Chris!" Chika cursed. "Tell me everything."

It took Kelenna two minutes to recount the events of last Thursday. She was surprised Chika let her finish her story without a single interruption.

"I'll be damned. It's the oldest, most chivalrous trick in the book."

"What is?"

"Chris is totally testing out the butterfly theory."

"Butterfly theory? Do you mean butterfly effect?"

"No, not math. I mean the butterfly theory. You know, like the Mariah Carey song."

Kelenna looked heavenward. "What do you mean?"

"Hear me out," Chika began, sounding way too excited to share what Kelenna was certain she'd made up on the spot. "Anyone who's ever been in love with a clueless person has had to do this at some point or the other. Let them go. If they come back, they are meant to be yours. If they don't . . ." she trailed off.

Kelenna frowned. She didn't know what to address first. The fact that Chika had just called her clueless, or that she had implied that Chris was in love with her? She shook her head and tried to wrap her mind around Chika's logic. "So he let me go to Baltimore, to another man, cut off contact with me for three days, hoping that I would return to him if the feelings are real?"

"Yes, butterfly! And I have to say, girl, it's clearly working. You spent an entire weekend with Dr. Landon and you haven't said a word about it. How *is* our hot doctor? If I wasn't clear before, I'm on Team Landon in this love triangle. How Chris inserted himself into this is beyond me."

"Nobody's in love with anyone! I just . . ." It was her turn to trail off.

"You just what?"

She groaned in response. "You have to understand, Landon was the perfect host."

She told Chika about how he'd sent a car to pick her up from the airport (who called cars anymore?). He lived in Baltimore, but they spent most of the weekend in D.C. where he took her to see all the sights. They walked around famous monuments and in and out of museums until she was sure she'd clocked ten thousand steps on her smart watch. On Saturday night, they dressed up and went to a really fancy restaurant on The Wharf. It was the kind where there were no prices listed on the menu, because if you had to ask you couldn't afford to eat there. The food was so good that she had to physically stop herself from ordering an entire second meal.

"I'm waiting to hear about the bad part of the weekend." She could almost hear Chika tapping her foot impatiently.

"There was no bad part! He was the perfect gentleman. I just—" she cut herself off with a sigh, trying to find the most accurate way to relay her thoughts. "I couldn't *see* him."

"What do you mean you couldn't see him?"

"Just that. I couldn't. All I could think about was Chris," she admitted. And once she did, she couldn't stop. "I wanted to see him, talk to him, be around him. I almost called Landon Chris. Twice!" She paused and sighed again. "Landon was great, but I couldn't see him. Chris was there the entire time."

When Chika didn't say a word for what felt like an eternity, Kelenna called out her name.

"I'm still here. What did Landon say when you told him this?"

Kelenna scoffed. "I could hardly tell him I was thinking about another man the entire weekend, could I?"

He'd called a car to take them to the airport. "Circle around the terminal," he instructed the driver. Then he picked up the handle of her suitcase and dragged it on its wheels as he walked her into the airport, right up to the security line. He took her hand and pulled her in for a hug which she returned as warmly as she could.

"I had a great time," she whispered.

He pulled back from her. "Kelenna, when you get to be my age, doing what I do, you've seen it all. The gold diggers, social climbers, status-seekers. When you come across someone who isn't moved by everything you've done

. . . who is real, you want to hold on to it. You're just the kind of girl I want. I think we can do big things together. What do you say?"

"That's a hell of a lot better than Chris tricking you into even thinking about him," Chika snapped after Kelenna was done. "Please tell me you told him yes!"

"I couldn't! How different would I be from the other girls he's dated who were with him for what he could do for them? I wasn't fully committed to him in the moment, and I couldn't lie about it."

"Damn it, Chris!" she heard Chika say through gritted teeth.

"I told Landon that I wanted to think about it without the amazing weekend clouding everything."

"But your mind wasn't clouded at all, was it?"

"No, but what else could I say? He'd already dropped hints about all the great hospitals I could work at in Baltimore and all the connections he had! I couldn't disappoint him."

"A man with a plan," Chika said with a sigh. "He's already thinking ahead. He's not giving you the silent treatment like some twelve-year-old."

"You called it chivalrous five minutes ago!"

Chika mumbled that there was no way to know for sure. "What else did Dr. Landon do?"

He'd kissed her then. It was a pleasant kiss; all his kisses were. But they didn't overwhelm her like Chris' did. They didn't surround her and make her forget. When she told Chika this, her friend groaned.

"Chris is just a good kisser, Kelenna! It means nothing! You said so yourself!"

"I know what I said," she said softly.

"He's going to win, isn't he? He's going to win because you don't want to leave Georgia, and because he kisses so well."

Kelenna wanted to say that it wasn't a game, and that there wasn't going to be winners or losers, but she didn't. Something about what Chika said bothered her. It reminded her about six months ago, the exact moment after she'd learned of a certain engagement. She'd felt like a loser then, but had she really lost? There was only one person who could shed light on that feeling. That night at the Westin with Dev, she dodged having a conversation about it, but maybe she was ready now.

"I have to go," she told Chika.

"Don't do anything crazy!" Chika warned as she hung up.

Before she lost her nerve, she found the right number and dialed it.

"Perry," came the response after the second ring.

"Why did you send me a save-the-date to your wedding?" she blurted out.

That was not what she'd planned to say. She'd planned to say hello first, then apologize for calling him at ten o'clock on a Tuesday. And then, she would have figured out a way to bring up his engagement. Subtly. His long pause told her that she should have gone with her original plan. She could practically see him shifting her question in his mind, wondering if he should even answer.

Before she could take it back, his voice came through the line. "To be honest, Kelenna, I didn't even realize you'd gotten it until you texted me to say congratulations. I kicked myself when I saw how careless I'd been, sending out a save-the-date without double-checking my email list."

An accident, she thought. She didn't know if she was glad that he'd sent it to her, or if she would have preferred to not know about it. In that moment, her mind's eye conjured a picture of herself running into him and Amara St. John at Lenox mall, pushing twin babies in a double stroller ahead of them. No, thanks. She was definitely glad that she wouldn't be shocked if that visual ever came to fruition. His answer emboldened her, and she took a deep breath as she prepared her next question. She didn't even care if he was working late, or if Amara St. John was in his bed next to him. "Did you . . . was she in the picture while we were . . .?"

"You're asking if I cheated on you?" Will clarified.

"It was so quick," she said lamely.

"Not once," Will said emphatically. "She wasn't in the picture while I was with you. No one else was in the picture while I was with you."

She believed him. On the night she received the save-the-date, Chika planted that particular theory in her head. Kelenna told her then that Will had a faithful streak a mile long when he was in a relationship, but when he was out of it, anything was fair game. Still, she wondered. "How was it so easy for you to move on?"

She heard Will's sigh then. "There really isn't any way for me to say this without sounding like a stuck-up ass, so here goes. 'Mara and I had history. We'd almost always been *it* for each other. There was a period of time when I thought she wouldn't be *it* anymore, and that was when I was with you."

An audible gasp escaped her lips. He most likely heard it, but she didn't care. He'd called Amara St. John *it*, and then mentioned her in the same sentence. *It* had a much stronger connotation than *'The One.'* It meant something deeper than a soulmate. *It* was final. She cleared her throat, and even though he couldn't see her, she shut her eyes against the whininess of her next question. "Did you ever love me?"

"Kelenna, I knew I could love you. I think a part of me actually did. But there was this other part that kept telling me to hold off. Because I was never sure if you could love me back, or if you would just go along with me. I was never sure if I was seeing the real you."

Her eyes flew open. He didn't think she'd been real with him? "You never told me that," she said softly.

"Told you what?"

"I didn't know that you doubted how I felt about you. I would have worked on being more open. Will, I was this close to being in love with you. I was right there. If you'd said the words, it would have validated my feelings."

"That's my point Kelenna, I didn't want to be a validator. I didn't want to dictate the pace every time and—"

"But you set the pace for our entire relationship!" she said, cutting him off. "All of a sudden you didn't want to do it anymore? How was I supposed to know?"

"God, there's really no good way to say this," he mumbled.

"Can you try? Please?" She was desperate. She felt like she was so close to hearing what she needed to hear, even if she didn't know what it was. Besides, he'd always been able to explain anything. It was part of what made him a great lawyer.

"You know, I hate that society makes it look like we men hold all the cards when it comes to love, marriage and settling down. We have to be ready before we can commit, and it may not matter if we meet the most spectacular woman." He let out another sigh. She didn't think she'd ever heard him sigh so much. "'Mara isn't easy. She never was. But she gives as good as she gets. She can hang with me. She lets me see *her*."

Kelenna let out a reflective snort. Everything he just said implied that she was the opposite of Amara. But could he blame her? Did he not realize what a force he was? He accused her of going along with him, but she'd had no choice. He was like a strong tide, and to keep up with him, you had two options: either let the current carry you along, or get left behind. He *had* dictated everything they'd done, even down to their break-up. Oh, she'd rationalized that it had been mutual, but she knew she would have been content for them to carry on with their relationship if he'd been content as well.

As if he could hear her thoughts, he cleared his throat. "I didn't want you to want us because I wanted it. I wanted you to want us because *you* wanted it."

Suddenly, a light bulb went off in her head. She was assertive by nature, or at least she thought she was. She asserted herself at work, and with her friends and family. She knew what she liked and what she didn't, and she let people know it. Why had she not done that with Will? Suddenly, John's words from over a year ago floated through her mind.

You're not you around him.

Well.

"It wasn't easy being with you," she admitted. "I think you intimidated me."

"That first day in that woman's office, I didn't think I could intimidate the girl I saw. You were feisty as hell and I wanted some of that fire. But it burned out, and I'm not sure why. Hell, I saw more of it that day when Dev had his work problem than I did the entire year we were together. Whoever doesn't make you hide that fire is the right person for you."

It was in that precise moment that she truly understood what he was telling her. She'd crowned him as *'The One Who Got Away,'* but that wasn't who he was. They hadn't really . . . fit. Not if he didn't really know her, and certainly not if she'd subconsciously hidden who she was with him.

"I'm sorry for calling you so late," she said sheepishly.

"Now she tells me."

She burst out in laughter then. On the day she got the save-the-date, she didn't imagine she would ever be able to laugh at anything Will Perry said. Now she felt like maybe they could be friends. Or maybe amicable acquaintances. Plus, she got what she wanted. Clarity. "I really do wish you and Amara well. I hope you're truly what the other needs."

"Thank you, Kelenna," he said in a hushed tone.

"Goodbye, Will."

* * *

At 2 p.m. the next day, Kelenna was seated at the conference table in Meeting Room B for the pain management meeting. Also around the table were Dr. Schwartz, the CMO, Dr. Montgomery from general surgery, several of the nurse directors, and Bertha from quality. Kelenna brought her students, Tracy and Parker, and made them sit at the table beside her. She was excited for them to experience the satisfaction of seeing their hard work come to life.

She listened half-heartedly as the nurse leaders spent the first fifteen minutes describing their use of unconventional methods like music, dogs, and essential oils to help alleviate patients' pain. She was happy that they were making efforts to tackle the epidemic from a different angle, but she was too distracted by the last-minute adjustments she was making in her head, and the absence of her co-lead on the project. Was Chris really not going to show up?

They went down each agenda item, and soon it was her turn to speak. Gina, the committee lead, stepped aside from the podium to let Kelenna control the slides that she had prepared for the meeting. She spared one more glance at the door, willing it to open. It would be right on par with his usual behavior. He was always running behind for meetings. The door didn't open.

"I'm excited to share this project that Dr. Tari-Douglas and I have been working on," Kelenna began. "Before I start, I want to say thanks to my students over there. They pretty much put all of this together." She paused and smiled proudly as Tracy and Parker shyly waved away the acknowledgments from everyone around the table. When the noise died down, she continued. "We did this in light of what happened in our ER this past December, and the opioid crisis in general." She knew she had their attention then. Ashleigh was still on everyone's minds. "Dr. Tari-Douglas and I wanted to create order sets that would force the ER doctors to provide alternatives to opioids. This is what we've been missing in our ER all along. We've asked the doctors to cut back on opioid use, and told them to use alternatives, but for the first time, we're going to be intentional. We've created a list of several drugs, and have categorized them by what kind of pain they're suitable for treating. You'll recognize some of them, and wonder if they're appropriate, but what I want you to understand is that they're all evidence-based, effective, and most importantly, non-opioids."

"Chris and I talked about this on Monday," Dr. Schwartz said. "He talked about trigger point *lidocaine* injections for headaches, *ketorolac* for kidney stones, and *ketamine* for abdominal pain. This is very important for Preston, and I'm glad to see it taking off."

"He wanted to be here," Sarah, the ER nurse director added. "He just texted his apologies. He is seeing patients today."

Kelenna felt like a weight was lifted off her chest. She felt so light that she almost laughed out loud. She realized then that she must have considered his absence to be an extension of his silence. The silence that confused and frustrated her. Hearing that he'd talked up their project to the CMO, and that he would have been present at the meeting if he could, made her feel good. He was thinking about her.

The rest of her presentation went without a hitch. Even Dr. Montgomery, known for being an ornery and disagreeable surgeon, gave positive comments, albeit in a backhanded way.

"I don't know which is crazier, using music to treat pain or giving *ketamine* for abdominal pain, but I hope you're working on something similar on the inpatient side. Pain isn't limited to the ER, you know."

"Absolutely," Dr. Schwartz put in. "I'm sure Kelenna will come up with something similar for the inpatients, once we've got the ER in motion."

"Of course," Kelenna replied with a smile. She knew a mandate when she heard one. Dr. Schwartz wasn't asking her, he was telling her. And she loved it.

After the meeting was adjourned, she walked back to her office with Tracy and Parker, barely listening to their excited chatter. They were proud of themselves, and rightly so, but she had other things on her mind. She gave them the rest of the afternoon off and sat at her desk to begin working on the next steps for the R-O-I project. There were emails to be sent, and education materials to be developed. She was working for an hour when her landline rang. She picked up the phone with record speed when she read the caller ID and saw it was from the ER.

"Hello?" she said breathlessly, and probably a little too hopefully.

"This is Dr. Ogden from the ER. This is the pharmacy, right?"

"Hi! Yes!" she replied, a little flustered at having neglected to answer the phone in a more professional manner. "How can I help you?"

"I need help ordering a *mannitol* drip for a patient we'll be transferring out soon."

"Sure. Go ahead and give me the patient's name, please."

A minute later, she was off the phone and letting out a sigh. She told herself to get a grip as she returned to her work, but she soon began to feel restless. Who was she kidding? She really only wanted to do one thing. See one person. The feeling persisted until she was almost bursting with it. When she couldn't take it anymore, she popped up from her chair and left the department.

Her feet led her straight to the ER. It was going through its early evening busyness with a lot of staff walking purposefully, responding to something or the other. There was an EMS team throwing their things onto a gurney in front of a trauma room, as if they had just dropped a patient off. In the doctors' dictation area, there were a few people working at the computers. She walked around to the nurses' station and saw a sea of blue scrubs. Nurses were talking to each other while they worked. There were forty ER beds at Preston, and he could be busy at any one of them. She felt like an idiot for coming all the way up there just to see him, as if she were in a *Grey's Anatomy* episode. How dramatic of her. She was about to head back to her office when she heard her name called from behind her.

"Pharmacy!"

Well, close enough.

She swiveled around to see a tall nurse trying to get her attention at the entrance of one of the rooms in the far corner.

"I'm glad you're here," he said when she got to him. "This bag won't scan." He handed a bag of fluid to her. "Y'all just sent it and I'm trying to hurry and start it before we transfer the patient out."

She looked down at the bag. It was the *mannitol* for the patient she'd just talked to Dr. Ogden about. She couldn't believe it hadn't been started already. *Mannitol* was used to reduce swelling in the brain, so time was definitely of the essence. After inspecting it for an additional second, and determining that it was properly labeled, she handed it back to him and pointed at the computer screen. "Go ahead and show me what you were doing."

She watched him scan the label on the bag, but the computer wanted more than that from him. It was asking him to scan a filter as well.

"Okay, now scan your filter."

He looked confused. "Y'all didn't send me any filter."

"That's why it's not working. It's stopping you from going forward because you don't have a filter," she admonished lightly. *Mannitol* was notorious for forming crystal-like complexes that looked like broken glass, especially in cold temperatures. "If you infuse *mannitol* and try to send the patient out in this weather, it could crystallize in their veins and do some real damage."

When he was still standing there almost in shock, she gestured for him to leave. "Well, go get one from the medication room! It's beside the ADM."

He ran out so fast that she shook her head. At least her trip to the ER wasn't a wasted one.

"You're bossing my people around now?"

She spun around to see Chris behind her. He was just standing there, wearing his glasses and his signature black scrubs, sans white coat. She didn't think she'd ever seen a better looking person. She couldn't stop the smile that started slowly on her face.

"I wasn't bossing him around, I was helping him."

Chris narrowed his eyes. "It sounded like you were shouting at Mike."

Kelenna covered her laugh with a snort and looked up at him. "I just saved that patient's veins. Mike will appreciate me yelling at him."

Chris looked impressed and nodded. "In that case, yell away."

She grinned at him. She was really so happy to see him, it took all she had to not throw her arms around him. Instead, she cleared her throat and changed the subject. "They really liked the R-O-I project at the meeting today."

"ROI," he corrected with a grin of his own, and laughed when she shook her head in a gentle reprimand. "I heard. Sarah said you killed it. Wish I could have been there."

She nodded, agreeing with him. She wished he had been there too. They stared at each other in that corner of the bustling ER for a moment, not saying a word, just acknowledging another moment between them. This time she wasn't uncertain about what she saw in his eyes.

"Did you know that you look at me funny?" she blurted out softly.

He arched a brow, probably thrown off by a second change in subject. "Do I?"

"Yeah. Landon said so after the gala. He thought there was something between us because of how you looked at me."

"Did he now? Smart man." He chuckled, then sobered up immediately, looking down at his feet, then back up at her. "How was Baltimore?"

She exhaled. "It was . . . eye-opening."

He nodded knowingly. "Eye-opening enough for us to see each other tonight?"

"Yes."

He nodded again. That tender smile was back. She cocked her head slightly, and sighed as she looked directly into his eyes. Unwaveringly. "I think I can sort of see it."

"See what?"

"The way you look at me," she said, her voice taking on a tone of wonder. "You look at me like . . . like I'm the person you want to see the most."

"Well." He gave her a lazy grin, taking a tiny step towards her. So tiny that she would have missed it if she hadn't been hyperaware of his every movement. "At least you're looking at me now."

24

The weather on Super Bowl Sunday was simply perfect, especially for early February. It was dry, sunny, and the only chill in the air was the nervous energy coming off all the Falcons fans in the city. Kelenna felt it all around her. From church, where the entire congregation was decked out in red and black, and the pastor said a prayer for the team, to the grocery store, where she stopped to buy items for John's Super Bowl party. She couldn't keep track of how many times she heard people greet each other with, "*Rise up*," or the number of conversations she overheard about the game. By the time she got to her brother's condo, her own nerves were shot. Although in her case, they were shot for reasons other than the big game. She looked down at the hand that had been intertwined with hers for the last twenty minutes, now resting on the console in between them.

"It feels like a weird '*meeting the parents*' moment," she said as they sat in the parked Mercedes.

Two people had never moved as fast as she and Chris had these last few days. If she was on the outside looking in, she would have advised herself to slow down, to not commit herself too quickly. But as one half of the duo, she was all in. Wednesday in the ER had been the turning point, and she hadn't looked back. It was crazy how after you made a decision such as the one they made, you always wanted to be around the person. They spent every waking, non-working hour—and probably part of what should have been their sleeping hours—together. She learned things about herself that she hadn't considered. For instance, she knew that Chris was tactile and attentive at baseline. Whether it was with his hands, his voice, or his eyes, it was second nature for him to try to put people at ease. But she had no clue that being the object of that attention would give her such a heady feeling, one that she would crave when it wasn't there. Perhaps that was why she was nervous about bringing other people into their space. Those three days had been precious to her, and she would have loved more than anything to extend them. But Chris did not agree.

"I already have to keep away from you at work," he said the night she suggested it. "I would prefer not to do it in my personal life."

She pursed her lips in frustration because the comment, while sweet, did not help matters. He kissed her and told her to stop worrying about what others would think.

"Besides," he said, "I find it hard to believe that no one in your family has ever thought about the possibility of you and me. Especially your mother."

"Maybe she doesn't think you're good enough for her precious daughter," she teased.

"Nah, your mother loves me," he replied dismissively, not taking the bait.

"That's because you suck up to her and speak Igbo to her every chance you get," she retorted in mock disgust.

He grinned at that. "It's good for my practice. You're welcome to speak Kalabari to my father if you like."

"And when would I have learned the language? When I can barely speak mine?"

He kissed her lightly on her forehead then. "I'll teach you."

She blushed. She probably blushed more in those three days than she ever did before.

"Something doesn't add up though," he continued. "Especially when you factor in your age, and the fact that my mother has brought your name up once a month since I finished residency."

"Really?" She was genuinely shocked by that admission. His mother and hers had grown up together, and gone to the same finishing school in Nigeria. How could his be overly vocal, while her mother was deathly quiet about the two of them? Something definitely didn't add up, but she couldn't put her finger on it. "You didn't listen to her?"

"Oh, I did. I told her you wouldn't give me the time of day." He grinned at her. "I was wrong, wasn't I?"

"Mhmm." She smiled back at him. But then his comment about her age dawned on her, and she slapped his chest in mock anger. "Hey, what did you mean about my age? You're much older than I am, you know!"

He pulled her back to him. "You're a woman. Why hasn't your mother been bugging you to get married all this while?"

She leaned away from him once more and sent him as ferocious a glare as she could manage. "My mother is one of the most progressive women of her generation! For goodness' sake, she still goes by her maiden name professionally. That was unheard of thirty years ago! Maybe she doesn't think I need to be married to be fulfilled." She could hear her mother's voice chiding her for that little stretch of the truth.

Chris, to his credit, didn't buy it for a second. "No Nigerian mother is *that* progressive," he replied with a snort.

Now, in front of John's condo, they got the drinks they'd purchased out of the back seat of the car, and went up to the door.

"Hang on." Chris stopped her from ringing the bell. He put the things in his hands down and reached for her. "Before everything changes." He leaned down to kiss her. She knew it! He was feeling that same apprehension about letting others into their space. As she'd done in the last few days whenever he got near her, she leaned into him and returned the kiss with as much passion as she could muster. She was on her toes, with her hands wrapped around his neck when she heard someone clear their throat behind her. She froze, releasing Chris and resting her head on his chest for a moment, before spinning around to face her brother. His brows were raised in shock as he looked at her and then at his best friend. For the first time since she could remember, he was too surprised to actually speak.

"Hi John!" she said as cheerfully as she could manage, picking up the bags of drinks from where Chris had placed them, and ducking under John's arm to walk through the door. When she got in, she turned to watch the two friends' interaction. She was a coward, she knew, but she couldn't help it. This was uncharted territory for her and John, and she had no clue what to expect. In all the years they'd been classmates, she'd never dated any of his close friends. And even though she'd discussed the bro code with Chris, she had no idea how John would truly react.

They'd planned everything carefully, she and Chris. They were to show up at John's condo together (they both lived in Marietta, so a carpool wouldn't be too farfetched), and do their best to watch the Super Bowl while keeping their hands to themselves. The manner in which they would reveal their relationship would depend heavily on the results of the game. A victory would make things very simple. Nothing would dampen John's mood if the Falcons ended up with the Lombardi trophy. And a defeat? Well, they would wait till all their friends left, help with the cleanup, and then sit him down to tell him.

Now, they had to move to their nonexistent plan C because she and Chris couldn't refrain from touching each other for two seconds. She looked at John still standing by the door, looking like he was still processing what he just saw. Will he approve? Or would he and Chris have a shouting match? Would they have to leave after she jumped in to defend Chris? Because she would. Jump in to defend Chris, that is. Finally, she looked over at Chris. He was looking right back at her, wearing one of his amused smirks. He walked in then, past John, forcing him to turn around and face them.

"So you two are—"

"Yep," Chris replied smoothly, like he had an actual plan C in his head.

"How long?" John asked.

"A few days," Chris answered.

John nodded slowly. "And it's not a problem at work? I mean, you guys technically work together."

"We barely work together!" Kelenna blurted out, getting her first words in. She let out a breath. She really needed to relax. "Either way, it's not a problem. I checked. We don't work in the same department, and he doesn't have a supervisory role over me."

"You *checked*?" Chris sent her an incredulous look that was dripping with patronization, like it was the cutest thing he'd ever heard. She rolled her eyes. Of course she'd checked. At least one of them cared about potential roadblocks to their relationship.

"I would never have thought . . ." John trailed off. "I mean, Kels, you've always acted like you could see right through him . . . I thought you hated him."

Kelenna gasped. "I've never hated him! I just . . ." It was her turn to trail off. "It's different now," she concluded softly. She looked at Chris standing a few yards away from her. When he winked at her, she grinned. She itched to close down the space between them, but she didn't. She knew that he understood that she was done assuming things about his character. They'd talked so much in those three days, and they'd agreed that there would always be honesty between them. She turned back to her brother. "John, are you mad?"

John looked pensive. "Mad that I never saw it," she heard him murmur before he let out a deep sigh. "I'm not mad, why would I be?"

"Bro code, bro," Chris said quickly.

John gave him a quizzical look before turning to her. "Bro what? What is he talking about?"

Kelenna looked between her brother and her boyfriend. How did she know two men who didn't know what the bro code was?

Chris walked up to John and placed a hand on his shoulder. Kelenna couldn't hear what he was saying near John's ear, but she saw John's eyes brighten in realization. "Of course!" he said, then cleared his throat. "Chris, you know that I . . ."

"Mhmm."

"And that if you—"

"Yep."

"And also that you—"

"You don't have to spell it out, bro."

"Good."

Kelenna rolled her eyes at their performance. "I hate you both. So much."

John laughed and walked up to her. He put both hands on her shoulders and shook her gently. "I love you, sis, and I want you to know that if it ever came down to choosing between you both, it would be difficult, but you would edge him out. You hear me?"

"Edge him out?" she said with a laugh, reaching up to give him a really tight hug that made him yelp a little, then kissing him soundly on his cheek. "It shouldn't be close at all!"

* * *

The game was intense right from the start. Both teams remained scoreless after the first quarter, each punting the ball multiple times. But when the second quarter came around, the Falcons began to show why they were ranked number one in offense. They scored three touchdowns in quick succession, and their defense was able to snuff out the Patriots' offense and hold them to a lone field goal. The condo, now filled with a combination of John and Chris' medical school classmates, and Kelenna's classmates, Zoe and Nichole, was buzzing as loud as any rowdy sports bar. Chika came in at the stroke of halftime, but wouldn't admit that she'd only come for the halftime show.

"I can't stomach three hours of a football game," she said, taking a beer from John and sitting down on the arm of Kelenna's recliner. When she noticed the score line, she let out a squeal that drew attention from all the corners of the living room. "If I had known Atlanta would be this dominant, I would have gotten here sooner!"

"I know, right?" Zoe chimed in gleefully. "We're up by eighteen points! We're winning the Super Bowl!"

"I would be a little more hesitant if I were y'all," Nichole cautioned. "Atlanta teams are known for choking!"

Kelenna snorted while Zoe and Chika turned on Nichole to fight for the Falcons' honor. She tuned them and their chatter out, letting her gaze land on Chris clear across the room. She smiled at the hand gestures he was making, and how he was really into the discussion he was having. Whether it was subconscious or not, they had stayed away from each other since everyone came in. She knew it made no sense, but she missed him. How had they thought they could keep their relationship a secret from John until the end of the game?

"What do you keep looking at?" Chika snapped, breaking into her thoughts.

"Chris," Zoe said simply.

"What?" Kelenna turned sharply to her.

"What?" Zoe asked, bemused. "He's totally staring at you too."

Chika's eyes widened and her mouth dropped. She pointed at Kelenna and then at Chris, and started talking about butterflies returning to their senders and love triangles. Eyes were beginning to turn their way and Kelenna pulled Chika's arm and began to drag her in the direction of the kitchen.

"What's going on?" Nichole asked. "Is butterfly some kind of code?"

"Come on, guys." Kelenna eyed Zoe and Nichole and nodded at the kitchen. Despite being where all the food was, it was surprisingly empty.

"You chose Chris over Dr. Landon, didn't you?" Chika asked the second they were all alone. "You fell for the butterfly trick!"

"Why do you keep saying butterfly?" Nichole asked.

"And who is Dr. Landon?" Zoe added.

"Only the hottest pediatric neurosurgeon in Baltimore!" Chika exclaimed. She whipped out her phone, and in two swipes, she had a picture of Landon on her screen.

"You did not save a picture of him on your phone!" Kelenna cried.

Meanwhile, Zoe and Nichole were examining the picture and giving approving nods. A deliberate peek told her it was a photo of Landon in a white coat, standing beside his colleagues with his arms folded across his chest.

"I had to see what he looked like," Chika said with a shrug. "This man wanted to be with her," she added with a sigh. "But she's chosen Chris over him."

"You're dating Chris?" Nichole said disbelievingly.

"You've been holding out on us!" Zoe practically yelled.

"Guys, keep it down!" Kelenna whispered harshly.

"Is it a secret?" Nichole asked.

"No, it's not a secret." Kelenna sighed. "It's just new." She raised a hand when it looked like Chika was about to spew out some more of her team Landon rhetoric. "It was never a contest, Chika. Once I stopped overthinking it, it became fairly obvious. I am my realest self with Chris, and the way I feel about him validates that."

"Haven't you known him all your life? You're just finding out you're this into him now?" Nichole asked.

"She's always been into him," Chika said before Kelenna could utter a word. Kelenna shot a questioning look at her friend. She had a long time to think about it, and she arrived at that same conclusion, but she was surprised that Chika felt the same way. Especially considering how relentlessly anti-Chris she'd been. Chika simply shrugged when they locked eyes. "I just wanted you to be sure that this isn't some fulfilment of a fifteen-year-old crush."

"It's not!" Kelenna protested. "It feels new and familiar at the same time. It's the best feeling, actually."

Zoe gasped as her hand went to her chest, almost like there was a string attached. "My little Kelenna is in love!"

Kelenna blinked. In love? Wasn't it too soon to say that?

Just then, her cell phone rang in her back pocket. She pulled it to look at it. It was her work number. "I have to take this."

Her friends left her alone in the kitchen while she answered the call. It was Mona, one of the evening shift pharmacists, and she was calling to tell her about a surgeon's request for a drug that was typically reserved for outpatients. As Kelenna walked her through how to handle the situation, she felt familiar hands wrap around her waist from behind. She smiled and leaned back against Chris. Mona was rattling off about her concerns with the approach Kelenna suggested, which were mostly centered around the fear of ticking the surgeon off. Apparently, the surgeon had already yelled at her twice. Kelenna was surprised that she could focus on what Mona was saying while Chris' lips were on her neck.

"It's almost nine o'clock on a Sunday night, Mona. Tell Dr. Thom that it's against hospital policy to use that drug on an inpatient. We can do a drip or give it every eight hours until he can discharge the patient. If he has a problem with it, he'll have to go over our heads to the CEO. But not tonight. Tomorrow. Those are his options."

"You're scary when you get in boss mode," Chris said in her ear when she got off the phone.

"I'm not bossy," she said, stepping away from his embrace. "I'm just firm, so that people do what I tell them."

"The exact definition of bossy," Chris chimed in.

She gave him a look. "Fine, I'm bossy! But your doctor colleagues are so—argh!" She clenched her fists. "Why are they trying to bully my staff over a non-emergent, non-crucial drug?"

Chris sighed. "You're not going to like this, but we docs don't care about your policies if we want a drug and think it's necessary. That's just the way we roll, baby."

"And that's why we're around. To make sure we can give you reasonable, cost-effective alternatives that neither compromise patient care nor our policies. It's bad enough that the drugs are so expensive without us using them when we don't have to. Someone has to be looking at that, and unfortunately, that someone is me."

"And you're great at it. I'm just saying, know that it will be never-ending. As long as there are expensive drugs, and there are doctors and patients, you're going to be tasked with policing us. And we're probably going to put up resistance from time to time."

"Really?" she asked, hooking an arm around his neck, and forcing him down to whisper sultrily in his ear. "And what about you? Will *you* be able to resist me?"

He chuckled softly, wrapping his arms around her once more. "I don't think I can."

"Good."

"Ready to take a break from work and come and watch the game? I need to hold someone's hand, and I would rather it be yours. The Falcons are putting us through it."

"What?" She gave him her hand without a second thought. "We're not losing, are we?"

"No, but the Patriots are mounting a comeback. It's 28-20, with less than five minutes to go."

Kelenna's free hand rose to her throat as she followed his lead back into the living room. The occupants were staring at the TV, hearts in mouths, watching the Patriots slice through their team's defense like a knife through butter. If anyone thought it was weird that Chris was holding her hand, or pulling her down to sit beside him on the floor, and anchoring her close with his arm hooked around her raised knee, they didn't say anything. They used the wall as a back rest, and he kept hold of the hand she'd given him seconds before. She soon regretted giving it to him, because that hand experienced the full range of his emotions over the next few minutes. She was right there with him though. They celebrated near-misses, berated the refs and yelled at the TV. But it didn't matter, because they watched their team capitulate like a slow train wreck. When the whistle blew for full time, the game was tied at twenty-eight a piece.

"We're witnessing history," John said in wonder. "First overtime at the Super Bowl. We just need to win it."

"The Patriots have all the momentum!" Zoe wailed.

"Falcons haven't scored another point since they got to twenty-eight," one of John's med school classmates said. "You think the Patriots are going to lose this? It's a wrap."

Just like disgruntled fans would at a stadium, John's friends shook hands with him and left the party, one after the other.

"Guys, the game isn't over!" Chris called out from beside her.

"You think we can still win it?" Kelenna asked hopefully.

"Oh, hell no. Give the Pats an inch, they'll take a mile. The game is done. But we're going to sit here and watch it till the end." He squeezed her hand.

The Falcons won the coin toss at the start of overtime and elected to receive the ball.

"Yes! That's the best move!" John jumped up excitedly. "Keep the ball out of their hands! Rise up!"

Kelenna looked on as the people left over stood up one after the other, in the most dramatic fashion.

She leaned closer to Chris. "Should we be standing up as well?"

"No, stay."

The Falcons moved the ball down the field for forty yards, and were stuck at the fifty-third yard line, trying to make a play on third down and seven.

"Can our kicker make a field goal this far out?" Chika asked. She was clutching John's arm and was more invested in the game than Kelenna had ever seen her.

"We need to protect the ball more than anything else. If we lose the ball to an interception, we're done. Just play it safe and get the ball a bit closer," Chris said.

The next play was a rushing play that ate up six yards.

"Fourth down, oh my God!" John said, covering his eyes. "Are we going for it?"

"We have to go for it!" Zoe yelled.

"Absolutely," Chris agreed.

"If we go for it and miss, we're done!" Kelenna warned.

"If they miss on fourth and one, they deserve to lose the game!" he snapped. "Hold on," he said, turning to her fully. "Are you shaking? Nerves?"

"Yes!" she cried, trying but failing to still herself. "I didn't even know I cared so much!"

Chris laughed, and she could hear his own nerves. "You're supposed to be calm for the both of us."

"I'm trying!"

When the Falcons rushed the ball for one yard, Kelenna let out the breath she didn't realize she had been holding. "Oh my God, first down! My favorite words in football!"

"Oh yeah? Why?"

"Because of what it signifies," she said softly. "Progress. Hope. Something new. There's always a chance when you have a first down."

She had no idea what part of her statement made him do it, but right there and then, against John's living room wall, in the thick of the most dramatic game in football history, Chris told her he loved her.

"And I plan to marry you one day," he added.

"Is that a proposal?" she asked as lightly as she could, even though the emotions welling up in her caused her heart to thump loudly. She couldn't believe how they'd gone from being a non-item to talking about marriage in under one week. And more than that, that she was at peace with it.

"Oh, you'll know when I propose." His voice held a hint of a smile as he turned back to the TV.

With a fresh set of downs, the Falcons lined up and were ready to go. Kelenna could feel the energy from all the brave fans left in John's condo, willing their team to victory. Most of all, she could feel the presence of the man beside her, calm and certain, grounding her. She thought about John's words when they'd first walked in. "You could always see right through him," John had said. Well, she was done looking through him. She was only interested in *seeing* him. She may not be fluent in the Igbo language, but she knew the words for 'I love you,' *Ahuru m gi n'anya* translated in English to 'I see you.' Did she really have any doubts about what he was to her?

"Hey." She tapped his knee, and he turned to her, brow raised, eyes focused on her. "I love you too."

He didn't say a word in response. All he did was lift their conjoined hands to his lips and place a lingering kiss on it. She didn't know how long they sat there grinning at each other, but soon there was more uproar in the room. They looked up to see the quarterback throw a pass directly to a well-covered wide receiver. There were audible gasps when the pass was caught, and more cheers when the receiver landed on his feet, turned and ran straight to the end zone.

The silence that ensued was deafening. It was disbelief turned into paralysis. As though they were afraid that if they said a word, they would jinx it. Zoe's screech cut into the silence, and that was the trigger for the room to erupt in celebration. Chris gave Kelenna a quick kiss on her mouth before jumping off the floor to tackle-hug John. Kelenna ran to hug her friends. The touchdown was still under review, but it didn't matter. Helmets were off, and confetti was on the floor. The Falcons had won the Super Bowl.

EPILOGUE

Six Months Later

Kelenna was the last to arrive at The Bistro, and when she did, she walked straight up to The Table and slapped down a rolled newspaper on it.

"Guess who made the news!"

"Uh, Kelenna, you do realize that nobody reads newspapers anymore, right?" Zoe picked up the paper, and scrunched up her nose as she looked at it. "And certainly not the *Preston Herald.* What is this?"

"Hey, the *Preston Herald* has a good reach!" Kelenna pulled out the last empty seat at The Table and sat down. "It has a good online following too."

"Hand it here," Dev said as he reached for it. He opened up the paper once Zoe handed it to him.

"No, no, no, Dev. Front page."

"Oh, excuse me." He closed the newspaper and began to read out loud. "Preston Regional Hospital Takes On Opioid Crisis." He paused to look at her. "These are your people?"

She nodded. "Keep reading."

"Preston Regional in the heart of Preston, Georgia is tackling the opioid epidemic head on with new measures designed to reduce access to the dangerous drugs in the ER. The campaign, dubbed: Reducing Opioid Initiative, or ROI project, was implemented about five months ago, and the changes are already dramatic."

"Let me see." Pete took the pages from Dev and glanced over it. "Kelenna, this is great! You're quoted in it. It says, *Kelenna Jordan Agu has been the pharmacy clinical coordinator at Preston for four years, and was instrumental in rolling out the project. 'With the regulatory changes made to opioids at the national level, we had to do what we could to change opioid use habits at Preston. In the five years before the project, one out of every four patients received an opioid in our ER. In the last three months alone, that number has changed to one out of eleven.'* This is nice, girl."

"I'm glad they gave you a quote," Sharon said, peering over Pete's shoulder before commandeering the newspaper altogether. "Usually, they only take quotes from the physicians. And look at that, right on cue." She laughed. "*Dr. Christian Tari-Douglas is the ED medical director at Preston, and had a more personal reason for wanting a program like this in place. 'After we lost one of our staff to the opioid epidemic, we knew we had to act. It was important that we get buy-in from all the physicians, the nurses, and even the community. We're making a more conscious effort to assess pain properly, and have increased the number of referrals to addiction specialists and pain clinics. This non-conventional treatment of pain has been effective thus far, and has changed the culture in our ER.'* Your fiancé sounds good."

Kelenna didn't think she would ever get used to that word. Fiancé. When Chris told her that Super Bowl night that she would know when he proposed, she lived in fear of him staging an elaborate proposal, complete with balloons and streamers and everyone they knew. She should have known better. It was the most understated but meaningful proposal.

The month before, they were at her parents' for Wednesday night dinner when John let it slip that he would no longer bet against their mom. It turned out that they had a long-standing bet from a year before about Kelenna and Chris ending up together. Well before that snowy evening that had changed everything. She should have known that something was up when her mother showed no real surprise the first time she announced that she and Chris were an item, nor any disappointment that she didn't follow through with Landon. All she'd done that first time was beam at Chris and say, "Welcome, my son," in a weird Godfather kind of way. On their way back to her apartment after the bet revelation, Chris did a good job staying calm as Kelenna tore into her mother.

"Do you realize that she's been manipulating me the entire time? She throws Landon at me, knowing that I hate parental interference, and tells me that a doctor would be good for me. She says I'm such an overthinker, that I could have already met the guy, but probably wouldn't even know it. That woman actually told me that she wanted me to figure it out on my own, when all the while, she had this bet with John. And don't get me started on John." She was probably fuming more from embarrassment than anything else. That the whole scene had transpired in front of Chris made it more annoying. Her family was weird, plain and simple.

"I'm surprised John didn't say anything," he said thoughtfully. That was probably the most upsetting part to him, since John usually told him everything. "But babe, I tried to warn you. No Nigerian mother is that calm when her daughter is single past twenty-five. Hell, my mother did the same thing with my sister! Belema was dating her boyfriend for eight years when my mother pulled him aside and told him to either marry her or get out. They were both only twenty-six."

She laughed appreciatively at his attempt to calm her down. "I wish my mom was more upfront like your mom and not always trying to play these games. I wish she wasn't always two steps ahead of me."

He simply shrugged and said something about the grass being greener on the other side. "People tend to wish for what they don't know. I love my mother to death, but her nagging me about you was more annoying than anything. It didn't make me choose you any more than your mother's avoidance of me made you choose me." He paused and she knew he was ruminating over his own words. She smiled as she watched his mind work. "Did that make sense?"

"Yes."

"Good." He parked in front of her apartment and they got out of his car. As he walked her to her door, he confessed that he had made a bet with John back when she was dating Will Perry.

"What about me screams that I need to be the subject of wagers?" she groaned as she unlocked the door and walked in, "I don't want to hear it."

"Are you sure? John lost that one as well—"

"No more bets!"

"What if I make one with you?" he said softly from behind her.

She turned to look at him with narrowed eyes. "What would we bet about?"

"I don't know. We could bet about anything." He took a step towards her. "Like how many children we would have."

"Two," she said without thinking. If she had, she would have wondered why they were even talking about children.

He gave an infinitesimal head shake. "Three," he corrected.

"Come on, you only need two children! One child for each hand. Any more than two and you're outnumbered. You run out of hands." She grimaced when Chris laughed at her logic. "Also, it would be a discussion, not a bet!"

Chris took another step towards her. "Gender of the first child?"

"The odds are fifty-fifty!" she said exasperatedly.

"But if you were betting?" He arched a brow.

"A boy."

"Girl," he corrected once more, as if it was a no-brainer. As if he could control the gender of a child just by speaking. "I want a carbon copy of the most beautiful woman I know."

From anyone else, it would have been the cheesiest line ever uttered, but from Chris, she could actually feel that he was being genuine. She snorted to keep the emotions at bay, but her voice cracked with her next words. "Okay, now you're just picking the opposite of what I say."

"Maybe you're right," he whispered, closing the gap even more till there was none. He took both her hands in his. "How about we bet on something we both can agree on, sweetheart?"

She knew then. And he knew that she knew. And she knew that he knew that she knew. A slow smile spread across her face.

"Yeah?" he asked, looking directly into her eyes.

She grinned up at him. "Yes."

"Do I still need to get down on one knee? How does this work?"

"Oh yeah," she said through laughter.

He got down then. He brought out the most beautiful sapphire blue ring she'd ever seen.

"I love it," she gasped as he placed it on her fourth finger. "Chika?"

He scoffed, holding on to her hand as he rose to his feet. "That girl wasn't helpful. She told me to get some big, princess cut whatever diamond. The pictures she sent just didn't seem like you."

Kelenna thought about it a bit more and knew without a shadow of a doubt. "My mother."

"Yeah, baby," he said softly, squeezing her hand. He probably noticed that tears were threatening to spill from her eyes. It was the sweetest thing to include the person who knew her the best. Even if she had just spent the entire evening being upset at her. No one else had the foresight to see her here at this special moment.

"I'm going to have to call her." She smiled, rising to put her arms around his neck and meet his lips for a quick kiss. "I love you so much."

He hugged her fiercely and released her gently. Before she could go too far, he captured her hand in his, and held it against his chest. She felt his heart race beneath her palm and she looked up questioningly at him. "I've always known that it would feel special to be the person you choose to love," he told her softly. "Most days I can't believe I'm that person." He lifted his left hand to palm her cheek and simultaneously swipe at the tears on her face.

He smiled at her. She smiled back. "I love you too, babe. You and I are going to be family."

Now at The Bistro, she watched Nichole as she read through the rest of the newspaper article. "Looks like you're working on spreading the ROI project to the rest of the hospital. Your chief medical officer says so here."

"Yes, we've already begun educating our hospitalists about the new orders." It was going to be a bit more difficult, but they were going to go for it.

"It's impressive." Nichole closed the newspaper and folded it. "This is what I wish I could do. I want to feel like I'm doing meaningful work."

Kelenna frowned. "We're all doing meaningful work in our own ways. Saving lives."

"Not like this," Nichole sighed. "I've been thinking about seeing a therapist. Ever since the robbery, I just haven't felt satisfied at work. Or even wanted to be there."

"Oh, Nichole," Kelenna said, saddened that there was still such a contrast in the way they both felt about their jobs.

"I'm sorry you feel that way, Nic," Zoe said. "But I think it's a good idea. It's always good to seek help."

"Exactly," Pete added. "I'm sure it will give you some insight into what your next steps should be."

"You know we're here for you," Sharon said.

"Thanks guys," Nichole said, emotions choking her voice. She began to fan her eyes to stave off tears. "Okay now, I didn't mean to bring everyone down. Somebody, please change the subject."

"Priya and I are official," Dev blurted out at the same time that Sharon said: "We're pregnant."

"What?" Kelenna asked, and she knew her eyes were bigger than saucers. It was so much to take in all at once.

"I'm so happy for you guys!" Nichole clasped her hands. Her smile was big, but Kelenna had known her long enough to know that she was still a little down.

"Oh, we have to have a toast!" Zoe picked up her cup. Kelenna looked around for something to pick up, and settled for a cup of water in the center of the table that hadn't been touched. "To new relationships, a new baby, killing it at our jobs, and to knowing that we will all make it to where we need to be . . . I really mean that, Nic." Zoe lifted her glass to her. Kelenna leaned over to her left to give Nichole a quick hug.

"Thanks, girl."

"Yamas on three. One, two—"

"Wait, why yamas?" Pete asked

"Because I'm Greek, and the toast was my idea! One! Two! Three!"

"Yamas!!"

THE END

Read on for an excerpt from Nichole's story . . .

PROLOGUE

"Welcome to Dexter's pharmacy!" Nichole said in as cheery a voice as she could manage. It was 8:30 p.m. and she was in the home stretch of her work week. The pharmacy was closing in half an hour and she had the next two days off. She was already counting down the minutes to when she could head out, catch up with her friends, and most importantly, sleep. But first, she had to take care of this customer. "How can I help you?" "I need to pick up a box of needles." He had on a black hooded jacket that was raised to cover his close-cropped hair, and a pair of tinted glasses that was out of place for an evening trip to the pharmacy. The hairs on her arms stood—a tell-tale sign that she didn't trust that he had legitimate use for those needles. Still she wouldn't presume. "Do you have a prescription for insulin?" "I don't think so." Nichole hid an eye roll. It was too late in the day for obtuse customers. "How about you just give me your last name and I'll look up—"

"No, no, no," the man said hurriedly, lifting his glove-covered hands to stop her in her tracks. Those hands made her pause. Why was he wearing gloves in the middle of September? Before she could think about that any further, he grinned at her—far less reassuringly than he was probably going for. "You see, they're for my grandmother. She's run out, and she needs them for her insulin."

Nichole couldn't stop herself from nodding disbelievingly. It was always either a grandmother or a daughter. She could humor him.

"I'm doing her a favor," he continued. "The poor woman is damn near blind and can barely walk. I'm all she has and I don't want her to end up in a hospital. Listen, if you can just give me a box, I'll be on my way." He pointed in the general direction of the back wall. Her eyes followed his hand gesture to the wall where several boxes of needles were stacked.

"Not a problem." But instead of going to the back wall, she walked over to the verification computer and tapped on the mouse to clear the screensaver. "Tell me your grandmother's name and I can look at her records to see what type of needles she uses with her insulin." When she looked back up at him expectantly, he was fidgety.

"She doesn't use this pharmacy."

Now she knew he was up to no good. She didn't want any confrontations with a likely intravenous drug user, and the best way to avoid one was to make him choose to leave rather than ask him to do so. "I would be happy to call the pharmacy she uses and have it transferred over here."

Before she could blink, the man jumped over the counter and advanced upon her. Her quick reflexes made her reach for the phone, but his next words made her freeze.

"Don't touch that. I have a gun and I won't hesitate to use it." He must have taken her shock as a sign to continue because he gave her another grin. "Good. Now let's forget about the needles since you care about them so much. Go on to your safe where you keep the good stuff. I want every form of Oxy you have in there."

She was shaking as she walked over to the safe. Her fingers were almost vibrating as she punched in the code to open the gray cabinet and withdrew bottles of the drugs he wanted.

Obey, obey, obey. Put up no resistance. The words from the annual training videos Dexter's made the pharmacists watch ran through her mind. She never thought she would ever have to use them.

"Why don't you throw in some Adderall while you're at it?" he told her. "And hurry up, I don't have all day."

He didn't catch her hit the panic button beside the safe. Nothing happened when she did, but she wasn't sure what to expect because she'd never had to use it.

"Please don't hurt me," she whispered as she rose to place the bottles on the counter.

"Where are the cameras in this store?" he barked, ignoring her plea and shoving the bottles into his jacket.

"I-I don't know, I-I'm just filling in," she stammered.

His sneer told her he didn't believe her for a second. He was right not to. All the Dexter pharmacy layouts were the same. There were cameras discretely built into the ceiling tiles and he was being recorded from several different angles.

The phone rang. It was louder than she'd ever heard it, and it startled her so much that she physically jumped. After she calmed down, she looked at the caller ID. It was the store manager. Was he really calling her in response to the panic button she'd pushed? Instead of calling the police? She had to hide her groan as she reached for it.

The man pulled out his gun and cocked it. Her breath left her. "I swear to God, if you touch that phone, you're dead."

She nodded mutely, her eyes wide with fear as she stared down the barrel of the gun that was aimed directly at her.

This is how I'm going to die, she thought. At a job she hated. After ignoring her mother's last few texts. While still not speaking to her dad. Having never experienced true love. This was how she was going to die. The next thing she heard was the sound of police sirens cutting through the air. Then there was a roar from a—a tiger? Why was there a tiger in the pharmacy?

Nichole jerked upright out of her sleep. She clutched at her chest and took in quick deep breaths to reorient herself. She was in her all white bedroom that never quite managed to get completely dark. Her phone alarm was blaring on the nightstand beside her bed and she blindly reached over to dismiss it. Time to get ready for work. She turned to the form under the covers beside her. Shawn hadn't even flinched at any of the noise she'd made. Not for the shriek she'd let out, nor the alarm that had just gone off. No, he just lay there drowning out every other sound with his own snores. Like a tiger's roar. Ah, that explained the tiger in her dream. Nightmare was more like it. It was the same one she'd had since the actual robbery incident she'd experienced at work about a year ago. Every nightmare had a new twist. Sometimes the robber would metamorphose into someone she knew. Like one of her exes or her tenth grade chemistry teacher. Sometimes the location would change from the pharmacy to the auditorium where she'd sat as a first-year pharmacy student. Sometimes the thoughts that floated through her head as the gun was pointed at her would change from serious thoughts about her family and friends, to frivolous ones about her hair or a cute pair of shoes she'd neglected to buy.

But one thing never changed. In every version of the dream she'd had since that incident, she'd realized that she was going to die for a job that she didn't even like.

1

Freud himself would have been proud of the way the office slash counseling room was designed. It was rather dim, kept even more so by the heavy curtains that lined the windows. A large office desk that looked like it was made from some rich lumber, like mahogany, stood to the left of the room. Behind that was a leather office chair, slid closely under the desk, almost as if no one had sat in it in a while. Serving as a backdrop was a shelf with rows that seemed to emerge out of the wall. It was stacked with a ton of books from the ceiling to the floor. On the right-hand side of the room was a three-seater couch which she was now sitting on, and across from her, separated by a short coffee table, was a fabric upholstered arm chair. Potted plants accented the room at every corner. They looked nice, but they were plastic. How ironic that the things that were probably bought to bring life to the room were lifeless themselves.

Dr. Marie sat in the arm chair with her legs crossed. She wore her natural hair short, and it was mostly gray, giving her a very distinguished look. She wore a stiff white shirt tucked into a pair of dark pants that stopped just short of her ankles. It was the same outfit she wore in all the online photos on her website. Maybe it was some sort of uniform. Maybe she preferred not to waste brain matter thinking about outfit changes. Like Steve Jobs.

"Nichole?" Dr. Marie started, cutting into her thoughts.

"Yes?"

"I asked if you were ready to begin."

"Of course." Nichole rubbed her palms together and put her thoughts about her therapist's wardrobe to the side. "Yes."

"Good. If you don't mind, I'll take some notes as we go along." She whipped out a pen from behind her ear, and picked up a notepad from a small side table. "I understand you found me online. The notes my receptionist took down said you believe you have Post Traumatic Stress Disorder, and you wanted to talk about that?"

"Yes. I recall from when I was in school learning about psych medications, that it graduates from Acute Stress Disorder to PTSD if you continue to feel the after effects past thirty days. Right now, I'm over the one year mark. I wanted to see someone because I feel like it's taken over my life. I feel like I can't move forward."

"Hmm," Dr. Marie said. Then she leaned forward so abruptly that Nichole jerked back a little. "Well, Nichole, let me first of all say, I'm glad you decided to seek help. That first step is the hardest, but it is the most important one. I can promise you that I'll be committed, and if you'll be committed too, you will move forward."

She had kind eyes. That was what had drawn Nichole to her in the first place. When she'd gone scouring the internet for a therapist that she was going to bare her soul to, she'd known that she wanted it to be someone who was kind. Those eyes edged out the fact that she was a first name doctor. Nichole had always dismissed people who referred to themselves as Doctor 'whatever their first name was' as quacks. She was already glad that she hadn't done that with Dr. Marie.

"I would like for us to start with the traumatic event. How comfortable do you feel talking about it, Nichole?"

Nichole shrugged. That was why she was there after all.

"Good. Tell me what happened."

"I've worked at Dexter's Pharmacy in some capacity since I was seventeen. I'm thirty-one now, so that's what? About fourteen years?" She took a deep breath. "I was a technician for the first five years, an intern for the next four, and a pharmacist for the last five."

"A pharmacist? That's nice. Some of my very good friends are pharmacists. How do you like it?"

"Like what? Being a pharmacist?" Nichole let out a derisive snort. "Depends on the day."

Dr. Marie made a show of looking at her watch. "Thursday, November seventh."

"Well, I'm not at work right now so I like it just fine."

Dr. Marie arched a brow and smiled at her. "I see. Forgive me for cutting you off there. Please go on."

"About a year ago I was covering a shift at one of our Buckhead stores when it got robbed." She paused to collect her thoughts. After all, she was sure Dr. Marie had heard countless other traumatic encounters that were more serious than getting robbed.

"I'm so sorry to hear that. Were you physically harmed?"

"No, I wasn't. Luckily," she said, waving away her concern. "I got marks from when he handled me roughly, but those are long gone now." Those marks had taken their time to fade away. Her light skin showed bruises more easily than most.

"Tell me more about what happened."

Nichole began to describe the events of the day, from when she'd walked into work that morning up until around 8:30 p.m. when the man showed up at her counter. She couldn't remember every single detail, but she knew that it had been relentlessly busy. The Buckhead store was always busy. The customers were always impatient and had that air of entitlement that you would expect from people who lived in the affluent part of town. The doctors who called in prescriptions over the phone were always rude. There'd been no reprieve until it was almost time to close. And even that had been dampened by the robbery—the icing on the cake of what had been a truly crappy day.

"I did everything I was supposed to do. I obeyed him, I handed him everything he asked for. I even pushed the panic button. And still, I ended up with a gun in my face."

"Mmm," Dr. Marie said slowly.

Nichole followed the older woman's eyes as they assessed her. Was she looking for signs of a gun-inflicted injury? "He didn't use it," Nichole clarified quickly. "But I was terrified enough to think he would. I mean, the only reason he brought it out in the first place was because he heard the sirens outside. The police was responding to the panic button I'd pushed. He became paranoid and wanted me to walk him out of the pharmacy."

"And you did?"

"Yes. All with the gun pressed against my lower back." She reached around her back to feel for the imprint of the mouth of the gun. Sometimes she swore that she could still feel it.

"And no one saw you?"

"Dexter's was practically empty. If anyone saw us, they ignored us. I don't blame them though. I think we looked like a couple. He was huddled so close to me. Close enough to lean down and whisper things in my ear."

"What things was he whispering?"

"He told me to smile and not make a sound. He sounded almost encouraging. I felt like a victim and an accomplice at the same time."

"Hmm. Talk me through what else you were thinking as you walked him out."

She let out a breath as she accessed her memory bank. "I was thinking that I didn't want to die. I didn't want to die because of Oxy and Adderall. I didn't want my last memory to be at Dexter's."

Dr. Marie nodded as if she understood. Although that may have been her psychotherapist way of asking her to continue. Nichole decided to roll with the latter.

"Anyway, when we got to the front entrance, there were cops out there. Their guns were drawn and were pointed at me—well, us." She paused and let out a snort. "At that point I was worried there would be a shootout and that I would get hit in the crossfire. Or worse, that they would actually assume that I was an accomplice. So when they yelled out to the entire store to get down, I dropped to the ground. I was so quick that I must have startled the robber because his gun fell on the floor. They took him away in handcuffs, and a cop took my statement before I had to go back to the pharmacy to close up."

"I'm glad you're physically fine, but we both know you wouldn't be here if you were okay in other ways. Had you been robbed before, or ever since?"

"Only in my dreams," Nichole muttered.

"I'm sorry?"

"I've been having dreams—well, more like nightmares—about this. They come often, maybe a couple of times a week. I'm used to them now, but sometimes it's just—ugh! It's hard going to sleep wondering whether that's the night I'm going to have yet the same dream. It's hard falling back asleep after I wake up from one."

"And you're going through the same robbery in these dreams?"

"There are variations, but for the most part, I end up with a gun pointed at me. Sometimes, I get shot, other times I don't."

"When was the last time you had this dream?"

"The day I made this appointment. Last week." She gave a self-deprecating chuckle. "I guess I'm due for one."

"Hmm," Dr. Marie said sounding thoughtful. "You've had these nightmares for an entire year, but what about real life? Are you afraid to be alone at work?"

Nichole grew pensive. She hadn't been back at the Buckhead store since the incident, but she didn't think her answer would change much even if she had. "No. I had the weekend off after it happened, and by the time I got back to my home store in Dunwoody, I felt fine. I haven't had to close the pharmacy by myself since then though, so I don't know. That day was an anomaly because I'd sent my tech home earlier. She had to go pick up her kids or something. Dexter's usually has two people to close during business hours. I stay longer to wrap up after we've officially closed, but I put up the gates in front of the pharmacy when I do that. I've never really felt unsafe at work."

Dr. Marie nodded, still taking notes. "Apart from your dreams, is there anything that triggers the memory of that night?"

"Getting ready for work. Driving to work. Being at work. And oh, white men in dark hoodies."

Dr. Marie spared a small smile. "We only have a few minutes left, but before I let you go, I want to touch a bit more on your apparent disdain for your job."

"Is it that obvious?" Nichole asked with a wry smile.

"Yes," Dr. Marie replied seriously. "I'm sensing there's a lot to unpack there. I want you to be ready to talk about it at your next appointment. We'll get Kendra to set you up for next week."

"Um, next week doesn't work for me. My friend's getting married and I'm in the wedding. It will be a whole thing."

"Oh, a wedding, how nice! A break of some sort to distract you is always a good thing."

"Yes, I'm sure it'll be perfect. Everything about my friend is perfect. Now if you're looking for a pharmacist who loves her job, look no further. She even found her fiancé at work without trying. If she weren't my friend, it would be nauseating." She caught Dr. Marie's raised brows and smiled. "Too much?"

"Nothing is too much within these four walls if it's how you truly feel. I don't want you to go too long without seeing me though. Let's try to get you in the week after that. Give Kendra a good time for you. She knows my schedule better than anyone. Until then I want to give you a simple assignment. For the next two weeks, I want you to keep a journal. Write down every time you have a dream about the robbery. As much detail as you can remember. And as a secondary exercise, I want you to stop thinking negative thoughts about your job. Every time you have those thoughts, make a conscious effort to stop them. Positive thinking is like a muscle. You have to train it. If you don't you're left with atrophy. It's important that you exercise that muscle. Do you think you can do that?"

"Piece of cake."

* * *

It was anything but a piece of cake. In fact, keeping up with the journal made her almost late for work a week later. She managed to park her Lexus RX350 and simultaneously grab her purse, lunch bag, and white coat from the passenger's seat. As she jogged lightly through the front door, she caught Alan, the front store manager, notice her and then eye his watch like the loser he was. She was sure he would relish writing her up for being late. Luckily, she didn't give him the satisfaction because she'd made it with a minute to spare. Dexter's had a tardy policy that was so harsh it was unbelievable. Two strikes and you were out—as in fired. As she strode past Alan, she gave him a sweet smile. He was barely taller than she was—she was five-three, which wasn't tall at all—and wore the nerdiest pair of glasses. He had a full head of hair that he didn't know what to do with and was beginning to develop a pouch around his middle. The man lived and breathed Dexter's. First one in and last one out. Not like it got him anywhere. He'd been at that store longer than she had, and she was sure he would be stuck there well after she found her way out.

"Cutting it close today, aren't we, Nichole?"

He always used the collective we in the most annoying way. Especially when he was giving out instructions. God forbid that he man up and be clear about what he wanted, no, that was too much to ask. Instead, he would say things like, 'I want us to do this' or 'can we make those calls more frequently?' when he really means that he wants *you* to do it. She almost wanted to ask him if he was late as well.

"Think of it as one minute early, Alan!" she called out, keeping up her brisk pace as she approached the small side door that led into the pharmacy. She punched in a code and closed the door shut behind her. Then she went to the gate that covered the face of the pharmacy, unlocked it, and rolled the metal bars open from one post to the other. She unlocked the bulletproof drive thru window and went to power on the computers at the pharmacist station.

"Kill me now," she muttered as she noticed the blinking light on the phone beside her. The screen on the phone showed that there were fifteen messages on the doctor line. Were they working from home now? She decided to address some of those calls first. There was no doubt in her mind that some of the patients whose prescriptions were called in would be at the drive thru window or at the counter the minute the pharmacy opened officially at eight o'clock.

Ten minutes later, Sharonda, an African American woman in her fifties and Nichole's favorite pharmacy technician walked in through the half door at the front of the pharmacy.

"Good morning, Nichole," Sharonda said brightly. Her disposition was always so sunny, it was like she was on Prozac. She was one of those women who saw the glass as full even when it was clearly empty. That would ordinarily annoy Nichole, but it didn't. Perhaps because the older woman also had a sharp tongue to go along with it. Besides, she was so efficient at her job, it was like working with two people.

"Morning, Sharonda."

"And how are you doing this wonderful day?"

"Well, let's see. I dreamed that Alan tried to kill me." If she was going for shock value it didn't work because all Sharonda did was laugh.

"You need to give that poor man a break," she said as she immediately began to make herself useful by filling some of the prescriptions that Nichole had entered. See? So efficient.

"I'm not joking! He pointed a gun at me and actually pulled the trigger!"

It was why she'd almost been late to work that morning. She'd woken up with such a start that she'd managed to even stir Shawn out of his slumber. "Babe, go back to sleep," he'd mumbled before turning over and continuing to snore. She'd rolled her eyes and climbed out of bed. It had been practically time for her to get ready for work anyway, so it would take nothing to spend a few minutes documenting her dream in the notebook she'd bought only the day before. She sat at her glass dining table and began to jot down the twists and turns in her dream that ended with Alan shooting at her.

She was closing up shop at her store when Alan came to the counter looking sinister as hell. Instead of his usual button down shirt and slacks, he was wearing the robber's signature black hoodie and black gloves. "I want our metrics to be good this month, Nichole," he'd said in an evil tone that didn't match his simple words.

"Our metrics are always good," she countered. Dream Nichole knew she worked hard to meet their company's goals, no matter how unrealistic they were.

"I want us to be number one in the district. We could be number one if you and Tom got off your butts and start giving out more flu shots."

"Have you told Tom this? The actual pharmacy manager?"

"He's not here now. You are. Make more calls today, Nichole."

"It's time for me to go home, I'm not making any more calls!" she snapped indignantly. He was being unreasonable. "Also, I don't give a damn about your number one spot or whether or not you get your bonus this year."

"You better give a damn Nichole, or else—"

"Or else, what?" she said with a taunting gleam in her eye. "What are you going to do? Shoot me?"

A gun materialized out of nowhere into his gloved hands. He aimed it at her forehead.

"Put that away, Alan. Go home."

"You'll do what I say. I'm your boss."

"You're not my boss, Alan! Look at the store out there. That's your jurisdiction. You handle the candy and the magazines, okay? We'll handle the drugs back here."

Even in her dream she'd known that was a lie. Dexter's hierarchy went store manager, pharmacy manager, then lowly pharmacist. And she was fine with being the lowly pharmacist, by the way. She didn't care to be the pharmacy manager. Been there, hated it.

"I am your boss," he said, the click of his gun paralyzing her, just as it had with the robber.

And then he pulled the trigger.

Sharonda cackled. "I can interpret this dream better than that shrink of yours. It's so simple. Don't run your mouth and you'll stay out of trouble."

Nichole choked down on a laugh. Sharonda was one of the few people who knew she was seeing a therapist. Her own mother didn't know yet and she was a guidance counselor at a high school in Nashville with plenty years' experience. She would probably be upset that Nichole didn't see it fit to let her know she was feeling bad enough to see a therapist, but Nichole wasn't in the mood to bring her in. Sharonda was not a hundred percent in support of her 'telling her woes to a shrink,' as she put it. The older woman felt like she just needed to choose a different approach to life and that she didn't need to pay someone a hundred dollars an hour to do that.

"My therapist isn't a dream interpreter," Nichole said firmly.

"Ain't that what you wishing she would do for you? All them dreams you keep having are a sign. We don't just dream for the sake of dreaming, girl. I've told you this before."

"It's a sign that I have trauma from when I was robbed."

"Girl, you ain't afraid of nothing. I do like this exercise though, what your shrink got you doing. And I'm glad you told me, so I can be the enforcer. Expect a pinch on your side anytime I hear you whine about your job."

"Oh, Sharonda, I wish I never told you," Nichole said with a laugh. She looked up from her computer just in time to see their first customer approach the checkout counter. "I'll get this, Sharonda. Exercise my new job-loving skills and all." She wiggled her eyebrows.

Sharonda scoffed as she kept counting pills by fives and tossing them into amber pill bottles. "Mrs. Williams is so pleasant, it's practically cheating."

Nichole ignored her as she walked up to the counter. "Mrs. Williams, good morning!" she said jovially. "You're looking good."

Mrs. Williams was well over eighty but she didn't let that hold her back. She was spry and always on the move. She'd been coming to the pharmacy since before Nichole started working there and was easily her favorite customer. Sometimes she would stop by to chat while she was milling about the store. Other times she would pop in for her medications and run off.

"Thank you, darling girl, so do you. It's so nice outside today, I just couldn't resist walking down here to pick up my medicine."

"Now Ms. Williams, you gotta take it easy!" Sharonda called out from the filling station.

"Nonsense, I live half a mile the other way." Ms. Williams pointed a wrinkled hand behind her. "A brisk walk first thing in the morning does a body good. If I didn't come here, I would have gone somewhere else. Now, pretty girl, can you get me my medicine? I'm almost out."

Nichole was already a step ahead of her. She'd collected the paper bag with the woman's medications and had been holding on to it for some time.

"Here they are. Same as last time, your blood pressure medicine, *amlodipine*, and your cholesterol medication, *atorvastatin*. What problems do you have taking these medications?"

"None," Ms. Williams said proudly. "I take them every day. My blood pressure runs a little high, but the doctor doesn't want to make any changes right now."

"Oh yeah? What's a little high?" Nichole pressed.

Ms. Williams shrugged. "One-forty, one-fifty."

"Okay, that's not too bad for now. Just remember to keep taking your meds. Keep exercising, and keep eating right. You're doing a good job, Ms. Williams, you look great." She scanned the label on the bag and a receipt printed out. She stapled the receipt on to the bag. "Your copay is zero dollars. Sign right here, ma'am." Nichole handed her a stylus and let her sign the screen to acknowledge that she'd picked up her medication.

"Thank you, dear. Y'all have a good day now!"

"Bye, Mrs. Williams, say hi to Mr. Williams!" she said to her retreating figure. Her gray hair bounced as she—was she speed walking?

"I believe Mrs. Williams is speed walking out of the store!" Nichole said to Sharonda. "Oh, it's so cute! Like one of those geriatric Olympic competitors!"

Sharonda laughed. "Well, good for her! I know no one's ever accused me of exercising!"

Nichole failed to stifle her laugh as she glanced at Sharonda. Sharonda was *healthy*, very much so. She could stand to lose a couple thirty or forty pounds. It wasn't like Nichole couldn't relate to being on the heavier side. All she had to do was look at food and her weight would fluctuate wildly. She'd tried every diet craze in the book, always seeking a way to drop some of the extra pounds. She was currently intermittent fasting, but she already knew that wouldn't be too sustainable. Her breasts came in when she was twelve and did nothing but grow to the double Ds they were now. Her hips came in a few years after that and gave her a figure that looked more hourglass than anything else. At least it distracted from the fact that she was soft around the middle. She'd had to learn the usefulness of high-waist pants and control undergarments. Right now, she was the slimmest she'd ever been, which at five-three and one-fifty wasn't that slim, but at least she could force herself into a size eight or ten, and that worked for her.

She walked back to the pharmacist's station and began to verify some of the orders that had come into her queue. Her job was to review everything the techs did, make sure the drug in the bottle matched the prescription written by the physician, and sign off on it. She was the final check to make sure that there were no errors, and she took it seriously. After all, her license was on the line every time she looked at a prescription.

Like an assembly line, they worked together in silence, stacking up the filled prescriptions until the first wave of busyness swept through. At the top of the hour, their second morning tech, Marty would come in, and by noon, Tom, the pharmacy manager, along with their evening shift tech Desi would come in. Their store was usually a circus during lunch time and in the evening after five. Her shift would be over by four p.m., so all she had to do was get through the midday craziness in one piece.

But for now, she could enjoy the tranquility. Tranquility made her forget she hated her job. When she let out a sigh, she felt a pinch on her side a few moments later.

"Ow! What was that for?" She turned questioning eyes to Sharonda.

"I know what that sigh means!"

2

Nichole waited in line at the front desk of the W hotel in Buckhead to check in. She thought it was over-indulgent, staying at the hotel when she lived five minutes away, but the bride wouldn't be swayed. She wanted her wedding party in the same space for the weekend, and she was footing the bill for it. The agenda for the day was as long as her arm. Nichole and the other bridesmaids had just got done hosting a bridal shower brunch at a small teahouse off Peachtree road. It was cute watching the bride blush at all the lingerie that she'd received as gifts. It almost made Nichole abandon her theory that the quickie wedding was covering up an unexpected pregnancy. In a couple of hours, they would all be at the Episcopalian cathedral for the rehearsal. After that would be a pre-wedding party, followed by a tame version of a combined bachelorette and bachelor's party at an afrobeats lounge. It was almost as if the couple couldn't trust their guests to occupy themselves for two nights. Nichole planned to check into her room and sleep for an hour before the evening shenanigans. She was already looking forward to a white chocolate mocha from Starbucks when she woke up.

"Welcome to the W, how can I help you, ma'am?" The clerk at the front desk signaled to her.

Nichole's heels clicked against the shiny floor as she wheeled her small suitcase to the counter. "Hi Beth," she said after a quick glance at the clerk's name tag. "I need to check in. Nichole Masterson." She slid her ID across the counter.

"Certainly." The blonde hit around on her keyboard and looked back up. "I have a king, non-smoking room for two nights? That sound good?"

"Perfect."

"The room is covered, but we require a credit card to hold on file for incidentals."

Once she was done, she made her way across the fancy lobby and right up to the elevators and pushed the button. She dragged her suitcase in behind her and pushed the button for the fourteenth floor. Right as the door began to close, she heard a shout to hold the elevator. She stuck a fist between the doors to stop it. It sprung back open mere seconds before it would have hit her hand. She withdrew her hand and gave the man who walked in a small smile. When he neither returned her smile, nor thanked her for holding the elevator, she turned to face the doors as they began to ascend.

From the corner of her left eye, she could see him staring at her. She glanced at him a couple of times, but that didn't deter him. He was tall with brown skin that contrasted the white t-shirt he had on. She knew she looked good in the tea-length summer dress that hugged her chest and flared out from her waist—totally inappropriate for November—but somehow his gaze didn't reflect any interest in her. He wasn't her type anyway. Even though he didn't look too bad, he was far too thin.

Finally, she lifted a palm in a questioning gesture. "Is something wrong?"

He tapped one of those obnoxious wireless earbuds on his ear. "You shouldn't stick your hand through an elevator. These things malfunction all the time. People have lost limbs doing that."

She frowned. Was he not there a few moments ago when he asked her to hold the door? "You asked me to!" she said defiantly.

"It doesn't matter. There're like eight other elevators down there. I could have waited for the next one. You don't risk getting your arm chopped off for a stranger."

Her mouth was agape as she listened to his gentle chastisement. He sounded as though he were talking to a twelve-year-old. He couldn't have been much older than she was, if he was at all. It was impossible to tell a twenty-three-year-old from a thirty-year-old man these days. And he was one to talk about strangers! How did he feel so comfortable talking down to one?

"Lesson learned. Next time I'll just hit the close button." She smiled sweetly as they approached her floor.

"Or just hit the open button."

She had to ball her fist to stop herself from showing him her middle finger and stayed mute as she dragged her suitcase out of the elevator. She heard footsteps behind her and turned to see him following her. She stopped and turned around fully.

"Are you following me?" Was he going to lecture her on how to open her room door? Or worse, attack her?

"What's more likely? That I'm following you or that my room is on this floor?"

She rolled her eyes and turned around to keep going to her room. She did not give him the satisfaction of looking back again. What a jerk!

* * *

Nichole woke up from her nap so disoriented that she needed a minute to get her bearings. When she finally did, she grabbed her phone from the nightstand and looked at the time. She breathed a sigh of relief when she realized that she'd not overslept. Just then a text came through:

Ride together to the church? Meet you in the lobby in thirty.

She responded in the affirmative and slid out of bed to get ready. She had half an hour to brush her teeth, touch up the makeup she'd put on earlier for the bridal shower, and change her clothes. When she was done, she assessed her appearance. She'd straightened and curled her 4a hair and it felt light and super bouncy against her shoulders. Whether it was in its natural state or straightened as it was now, her hair was her favorite feature, second only to the dimples on either side of her cheek. She looked casual but chic in her blue jeans and the black loose fitted blouse that she'd tucked into them. She wore a pair of flats to complete the look. There would be plenty of opportunity for heels to complement her height with the multiple outfit changes she had planned for the rest of the evening. She sprayed two puffs of perfume on either side of her neck and picked up her things.

When she got downstairs, she made a beeline for the Starbucks in the corner of the lobby. She had ten minutes to spare before Zoe Callas, her friend and one of the other bridesmaids, would be looking for her.

"Two steps ahead of you, darling," she heard from behind her. It was Zoe and she held out a cup of coffee in her outstretched arm.

"White mocha?" Nichole asked hopefully.

"Non-fat milk, no whipped cream."

"God bless you." Nichole grabbed the cup and took a quick sip, and closed her eyes as she let the coffee flow through her bloodstream. She could feel more alive with just that one sip.

Zoe shook an amused head at her. "You ready? Our ride is outside."

"Uber? I can drive, you know. My car's in the garage."

"So is mine. But no, we're hitching a ride with Kam." Zoe turned and began to walk to the hotel's front entrance. She always forgot her long legs gave her an unfair advantage. All she had to do was take three steps and she would cover more ground than Nichole could with ten steps.

"Who the hell is Kam?"

"One of the groomsmen. You would know if you paid closer attention in the group chat."

Zoe wasn't wrong. Nichole was very unresponsive in the bridal party group chat. It was hard to contribute when everyone in the group talked so much. A comment could multiply to fifty after only ten minutes of looking away from her phone, and she never had the energy to go back and read everything she missed, so she just didn't bother.

Zoe glanced back at her. "Come on."

Nichole had to gallop just to keep up. She caught up only when Zoe stopped to find their ride amongst the line of cars in front of the hotel.

"Over there." Zoe pointed and started to walk at a brisk pace once more. "The black Volvo."

"Who drives a Volvo under the age of fifty?" Nichole muttered. As she walked behind Zoe, her eyes were drawn to one of the drivers of the cars. It was the elevator police! She frowned as her eyes locked with his, and it deepened when she noted the Volvo symbol on the front of the SUV. She'd been looking for a much less stylish sedan.

"Oh, hell no, Zo, we're *not* riding with that guy!"

"Why?" Zoe looked alarmed. "What's wrong with him?"

"He attacked me in the elevator today!"

"He *what*?"

As Nichole relayed the elevator incident to Zoe, the man actually had the nerve to honk at them. Zoe raised a finger at him as she continued to listen patiently. Nichole could see a smile threatening to break and she wasn't the least bit pleased about it.

"Nah, don't minimize it. What he did wasn't normal!"

"Come on, Nichole, he didn't attack you. I thought I was going to hear a 'me too' story. Not putting your arm through an elevator door is just good sense. Come on, I'll introduce you."

Nichole sulked as she walked behind her. She opened the door to the back seat at the same time Zoe opened the door to the front seat of the car.

"Kam, Nichole. Nichole, Kam," Zoe said and all but ducked.

Nichole rolled her eyes and decided to be the bigger person. She stretched out her hand towards the console for a handshake but he didn't reciprocate.

"I would shake your hand, but I'm afraid it's probably hanging on by a thread after you almost lost it in the elevator."

"Oh my goodness," she said as she made to withdraw it, but he was quicker. He caught on to her hand and chuckled.

"Just kidding. It's nice to meet you, Nichole." He was cute, but he was also irritating, and the former only slightly edged out the latter. She rolled her eyes again, but this time it was accompanied by a small smile. "Nerd," she mumbled under her breath.

"Guilty," he said, and her eyes widened catching his in the rearview mirror. How had he heard her?

"Nichole, be nice to our ride at least until we get to the church in one piece," Zoe said dryly.

"Fine," Nichole grunted in resignation. She turned her head to keep her eyes on the scenery as the car made the short trip to the cathedral. She was listening half-heartedly as Zoe asked him questions she would have asked if she was in a friendlier mood. The only thing she caught was that he had gone to high school with the groom.

He parked the car in a lot half a block away from the cathedral, and they got out and began the short trek. She was silent while they kept yammering, gaining more ground ahead of her. She didn't mind walking alone though. She could take in the sight of the cathedral better without their distracting chatter. She'd always admired the majestic building but had never been in it. She didn't realize they had both stopped until she almost walked into them.

"Kam doesn't think you should walk behind us," Zoe said, locking arms with her and essentially putting her in between them like she was a child at risk of running away.

"For someone I've never seen before today, Kam sure does have a lot to say about what I should or shouldn't do." When he said nothing, she glanced up at him and he was looking straight ahead, a small smile playing on his mouth.

"Relax." Zoe patted her hand. "It's going to be a fun weekend, you'll see!"

"I hope so," Nichole said with a scowl. "The last wedding I was in was my friend, LaDan's in Nashville. It was a nightmare."

"Is she always like this?" Kam asked over her head.

"Mhmm," Zoe replied with an aggravating chuckle. Nichole rolled her eyes and began to angrily stomp up the stairs that led to the entrance of the cathedral.

"You know you can talk to me like I'm actually here, right?"

He was quiet once more and she had to look up to the sky for the strength to not tell him off. It worked because she was actually able to keep shut.

Zoe threw open the heavy doors. "Let's do this!"

* * *

Inside, the cathedral looked even better. Like the kind of church a royal wedding would take place in. There were rows of impossibly tall arches on either side of the aisle, from the entrance all the way down to the altar. The windows were made of stained glass with depictions she couldn't decipher from her vantage point. The pews seemed endless as the trio walked down the aisle to the altar where everyone was already standing. The altar was elevated and dark, probably because it wasn't in use. She could just imagine what a Christmas or an Easter service would be like in this building.

"Kamili!" Nichole heard when they got close to the head of the church. It was Chris, the groom, and he ran down the stairs to jump on Kam. Nichole looked back and forth at the men as they embraced for longer than was probably appropriate and shook her head. John, the best man and the bride's brother came to her and greeted her with a quick hug. Over the years, she'd caught John's eyes lingering on her. As though he would be interested in her if she gave him any encouraging signs. She may have gone for it if he wasn't her friend's older brother. He was good-looking, and he was a cardiologist, what more could a girl ask for? But it was always a bad idea to mess with a friend's family member, especially when you had a track record like hers. Plus, John was too clean. She needed someone with some grit; someone who was a little rough around the edges. Someone like Shawn.

When they'd all exchanged hugs, Nichole and Zoe went to the bride's corner. Kelenna looked taller than usual in a white Grecian maxi dress that she paired with gold sandals. She'd proclaimed months before that her plan was to wear white the entire weekend, and so far she was pulling it off so well. Her matron of honor and best friend, Chika was right beside her on her phone. She was definitely a bit loony, but Nichole had always liked her.

"We're all here except for Mark," Kelenna announced. "He has five minutes before they'll make us start."

"Who is Mark?" Nichole asked when no one did. She really should have paid closer attention in the group chat.

"My brother," Chris said with a frown, looking down at his phone. "He drove in from Athens. He said he just left the hotel. He'll be here in a few."

Nichole wandered away from the group towards one of the stained glass windows. She spent some time admiring the designs and reading some of the inscriptions. Before she knew it, she'd walked down several pews and had reached the halfway point between the altar and the main entrance. She saw a tall, well-built man burst through the doors and jog down the aisle towards the group. *Mark*, she thought. Where had Chris been hiding that? She had known Chris for some time now, and she didn't know he had a brother. She couldn't take her eyes off Mark as she started to make her way back to the group. She watched him exchange hugs with everyone, and as she slipped in beside Kelenna, she saw him literally lift the six feet, two inches tall Chris off his feet in a bear hug, and put him back down. He was clearly super strong.

From beside her, Kelenna was smiling as wide as Nichole had ever seen her. She even stretched out her arms to him.

"Hi Marky!" she said.

"Hey, beautiful." *Marky* took both of her hands in his and actually leaned in to kiss her cheek. "You look great. Are you sure you're ready to marry my brother?"

All eyes turned to Chris but he only had eyes for Kelenna. It was nauseatingly sweet. Even more so when Kelenna winked at him and nodded. That was totally a Chris move that she'd adopted. God, they were beginning to share mannerisms.

"Uncle Mark!" Two kids, a boy and a girl, who had been sitting silently on one of the pews jumped up to hug him.

"My babies!" He stooped down to a squat to get eye level with them as he gathered them in his arms. Nichole was mesmerized watching him interact with the children she'd been told were Chris' older sister's kids. When he stood up, they ran back to the pew they'd been sitting on.

"Well, sis," Mark said, turning back to Kelenna and rubbing his hands together. "I'm here, so let's do this. Where do I stand?"

"You'll be with Nichole," Kelenna said, putting an arm around her. "Nichole, this is Mark. Mark, this is Nichole, one of my dear friends. We met in pharmacy school a long time ago."

When Mark turned around to look at her, she was arrested by how focused his eyes were. On her. It was almost as if he was drinking her in. The way he looked her up and down without undressing her was perfection. It was the most polite perusal she'd ever been under and it immediately endeared her to him. She found herself stretching out a hand to him. Instead of shaking it, he surprised her by picking it up and placing a chaste kiss on the back of it. Unable to help herself, she snort-laughed.

"It's nice to meet you, Nichole."

"My God, Mark, when will you change?" Chika cut in. Her eye roll could be heard in her tone. "Careful with this one, Nichole. He's a hopeless flirt."

"Hi Chika," Mark said dryly amid laughter from the wedding party. He was still holding on to her hand and Nichole gently tugged it out of his grip. He smiled at her as he released it. Even his smile was refreshingly disarming. She couldn't stop her mind from drawing comparisons between him and Shawn. Physically, they were both big and tall, and she liked that. She liked men who could make her look small, and who weren't likely to drop her when they picked her up. She knew nothing more of him, but she was certain that she would be helpless if he made any attempt to woo her. Hell, she gave Shawn a shot simply because he'd been bold enough to message her his number through a food delivery app after he'd dropped her order off. She'd called him on a whim, and voila! Five months later, he was spending more nights at her place than at the apartment he shared with his friends in Smyrna.

At ten minutes past five, a priest appeared at the altar. It was time to begin.

Acknowledgments

This book would not be possible without my job. My experiences as a pharmacist at Cartersville and the people I've worked with, in and out of the pharmacy department, inspired this book. My coworkers, who have been supportive since the day I was hired into a leadership role as a green pharmacist, and through the years I've spent writing draft after draft of this book, have held me accountable in ways they may not even understand. Thanks for being sounding boards, listening ears, beta readers and hype people! I know the camaraderie we have in our pharmacy department is unique, and I am lucky to have such a great group of coworkers!

To my parents, Stan and Ijeoma, thanks for feeding me and my siblings' voracious appetite for reading, and for pushing me in the direction of pharmacy at a time when I was considering other career options. My little brother, Enyi, I know the world will get to see your talents one day! To my three sisters, who have read every story I've written since I was ten years old. Your indulgence of my obsession with this project, and allowing me to harass you for opinions concerning every aspect of this book, got me here. Ivy, you were insightful and encouraging. Crystal, you were a sounding board and an editor—no one can fix a sentence quite like you can. Denise, you paved the way for me to get here. I've always followed in your footsteps, and when I followed you into novel writing, I knew you would make the journey easier for me. From the bottom of my heart, I thank you all.

To my friends who gave their time to read drafts of the book. Oby, Chidinma and Courtney, thanks for the pharmacy perspective! Mikkie and Ona, your feedback and inability to finish the first draft encouraged me to work harder on improvements. I've always valued your opinions and I'm grateful for your ability to give them without sparing my feelings. To the best crew: my ATL Crew, and my Nashville crew, and my own pharmacy school classmates who I've remained friends with all these years later, you've all inspired me to write about the dynamics of friendships. Thank you!

Finally, I would like to thank God for seeing me through to the end of this project. I may not be a trained writer, but You've given me a storytelling ability and an interest in putting words on paper. I know I'll get by.

A Letter from the Author

As someone who has never subscribed to the notion that all pharmacists have a little OCD, I was surprised when my venture into novel writing revealed that I was part of the rule, and not one of its exceptions. It took a while for me to stop tinkering with my project and get comfortable enough to put it out there and let it fly. Thank you for starting this journey with me.

This novel—like any other one I imagine—started out as a simple idea. It came to me one afternoon at work, after I had spent a long time ensuring that a woman with a rare condition would receive the treatment she needed to save her unborn child. I had gone beyond the scope of my job to pull this off and I wanted to share a piece of that with the world. What does the public really know about hospital pharmacists? We aren't nurses or doctors who, based on medical dramas, are the only people who work in a hospital. We are relegated to the basements of hospitals in real life and completely hidden in media and works of literature. I thought about how unfortunate that was. We are the drug custodians and the mediation experts! We put out little fires in hospitals every day! We keep patients safe! Without us, hospitals would not function! Those thoughts birthed the beginnings of this novel.

Oh, but I didn't realize how difficult it would be to write about a pharmacist hero/heroine. I didn't appreciate that pharmacy jargon was not widespread, nor how hard I would have to work to translate my experiences into something book worthy. It took me a while to come to the realization that I had to keep it simple. Stick to one issue and expand upon it. For me, it was the opioid epidemic.

I chose the opioid epidemic not only because I felt it would be recognizable for many readers, but also because I knew that the idea of it affecting a hospital pharmacist would be a novel one. In 2017, the DEA did cut back opioid production quotas, and just like I portrayed in my novel, every hospital pharmacy in the nation had to come up with a response. But just like a drug needs a vehicle to help the body absorb it, I knew that I needed something to make my novel about pharmacy more palatable to readers. Enter romance.

I chose romance as my vehicle because I've always been a huge fan of romance novels. They reach down and grab at what everyone truly desires: to love and be loved. So even though I was advised to stick to one lane: love or pharmacy, I didn't listen. Even though I was warned that trying to weave the two concepts into one tale would take away from either, I stuck to my guns. Call me naïve, but the decision to not listen birthed an even bigger idea. A series. What's better than one novel about a hospital pharmacist? Five novels about different kinds of pharmacists! Each one with a unique perspective about how life, love and pharmacy intersect. I am so excited to get to work on all these books like you wouldn't believe! But back to *The Way You Look at Me*.

Once I settled in, I knew I had to go with a theme that involved seeing and making connections. We hospital/clinical pharmacists may not be overly visible to the patients we care for, but we must not let that stop us from seeing them and finding ways to connect to them so that we can help them get better. And, as I wrote in the book, the words 'I love you' in my mother tongue, '*A huru m gi n'anya*,' translates to 'I see you.' I don't think you can have love without seeing a person for who they are. In *The Way You Look at Me*, Kelenna learns that lesson and it helps her with her job challenges and in her quest for love. The way we look at people, and how we allow others to see us informs every decision we will make. I can only hope I have conveyed that message through this book.

So please be gentle with me as you read my attempt to put my ideas down. Leave me a note and share your thoughts. And welcome to the subgenre of pharmacy romance! This is only the beginning!

About the author

Born in Nashville, Tennessee, EeJay relocated to Lagos, Nigeria with her family shortly after she turned four years old, and spent her formative years in the heart of the city. Some of her fondest childhood memories involve her reading everything she could get her hands on, and writing stories to entertain her sisters and friends.

At sixteen, EeJay returned to Tennessee to attend university. Eight years and two degrees later—a Bachelor's in Chemistry from Middle Tennessee State University and a doctor of pharmacy from the University of Tennessee—she moved to Atlanta, Georgia where she began her career in clinical pharmacy. She completed a one year, post-graduate residency at the former Atlanta Medical Center and was hired on at Cartersville Medical Center into the clinical pharmacy manager position. For the last eight years, she has worked to ensure the safe and appropriate use of medications in hospitalized patients while serving as adjunct faculty for nearby pharmacy schools, precepting and training future pharmacists.

Despite choosing a science-based profession and enjoying her career thus far, EeJay never truly abandoned her story writing habits. The six-year-old who spent an entire summer vacation in England traipsing in and out of libraries and reading novels, and the teenager who would fill notebooks with handwritten stories was always there. She began working on her debut novel when she realized that pharmacists were underrepresented as leading characters in media and works of fiction.

EeJay currently lives in Atlanta, Georgia, and when she's not at work, she's reading, writing, playing tennis, or watching sports: Futbol, football, basketball, tennis, you name it. Go Gunners!

Made in the USA
Columbia, SC
20 November 2021